Son of the Moon

JOSEPH G. HITREC

★

SON
OF THE MOON

London
MICHAEL JOSEPH

First Published by
MICHAEL JOSEPH LTD.
26 *Bloomsbury Street*
*London, W.C.*1
1949

*Set and printed in Great Britain by Tonbridge
Printers Ltd., Peach Hall Works, Tonbridge,
in Times nine on eleven point, and bound by
James Burn*

He that abstains to help the rolling wheels of this great
world . . . lives a lost life. . . . For the upholding of thy
kind action thou shouldst embrace.

Bhagavad-Gita,
chapter called 'Karma-Yoga'

In the poetic annals of the Rajput we see him check his
war-chariot, and when he should be levelling his javelin,
commence a discourse upon ethics; or when the battle
is over, the (Chief) of the host converts his tent into a
lyceum, and delivers lectures on morals and manners.

Colonel James Tod

An attempt has been made in this book to minimize the number of Indian words necessary to atmosphere and principal tradition. Except the following, all such words have been explained or paraphrased in their proper places in the text, while for the conscientious reader a glossary is attached at the end of the book.

> *ama:* mother.
> *pita:* father.
> *bhai:* brother.
> *-ji:* suffix of respect and endearment (as in *pitaji*).
> *arre:* a sound of expostulation, meaning, loosely:
>   Well then, but.
> *jee-huhn:* loosely, Yessir (*huhn* pronounced gutturally, rather like the English 'huh').

The Indian race of Rajputs is said to be the medieval and modern equivalent of the old Hindu Kshatryas, the princely and warrior caste. Legend has it that they are descended from the gods Sun and Moon and that they are equal in rank to the Brahmans.

The main quotations from the Bhagavad-Gita are from Sir Edwin Arnold's verse translation.

TO LEYLA—MY WIFE

AUTHOR'S NOTE

The realities of Indian life are indistinguishable from the four hundred million people that make it. This book—like many others before it—is an imaginative version of that axiom. It would be a grave mistake to look upon its characters and incidents as anything but pure invention: fictive montages against the larger search for truth. The background of politics, tradition and ritual is, of course, common knowledge, and on that I have drawn freely.

There is an India for each person. The following pages are the fond memory of one such. It so happens that he was happy there and liked what he saw.

First Chapter

❧❧❧❧❧❧❧❧❧❧❧❧❧❧❧❧❧❧❧❧❧❧❧❧❧❧

1

IN THAT January of 1936 the face which India turned to a new arrival was still bland and well enough composed, and over it the fresh breezes of the cold season still wafted scents of jasmine and tuberose and, of an evening, the plaintive otherworldly tolling of shrine bells.

As yet no earthquake, flood or famine had made the year memorable. No Muslim had yet ambushed a devotional Hindu procession, nor had any misguided Hindu caused a riot by trumpeting a conch shell outside a mosque at the hour of Allah. Young though it was, it was a quiet year. A few more temples had been thrown open to the untouchables in the South where the Brahmans held sway and the event had been accorded due praise in the *Harijan*, Mr. Gandhi's own newspaper, and in the nationalist press generally. Preparations for a mammoth Magh-fair at Allahabad were already afoot and on the banks of the Ganges at Hardwar, one of the seven holy cities, ascetics of all denominations began to assemble for the annual pilgrimage to the holy sources in the Garhwal Himalayas. The crops were doing well, marriages were on the increase, moneylenders had every reason to feel well disposed towards Ganesh, their elephant-headed god of success. Vasant was in the air—a Spring so throbbingly different from any other as to be a climatic feature of the peninsula.

When Vijay Ramsingh walked down the gangway of S.S. *Kistna* and on to the stone quay of Ballard Pier at Bombay, the hard outer crust of his home land, he felt like a tourist renewing a half-forgotten but indelible old experience. Neither the pier nor the colour of the crowd on it seemed to have changed since he last saw them; the port buildings were still topped by a Union Jack and gay streamers of maritime signals; a typical Indian crowd boiled all over the quay, hot, voluble and breathless as usual.

His family alone seemed a little strange, though he had spotted them quickly as soon as the mail steamer hove to. The group included Jagnath, his father, Tara and Munu, his sisters, the uncle called Premchand and Salim Haq, the Muslim friend of his flying days.

9

Jagnath was the first to come forward with raised arms.

'Welcome home, son! It has been so long.'

'Pitaji!'

Vijay bowed lightly over his joined palms, in respectful Hindu fashion, and Jagnath returned the greeting and followed it up with an embrace on both sides of his son's head. 'Welcome back to the land of your people, Vijay,' he said gruffly, patting his back. 'This is a very happy day indeed.'

'It is good to see you, pitaji.'

Holding hands, they looked into each other's eyes and smiled happily, the older man on the verge of tears.

Then Tara came up and hung a garland around her brother's neck with an awkward but determined swing of arms, blushing darkly; she was quite unexpectedly grown-up and pretty. 'Oh Vijay bhai, is it really you?' she said after they embraced. 'We were all so thrilled when you wrote that you were coming back at last. I am so happy to see you. . . .'

'So am I, Tara! I thought of nothing else for the last two months.'

'You look so different . . . so European.'

'You too, believe me. So pretty and big . . . not at all like the girl I left.'

Then it was the turn of Munu, the shy fourteen-year-old, still bareheaded in the manner of school children, whom Vijay could remember even less well. She threw her arms about him and stepped away abruptly, stammering, 'Vijay, bhai!'

'At last, dear boy, at last! We thought you would never come. Welcome back to India!'

'How very good to see you, uncle!'

Uncle Premchand's hug gave no impression of awkwardness, only of pleasure and a prepossessing joviality. His breath was pan-scented and behind the thick gold-rimmed lenses his look seemed to say, Just as I thought, another Indian youth lost to the wanton West. His poise had something of the public-address air about it as he broke away, pushing the glasses farther up his nose, smiling shrewdly.

Salim Haq was the last. He was not of the family, only a boyhood friend of Vijay's. He hugged him powerfully in the Muslim fashion. 'How are you? What have you been doing? This town has not been the same without you.'

'And you, dear Salim? How is everything?'

'As well as it could be. Welcome to Bombay.'

'Thank you. You will have to tell me everything, Salim.'

'I will, I will. . . . So will you.'

And that was all he would remember in the future, and it would be very little to go by even though the moment was one he had looked forward to with some trepidation.

While new arrivals still poured down the gangway and tore around them

10

grinning and mumbling excuses, and while the crush grew hotter and more odorous, and coolies staggering under huge loads made any orderly progress hard of achievement, they somehow inched their way towards the custom-house and went through the formalities. Uncle Premchand took charge of the baggage and steered it through without duty; Salim took the girls into the waiting hall, alerting the family driver at the same time. Jagnath braved the tumult and stuck to his son until all the red tape which the Indian government lavished on a homecoming national was successfully overcome. Even as they elbowed towards the exit, free to go as they pleased, three press reporters and a couple of photographers held them up for a pose and and interview.

'They still remember you, Vijay,' Jagnath said with a proud grin. 'Yesterday there was an article saying that you were coming back with an important new plan.'

'I am, pitaji . . . though it is not what they think.'

'You must tell me. . . .'

Finally they came out of the building, just as the sun fell beyond the western ramparts of the city and the last of daylight seemed to gather in streaks of orange and mauve over the sea. They drove into the greying town and on to Worli and home. It was then that Vijay asked about mother.

'She was not well enough to come, son,' Jagnath said. 'She is waiting at home . . . and that is why I hurried you so much. It is nothing for you to worry about. She has been ailing lately . . . not really ill. We thought it best that she wait for you at Worli.'

'Why didn't you write and tell me?'

'I did not wish to alarm you.' Jagnath wiped his forehead and the rim of his topee. 'We do not know what it is . . . only that it is some kind of kidney trouble. You see, Vijay, it is actually an old complaint, but she has never paid it much attention. You know how ama is . . . she talks very little about herself . . . and does not wish us to talk either. And for that reason,' he added, putting his hand on Vijay's knee, 'we in the house don't talk about it. I wanted to ask you to remember that when we come home.'

'Yes, how like ama . . . always the same,' Vijay said softly, the past leaning over his shoulder for one brief moment. 'I should have thought even she would change at least a little. . . .'

'Not she, son. It is a miracle we are as modern as we are, with her so unshakable.' He stared out of the window, as if caught unprepared by his own statement and overtaken by its truth; then he recalled himself, smiled almost shyly and concluded: 'Anyhow, it is such a little thing after all. If she wants us not to mention it, the least we can do is to obey her.'

'Of course, pitaji.'

'That is good,' Jagnath said, relieved. 'I knew you would understand.'

11

Turning again to the window he fanned himself with his topee and his look roved restlessly over the oval maidan, on which, at this hour of the day, youngsters played ball games and elderly people lay on the grass watching them. The late slanting light set his hair aglow and made it seem greyer than it really was, and it gave his face a trembling, almost scholarly vacuousness. He was now in his late forties—a time when most Indians looked back on life and studied sacred old texts—but old age was about to surprise him while his eye sockets were still unwrinkled and the skin of his cheeks was still firm. He wore his European cotton suit with the studious ease of a government official and betrayed it on occasions with a clashing tie or an unsuitable colour of shoes. At this moment, though for the merest split second, time and separation enabled Vijay to see in him a characteristic product of the long and pervasive attrition which a distant culture had brought to India.

Now the car surged towards the sea wall on New Marine Drive and towards an overripe sun. A gust of cool evening breeze blew into the car, inflating Tara's sari and causing her to wrap it more tightly around her neck. Vijay smiled at her, delighted with the old familiar movement and the jingle of her silver bracelets. 'You know, I can't yet get over it,' he told her. 'You were only a cross-tempered little girl when I left. Now you're a lady . . . and a very pretty one.'

'Bhai, how much do you really remember?' she said with a toss of the head.

'Everything.'

'I wonder. You go away a boy and return an Englishman. I was sixteen when you went.'

He looked at her fondly. She had stuck a red hibiscus in the tuft of hair showing under the sari border; this and the double coral necklace above her blouse made up for the grey plainness of the garment. She was less fair than either Jagnath or himself, but her lively long-lashed eyes and pouting mouth made the fact seem insignificant; a quick, ready smile, the more dazzling because of the contrast, achieved the rest. The ebony-black freshly oiled hair was parted at the middle of the forehead and fell with a single ringlet over each ear; the plaits, now tucked under the sari, were flower-braided and tufted at the ends.

'Am I so very changed, then?' he said.

'Yes, you are, very much,' she said. 'Your accent is foreign . . . you have become so sure, like a European.'

'When you get to know your sister a little better, you will know that this is not a compliment,' Jagnath said. 'The cheek of it! She has been to a few Congress meetings and now no one can be patriot enough in her eyes.'

'Are you a party member then?' Vijay asked.

'Certainly I am. We Indians must fight for our freedom . . . it will not be given to us on a tray.'

'Now you know,' Jagnath said to his son. 'It is what happens when there is no brother in the house . . . the girls think that they must take his place.'

'That's not true, pitaji. I joined the Congress because I wanted to.'

But Jagnath went on smiling to himself, saying nothing, satisfied that the balance missing from the house would presently be restored with the return of his only son. Vijay laughed a little and all his worries and tension left him.

This was more like the reunion he had imagined—his elder sister bickering half-playfully, half-earnestly, his father admonishing with an authority which he no longer knew how to wield save in defence of appearances. In a family where women predominated, this was an appreciable blessing—at any rate to one fresh from a long absence. Only too often were the Hindu households either over-feminine or over-masculine, and one or the other side found itself smothered. Here, Vijay thought, a fine level had been raised because women dabbled in the traditional pursuits of the male and yet managed to keep their womanliness.

'Many things you knew so well are no more the same,' Tara went on as the blurred tongue of Malabar Hill floated in sight.

'How so?'

'When you left the people were still . . . they were afraid of the police and jail. But no more, bhai. To-day they sing *Bande Mataram* and wear Congress badges quite openly.'

'Yes, that is quite true,' Jagnath said. 'Your Uncle Premchand has become an important man, almost a leader in this province.'

'Good luck to him,' Vijay said. 'What about our friends?'

'All running after the people,' Tara said quickly.

Jagnath gave her a distrait look. 'What she means, son, is that no one has been idle while you were away. The good old Mr. Varma, for example, is now on the local committee of the party. Your friend Salim Haq is a reporter on Uncle Premchand's *Morning Herald*. This provincial autonomy which the British have given us looks as though it is coming through. . . .'

'Tell me about that,' Vijay said. 'The London newspapers were full of it even when I left.'

'Nothing to tell as yet. The new act became law a few months ago. If the Congress and the Muslim League will accept it, there will be elections this winter. Then we shall know our strength and act accordingly.'

'And how is home and everyone in it?'

'That at least has not changed. You shall find out yourself.'

On the sands of Chowpatty Bay the evening crowds were already gathering round the hawkers' stands. The noise was like the merry sound of a fair. Vijay saw the coconut piles and the children in various stages of undress milling around them and also the familiar loafers clustering under a loudspeaker extolling the curative magic of a herbal preparation, and he smiled indulgently. In the breakwater men in loinpieces and women in wet saris worshipped the setting sun. Somehow he found it impossible to think of them as people of his religion.

'Look!' he said to his father and his sisters. 'This hasn't changed either.'

'It never will,' Jagnath said. 'This is true India.'

Then they swerved inland and raced towards Cumballa Hill where the dusk was already inseparable from the thick crowns of fig and plane trees. The weird and ornate Parsi castles streaked past in a dapple haze, then the road tumbled again seaward and they skirted the walled precincts of the Mahalakshmi Temple. The smooth black avenue stretched to the end of the shallow bay, and above it a line of palms strained over backwards, the breeze full in their fluffy heads.

'Still the same!' Vijay pointed to the low mosque out on the reef.

The tide, rolling in loudly, already washed the causeway that bound the mosque to the shore; along it the last worshippers now scurried towards dry land and their women lifted their skirts up to their knees. In the east, the smokestacks of the cotton-mill section blackened the sky into virtual night. Farther along the road a shrine-hut teetered precariously on a steep cone of rock, its worn flags flapping in the breeze. And where the sun had been was now only a crimson half-halo and even this was already fading into soft lilac and pale turquoise green.

Father and son smiled at each other warmly, and the former threw his head against the cushion and sighed feelingly. 'Almost home,' he said.

Home, Vijay thought, leaning back with a touch of breathlessness. Up to this moment he had been happy just to look and listen, but now his exhilaration became lambent; it flitted from the car to the darkening landscape outside, from there to the home ahead and to his mother Kandubai, and then back to the swarming town they had just left. What was home and how did one prove it to oneself? Was Bombay his home?

He had believed so back in England throughout the last two years, and whenever the vision had showed signs of dimming he had tried to remember the words of Mr. Varma, a friend of his father's, who had been born here and loved Bombay very much. 'Look inland from here,' the old gentleman used to say, 'and you are on the crest of an enduring Aryan wave. Look southward at the Dasyus of the Vedas, probably the oldest race in Asia, and then up at the Karakorum out of whose craggy valleys these same Aryans have issued to make our civilizations what they are . . . and then raise yourself beyond the forbidden Himalayas and you are in China, another spawn pool of civilization. In Bombay, dear boy, you are privy to the glory of the Palis, Kushans, Mings, Chings and Moguls, all of whom have ruled more and longer than Rome ever could, and given the world quite as much, if not more, than Hellas. . . .'

14

It was an awesome picture, one that weathered all Vijay's European impressions and new ideas—to be pegged down to size only now, when he no longer needed its help, by the inevitable processes of a young man's photographic memory. For now Bombay seemed to have shrunk as no town ever had. After London, Edinburgh, Dublin and Paris, its size and beauty were no longer wonderful, as once they had seemed; the vision had dimmed suddenly, almost imperceptibly, between one end of the town and the other.

He looked at his father and found him talking. He had replaced the topee on his head and buttoned himself up. There was an air of relief on his face and a new conviction in his voice as he made a last announcement:

'The main thing is that we are complete once more. What is the point in having a family if they are not together in one place? The truth is, son, we have missed you. . . .'

2

VIJAY found the house as he had left it two years ago: Three storeys on the road side, two on the hill side, the flat roof adorned by a gay red and white garden umbrella and marred by a water tank and two shaky radio masts; to the west a squarish, bushy garden, in which a long line of gardeners had been plainly experimenting, enfolded a small lawn; a narrow cement path joined the house to the road, while at the southern boundary of the plot a gravel drive led to the garage. Save for the lawn and the building, most of the ground sloped towards the road, below which the rock again deployed southward, lashed by the rains in the monsoon and heated by the harsh afternoon sun throughout the rest of the Indian year.

'There you are . . . the same old zenana palace,' Jagnath said as they crossed the lawn.

Vijay grinned—'ladies' quarters.' How well the name fitted the house! Even now it seemed to address the scattered pseudo-modern locality like a purdah lady whose antecedents needed no proof. Like a purdah woman sure of her standing, it could also be aloof when it felt like it. When Jagnath Ramsingh first began to build it in 1923, he was motivated by a vague urge to make it a comfortable home for many generations of Ramsinghs, of which Vijay was to be the first cornerstone. But new trends intervened, 'simplicity' gained the upper hand with the architect and time-honoured Indian design floundered in a muddle of 'expert' argument. Villa Ram grew up a wonder child; her bleak exterior spoke of Function's arrival in the East; her floors were sensibly planned, rooms light and airy. When Jagnath and his family first moved into it, they found it hard to

15

behave naturally. He had had to sell a portion of his inherited lands in Indore to build it, but now it gave him a feeling of sitting naked in a public place. It took tradition many years to reassert itself. With each post-monsoon whitewashing the conversion grew a little more hopeful, a little jollier. Old Hindu swastikas appeared on the balconies and along ledges, green bamboo shutters on the windows; unwieldy Chesterfield suites gave place to plain Indian lounging couches, tile tubs vanished in favour of roomier shower-baths. In the garden, too, the malis recaptured the spirit of the past—by lumping together figs, temple trees, bougainvillæa and mimosa, in happy disregard for consequences. Gradually but successfully, the young matron retired again behind a purdah of her own making and put everyone else at ease. She was now what she ought to have been from the outset: a livable compromise between the past and the present.

The old carved teak furniture was still in the hall and in the rooms of the ground floor, but its fusty old soul had been given quite a fillip by a riot of fresh garlands and streamers of coloured crepe paper. The statue of Radha-Krishna on the dining-room cupboard was smothered in tuberose and twigs of frangipani. All divans had clean covers and above one of them Vijay's graduation photograph sported a huge rose garland all to itself; the paper cut-out along its base bore the inscription W*E*L*C*O*M*E* B*A*C*K and on the divan itself was a large package tied with silk ribbons.

'Go on, son, open it,' Jagnath nudged him. 'It is a present from all of us.'

Vijay tore it open. From the successive tissue wrappings emerged a portfolio of maroon leather, with the initials V.R. embossed on the cover—a collection of Indian newspaper clippings of his flight to England and his subsequent triumph. A picture on the frontispiece showed him and H.H. the Aga Khan at the prizegiving in London.

'Believe me, we enjoyed doing it,' Jagnath said, beaming for the entire family. 'Mother and I did the reading, your sisters clipped.'

'We must have gone through a thousand magazines and papers,' Tara said.

Vijay thanked them and hugged them one after another, assuring them that it was the finest gift anyone could receive. Then he took off his jacket and tie and climbed to the first floor. The door of his mother's room was open; he saw her propped against the pillows of her bed, both arms raised towards him; she smiled faintly and sweetly.

'Ama!'

'At last, son!'

He made the traditional obeisance, touching her hands and feet, but did not kiss her. Then he stood up again and smiled down on her, waiting for her to speak first. Tearful, gripping one of his hands in both hers, she gazed back for a while. In her spotless white sari, smelling delicately of incense and rarefied musk, she lay on the bed, not in it; close to her head two joss sticks burned with a blue coil of smoke. On a home-built stand near the window was another statue of Lord Krishna, a clay one this time, and at its base lay a brass bowl of rice, some pieces of coconut shell and a brass dipam—oil lamp. The rest of the room was typical of orthodox Hindu ladies: Two camphor chests contained all of Kandubai's clothes and heirlooms, while one almirah held all the linen for the house. The Kashmir rug on the floor was in the usual walnut-leaf pattern.

'You have grown taller . . . taller even than your father,' she said presently. 'No longer the boy Vijay.'

'I am twenty-four, ama. Have you forgotten?'

'No, son, but the years away from home are the longest. We shall have to get used to each other. . . .'

With her knees drawn up, lighted only by the pale-mauve oblong of sky beyond the open window, she looked almost as fragile as Tara had looked when he left. He thought, Was she always so tiny? and the thought faded in a swift access of warmth. Then she turned to the window and spoke again, and he saw that she had lost another front tooth and was a little conscious of it.

'I wanted to come to the steamer,' she said, 'but they told me I should wait here. Anyhow, this way is better . . . we shall not be disturbed.'

'Father told me, ama. It is better.'

He put her hand to his cheek and waited for the next question, as became a well-brought-up Hindu son.

Her pallor set off the high cheekbones and gave the rest of her face a vaguely fallen-in look—something he did not remember. She was not beautiful as Rajput women could be, perhaps not even handsome, but she had over a period of years repaired that with an expression which was one-half dignity and one-half the peace of a confirmed dreamer. What her dream was, Vijay had not yet learned, and now he wondered if she knew it herself. When Hindu matrons belied the ironical adage and desisted from ruling the household with an iron hand and a loud voice, they often grew such airy graces. Perhaps the manner was a fabric thrown over a keen inner sight that might have been uncomfortable otherwise—for it was inconceivable that a mother of three children and a wife of long standing would not have pieced together the usual wisdom or profited by the usual mistakes.

'Did they like you in England?'

He sat down at the edge of her bed and tried to divine her look.

'They were kind,' he said slowly. 'They met me as equal and spoke frankly.'

'And you think you have got to know them?'

17

He hedged, wiping his face with a handkerchief—it was a question he had wanted to leave for later.

'I think I did,' he said, 'as well as an Indian ever can.'

'And you are still an Indian . . . and a Hindu?'

'Of course, ama. You must never doubt that.'

'I will not . . . when you have proved it.' Now she began to look at the window after every sentence, as though recalling a faded image. 'When a Hindu crosses the water, he must arrange for a proper return. We in this house are not Brahmans, but we are good Hindus all the same.' Softly but clearly she added: 'A return is made proper with worship and purification.'

'Ama, we are more modern than that,' he said. 'I thought we were no longer superstitious.'

'It is not a superstition. It is being a good Hindu.'

Her voice did not change, so she disarmed him in advance. If she had insisted or argued, he might have argued back and explained his viewpoint patiently. The idea that a Hindu lost caste and needed formal purification after an absence from his soil impressed him not at all any more; what was more formidable than an old prejudice was this weight of her conviction and her sure instinct for timing. Could he now deny her first wish after reunion.

'Don't rush me and there will be time for everything,' he said, improvising. 'Let me first feel my home.'

'I will not rush you, Vijay. It is your duty more than it is mine.'

He put on the light and had a better look at her. 'You've become much thinner,' he said.

'Old age, nothing more. Doctors cannot know better about a woman than the woman herself.'

'So there are doctors?'

'There are, because your father wishes. They come and go, but cannot agree among themselves. That is not what I wanted to speak of,' she said. 'How do you find your father and sisters?'

She pulled herself up and sat higher, and the impression of minuteness faded.

'The girls are not to be recognized. Tara has become very pretty.'

'Also very restless, son. She cares too much for politics and too little for studies. Twice already we have had the police in this house . . . questioning, searching, as though she were a revolutionary.' Then, an edge of plaint creeping into her voice: 'Sisters are not like brothers. . . . They have no secrets between them. What Tara does, Munu wants to do too. It is good that you are back. Two such sisters need to have an older brother in the house.'

'Tara is a true Rajput, I think.'

'How well it were if she didn't know it! Some Rajput traits do not stand up to the new times . . . false pride, to name one. Tara looks ahead and sees only a free India. Your father and I see other things. . . .'

'Which, ama?'

'Sold lands, debts in the future . . . maybe the sale of this comfortable house. It was not necessary that you should know this so far, but now I can tell you. Half of our land in Indore has already gone to pay for your education . . . and that of the girls. Tara's mooning is therefore a double worry. She wants to be a rebel . . . not realizing that a college degree makes a rebel more useful. And there is her marriage, now very near, which must be arranged suitably, according to custom. . . .' She began to gather her sari into folds, pensively.

'What else?' he said. 'Your letters never told me anything.'

'Oh, many other things . . . who would know where to begin! These reforms the British have given us . . . who knows but your father may have to join the Congress and lose his post with the government . . . just now when he has at last been promoted. . . .' She told him of Jagnath's new duties in the agricultural department of the provincial government, to which he had lately been assigned as adviser, and of the change all Indian officials might have to fear if Congress won the coming elections and decided to infuse new blood in the existing ministries. Not that Jagnath was not a patriot, she said, taking up the cudgels on behalf of the Ramsingh type of quiet nationalism, and doing it instinctively—but patriotism in these days of 'Acts' and local autonomy was apparently not enough. One had to be a party member and go to jail to prove it. 'This has become a new country since you went away,' she summed up diffidently, as though the handling of long technical terms had left her weak and more bewildered. 'If the British are sincere this time, there will be Indian government in every province by spring next year. And still,' she added with a shake of the head, 'I cannot imagine it. We have waited too long and seen too many broken promises.'

'They are sincere, I am sure,' he said. 'I talked to many and they were all for it.'

'I hope so . . . for the sake of you young ones,' she said.

Something was happening almost every day, in all parts of the country, she went on. One couldn't recognize old friends or be sure of the new ones; one barely knew whether the past or the future was more important. She understood very little really, and that was why she fell back again and again on the one topic she was most at home in—family. 'Your return will make this home what it used to be,' she said. Maybe the mad rush would cease for a time and the girls would accomplish what was expected of them: dignity and honest judgment were more desirable than brief thrills. All of life was not on the streets; there was also the day-to-day traffic between people of the same blood, there was love and piety, devotion and learning, also the sixteen milestones of a full Hindu destiny, the sanskaras or sacramental rites, to which they owed their first allegiance. She mentioned three specifically—completion of studies, marriage, family life.

He saw how much farther back into orthodoxy she had drifted in the time he had been away. Outwardly, she was in voluntary semi-purdah, but within herself she had begun to lean heavily on the solid keel of her religion, the ritualistic view of life, and her patience with innovation had become exhausted for all practical purposes. He wondered anew how true was the Anglo-Indian belief that if you scratched a Hindu of the motor car, the Hindu of the ancient Vedas showed through soon enough.

'But I am forgetting my guests and my duties,' she said, flicking the ashen tops from the joss sticks. 'I should have told you earlier . . . there are people in the house . . . Shreemati Rana Prashad, her daughter Chanda . . . also your Uncle Uday. They have come to Bombay especially to see you. Go now and get ready to meet them. . . .'

'How annoying for you, ama,' he said. 'You could have rested longer and we could have talked.'

She got out of the bed on the other side, bating her breath ever so little, then smoothed the skirt of her sari and found her sandals. She smiled again.

'I have rested enough, and guests are a law in the household.' She took his hand and went to the door with him.

He tried not to show his disappointment as they walked out on the landing, still hand in hand. He had hoped to be spared the outer branches of the clan at least on the first evening. He had wanted to go slow and tactfully with all his news, for he knew, even if they didn't as yet, that two years were a separation greater than in calendar only. In a lively crowd such caution was bound to be a strain on everybody. He knew his people and was pretty certain that they would not let him keep anything back; a skimming gay curiosity was as much a part of them as his new, painfully won reserve was a part of his long absence. He sighed inwardly. Now it was plain to him that his freedom of movement and behaviour had drawn to a close, that indeed from this night onward all his plans would have to be laid in the shade of this master plan called the Indian family.

3

MEANWHILE there was much banter and a frank show of pride soon after the first greetings, and the family, almost to a man, took a lively interest in his luggage and trophies. He had left Bombay with a map and a small suitcase; now his possessions added up to a pile of shop-new trunks, a whole wardrobe of English suits and two planes, one new, the other old. There was that enormous silver cup presented to him by the Aga Khan and heaps of other mementoes, ranging from letters of congratulation and commemorative scrolls to engraved salvers, signed menu cards and newspaper clippings, all personal junk of very pleasant association but crying out for an editor. Showing it to them turned out to be a delightful and exhausting task. They were resolved to bask in his successes and trade that exhilarating privilege for a flood of advice—just as he knew they would. Success was everybody's business. Above all, it was the romping preserve of the entire family right down to the shyest and greenest collateral. And he had forgotten how many there were!

'I wish that your uncles from Indore could have been here,' Jagnath said. 'They would see how the name Ramsingh has travelled!'

They all agreed that it had. It was no longer the concern only of the clan, of which the parent root still eked out a bucolic sort of existence in Indore, or of the Ramsinghs, who had long since moved to other parts of India in a restless spirit of expansion, or even of the Rajput tribe as a whole. It had now become a name of India, a bearer of fame and importance; it gave the lie to the popular belief—among the castes not twice-born, of course!—that the living Rajputs betrayed their martial heritage, lived only on borrowed pride, and that their initiative and daring were a thing of the past. It warmed and it gave hope; it cast a fresh glow on the memory of Jaswant Ramsingh, their bright and towering progenitor, whose forays against the last great Mogul, Aurangzeb, were already in the safe-keeping of the minstrels. To Jagnath it was another proof—if any more were needed after all these years—that he had done well to leave the rut of Indore State and move on to Bombay and new horizons.

Jagnath still remembered how difficult that step had been. Not one of his children knew what trouble and anguish the very thought of it had caused him at the time, for no Rajput, not even a forward-looking one, would ever find it easy to abandon his ancestral home and branch out on his own, even though ambition and common sense might be on the side of the move. It had taken years of vacillation and one rather sordid scandal to make the vital decision, but make it finally had to.

Jagnath had inherited a landed estate and a friendship with the ruling family of the state, and his own contribution to the Ramsingh welfare had been a degree in agriculture, then a new and untried field of endeavour. But came the children and the need for a reorientation, followed by a bad failure of the monsoon in which he realized that land was a groove as well as a boon and that if he wanted his children to benefit by the spread of Western ideas, he must cut himself loose from it and go where 'progress' was to be made the most of—Bombay. So he put his brother Viswanath in charge of the estate, moved forthwith to Bombay and took a job with the government. Vijay was then a growing boy, Tara a precocious baby. The Great War had lately been concluded in Europe and Mr. Gandhi, who had helped Britain with Indian money and volunteers, was confidently awaiting the redemption of the British promise to speed India on the road to self-government. The Act of 1935, embodying a partial fulfilment of that promise, was still fifteen years distant.

Bombay became a landmark, and no Ramsingh would ever be able to disentangle it from his consciousness as long as he lived. To the father it brought a revelation of the ingenious scheme by which a couple of thousand officials ruled a country as large as Europe. For Kandubai it became a time of slow adjustment, the more trying for Bombay's frank indifference to Rajput life and ritual. The Ramsinghs worshipped Siva, Krishna and Gauri, and the festival of Dasara was to them the one true red-letter day in the Hindu year, but the Marwaris and Gujeratis of Bombay seemed utterly devoted to their elephant-headed god of success, Ganesh. So she spent a few years with an intricate plan of compromise which would assure a continued tradition for the children and also fit the family spiritually into the new surroundings, only to find that she need not have bothered. Bombay was so busy becoming a true 'Gateway of India' that its religious broad-mindedness amounted to disregard. When Vijay was enrolled at St. Xavier's College and Tara began to go to a girls' school, the family's pantheon had even to find a temporary niche for such claimants to god-hood as Christ, the Pope and Mohammed, though fortunately the rash soon died down leaving no scars. That was when Vijay began to use the handshake as a form of greeting, instead of bowing over his joined palms as he had been taught; when he first began to bring home Eurasian, Sikh and Parsi playmates and thought nothing of befriending a Muslim, that old and vaunted enemy of the Rajput race, or saying that only an India without caste or religious barriers deserved to be free. How she trembled over that boy, and how soon the devil of 'modernity' ate its way to his inquisitive little brain!

'There is no India without caste,' she used to tell him, hoping against hope that it was not too late. 'Caste has made us what we are, my boy. . . . Never forget that you are a Rajput, a twice-born . . . an equal of the Brahman . . . that gods and holy books have made you so. We hail from the moon . . . to fight and rule the earth . . . to remember our forbears and our dharma. These things are as hunger and thirst . . . a part of ourselves that we must satisfy.'

'Why don't we fight the British then?'

'We have and we have lost. They were stronger.'

'They were stronger, ama, because they have no caste. India too will be strong when there is no longer any caste.'

This kind of glib logic had an irresistible appeal to the Indian boys of that time. Vijay was beginning to hero-worship Mr. Gandhi and Jawa-harlal Nehru and lap up nationalist writings by the satchelful, and his literal mind was apt to linger on anything flamboyant or polemical. The campaign against untouchability, passive resistance against the British, high-caste abuses of their privileges, starving to death in a noble cause—these readily impressed him as the pathway to greatness. They also impressed Nand, a schoolmate of his and a Maratha of soldierly lineage, whose favourite daydream was a Bharat Mata—motherland—without priests and foreigners, in which the young had complete freedom of political action and old men confined themselves to the study of sacred texts. The two boys fell out once or twice over the spinning-wheel, the *charkha* of Gandhiji's, for Nand believed that Indians must master the machine in order to lead the world once more, while Vijay tended towards the Gandhian 'back to nature' ideal, but Nand, being the older, prevailed in the end.

At fifteen, the boy Vijay's Bharat Mata emerged as a nation of skilled mechanics and engineers planning boldly but reverencing their humble origins, of men and women steeped in the past and therefore equal to any foreigner, proud of one another and generous to a fault towards the not-so-well-endowed. Among these last the Eurasians were to be found increasingly often, because at that time both Vijay and Nand got into the habit of meeting Eurasian girls after college hours and walking them along the sea wall at Colaba or through the Victoria gardens, and because it was during such a walk on the reclaimed land in Colaba that Vijay staged his first seduction and broke a nail on the mysterious buttons of a girl's bodice. The agony of that event could still burn a small hole in his consciousness. When he would want to remember his adolescence in later years he would seldom be able to hush up the frightened Eurasian singsong of the girl when she said, 'No, no, don't . . . what are you doing?'

However, sex and Bharat Mata were not all of his boyhood. There were also the tall and dusky corridors of St. Xavier's College, those absurd Gothic tombs forever shying the smiling tropical daylight, and those Italian fathers who never could say 'the' without a faint snarl, who wore their cassocks tucked in at the waist whenever the weather warmed up and had the lavatories whitewashed every time the wall scribbling showed a really interesting turn of mind. In the teashop at the bottom of the courtyard, Hindu, Parsi and Christian boys mixed freely and learned the promise of a new trans-caste unity, the unity of common anti-British emotion. There was Father Antonio's voice when he came down the rostrum on graduation day—'You have stopped waiting for life, life is now waiting for you.' It was as if the one had ceased being a Hindu and the other Christian and the two races had fused somehow for a brief moment—a different kind of unity, both larger and brighter than the first, one he was never again to perceive so intimately save in Connie's bed, and this would only be ages afterwards.

But if life did really wait, it seemed awfully careful not to give itself away. At home it was still a processional of rites and remembrances, of Holi's swings for Lord Krishna, Divali's oil lamps and Dasara prayers, each exactly as in the year past and the year to come. His father was now apt to say, 'Vijay, you have come of age . . . I shall have to look for a bride for you,' and mean what he said. Vijay's degree of M.S. would have been enough for most commercial and government jobs, if he had wanted them; instead, he decided on a further study of mechanical engineering, because that was what Nand was doing too. 'India cannot revive without experts,' Nand used to say during the long arguments at Villa Ram, at which Jagnath pleaded for moderation and common sense. 'This country must be rebuilt from the bottom up, and we must learn how to do it'—Vijay echoed him in his spare moments. Later Uncle Premchand, the newspaper owner, added his weight to Jagnath's and the argument became more specific.

'There are good business openings nowadays for a young man of your talent and education. All engineering is in the hands of the British. There is too much foreign competition for an Indian.'

But Vijay thought he would take it up all the same. After one such harangue in the Premchand house at Juhu, he and Nand walked over to the Flying Club and met Salim Haq, who flew them over Bandra, Santa Cruz and the island lakes. When Vijay came home that night he found that his sense of fitness had been strangely meddled with and that among the values until then immutable a new travesty had taken place. A fortnight later he and Nand started a course with Salim.

'It is still a game for the rich,' Salim confessed soon afterwards, 'but wait another few years and you shall see.'

Salim, the tall, big-faced Muslim, with a gait and manner so deliberate that they seemed to Vijay octopal in the beginning, knew what he was talking about. He then combined the duties of chief instructor, chief engineer, chairman of the managing committee of the club and, in his spare time, confidant of pupils younger than himself; sometimes, too, he was a bad influence in their lives. He was then in his early thirties and had already managed to go through a considerable inheritance left to him by his father. Flying was his last belief; on it he was willing to stake the last good will of the name Haq and his best energies.

In those days the club was still a low shack slapped together out of brick, piles and palm matting, a separate higher shed for two sports machines and a thatched lean-to for members' cars; this last also sheltered stray cattle during the long months of rain. On Saturday and Sunday evenings its green roped-off lawn would be full of week-enders who had spent the day at Juhu

Beach and wanted either a drink at the bar or a ten-minute spin over the island of Salsette, but during the week the small field was quiet and the training went on in a chaste pioneering mood. Vijay began to experience a new kind of exhilaration. The air seemed to be ruled by an independent code of its own, as binding as the codes of the ground, and its single condition of acceptance seemed to be the wholehearted submission of a newcomer. There were so many different ways of looking at it if one happened to be a Hindu! Its thrill was a reward in itself; its detachment, though only partial, made it possible to see oneself as never before, so that many events whose early impact had appeared haphazard gradually took on a more or less smooth pattern of sequence. Uday Ramsingh, the ascetic uncle of Vijay's, had once said that the approach to detachment was immaterial as long as the outcome seemed real enough, and this now rang true for Vijay in a way he had never expected. Not even Salim Haq's fanciful definition could muffle that ring for him.

'Up there my roots are trimmed,' Salim tried to explain one evening, after they had come down and reviewed the lesson over a cup of tea. 'I am reduced to what I see before me . . . and nothing else. When I close my eyes, I forget even that. I become everything . . . and everything becomes me. Once I was Emperor Asoka, dictating my memorial plate . . . I swear to you, my friend, it was quite real. I even worried about someone . . . I don't know who he was . . . who thought that Buddhism would die out in India and that Brahmans would again be strong . . . and me a Muslim, imagine! I wrote him a letter on a piece of parchment and told him how mistaken he was! All the time I was completely awake . . . I put on my sunglasses and listened to the engine. . . .'

That sounded rather obscure and he didn't grasp it at once. 'What else do you remember?' he asked him curiously, discovering the real Salim for the first time and attracted by the discovery. 'Nothing,' Salim told him, 'except that I was Asoka and not Haq. I did not bother my head about the club debentures, which is a favourite pastime of mine. Being a great emperor, I had other worries . . . but not being Salim Haq, well . . . there was nothing. I don't remember that I was blissfully happy . . .'

'Some people are not supposed to remember,' Vijay then said, voicing a garbled version of the Hindu belief in preordination which, to his way of thinking, left non-Hindus to their own fumbling devices. But Salim missed the point, or chose to miss it for reasons clear only to himself. He said: 'You had better not think about that until you have flown a little more'— and there the matter was left to rest until much later. From that day on the mechanics of flying quickly gave place to a growing exuberance which was to dim many of his plans for a new India and refurbish others in a quite inimitable fashion, so that his father Jagnath would be tempted more and more often to call the airplane a curse of the Ramsinghs and Kandubai would sigh for the quiet safety of her beloved Indore.

Then Mehta and Nirula joined the circle under Salim's heavy-footed tutorship. A drive for new members raised the roll to over two hundred and the ramshackle club burgeoned into a respectable meeting place, where the neighbouring rajas and maharajas could display their own dapper new models without losing caste. He piled on his flying hours and struck up some permanent friendships, as with Salim Haq, while at home the wrangles with his father and uncle took on a new hue of pettiness and futility. He was then twenty-two—a highly marriageable age for a Hindu; apart from Nand, all his college mates had already married, gone into suitable jobs and acquired a fairly sensible view of their place in the community; to a father's way of thinking, they were past mischief. Vijay spent many months painting the aerial future of India in lurid colours and his arguments were nearly always emotional.

Nand's death at that time blasted open a youth that had almost rounded itself, if not in a flawless whole, at least in crude likeness of it. Nand crashed late one Sunday evening doing a 'teacher and pupil' turn for Bombay's first flying gymkhana, leaving Vijay very much shattered and exposed.

Even now he could see him lying in the surgery of that municipal hospital at Bandra, the Indo-Christian doctor bending over him and repeating, 'Too late . . . what a shame,' in a voice so resigned that it was maddening. There was a message in Nand's passing which was its meaning, which did not fade because the good doctor could diagnose one part of it alone—the hard one. Even now he remembered the weeks that followed, in which he toyed with the dualistic view of life and human beings; perhaps every man was made of two parts, a live and a dead one, and was not a compact entity as Hinduism pretended; perhaps there was absolute knowledge and absolute ignorance, as well as absolute friendship and absolute enmity . . .? To Vijay, Salim and the others, Nand's going became an event singled out for their notice by a casual fate, and it built a wall between life at large and its intimate significance. Salim brawled himself out of most Bombay clubs, Nirula rushed into an imprudent marriage and he himself lay on the Juhu Beach all day trying not to think. But unlike pledges, loyalties failed to break even in death. Nand's death did away with the last need to rationalize their bond; he went right on existing, virtually if not in fact. Months later, when this belief mellowed into a more bearable emotion and he began to patch up Nand's absence with a greater attachment towards Salim, Vijay came out of his spiritual shambles and went back to the patriarchal monistic house which Hinduism had put together so painstakingly from sundry opposites—with one reservation. It did not matter whether life and death were separate or simply two visages of the same thing; the important issue was that they sometimes merged and cast fleeting light upon each other. When a Hindu gathered that much despite his youth, he was apt to become fidgety in the cramped little niche which his slow-moving community had assigned him.

At that hopeless stage the Flying Association of India announced that H.H. the Aga Khan was offering a cup and two thousand guineas to the first Indian who flew solo to England, and Vijay pounced on it vehemently. It took a week of impassioned argument and flourishes of the association's letter to convince Uncle Premchand, who alone had money for such a venture, that he should back it. When the hardheaded uncle finally gave in, it was from exasperation, not conviction. Vijay hired the club's older Gypsy Moth over his guarantee and Salim threw a party for the local press. Jagnath bore the feverish preparations with a quiet dudgeon that was more withering than any spoken reproof. To Uncle Premchand the plan may well have been a fool's errand, but no true nationalist could think of it without a frank thrill.

'By all means let us have an example of Indian initiative,' he said to Jagnath, justifying his own temporary lapse of balance. 'It is time the world learns that this nation is no longer a sleeping beauty!'

For him, as indeed for all the family members holding his wealth and singular influence in awe, any illustration of that fact soon became a legitimate aspect of patriotism.

4

322 *hrs.* 17 *m.*, he wrote in his logbook on the day of take-off. *They think me crazy—and perhaps I am—but Nand would have understood.*

Some memories were a scramble of images, but this one was an orderly march.

With a boundless landscape slipping steadily beneath him, names and words reverted to their primal awkwardness. Jask, Basra, Shatt el Arab connoted next to nothing; in real life they were large spiders on the fringes of Persian Gulf or banks drenched in deep green, sometimes very wide, often narrow and ephemeral. Baghdad was a rash festering on the sallow skin of the desert, the pale mirrors of the Mediterranean eluded all definition; away in the distance, the spilling cones of ice-cream were Switzerland. A tapeworm lay crinkled in its first sunlight and the map said 'Rhine.' On the last day an unexpected white padding covered all but a few tongues of Southern England. He had no mishap, no engine trouble, not even a strong contrary wind; it seemed almost too simple. He crash-landed on the Downs, sustaining only slight damage, and that same evening faced his first reporters and posed for his first photographs. A logbook entry summoned it all up rather breathlessly, though faithfully too. *Cables from Bombay, Delhi and other parts of India. Personal note from the Aga Khan—flying from F. Riviera to meet me. I am in all the papers. They say I have done it!*

Did the tabloids play him up for lack of better material? Would any other piece of good luck have served their purpose as well as this fluke of his? Had he started a trend for Asia? He puzzled about it for days and finally gave up, for it soon became obvious that his own estimate of the achievement mattered less than that of other people. The Indian Association in London installed him in a fashionable hotel and he posed for a photograph with the members of the committee.

'In our struggle for freedom every little bit helps,' the chairman explained. 'I think the British are pleased that you are not a politician . . . they can give you a rousing reception without committing themselves.'

He accepted that and the later events seemed to bear it out fully.

The Secretary of State for India sent him a sealed letter of good wishes and an invitation, and in the wake of that, other interesting contacts followed. Vijay met His Highness the Aga Khan, received his cup and the prize-money and was then sent on a tour of the Midlands and Scotland. A round of visits to the aircraft factories yielded a most unexpected present, a new-model sports plane. He met a leading aircraft designer and the experience was stimulating beyond words. By then reports of his goings-on had found their way into the home press and the letters from the family reflected a due upheaval. Three months later he wrote to his father of his decision to take a course in aeronautics and aerodynamics, and the reply was a bewildered plaint. He went into an aircraft firm near London and remained studying almost a year. Jagnath and Uncle Premchand expostulated in vain; Vijay had taken to Europe as had other Indians before him, and Europe for once turned her best face forward.

The English at home seemed so different from those back in India! They respected his beliefs and listened to his nationalism seriously, almost sympathetically, and if some of them still favoured colour bars the majority were willing to take an Indian as an equal and a future friend. They knew little of real India, it was true, but they were fairly and soberly disposed. He was impressed by their dispassionate public life, their art of understatement and their unshakable individualism, so vastly more robust than the peepsqueaking which the Indian caste system allowed its young. The warning of the chairman notwithstanding, he thought that no people heir to such an impressive record of freedom and perception would pooh-pooh the suggestion of a free India, if they were only made to see how the Indian of the street felt about it and how deep-rooted was his tradition of government and civic responsibility. His endless talks on it were themselves an essay in parliamentarianism. He soon found himself answering fairness with fairness, harping less on the obvious and blatant than on the implicit, giving due in the right place rather than grudging it. He borrowed some of the laudable British reticence and tried to curb his sentimentality, while yet remaining Indian in all essentials. Over a period of months a new and earnest dignity replaced the bouncing daydreamer of St. Xavier's. Remembering Nand off and on, he began to feel that their joint debt to Bharat Mata now fell to him alone and that one sure way of paying it back in one lump sum was to make these people aware of India's past greatness and future promise.

About that time he got mixed up with a show crowd in London and this marked a new cycle of meetings and discoveries. This England was peopled by seedy-looking men who claimed a haughty knowledge of most things and by women who stormed in and out of rooms in supreme preoccupation. They talked art and riled each other with satisfaction and when this and allied subjects were exhausted, they turned to him with a magnanimity which was as crushing as their other impulses.

'We hear so much about your culture, but where is it?' one said. 'What went on before and after Tagore?'

The questioner, a scenic designer in a West End company, was Constance, a tall, languid girl of thirty, whose air of boredom could not completely disguise her sensual interest in the handsome young Indian. In talking to her, his sense of equality with the English took off from the uncertain rhetorical plane for the first time.

'It is all in the libraries,' he admitted honestly. 'Much of it has been discovered by you English.'

'I know,' she said. 'We've even had to write your history so that you would have it all in one piece.'

'Well, not quite so bad,' he said, 'but there is some truth in it.'

They ranged over the field for hours and while at the end of it Constance had already earmarked him for bed, he was moved to make this entry in the logbook that same evening. *We are a mystery to the outside world and pleased with it. Wherever I go the talk follows the same pattern. Where are you, let's see you! What do they know about us beside the few books they've written themselves? Very little. Of course the fault is ours too.*

It was then that the idea of a world tour first took shape in his head. He thought that if he could persuade a few cultured Indians to visit Europe and America with him, to lecture and talk about India to all who would listen, his debt to Mother India would be well repaid. If other nations could send their men abroad on missions of good will, India could—that is, real India, not the British government. His own mission would include lecturers, not politicians; they would be hand picked and grind no axe, yet would inspire confidence and tell the truth about their country. It was a fine idea, conceived in the grand manner, and Constance approved of it heartily. But a voice from another world jarred the exhilarating harmony for a short while.

'I am worried about you,' his father wrote in a letter. 'Never forget that the only margin rightfully ours in a favourable turn of events is that which we leave ourselves for later. Much of your success is capable of useful moulding, if you will it . . . which is to say that your present place is here at home. . . .'

He stilled it by going to bed with Constance—and replying to his father that his studies would take another half-year.

By the gentle accident of dealing with all his visions and misgivings on a cosily human level, Constance had come to mean for him all that he admired and disliked in the English, their best and their quite unnecessary worst. She was fair, and also disarmingly shameless when fairness no longer served her. As a love affair she was both novel and more disappointing than his Eurasian experiences back home—novel because, whether he avowed it or not, he had craved a white woman from his early adolescence and because in his urge there was the penchant of all coloured races for the fair skin, a penchant as old as Aryan India and almost a Hindu instinct. Disappointing, because after the first flare-up of passion her interest in him became almost wholly erotic. To her he was an experiment; for him, the consummation of the old urge fell far short of the tenuous ideal, and he couldn't help feeling now and then that in some obscure way he had let himself down. In it there was also a resentment beyond judgment, so vague as to be no help at all.

The nights spent with Connie altered, naturally and finally, his whole concept of white women, and through it his sense of parity with the white man received an unexpected, backhanded push. His possession of a white woman was a headlong pillage of the white man's inner fortress, and from then onwards not only would the romance of the white skin for ever be measured against Connie's promiscuous embraces, but the white man would have increasingly more to show for himself than his colour. Such was the ascendancy of emotional knowledge over that of intellect, however well intentioned. But he and Connie overcame the tension after a while and shared each other's bed like two people who have the need of it, though no longer a burning curiosity.

And from Bombay his parents wrote again that it was time he came back —and he realized that tarrying much longer was out of the question. He would like to have gone on with his work and his plans for the lecture tour, but the chairman of the Indian Association thought that India was the proper place from which to organize it. Then, too, winter was coming on again and he had unpleasant recollections of cold from the previous one. Connie's comment was in the line of least resistance: 'I suppose your people have a right to expect you, and that you'll have to go back.' For a brief spell she toyed with the idea of following him at the close of the show season, but he talked her out of it. England had become an indelible landmark, but he was beginning to feel that if he stayed close to it a little longer, he might no more see it. So the next unhappy letter from Jagnath sent him to book his steamship ticket.

He had his two machines crated aboard a P. & O. liner at Tilbury. In the small crowd that came to see him off he and Constance had little opportunity for a last talk.

'It was lucky my meeting you, sweet,' she said with an unnaturally bright smile, patting his arm and then embracing him. 'Try not to forget me so quickly. Remember, I'll still be here when you come with your lecturers.'

He waved to her when she climbed into a taxi and might have gone on waving had not the Brahman chairman taken firm charge of the proceedings at that moment.

'Carry on the good work,' he admonished. 'In a cause like ours every little bit helps. Why shouldn't India become air-minded? We can't bother our leaders with such things just now . . . it is up to you, the youngsters. Carry on and don't let it die on you.'

'I'll do my best,' he promised. The phrase was one of the many unconscious acquisitions of his long stay.

All the same, the wish to carry on was apt to stray in rather wild speculations on that homeward journey. The bank of white cloud which had been his first glimpse of England changed into a white line on the horizon, his last glimpse of it. Between the two were twenty-four extraordinary months from which it was as yet impossible to extract a design; he wondered what they would mean in the long run and he also pondered their pure content of good and bad. How would they affect the kind of life he was returning to? He knew that he had become different, but couldn't yet see it clearly. The colour of the residue was not yet discernible, as indeed it would not be for some time and the residue itself was a new substance. That alone was plain.

He found that the idea of going home filled him with missionary zeal, eagerness and apprehension one after another, and that the future, as the chairman had said, was indeed his own problem. It soon became quite a job to keep track of all the ideas and alternatives and the journey slipped by in feverish scheming, in daring projects that brimmed under his closed eyelids, in a chaotic relay of memories that brought him only headaches and sleepless nights.

But it wasn't until the colour of the sea had begun to change and the first fishing boats made their appearance just outside Bombay that the problem boiled up in his head in frantic earnest and he began to realize, as well as he ever had in the last two years, that the future was not so much a question of schemes as a choice of enlisting his family in his ambitions or else pining away in heroic isolation.

31

5

AND now his father Jagnath said:

'A tour of the world, Vijay . . .? Have you no desire to stay with us?'

And Kandubai, his mother:

'Son, they have changed you after all.'

And Uncle Premchand, the one who should have really grasped it:

'A friend of mine asked me only yesterday if you were going to stay in India or travel again abroad, and I told him your home was here and your first loyalty was to your own country.'

That was the seventh evening of his return and the first opportunity the family had of exacting their tribute in some sort of privacy.

There were, too, his sisters Tara and Munu, and Uncle Premchand's small and delicate-seeming wife Radabai. There was Ram Prashad, a friend of the Ramsinghs and a feminist reputed to be as bright as she was good-looking, and Chanda, the elder of her two girls. And Uday Ramsingh, a distant young uncle of Vijay's, the only one who asked no questions and was apparently immune to all upheaval; he was the family ascetic, whose mere presence would give the conclave a surpassing meaning. They either lolled on the ample divans and thick rugs of the living-room or lounged about with the varying flow of their interest and oratory. Their partly dressed and individually adorned shapes gave the earthy Villa Ram the kind of flashy excitement it had been lacking for some time.

The response was very nearly what he had expected.

Now that the word was out, he had to go through with it and hope for the best. Now it was a question of staying power, for he hoped that if he made a good impression on them they would in due course nod at his patriotic protestations and perhaps even appropriate them. They were given to generous impulses and could sometimes surprise themselves. Had he crashed in the Gulf of Persia and never reached England, some of them might have looked upon him as proof of the sin of deviation—had they not from the beginning regarded his flight as a rare folly? Not having crashed, he might in time become an argument for the value of initiative. Most promising for the time being was the notion he had given them that every young Indian could have done what he did, given the same chance and luck; this might ferment and make allies, he hoped ardently. When it came to pride and successes, Indians were really no different from other people. But, of course, they hated being rushed into a lot of initiative all at once.

'Son,' Jagnath now began humouringly, 'you have had your education . . . your travelling and your amusement. You are twenty-four a flier of

32

some experience. You have had more than your share of publicity . . . now is the time to do something final for your career.'

The occasion had given him a new kind of dignity, and the old Hindu tradition invested it with all manner of duties, both pleasant and stern. He was the father, the doyen, the host and the last authority to whom all issues would be put for evaluation; in his at times awkward bearing rested the unmistakable concern for his only son's karma.

'Why should you go lecturing to the world?' he said, unbelieving. 'Every day I hear the cry, Give us young Indians of talent! And what is the answer? Our boys either end up as government clerks at fifty rupees a month . . . or they go to Europe and come back wanting to tear everything upside down.'

'Please, pitaji, let me explain,' Vijay said.

He strolled over to the bookshelf, still laden with his English mementoes and newspaper clippings, and made a patient and coherent brief for his plan.

He told them of the hundreds of English men and women he had met and the sincerity with which they took him into their homes and often their confidence, and of their instinct to be just; of how incredibly ignorant they were about this country and how that handicap played them right into the hands of their better-informed but unscrupulous politicians; how they, almost without exception, wanted to learn more and meet more outspoken Indians 'like myself,' and how that led him to the idea of a lecture tour around Europe and America: it was a promise he must carry out at all cost.

'Of course,' he added at once, warming to it and feeling surer of his ground, 'I would only fly the little group, naturally. The lecturers would be the ones to talk, not I. We would get up a really interesting programme and try to do it well.'

'Whoever heard of such a thing?' Jagnath said.

'Who would finance you?' Uncle Premchand asked; he twirled his pencil a lot faster now and his thick lenses seemed to magnify his quizzical interest a thousand times; he slid his large and well-covered frame into an easy chair, gathered his dangling dhoti under his crossed knees and then began to shake them—a pointer to his concentration.

'Money would be found somehow,' Vijay said. 'Maybe even by public contribution. . . . I thought maybe you might help, uncle.'

'You would first have to prove that it would be a good investment. I am not convinced.'

'What I mean is this: We must put our viewpoint before the British in their own house. All along they have judged us just as they felt like . . . mostly by their own standards. All our misunderstandings begin right there. . . .'

'The British have been here for two hundred years,' the uncle said tartly. 'If they don't know us yet, it is their own fault.'

'But someone must put it right.'

'Quite, Vijay Our Gandhiji is doing it . . . leave it to him. You would do much more good to yourself . . . and, mind you, to India . . . if you were to start a small air service right here.'

'That would take even more money.'

'Why should it? I started my first business with one coolie in a small room.'

'It is not the same thing, uncle.'

Then Rajuram the Elder, an old family servant, brought fresh tea and while the pouring and distribution went on Vijay returned to his place on the couch and took a deep breath. The air felt several degrees warmer. Beyond the open windows a naked temple tree in bud seemed to be coming into blossom at the mere touch of the warm light reaching towards it in a fading tunnel.

Serving the country so that it and the server benefited—the dear theme of Uncle Premchand! It was not an infrequent view in this new India of businessmen and jute wallahs and in its own small way it was not unreasonable, but now he began to wish that his uncle had not been present at this stage of his return.

Like most successful business men Premchand had, after thirty years of accumulation, conceived a patriotic conscience. He had bought his three newspapers when they were on the verge of extinction and had built two of them into formidable pillars of the Indian press, it was true, but Vijay thought that he had certainly not done it for the greater glory of his country; patriotism had come much later, together with his other acquisitions. To that new horizon, he now seemed to persuade himself, he was directing his various ships of business, and the outward circumstances seemed almost to bear him out. It was small wonder that his opinions had also become increasingly rugged and that he thought enterprise to be basically the work of one man; it arose in the head of one man and grew with him. If one joined forces with other men for the purposes of enterprise, one openly confessed one's ineptitude; no working partner in a limited company could ever feel the pride of creation. Premchand would therefore plug for drudgery and 'starting on the ground floor,' and all the silly little irritations and nuisances which money, well employed, could spare one. None of this would make Vijay's going easier, especially since it was his plan to ask his uncle for money before he went to other people for it.

He saw them all, arrayed on the divans and chairs, stirring their tea or sipping it thirstily, and he thought, What a mixed family we are! He then took refuge in metaphor, remembering that pictures spoke to them more vividly than logical thought.

'If I stayed here my contribution would be like a pebble on the beach,' he told them. 'But this lecture tour would be a big thing . . . a real accomplishment. This is my choice as I see it. I would be unhappy if I didn't at least try it.'

'Vijay, my son, we ought to be realistic too,' Jagnath said plaintively. He had had enough of fantasy; the wanton rhetoric was beginning to upset him.

'I have never been so earnest in all my life,' Vijay said. 'Why don't you try to see that?'

Rana Prashad pulled her sari deeper over her head and said, 'Hear, hear!' cheerfully. 'Don't let them browbeat you, Vijay. I am on your side!' She turned to Jagnath and smiled beautifully. 'If he were my son I would let him cross his bridges when he came to them.'

Jagnath pondered this in vain, and his eyebrows came together.

'Has he not come to one of them?' he asked—for in his world of solid deeds safety counted more than its cost in æsthetic values. It was all very well for this handsome Rana Prashad to take ideas as they came—was she not such a singular exception to most of them, at any rate in this country? For one thing, she was a widow, a person of traditional humbleness and inconsequence on the Hindu scales, except that she refused to feel humble about it; for another, her life was quite a heap of flouted rules and trampled convention. It was very well for her to give her blessing to anything unusual—but here was this boy Vijay, a man in every respect save the good old conventional, whose course must be plotted with a steady hand and much clear thinking.

So he added firmly and respectfully: 'If it were not so important for a man of his age, we would not be discussing it, would we?'

But she smiled again, playing with her many bangles.

'And I would rather my son went abroad as an ambassador of good will,' she said, 'than that he shouted himself hoarse in the streets of Bombay. Everyone according to his lights. I often wish I had a son.'

'Thank you, Shreemati,' Vijay said, smiling back.

'And what is more,' she added, 'we need all the good will we can get. Look how the Americans sold themselves through their films alone! Look at the legend of the Irish! This is a lazy world, my friends. Good neighbours don't fall from the heavens . . . they must be made the hard way.'

Influenced by home gossip, Vijay had once thought that her modernity was no more than an emotional rebound from orthodoxy. Now he gathered that she denied the die-hards intellectually as well—a daring thing even for a truly emancipated Indian woman. She painted her nails, used facial make-up and smoked cigarettes in the presence of men—all outrages of the old notion of Indian woman, that shy, self-effacing form stirring in the shadows! She wore lovely sheer saris of quiet colours above which the oval perfection of her face shone like a hill magnolia; she was thirty-seven, but seemed much younger, so that the apostles of purdah and those believing that sheltered home life was good for a woman had only to look at her to see how mistaken they were. She was not of the family either, though nearly as attached to it as an in-law, and she was a good friend of Ranjit Singh's, a cousin of Jagnath's. She had been married very early, lost her husband, then fought his family for the control of her two children and later become a rare combination, a jealous Indian suffragette mother. Although she argued only moderately, what she had to say happened always to be very much to the point; in the eyes of the Hindu males, though not in Vijay's, such lucidity was faintly in bad taste.

Now Premchand finished his tea, threw a turmeric seed in his mouth and came to the rescue of Jagnath. He said:

Supposing you do succeed, Vijay. Do you then propose touring the world all your life?'

'Of course not, uncle. When the tour is over I'll come back and do something else.'

'Well, frankly, I do not understand you. My meaning of the word realism is quite different.'

'Realism? At this time of the night? Who makes this depressing statement?'

Arriving at the threshold of the living-room at that moment, Ranjit Singh made a smiling general obeisance at the gathering and then raised his hands expectantly. He made no excuse for being late. He had on a natty tropical suit of English cut and looked very sleek and handsome to Vijay.

'I overheard the last remark,' he said, turning from the uncle to the nephew, using his long and live fingers picturesquely. 'A hero returns home after many years . . . he is in all the newspapers, everybody wants him to come to dinner . . . the world is happy to have him . . . and then this dismal word. Arre, my friends! Could we not be realistic to-morrow?'

Jagnath, who had got up to make room for the new guest, smiled hospitably. 'Vijay would like to go round the world lecturing. We were discussing it when you came in.'

'Lecturing? How very British that sounds. Lecturing whom?'

Jagnath, Vijay and Mrs. Prashad tried to explain all at once, then the father and son bowed out in favour of the lady guest. While Jagnath put on some more lights around the room and the servant brought more tea, she gave Ranjit a highly-coloured version of Vijay's idea. Just then Tara came in trailed by Mrs. Prashad's daughter Chanda, trailed in turn by two more servants loaded with betel-nut trays and plates of sweetmeats. The girls squatted at the feet of their mothers and one or two of the guests began to chew. Jagnath sat down again, satisfied that the wheels of hospitality turned according to the best custom.

36

'I am all for it, believe me,' Mrs. Prashad wound up, giving Vijay another smile. 'What is more, I think you are the right person for it, as long as you believe that there is some good in the British. I have no such illusions any more.'

'And may I be told what is so fantastic about it?' Ranjit asked.

The whole plan . . . from the beginning to the end,' Jagnath said. 'It is not only that he has not the money for it, but he wants to get it by public contributions.'

'Why not? We have contributed to everything else.'

'You don't realize, Ranjit. Such a thing would cost a fortune.'

'How much, Vijay?'

'About a hundred thousand rupees.'

'Arre . . . my goodness!' He sank on the nearest divan, mock-fanned himself with a sky-blue handkerchief, and a merry glint came into his eyes. 'My dearest Vijay, that *is* a huge sum!' he said. 'What a pity you did not need it five years ago, when I could have given it to you. Now the government is giving in to our propagandists,' he added, stuffing the handkerchief in his breast pocket and thwacking it. 'Now the land tariff has been reformed, unfortunately, and I am one of the oppressed minority . . . a mere landowner. Next year I may be a landowner without income, . . . maybe without land. Is there any other way I can help you?'

Vijay told him there might be, but he hadn't yet thought much about it; he would call on him when the need arose.

'I hope you will do so in Dehra Dun,' Ranjit said imperturbably, 'for I should be much honoured to show you to my friends . . . some of whom are rich beyond reason.'

The invitation was greeted with snickers from the younger people and some delighted laughter from the oldsters, and Vijay himself had to smile. In his mind the words of his young uncle conformed to an old and already accepted pattern.

Ranjit was thirty-two, an endearing wastrel and a puzzle to the family; an ornament whose fit was necessary but never quite comfortable. To the soberer among them he was an anxious hint of what a Rajput might become if the 'British peace' in India grew too long and Rajputs lost sight of their warring background. Ranjit's grandfather had been the youngest brother of Jagnath's grandfather, both of whom had known about the Indian Mutiny and learned to wield Rajput weapons from the great Jaswant Ramsingh, their forefather—but since then the two lines had separated and Ranjit's family had settled near Delhi in Northern India and amassed a good deal of valuable land, which the present heir seemed to do his utmost to neglect. He was fond of good Indian music and old Indian costumes and jewellery, and was not past dabbling in ladies' dress design on occasions—and a harrowing thing this must have seemed to the spirits of Jaswant and Gopal Ramsingh. But he had great personal charm and an impish wit which somehow blurred his failings and forced people to sigh in resignation: 'This Ranjit, what a great man he might have been!' Vijay wondered anew what had made him come all the way from Dehra Dun when all he would undoubtedly say would be in sharp contrast to the opinion and advice of the others.

'So for the present, my dear Vijay,' he now heard him conclude, 'you must address yourself to those who do not groan under advanced land policies . . . perhaps your Uncle Premchand here . . .?'

But Uncle Premchand had just finished folding a leaf of betel nut and pushing it into his mouth, and the chewing of it would render him unfit for any further discussion for at least ten minutes; he waved his hand in a vigorous and patent manner.

More laughter, and some malicious girlish squeals. Tara looked at Chanda and both raised the hems of their saris to their noses to hide their glee.

'And so once more India is divided on the issue of hard cash,' Mrs. Prashad said laughing. 'Next time you hear the word realism, Vijay, be sure that behind it tinkle the silver rupees.'

'I will, Shreemati.'

'And it is well that they do,' Jagnath said. 'Rupees must be made in order to be given away . . .'

An emphatic nod from Uncle Premchand, at that moment bending over the cuspidor.

'. . . and that is something I thought you had learned in Europe, where . . . I am told . . . a young man goes from the school straight into a job, so that he may take a wife as he pleases and become independent.'

'Shabash, lalaji! Well spoken!'

'How little you know, lalaji!'

'When I was in Europe things were certainly not so . . .!'

'But that was a long time ago . . .!'

'It was not. Let me tell you . . .!'

'Yes, let us hear it!'

Vijay drew up his legs more cosily and leaned on the cushions of the divan.

Now the air of the room seemed recharged with a fresh lease of the same old current and most of it swirled about itself and for its own sake. Now skirts rustled with a new and brittler sound, bracelets jingled more often, knees shook in a faster time. Even the temple tree seemed to crane closer to the window. He felt calmer now. He knew that they would waste hours, days and perhaps weeks in grappling with the real problem, only to find themselves probing it from a fresh angle through another chance remark. A good deal would be said for the pure joy of saying it, for they were born talkers and this was their talking holiday. They were in no hurry, despite their fervent protestations to the contrary. Talk was the original indoor sport of man.

They would eventually find themselves face to face with the core of the issue and wouldn't be able to ignore it any longer, and they would then, warmly and deftly, pass it around and leave him to make the last and only decision.

Back in England it had often been pointed out to him that this peculiarity was an Indian trait and that it was a good omen for the democratic future of India.

6

ONLY sadhu Uday Ramsingh, the austere among the smiling, quietly refrained from advising. Later that night, when Vijay found him on the flat roof, he said:

'I was wondering how soon you would come.'

The girls Chanda and Tara were already there, the latter in the midst of a story of the Ballard Pier arrival. From the lower floors came the composite hubbub of another debate and the breeze bandied it into the night. The sea broke over the reef with infinite gentleness; the sound was reassuring, like the creak of a bullock cart late in the evening. In the moonless sky a huge spread of crystals glittered largely.

'Yes, Udayji,' Vijay admitted. 'I wanted to know what you thought of my plan.'

'Sit down then and get your breath back,' Uday said.

He was the family ascetic, although a number of his relatives were still shy in using either the name sadhu or sannyasi in his presence. He was twenty-eight, another young uncle of Vijay's. He had renounced conventional family life while still a boy and now had no home except in the sense that he sometimes stayed with one or another member of the family, usually between two pilgrimages or after a prolonged penance on the road. It was his custom to straggle over the country and not bother to explain himself. A sadhu's life was nobody's business—an old Hindu truism. Destiny put all men in two categories, householders and men of spiritual occupations; while a householder was the pawn of his caste and community, an ascetic was his own law; renunciation of things dear to the hearts of most men exempted a sadhu from conformity—a concession which the West grudgingly made only to an artist and that but rarely.

He made that plain soon enough.

When Tara's story was over he sat up on his tape bed, on which he also slept at night, and slapped the pillow behind him once or twice; then he slapped his own shoulder, too, as the breeze was beginning to bring the mosquitoes all the way to the roof.

'I have only one opinion,' he said at length, raising a torpid arm to the stars. 'You could call these illumination from without. Our own illumination must come from within. This is true always . . . whether you are thinking of good will among nations . . . or simply of a chicken. I know what you are going to say'—he waved Vijay to silence across the space— 'We ought to get a new outlook . . . this one is old.'

'Well, isn't it, Udayji?'

The sadhu's arm fell slowly, touched the bed, then seemed to curl up, like a sleek young animal settling to rest.

'One must not forget,' he said weakly, 'that men go back to it again and again for its enduring comfort. But as you wish. . . . My opinion is: Where is the point in lecturing the world about us? Are we interested . . .?' After a long pause he went on: 'Is it not enough that we should first kindle the fire in our own chests? If that light is good the world will discover it in their own time . . . at their own pleasure. That is when they will most benefit by it.'

'Can anyone wait so long?' Tara said.

'You heard Mrs. Prashad downstairs,' Vijay said. 'This is a lazy world and we must make friends while we can.'

If Uday heard this, he didn't let it distract him. 'To conclude,' he said almost sleepily, 'we must believe in ourselves and be content with that. Each must worry only about himself . . . about his own dharma and his goals . . . and not meddle, if possible.' He paused and slapped again. 'But if you think it is your duty to tell the world about India, go ahead and do it. Who am I to say that such a thing may not be your destiny?'

'How simple that sounds!' Vijay said with faint suspicion.

He couldn't see Uday's face in the weak reflection of the roof lamp, but he could imagine it—a good face, numbed by a life of hard trying, in which the eyes, far from revealing, veiled a strange fire; in which the smooth forehead led the casual observer to assume that self-sufficiency in a human being was possible if he invoked it stubbornly and long enough. At that moment it was probably closed to all interference—a smooth trick he had spent many years in acquiring. If he were a squid retreating in a cloud of ink, Vijay thought, one would at least know where to look for him. But his technique was more slippery; he vanished neatly, like the dice under the cup of a gulli-gulli man at Port Said; one saw him enter, but one knew he was not really there.

'So you neither encourage nor discourage. Have you any other views?'

'None for the present,' Uday said. 'What I just told you was loud thinking . . . at your own invitation.'

'And this country?' Chanda Prashad asked. 'Don't you care what happens to it?'

'It is not that I do not care. It is that I *am* not to care.'

He shifted on the bed and pulled down the mosquito net, which he proceeded to tuck under the mattress on all four sides. His body became a dim shape behind the veil, burrowing, stretching and gasping. Then he lay down and yawned loudly.

'It is just as well that some of us do have to care,' Chanda said uncertainly, endeavouring to sound courteous, but not succeeding. 'Life of a nation is bigger than life of a man. If we all went to the Himalayas, we would always have foreigners in New Delhi.'

'And be their slaves too,' Tara agreed.

None of which, however, seemed to concern the sadhu any more. He sighed pleasurably, but the sigh became another long and relaxed yawn, after which he said only: 'The unlikely truth is, dear girls, that if we all lived in the Himalayas, we wouldn't care who was in Delhi.'

Lower down, the multiple voice became one—someone had put on the radio. Four bars of a doleful, quasi-oriental tune soared into the night, followed by the eager voice of the announcer. 'This is All India Radio, Delhi . . . here is the news . . .' The volume decreased, a few bars of Western dance music rent the air abruptly, then all was peace again and the mongrel in the Mahim cove could be heard once more in all his grievous wretchedness. To the north the glowing skyline of Bandra drew a line between the purple of the land and the purple of the sea.

'Uday bhai, are you sleepy?' Vijay asked. 'Do you want us to go?'

'Stay on here if you wish,' the sadhu said. 'I shall fall asleep presently.'

So the two girls held a whispered consultation, then rose and took their leave. Vijay hoped that he would sleep restfully. As they passed through the narrow doorway that led to the staircase, the creaking bed told them that the sadhu had finally settled down for the night.

It was only when they reached the second floor that Vijay gathered that his ascetic uncle had snubbed him. The shock was not a great one, but it rankled. Despite their kinship, in Uday's eyes he was still only a householder. His brain, achievements, fame as flier, ambition and sincerity apparently did not impress the sadhu. At that he rebelled instinctively. No Indian who had been lionized by the Europeans, as he had been these two years, could hope to fall in again with the hierarchical ways of his people with anything like his erstwhile blind acceptance. The break of these two years would sharpen his sense of national belonging in a hundred subtle and often clashing ways and even his inherited awe of the spiritual aristocracy of his countrymen would lose ground steadily in his eyes. Of course he would go on being respectful before sadhus, swamis and sannyasis, but this would call for an ever greater effort of will and patience.

Above all, he hated being snubbed in the presence of girls after all that had already been said downstairs. There was no getting away from it: He should have known better and not asked for it.

On the ground floor talk was still in progress, with Uncle Premchand holding forth at the top of his voice and Jagnath and Mrs. Prashad interrupting. Vijay suggested a walk in the garden and the girls agreed; he led the way to the lawn and from there to the young pipal tree near the outer hedge where Kandubai used to hang toy swings in honour of Krishna during the festival of Holi. There were some wicker chairs under the tree, and they sat down reflecting on Uday and his unearthly goings-on. Chanda was inclined to call him a brooding type, a dreamer, without whom India would never have become what she was, but who would yet be pretty difficult to live with, as a daily dose.

'Brooding in itself wouldn't be bad,' he told her, 'if it didn't make people believe that it was better than doing things. I myself brood quite often,' he added, lighting a cigarette. 'This is not to say that I am a lazy fellow.'

'I don't understand,' Tara said.

'Neither do I,' said Chanda.

'Let me explain,' he said, and went on telling them what he meant, not expecting them to follow him, anyway. Everyone said India needed a fresh outlook, a few departures from tradition, a fresh start, in fact.

'Please explain further,' Chanda said pedantically.

'All right.' He continued to explain how to his mind the weakness of spiritual induction was that it brushed aside the pace of life and left men acutely dissatisfied when they needed their hope most. He kept the talk on a homely level and did so patiently, as befitted an older brother.

'Not at all clear,' Tara said at the end.

'No?' he said, and shrugged resignedly in the dark; not for nothing were Indian girls said to be such shadowy companions of Indian men. 'Just look at Uday, a typical example,' he told her. While Uday pondered the ultimate answers in a leisurely way, three hundred million Indian peasants would probably agree that the abolition of land debt would be a fine thing.

'So it would be,' Chanda said. 'We all know that!'

Well then, there you were! It was in the first place a matter of proportion. It was fine for a man to try and measure the depth of life by draining it dry, but he could only do it because the others were willing to let him, don't you see . . .? If they refused to, or if they too forgot their mission on this earth in their own devil-take-the-hindmost fashion, where would that leave everybody—'you and me, for example, or my sister Tara?'

'Don't worry about me,' Tara said with much confidence.

'Or me,' Chanda echoed her. 'But listen, there is a dog here in the garden. Can you hear it?'

They listened and heard first a faint rustle, then a hiss. Tara was the first to recognize it. She said, 'Goodness, a snake!' and screamed. Then all three jumped and collided in the dark.

'Run back to the path!' Vijay ordered. 'Lift your feet!'

'Back to the house . . . run, run!' Tara called after her friend.

Vijay went on shouting orders and tripping over chairs, of which there suddenly seemed to be a fiendish multitude, and running across the lawn he nearly fell into a freshly manured bed of flowers. But they reached the house and in the hall Jagnath, Chanda's mother and Uncle Premchand were already surging forward to meet them.

'What has happened? Why did you shout?' Jagnath demanded.

Vijay started to tell him, but Tara was quicker and louder, and so he dashed upstairs to find his flying flashlight and on the way down grabbed his old tennis racket. He ran back to the garden and searched round for the reptile, while the family stood under the porch and superintended the operation with shrill concern. At last he found it, a sluggish dark-brown oldster of the rock-snake variety who had probably only just swallowed a mouse or frog, for it refused to budge in the intense glare of the flashlight, and he clubbed it to death furiously.

They all came and had a look at it, and Tara felt sick and had to run into the house. Jagnath said he would talk to the gardener in the morning and Mrs. Prashad wanted to know if anyone had been bitten and, on receiving a suitable assurance, thought that it was time for bed anyway. Premchand averted his head and said nothing; he was a Jain, to whom all killing was unpardonable. Little Munu examined the shining coil with a leer of disgust, found that it didn't wring her stomach, went upstairs to boast of it to Tara. Then they all went indoors.

'How good you were not a sadhu, but a man of action!' Chanda said to Vijay in the hall.

'Or a Jain,' he said. 'Just think of it!'

Ashamed of his excitement, he couldn't help thinking of Constance—now probably laughing again and maybe even flirting with other men back in the throes of the London show season, whose invariable comment in any upheaval used to be 'Easy does it, Vijay!' who believed that any emotion was absolute poison to human dignity. She had used those words on the street as well as in bed, and in time they had come to have a mesmeric effect on him; he had begun to associate excitement with the volatile oriental temperament and had started feeling ashamed of it. And here one little snake and two hysterical girls had made him lose his head and behave like a small boy! One had obviously to try and be alert all the time.

'You know, I agree with what you said before,' Chanda said trailing up the stairs after him. 'We Indians waste a lot of everybody's time . . . and the women are as bad as men.'

'I wasn't thinking of women down there.'

'Oh but I was, Vijay. And you should learn to, also.'

He glanced at her over his shoulder and thought, What do *you* know about women?

Her sari was of a simple white cotton, and she still left her head uncovered in the manner of schoolgirls. Her pigtails were long and braided with flowers of the season, but her prettiness was dulled somehow by her determined bid for intelligence. He had hardly looked at her since coming home, and this was not to be wondered at; her mother, Mrs. Prashad, was the kind of woman who would overshadow any other woman in the room, her own daughter included.

'I mean us, Indian women,' she told him on the first landing. 'We are the chattels of our men, not real partners.'

'Are you?' He looked at her more closely. 'Are you complaining?'

'No, not complaining. Only telling you.'

She sounded sincere, and he noticed that she wasn't such a chit after all —on the contrary, a rather demure and promising kind of adolescent, quite in keeping with the Prashad brand of good looks. He controlled his impatience and even managed to smile.

'I know what you mean, Chanda. You must tell me more about it . . . maybe to-morrow. Now we must all try and get some sleep. Good night to you and pleasant dreams.'

'Good night, Vijay.' She turned round quickly.

He watched her go up the second flight to the large guest room which she shared with her mother, her small henna-coloured heels bouncing up the stairs like two animated oranges.

Undressing in his own room, he decided that the day had not brought him as much success as he had hoped. The family were still rushing round in small circles—they couldn't help themselves, and now it was too late to reform them. To-morrow he was to go to town to a formal luncheon in his honour, the day after to a function at the Flying Club at Juhu, then to press interviews and meetings. And there were other invitations, among them one from his friend Salim Haq—and then he remembered that he hadn't yet talked to the Muslim and that that was probably what he needed.

If Salim had any advice to give, he wouldn't use long words to do it; he would think of the world lectures as a flier and practical man, and would look upon the plan as a job for its own sake. He and Salim had spent some very happy hours together in the early days of the Flying Club and if they weren't of the same faith and caste, they were at least of the same generation. And that, he now reflected in a sudden flash of lucidity, was the crux of all trouble for a young repatriate: No matter what he aspired to or did, to his seniors he would only be a mere young man on a rampage; here youth was axiomatically of no consequence. Here, once more, India was different from the rest of the world and the difference was regrettable and galling.

He peered into the mirror and wondered anew whether or not to grow a moustache and make a compromise. Connie had been against it on the ground that it would be an affectation. 'You're handsome enough without it,' she used to say. 'Don't be so unbearably vain!' But that was Europe; he was now back in his own circle, where it was useful to look older. He found a soft pencil on the writing-table and painted a wide black line across his upper lip, squinting at the result critically. The thing did after all change him into someone else, someone much more earnest-looking and more menacing, while at the same time it rather smothered his well-shaped mouth—'one of the nicest things about you,' Connie once said—and made light of his Rajput nose, that gently hooked, narrow-nostrilled legacy of the great Jaswant, of which the Ramsinghs justly boasted. No, this wouldn't do.

He wiped it off again with a moist towel and felt much relieved. Young or not, this is me anyhow! he thought, relenting towards the recovered image in the looking-glass. Now a strand of his thick black hair fell over one temple and gave his eyes a candid friendly look, and his pale-brown cheeks fitted more naturally into the smooth Rajput oval of his face. The mouth could have been more sharply curved, and maybe less sensuous and not quite so full, it was true, and he wished that Connie's descriptions of it had not been so extravagant, but all things considered it was a good and manly face, and he could look upon it as an asset and not fret so, even though its youth would plainly take some time to live down.

Then he switched off the light and lay down listening to the soft washing of sea at the bottom of the Worli rock.

Second Chapter

❦❦❦❦❦❦❦❦❦❦❦❦❦❦❦❦❦❦❦❦❦❦❦❦❦❦❦❦❦❦❦

1

ALL further thought of world tours was jolted by a series of leavetakings in the family.

Mrs. Rana Prashad, slightly wilted from too strenuous a contact with the militant womanhood of Bombay, had been called to Delhi by the militant ladies of that imperial city; and Chanda had to return to college in Mussoorie. Vijay, his father and Tara went to a dinner given in his honour in one of the Hindu hotels, and Chanda made the most of being his neighbour at the table by telling him that the family were old-fashioned and he right, and that he should most certainly go on his tour in spite of their views.

'You don't know how lucky you are to be a man,' she said. 'Imagine me trying to pack up and leave home without mother.'

'You would never be forgiven, would you?' he said.

'No, never. One has to be a woman . . . a Hindu woman . . . to know how lucky it is to be a man.'

Amused by her logic he said, 'You know, Chanda, sometimes I'd rather sit at home and have only the cooking and the priests to worry about.'

At which she jingled her glass and silver bangles and gave him a crushing look. Anger, he noticed, danced over her growing softness like a sprite at an uncongenial hour of the night, so that it was impossible to tell which of her tricks were native and which borrowed from the repertory of her mother. One thing was plain: Chanda took herself more seriously than most girls of her years, and she had acquired some of her mother's hostility towards the race of males.

'Wait till you've been back a few months,' she told him. 'Of all the good things you've learned in Europe you'll remember only those that are flattering to your person. You'll go back to betel nut and walking barefoot . . . and marry and use your wife like a piece of furniture. . . . You won't even know that she might have a soul and her own pride.'

'I don't think I'll marry, Chanda. If this plan of mine falls through I might even go into the forest.'

'You into the forest?' She fingered her lapis lazuli necklace and laughed. 'No one spends a few years in Europe to go into the jungle afterwards.'

'You sound as though the women did all the sacrificing in this world.'

'Well, don't they? I mean, in little ways, day in and day out . . . without holiness and high heaven.'

He would like to have known this strange girl a little better, even though she always seemed to be on the defensive about something. Now it was too late, and he had problems of his own. He wound up this last meeting of theirs by promising to be progressive and fair to women all his life, and she wished him good luck in his world tour. They shook hands under the table and later she turned pensive as suddenly as she had lost her temper. He decided that she would be a difficult girl to know and that it was perhaps just as well that the great mass of Hindu girls did not have suffragette mothers.

Mrs. Prashad's words of farewell were more to the point and also greatly heartening.

'Keep this to yourself,' she confided with one of her beautiful smiles. 'I have been quietly working on your father and Uncle Premchand. Your uncle might even be persuaded to count out some real money . . . I wouldn't put it past him. Everything is a question of approach. No, I am really very sincere'—this with a shake of the head when he nodded too readily. 'They are all deeply interested in your well-being, but they are apt to think of it in terms of their own. So go ahead, Vijay, and don't spare yourself.'

He conveyed his gratitude and told her that he was determined at least to have a try, and she added that any success he might achieve would be of very great interest to her.

'We're not related in the usual way,' she said, 'but I've known you most of your life. That gives me a certain right . . . yes, and expectations.'

Her smile was so beguiling that he couldn't help staring at it. Above all her sympathy at this stage was equal to a friendship unexpectedly come across, and he did appreciate it.

He tried to show it, too, by taking the mother and daughter to the station on the following day and seeing them comfortably established in the Punjab Express.

On the same train was Ranjit, making for his home in Dehra Dun. Like Mrs. Prashad, whom he was to look after on the twenty-six-hour journey, he had become bored with Bombay and its conflicting pretensions, but he had enjoyed Vijay's homecoming very much indeed and he frankly confessed it. 'I haven't had so much fun in the past two years.' Yet now he longed to be back in the sprawling and sleepy garden of his house, to which his friends came not for stimulation but for relaxation, where it was possible to be an Indian without having to hold some party card.

'The best about us is that we have managed to remain completely ourselves these five thousand years,' he told Vijay just before the train was whistled, steamed and flurried out of the station. 'The Arabs, Afghans, Moguls. British . . . none of them could really change us. But lately we seem to want to become someone else . . . a foolish mistake, if you ask me. You, for example!'—with a flourish of the finger that started as irony and ended in a diffident droop—'you also strain to be someone else. Why should you? We didn't invent the airplane . . . why should you waste your time on something so un-Indian? Why not on our old frescoes, histories, philosophies and so forth? These things make us a civilization . . . not your gadgets, certainly. Come with me to Dehra Dun and I'll show you how to be useful without having to borrow from abroad.'

'I will, sometime . . .'

But it was too late; the Punjab Express did finally pull out of the station.

He caught a glimpse of Chanda waving from her window. He waved back and wondered when he would see them again. He walked out of the station and drove home wondering, too, whether it was a good thing for these people to have so many contradictory notions about themselves. Were they not like the waving of a many-armed ancient idol? The simile was only partly accurate. Whereas each of the idol's arms was allotted a very special purpose, the present waving struck him as a confusion of feints on all sides, none prompted by very much more than a vague, unfinished reflex. But having other things to worry about, he could not warm up to the vision as perhaps he should have.

The last to leave was Uday, the sadhu. Coming home one afternoon Vijay learned that his ascetic uncle had suddenly tied his personal effects into a bundle and taken to the road. Only Kandubai and little Munu were home at the time, and to them he gave an appropriate blessing and also a message of good will for the absent members. He did not say where he was going—was not his territory without milestones?—only that he would look for a quieter place and a simpler life. Vijay was piqued, though not inconsolate; one more arm of the idol had apparently waved and vanished, and no one seemed to become the happier for it.

Then Uncle Premchand's visits to Worli petered out and stopped altogether. The great newspaper magnate had given the family his quota of opinioning and done his duty. Now his *Morning Herald* and *Free India* were about to launch a campaign against the Act of 1935—a new British dodge of Indian freedom, he called it—and his full-time attendance was necessary. Therefore, to talk to him as soon as possible about the world lectures impressed Vijay as more urgent every day, for once Premchand embroiled himself in politics his judgment would become entirely partisan.

This brought on the memory of Salim Haq, with whom he had not talked yet but without whose encouragement and help he could not hope ever to move.

48

2

THE long break in their friendship might well show to Vijay some of the kinks in Salim Haq's otherwise supple character, but one trait there was which would never change, on which it was safe to depend in any circumstance—the original adventurer in Salim. Once his objections were swept aside with suitable sarcasm or ferreted out of their crannies with a ringing call to adventure, the Muslim would turn fatalistic. This had occurred before and it would occur again, if Vijay played his gambits deftly enough.

Salim had learned flying in England, between erratically attended semesters of law at London, but his stay in that country had been cut short by the death of his widower father, a successful medical man at Bombay and interpreter of the Koran in his spare time. Salim and his sister Leela, then married to an up-and-coming motor car merchant, inherited a couple of weedy bungalows on Cumballa Hill, a good deal of valuable investment and a respected name. Since then neither had done much to edify that name; Leela had left her husband to cause a mild stir as a film actress and then vanish in obscurity, and Salim had launched his club at Juhu and taken up journalism as a hobby; his gossip column in Premchand's *Free India*—called Marut's Hour, the Ghost Hour—had given him a certain notoriety, because he was fond of imagining himself as a poltergeist in the better-gilded cupboards of the Parsis, that shrewd and wealthy community of Indian Zoroastrians who owned most of Bombay and a considerable portion of Indian industry.

His flying record was well known, though it made hardly a dent on his own community, the Khojas. About this time his loyalties were two: flying and Salim—from which stemmed all his other leanings and preferences, excitement being the chief among them. Life was apparently not a leisurely draught of solid well-being, but only so many potent drops of time to be enjoyed at uncertain intervals. To a Hindu such spacing of life between surcharged moments was apt to seem like a wilful foreshortening of perspective, but now Vijay was beginning to understand him better than in the past; now he also thought that Salim's mystical approach to anything new and beckoning was almost Hindu in feeling. The beliefs of Islam seemed no longer dynamic enough to occupy his intelligence, for since the fall of the Mogul dynasty in the eighteenth century Islam had lost its glamour and become the drab profession of a minority, suffering still further at the hands of Western rationalism in later years. His restiveness now dragged him from the low ebb of frustration to the high-water mark of fleeting transposition and he seemed to wait only for the next fraction of time that would make him forget himself.

This then was India of 1936, where, unknown to either of them, beliefs and temperaments for ever rubbed and worked upon one another, where the Muslim sometimes borrowed from the Hindu and the Hindu from the Muslim, with entirely reassuring consequences, where the only vital differences slept in musty old books and did not really loom very large save to those whose bread they happened to be.

Vijay presently ran his friend to earth at a tea party in Juhu. He explained his world lectures to Salim, stressing the adventurous sides of the plan, and told him that he proposed to go to the princes of Rajputana and ask them to back the plan each according to his means, and that his help was needed only for that one visit. The appeal was to run roughly: For the greater glory of India.

'Those people won't give you an anna, bhai,' Salim said and his eyebrows bristled darkly. 'If you were a tout for pretty dancing girls . . . then, maybe they would listen.'

Salim's scowl was that of a person for whose sole benefit the drama of human folly was being enacted once more.

Outwardly he was the same man Vijay had left two years ago—tall and large and beginning to stoop a little. For once his wild black mane was in place, uncovering a long slanting scar on his right forehead. Although he was now in his middle thirties, the wide purple rings under his eyes betokened a dissipation of nearly twice that time. Vijay had often wondered whether this point had anything to do with the fact that the Khoja Muslims, of whom Salim's family had been a prominent sample, were so inbred; long and fierce opposition to intermarriage with the other Muslim branches had branded their physiognomy so plainly that one could often think of their community in terms of a composite head. The highlights of that head were a strong, almost Semitic nose, large liquid eyes and a vague thickness of features that proclaimed strength but concealed foibles and uncertain personalities. He wore none of the usual coverings of a Khoja Muslim, but dressed in European white cottons of the single-breasted variety and occasionally open-necked shirts and loose white pyjamas.

Vijay came straight to the point: 'Listen, Salim, I want to go to them with at least one big name on our side . . . Uncle Premchand. I will probably get his promise of help on the condition that the princes come in too. Then, we'll go to them and say that Premchand and his newspapers are behind it. Don't you see, Salim? It's what Akbar did with the Rajputs . . . got the promise from one house and used it on the other. What can we lose? Nothing. And while we're doing it, you'll have a good holiday and enjoy yourself. Think of the fun if we do get away with it . . .!'

'It is crazy, bhai, but I will think about it,' Salim said.

'But time is getting so very short, Salim! Soon it will be spring, then summer. We don't want to come to Rajputana and find all the maharajas gone to the hill stations.'

The glib logic of the appeal had much less effect on the Muslim than its urgent ring. They parted promising to meet again soon, and Vijay considered the first round definitely won.

In the next discussion, which took place in Villa Ram in Worli, Salim was more captious—a good sign. They went into a hoarse all-night session in which Vijay stooped to every petty stratagem that would serve his purpose. Literature and maps lay on the floor; on the desk, a revolving school globe. with the capitals of Europe joined by red lines; on the bed, sheets and sheets of figures, estimates of cost, names of possible lecturers. Vijay made great play with the tentative itinerary of the tour. 'Look!' he said to the Muslim. 'England, France, Germany, Austria, Italy . . . all close together, all curious about India . . . all wanting to do business with us.' The partly shaded lamp over the bed gave the scene a flavour at once conspiratorial and weird. Salim waded through the litter on the floor, kicked about peevishly; his big nose registered all emotion from digust to near-capitulation. Obstinately he murmured: 'I cannot see it, bhai, simply cannot!' He slumped into a chair and crossed his bulky knees, shaking one of them violently, but to anyone who knew him this was clutching at straws.

Vijay therefore said, 'Let me show it to you once more, Salim,' and then abandoned frontal assault in favour of slow infiltration.

With infinite patience he outlined the route of the tour, his panel of lectures and all the incidental pleasure that would await such a mission in a strange country, and the sheer weight of it made the fancy seem earth-bound. Salim wavered between wanting to laugh uproariously and going home to sleep. Of all the things he had pictured himself doing, this was easily the most insane and the most captivating. Certainly it was adventure, of a kind that had no precedent even in his erratic career. One had to be an Indian to feel the true poetry of emotion—and Vijay was truly the most emotional young man, and his emotion truly contagious.

'Arre, it is still crazy, completely mad!' he said, even long after midnight. 'Have you talked to your uncle? Is he going to give you a single rupee? Do you really think the princes are patriotic . . .?'

'Some of them must be,' Vijay said patiently. 'I think you're being unfair . ... many have built schools and hospitals and looked after their people. And it is not as though a stranger were coming to beg for money . . . they know about me from the newspapers. And after all what more can they do than refuse . . .?'

'You don't know them, I am telling you.'

'Well then, Salim, I shall know them . . . after we make the visits.'

'You are mad, my friend, there is no other word for it,' Salim said with a shrug of his shoulders. 'And now I must go home.'

He didn't, however, and later there was a knock on the door and Tara came in with a pot of tea, which she had brewed on her own initiative in order to break up the noisy huddle. By then it was already four o'clock. Their voices, she complained, were to be heard all over the neighbourhood, and would they please give the other people a chance to sleep?

'All your brother's fault,' Salim said hoarsely. 'He is mad and now he is driving me mad too.'

And Tara, who had long nurtured a grudge towards the no-good wit of the Marut's Hour and believed that all Muslims were the natural collaborators of the British, was stung to rise to the defence of her brother rather explosively. She swept her loose tresses behind her and told Salim that if anything was the fault of her brother, and it would first have to be proved, it was sure to be not nearly so vicious as the shameful gossip-mongering of the Marut column. 'Is this what the Muslims are doing for the freedom of India?' she asked with blazing eyes and a contemptuous mouth.

To which Salim said, 'Look at the little revolutionary!' and poured himself a cup of tea. Then Vijay calmed her down, and she swung to the other extreme and told Salim that if he had any decency in him he would try and do something useful for a change. The interlude was resolved by the three of them sitting down to tea and reviling the Parsis, another torpid minority, and by Salim's admission that Marut's Hour wasn't pulling its weight and that he would certainly do something about it.

When Tara went back to sleep, the two men lay on the bed and had a last cigarette. Salim said:

'The reason I cannot be angry with you is that you are a barbarian. All Hindus are.'

Wryness flitted over his powerful nose like a mist over a crag; the Central Asian brigands who were undoubtedly his forbears visited his face for one unforgettable second.

'Any other race with so little appreciation of reality,' he concluded, 'would have rotted away in these five thousand years. You have absolutely no mission in this world.'

Vijay yawned. 'Then you are coming to Rajputana?'

'I shall tell you to-morrow,' Salim said. He sounded calmer, almost resigned.

Knowing that men on holiday were more malleable than in their offices, Vijay waited until Uncle Premchand moved out to his house at Juhu for the week-end. This proved to be a wise precaution.

He and Salim found the press potentate relaxing in a painted Mogul swing in the palm grove of his garden. He received them suspiciously. They lied that they had driven over from the Flying Club for a swim, then spent several hours on the beach, in redemption of the lie, and in that time Salim made two attempts to escape, of course in vain; later they played badminton on the uncle's lawn court, had a bath and cleaned up. Lulled into a sense of security, Premchand asked them to stay overnight. Next morning they took him to the beach and had another leisurely swim. From the club behind the grove someone chose that moment to fly a sports machine low over the surf—they could see the pilot waving at them—and the incident put Premchand in good humour. This was Vijay's cue; he took it up cautiously and did not let it drop for the remainder of the day.

The germ which Mrs. Prashad had lately put into Uncle Premchand showed signs of full incubation. Vijay produced his portfolios of selected English clippings, photographs of various functions and excerpts from some of the speeches made in his honour in England. An article in the *Manchester Guardian* actually deplored that 'rare sight, a cultured and outspoken young Indian in our midst.' Premchand had never been out of India, but he was well up on current affairs and he was impressed. The long and nerve-racking day drew to a close with his tentative promise of help for the lecture tour.

'If you get the backing of the princes, I will come in too,' he said. 'It will be a modest participation . . . I am not as rich as you seem to think. But if you fail . . .'

'We won't, Uncle,' Vijay said at once. 'Anyhow not altogether. But you could give us some letters of introduction.'

Premchand consented with a lameness that was more accommodating than they had dared to expect. 'I know one or two of those rulers fairly well,' he said. 'And it might help you. All the same, I would like you to understand this plainly: I will not stop thinking that there are better ways for a young man to make a start.'

'For me this is the best,' Vijay assured him.

'I know that I would never let one of my sons attempt anything so far-fetched,' Premchand went on. 'One can tarry after fifty, but not at your age. If you will have rice, you must see to the paddy while it is green.'

Vijay did not deny it.

They argued a while longer, now without passion, and later that night Vijay and Salim talked it all over once more. They drew up a separate itinerary of the Kathiawar and Rajputana native states, whose rulers included those they knew personally, and decided to fly to the main capitals by plane and cover the smaller states by train or car. By April-end, if they minded their schedule, they would be back in Bombay and ready to report to the uncle. Meanwhile, hurry was the order of the day; hot weather was around the corner and neither wanted to await it in such gruelling surroundings as the bare plains of Central India. Nor did Premchand believe in having the Marut's Hour filled by proxy longer than could be helped.

They drove to town on Monday morning, in the wake of the uncle, and Salim confessed to a certain amount of pleasurable anticipation.

This made Vijay completely happy.

Once more the Hindu and the Muslim shared the same thrill and felt like two brothers, and the thrill itself blunted their differences of upbringing in a way that would have astounded their parents.

For the Hindu, larger than the vision of a world tour and patriotic duty was this vibrant tingle that followed all decisions to act, to move on. The obvious enjoyable trimmings of the plan were certainly not all of it; Vijay could grasp that much in spite of the flurry which presently quickened all his thinking.

There was also an airy and lambent joy, a gift far in excess of the 'obligatory' action of the philosopher in the Bhagavad-Gita, the Song Celestial, the Hindu New Testament. Was he being a lesser Hindu for looking forward to it . . .? A moment's elated reflection convinced him that he wasn't, but that the Gita probably just overlooked this great emotion. Kneading a new idea and a brain child into a vigorous deed was not 'duty' in the Gita sense, nor a 'performance thereof'; it was not ethical like the need to obey one's parents or rear a family, and it surely was not something to be passed round from one birth to another as bail for one's soul—which was how the Gita looked upon all actions, under the name of karma.

No, he thought, remembering his ascetic Uncle Uday—it was new and immediate and his very own; it buoyed him and made him delightfully self-sufficient, much as his early flying used to. Whether that thrill was 'attachment' of the Gita variety or not, he did not stop to consider. The sheer animation of it precluded all hardheaded inquiry. He knew only that instead of fading out amidst bloodless phantoms, which was the alleged goal of all ascetic meditation—and also the probable future undoing of his sadhu uncle—he was surging out of himself on new wings and feeling very good indeed.

Was that the same as trying to be someone else, in the words of Ranjit . . .?

3

THE ruler of the first native state of Kathiawar was a member of the Bombay Flying Club. They landed on his private aerodrome late one evening and that same night Vijay wrote in his lately reopened logbook:

Dined with His Highness at the palace. Would like to 'assist' but the state finances are in a bad shape at present. Will let us know.

On the following morning they took off for Dragoda's big neighbour, Bijnagar, but the maharaja had gone duck shooting in the field and would not be back for some days. They borrowed a state car, drove after him and broke the front axle in the process, then waited twenty-four hours for a relief car and finally caught up with him. He promised to contribute two thousand rupees. *So much for the uncle's letter of introduction,* the logbook said. *I should have laughed in the man's face, but had to thank him instead.*

They went on to visit eleven more states of the first and second order, and the outlook failed to change. Three other maharajas promised one thousand each; the great majority were interested or sympathetic, but they refused either for reasons of state or from private difficulties. Vijay was at first inclined to believe them, but Salim was less impressionable; everyone knew that these princes spent many thousands of rupees on a single visit to Bombay or Poona during the racing seasons. It soon emerged that their carefully rehearsed strategy would not see them through and that what Vijay was looking upon as a patriotic plan for the greater glory of all his people was in reality a potential bone of contention.

Friday 22nd. Told H.H. we are going to lecture on Indian philosophy, religions, arts, politics, history. 'What?' he said. 'And you are leaving out the states, one-third of this country?' I said the states would come under history, but he wasn't pleased. 'British India can take care of itself,' he told us. 'I'm only interested in the states. If you can bring out that side, I can almost promise that some of my colleagues in the Chamber of Princes would sponsor the tour.' I told him that was out of the question, as foreigners thought India was one nation, and a contrary presentation might confuse them. 'I've given you my ideas,' he said. 'If you can see reason, I can make my promise. Otherwise not.'

One of the smaller rajas had the reputation of an art patron, and they explained the tour as a cultural mission from the East to the West. He nodded approvingly until the talk turned to cost.

'One hundred thousand is a lot of money,' he observed peevishly. 'I have given the University of Benares two musical scholarships for ten years and the cost was only forty thousand.'

'This is much bigger,' Vijay told him. 'It covers almost the whole of Europe.'

'Aside from that, it means a good deal of information spread far and wide,' Salim amplified. 'Something India has never done for herself.'

'True, true, I daresay. I am only trying to see my little corner of it. For example, with one hundred thousand I could give the Royal Academy in London a chair of Indian music . . . which I am very anxious to propagate. You can imagine the prestige of such a grant.'

'Very well indeed,' Vijay said sincerely. 'We Indians can do very much for ourselves, if we set our minds to it.'

'It is generous of you to agree with me,' His Highness said, 'but you must give me a little time to think about it. How can I get in touch with you?'

They gave him their addresses and a rough date of their return to Bombay, but he never wrote or did anything about it. Months later Vijay was still furious for letting him off so cheaply.

Afterwards the visits fell into a routine, now more now less depressing. They saw some twenty princes and their vassals, and behind the polite receptions and all-professed interest Vijay sensed a caution that was hard to square not only with his own now wounded enthusiasm but also with the lavish pomp with which the refusals were served—elaborate dinners, invitations to shikar, luxurious limousines and self-indulgence of the most expensive sort. He quickly fell into the habit of thinking that if the men spent so much money on themselves, a little more for the nation would not hurt them. Certainly, that kind of reasoning was petulant and highly subjective; the little more was always the stage at which the princes felt the need of economy. 'Do you see the point?' he began to inquire of Salim, and the latter admitted that he did.

'In fact, quite clearly, my friend,' the Muslim said, for his broad view of life was that the rich sucked the poor and that in India God had forgotten to take sides. 'They've heard of progress and they think that they can slow it down by a scholarship here and a memorial plate there. You have seen them and talked to them . . . they're not the least bit interested in the rest of the country. Arre, bhai, how could I not see the point? They are out of date . . . they wish to wring their privileges dry before they are snatched away from them. Did I not warn you at the outset . . .?'

From which outburst Vijay gathered that the Muslim was regretting his rashness in Bombay.

In the first fortnight of the trip Salim had tried to work on a novel of 'Parsi life and iniquities,' started, he now revealed, before Vijay's return from England, but as it became necessary to address the princes at greater length and more forcefully, his creative periods had shortened and grown less happy. A sluggish new grind had replaced the lively flow of his Bombay life, so repetitious that it looked like a conspiracy against his spirit. Dinner, argument, refusal—it was no holiday, and no adventure. To make everything worse, spring was changing to an untimely summer and heat and dust were becoming hard to bear, so that he would now more and more often sprawl in an easy chair of an evening and rail hotly against the meanness of certain individuals and against the Hindu breed at large.

From Baroda they flew to Rajputana. The heat battened the great plain into a pancake of jaundiced ochre, in which towns rippled in currents of hot air and dust vanquished every simul and tamarind grove; mud hamlets seemed like the abandoned excavations on the shores of waterless lakes; only the palace grounds, emerald stones washed up on the silt of the last seasonal flood, gleamed freshly. But the states of Rajputana increased their dejection.

Vijay began to wonder if by some obscure system of grapevine the purpose of their visit was not being relayed from palace to palace, in advance of themselves. The last letter of Uncle Premchand was delivered, read and ignored. Udaipur, Jaipur, Bikaner, Gwalior—all guest houses fused into one, all palaces merged. The trip began to resemble a travelling circus, with each new destination divided into the same fragments, each fragment a spiritless renewal of itself; pegs were driven into the ground, ropes tied to them from which canvas flapped hopefully until it sagged; the pegs came out again and only a few crumpled holes remained. He discovered that even in frustration one moved with a ludicrous kind of momentum, and for this there seemed to be no precedent in his past; one blundered on, sustained less by doggedness than by a failure to choose the right moment for stopping. Conversation now grated in a closed circle and he learned to wait for the phrase that would send the meeting to its familiar conclusion.

Perhaps they really think the idea far-fetched, he analysed at length. *I really don't understand them.* This was only partly true, for having listened to the opposite view so often he had come to accept its existence and therefore some of its validity. *All these princes travel to Europe and America every summer for their own pleasure. What is far-fetched about a few lecturers making the same journey for the sake of the country? Why don't they tell me straight away that the only far-fetched point is that the money should come out of their pockets?*

Sometimes—not too often—he wondered whether he wasn't being ridiculous. When all was said and done, he had really come to ask for money; if they felt like refusing it, it was their good right. Of course he obtained no comfort from such introspection. The heat had become too great, the interviews too exhausting and he was becoming too irritable himself for a thorough heart searching. One more entry in the logbook summed up his feelings accurately:

How can we jeer at the Katherine Mayos, or at the world for believing her calumny of India? If we don't care to have the world see us as we are, we can't blame it for getting its information second-hand. What is preposterous about a team of cultured Indians touring the world? Our tennis and hockey stars go to every international tournament and funds are always available. Our maharajas will send a cricket eleven abroad in the name of India's prestige, but a thing that has made us what we are, that is us, cannot be exported for lack of sponsors. I should weep, but I'm too disgusted.

Then May arrived in a dry, dusty hush, and he gave up even the logbook. Rivers and jheels shrivelled up and their gulches rent the landscape like some affliction of the earth's surface; the sky blazed more sharply every day. On the ground the simmering breath of the hot weather did away with all impassioned argument. They nodded listlessly over the glasses of raspberry sherbert offered to them, waited for the bad news, then departed. Salim began to receive urgent telegrams from the newspaper in Bombay, mostly over Premchand's name, and wanted very much to go back. He looked pale and seemed to have lost weight.

'After this call you drop me at Delhi,' he said suddenly one night. 'If I am to die, I should like to do it like a good Muslim . . . in my own house.'

They tried three more states and then Vijay gave up.

The whole labour had yielded just under fifteen thousand rupees, most of it in promises so laden with stipulations that they gave him a gripe. They had received no money outright, and could expect it only after the rainy season, when the donors would either descend from the hill stations or return from their European tours.

The trip ended at Delhi; Salim's furtive preparations for return deepened Vijay's gloom.

4

HE TRIED to picture the faces of his parents and his uncle when he told them of the failure.

Jagnath would probably say nothing, but his hurt eyes would be hard to by-pass. He himself would probably go on talking to cover his humiliation and there would come a moment utterly empty of all communication, a saturation of silence, as it were, in which they would eye one another stealthily and anticipate each other's thoughts, in which every new attempt at good fellowship would turn out clumsier than the last one. He could already guess the muteness of that isolation and he also knew that he would be helpless against it until the spring of bitterness within him gave out, for this would inhibit his sincerity and produce only sham. It was better to cool off, although this would need time and privacy; no bitterness would outlast the woolgathering breezes of time, those who knew had said.

'I'll go and stay with Ranjit at Dehra Dun, for a week or so anyhow,' he told Salim. 'He's asked me to come, if I ever came so far north.'

'But it is a mistake,' Salim said, cheered somewhat by his impending departure on the Frontier Mail. 'You are the brooding type, Vijay . . . I know you. The longer you delay it, the harder it will be in the end.'

But the thought of going to Bombay at this juncture verged on the harrowing, and he said merely:

'Maybe you are right, Salim, but it's the only way I know.'

He wondered, too, if the Muslim was right in calling him the brooding type. He had never thought of himself in those terms and no one had ever named them so bluntly; Constance had come nearest to it with that little phrase of hers—'take it easy'—but he had never taken it in the present context. Truth probably lay between the two: He felt that he must be alone with his failure.

It had come at a time when dismay didn't enter his thoughts, and it was on this plane that he couldn't bear facing his family. There were other reasons, too, which he might have cited in defence of his attitude—one of them: it was his first full-dress failure. It had come too soon after a real triumph; the events of the last two years had piled on top of each other too recklessly for such a bleak end. Was brooding an ability to realize that sequence clearly? Once in the old days Premchand had said that failure was joined to triumph by a frail causeway and that safe traffic along it was only a matter of learned negotiation. Not having learned it, before, Vijay could barely test the accuracy of his uncle's statement, the more so as it seemed to him that he had tumbled from one end to the other, mostly without warning and mainly through the air; he still felt giddy. That's all, he said to himself, sensing vaguely that it wasn't.

Now he also found that taking a frank measure of his failure was like the dazed murmur of a man who had tripped and fallen—I fell, I fell! . . . As a feeling it was simple enough, but it was not yet a wholly lucid perception. The man who fell started by not quite believing it; he moved his limbs and glanced round to see if anyone had watched him, then got up and dusted his elbows and the seat of his dhoti. Whether his behaviour was right or wrong was beside the point; he did it, that was the point. If he happened to be a Hindu, even a liberally schooled one, there would be the added temptation of looking for a sign in the tumble, for it had after all been written that no accident was ever purely accidental and that no one came to grief without a good reason.

This was a proposition which Salim should have understood, which he most certainly would have understood if he had only been less buffeted and exhausted. At this moment they were both too sick at heart for any real communion. It was therefore easier in the long run to allow oneself to be accused of brooding than to argue the toss. But when Vijay saw him off at the Delhi Junction on the following morning, he showed that he was more alive to it than he might have appeared.

'Arre, bhai, you will show them yet!' he said without anger or rancour. 'I don't know how you will do it . . . and you shouldn't ask me . . . but I know that you will. Those sons of she-camels and hyenas must not get away with it!'

The words were still there long after Salim's stooping frame moved out of the Station and the mail train clattered off towards New Delhi and Bombay Central. They were really quite suggestive. They turned his wrath on another course.

For ten whole days he dallied in the gardens of the Red Fort and cooled himself on its latticed balconies, pondering the rôle played by the sons of she-camels. On closer inspection, it turned out to be a large one. Their complicity seemed suddenly to shine out sharply, and his bitterness veered up at them and became personalized. Thinking in this manner became even faintly gratifying. As he loitered under some shady Mogul archway, fragments of past conversations would float into his mind and become banded in a greater meaning and this in turn would lead him to generalizations, another kind of adventure. He discovered that failure engendered a sense of crusade as soon as one apportioned it with any realism. The outcome did not make for an even mind, but it did bring him a kind of private comfort, summed up in the sneer: What could you expect!

June in Delhi is like wearing a frying pan for a hat, he wrote three days after his friend's departure. *Do nothing but loaf around and drink gallons of water. By the way! The Moguls failed too, but look at the scale of that failure! Trying to write home—can't make myself. Ranjit in Mussoorie. Will go and see him as soon as he comes down to Dehra Dun.*

Strolling along the cool corridors of the old Mogul capital he often remembered England and Connie, but the white Mogul marbles seemed more and more to butt in and say: We came before them, think of us! He did think of them, sometimes for hours on end, quite against his will. Throughout the day the sun and the shadows seemed to shift the white domes of Shah-Jahan's pavilions, while the breeze harped on the mango and asok crowns until it trapped itself, and the bronze bell in the old guard-tower chimed an hour more vivid and audacious than anything he had known since boyhood. In a neighbouring courtyard the Pearl Mosque slumbered in a precious but deathly stillness, undisturbed even by the ageing bearded guide and his five daily prayers. He sat on the spotless marble floor of the Hall of Private Audiences and thought he heard the murmur of another time. *Should I be hearing these things, being a Hindu . . .?*

He found later that it really made very little difference, and that feeling thus meant echoing the deep unity of India in a way that surpassed all learned assertions. The Moguls may have been Muslims and aliens but they became Indians in the end and *that* was the memorable thing anyone needed to know. Their exquisite marble, their red stone and brick, and the sun, stars, breezes and rains playing upon them, had always been and still were Indian—as was his growing realization that Constance was not of it, that indeed she was edging farther and farther into that limbo of his awareness which he now preferred to stir up as little as possible. He bought a picture postcard in one of the Fort's curio shops and filled it with the usual scribble, and the writing took on all the stiffness and none of the grace of the Pearl Mosque, to which his gaze stole again and again. But he sent it off to her all the same, feeling that it was the least he could do, hoping that the act would allay the last twitchings of his conscience.

Meanwhile, *Still haven't written home*, the logbook said. Each morning he took the pen and the writing pad with him, only to abandon it for a new view or another insidious daydream. First he condemned himself as lazy, then tried to blame the heat and justify his torpor. It is only a phase, he said to himself, as though the remedy lay without, in some as yet undivined event. I ought to make some kind of decision. Then he found that decision was another name for that wearying accumulation of postponements and excuses which had ceased to be convincing, the stage when he could languish no more without inward squirming; he gave in to it with the usual Hindu lameness, prompted merely by a vague desire to prove himself alive.

He sat down in his hotel one evening and wrote to his father, discovering in the process that there wasn't much that he could explain to him. He was not sure of the reason for that. Their reunion last January should have drawn them closer together, but somehow it hadn't done that; somehow it had cast their temperamental differences in sharper relief. No, it was no use deceiving himself—they didn't even speak a common language. He made that admission shamefacedly and with deep regret, but make it he had to. All that Jagnath had said and done since January went to prove that he still lived in the past and for the past—this was clear to him now. And Uncle Premchand, in spite of his martinet airs and thinly veneered grocer mentality, came much closer to what Vijay thought was his own advanced outlook; although his politics might at times warp his general sense of proportion, the man was still a 'modern,' with all his petty reservations and often in spite of them.

His letter to his uncle was therefore freer and longer, a restful task by comparison. Whatever else Premchand might think of him, he would never doubt his nephew's love of his country. On this dependable old target Vijay was going to group all his batteries in the future.

He outlined the Kathiawar and Rajputana visits in some detail, leaning heavily upon euphemism and omission. He made a clean copy of it, and the total impression was that some of the princes would welcome the plan if the enterprise were organized by an experienced hand—for example, Premchand himself. He posted the letter with a flutter of the heart; so much depended on how his uncle would read it! If he decided to be generous, the princes might be addressed once more and asked to review their contributions; if he withdrew, the scheme was off for the time being. Meanwhile, Salim would also prime the family at Worli as gently as he knew how, and then let him know.

Nothing to keep me here, he wrote on the eleventh day. *Ranjit is back. Going to-morrow.*

He spent the morning at the Willingdon Airport, servicing and refuelling leisurely, then took off in the early afternoon and watched the model neatness of New Delhi grow small and pleasingly inanimate. Its plaster-of-paris beauty was bathed in a strong glare and ringed by the bright silver of the Jumna Canal. The Round Assembly was a perfect navel, imperfectly placed. Over the Fort of Shajahanabad was a bank of dust blown from the seething dunes of the river and from the vast and melting plains of Central India.

Third Chapter

1

AT A mean and balmy height of two thousand feet, the plateau of Dehra Dun managed to combine the best of the Gangetic plain and the steeply-rising Himalayan ranges immediately to the north. It grew the finest rice in India, and also the only camellias; it had poplars, mangoes, eucalypti, papayas, litchi trees, bougainvillæas and poinsettias, side by side and often on top of each other, and it made a gardener of the poorest man. It had once been a part of the forbidden state of Nepal, from which the British had wrested it in a series of mountain wars but which, with their flair for usefulness, they had later befriended and made into a loyal ally; the Gurkhas of Nepal became the staunchest levies of the Crown, and Dehra Dun their chief Indian cantonment. The valley also gave room to the first Indian military academy, the finest forest research institute in the East and one of the most versatile botanical gardens in all India. Through its southern barrier, the Siwalik Hills, flowed two great rivers, Jumna and Ganges, and the range gazed straight at the frozen seesaw of the holy Garwal Himalayas in whose shade the Ganges turned from ice to water for the first time.

The winding hunched bazaars of the town lay clustered around the railway station, itself straddling the main Delhi highway, but their dust and odours seemed somehow cleansed by the lush greenery of the adjoining cantonment and forests. At one end of the highway lay Saharanpur and Delhi; at the other, Mussoorie, the gayest of Himalayan summer retreats. From this last Ranjit had lately descended looking the worse for his long and strenuous holiday.

'Arre, my dear Vijay, what are you saying! What talk is that of clashing!' he exclaimed when the former expressed the hope that his arrival would not clash with any previous engagements of the household. 'On the contrary, now that you have come, you must stay as long as you can.' He was expecting a few friends for Rakhi-Purnima, the festival of bracelets, and Mrs. Rana Prashad and her daughters were likely to be among them. 'I saw a good deal of them up in Mussoorie, where the girls go to school, as you remember,' he said. 'We are going to have such a jolly time together, wait and see . . .!' There was real warmth in his greeting and he obviously looked forward to the party with great pleasure.

Unlike the last time in Bombay, he wore plain white pyjamas with a dark-red cord and a thin muslin shirt that made him appear frailer and a little strange. His slippers were of an adapted Mohammedan design with silver tassels and fancy pigtail tops. The cool and comfortable Indian garb gave his movements a lissom new leisure, so remote from the pose of relaxation struck in Bombay.

Vijay was put up in the garden cottage and given a special servant. He loafed away three days without any difficulty, reading, writing to mother and Salim, often roaming through the huge and lovely garden to which wild jungle formed an outer ring of defences. Now and then as he sat and dozed on the lawn of the cottage a rippling chord would be relayed from tree to tree, plaintive in evocation and insistence, Indian music of an unknown softness, thrummed out of seedy-looking instruments so in keeping with the soul of the house, and he would try to listen to it with closed eyes only to find that, when he opened them, he was listening to the breeze in the eucalypti, blowing gently towards the mountain slopes. After a time he couldn't imagine it ever being different. Often, too, he would wonder if Ranjit expected that he should keep him better company, but this fitful insurgence of duty would soon be waylaid by the supine ways of the garden.

He had wanted time to himself, and time was a subtle prerogative of Ranjit's household. It wafted through the niches of the arched verandahs and perpetually dark passages, and it bristled uncertainly in the green bowers of the garden. The main building must have been intended as a forest refuge for a Mogul monarch; it was one-storied and meandering, and its many wings seemed to have been built on one principle alone: fusion with the trees. It lay a few miles to the north of the town, on the main road to Mussoorie, and one came to it through a stuccoed arch, late Jehangir in design and further dishevelled by bougainvillæa, and then by a drive first hemmed in by thick litchis and then colonnaded by pale and beautifully upright eucalypti. The front faced a round lawn and a maze of flowerbeds against a tall green backdrop, while the rear slunk away under bushy overhangs of mango and loquat, giving one the impression that it went on endlessly as if shying from evil eyes and daylight. If its existence didn't seem real that was not because its builder had willed it thus but because, with the plan of the house in his lap, he had probably fallen dreaming to the swishing whispers of the garden.

He was tempted to penetrate the shroud of easy friendliness which blood relationship was apt to pull over people in default of a more genuine understanding, and to find the inner person in his uncle, and the impulse was selfish rather than simply inquisitive. Ranjit was almost a stranger, despite his bland complaisance; to get comfort from him one would first have to learn his purpose. The prodigious bending of life to his own ends must have rested on some tried strategy, from which something might be learned, perhaps even copied? But when he did finally stroll over to the house to talk to him, Ranjit was unwilling.

'You made an effort, and you failed,' was all the reaction he showed to Vijay's story of Rajputana. 'Your fault or other people's . . . no one can really say without a fearful lot of speculation. You should say to yourself, My people are backward . . . and leave it at that. It will save you much anguish.'

'If I could, I would have gone back to Bombay,' Vijay said, regretting his confessions. 'I wanted to serve my people . . . in a way that suited me. Why should they think me impractical?'

'The same old question . . . why . . .?' Ranjit picked up a mounted watercolour which he was examining when Vijay walked in, and raised it to the light. 'A most attractive late Kangra, are you interested? Imagine, I have just come across it in the rubbish of my storeroom. It is called "Lady with Hookah and Attendant." Amusing too . . . look!'

Vijay peered at it silently; the Kangra belle was loaded down with jewels and her eyes were absurdly large and too wide apart.

'I have forgotten you do not care for Indian art . . . sorry,' Ranjit said. 'What was the topic . . .? Ah yes, service. Well, Vijay, different people have different notions of service. Yours is to fly . . . mine to save Indian art from the tourists. Our friends think us both lunatics. It can't be helped. You cannot please everyone.' He lighted a cigarette and blazed a wide circle with it, as if cutting a portion of space on which to fasten the present wisdom. 'The secret is to forget the other people and remember only yourself.'

'When you need their help . . .?'

'No, take their help if you need it, but don't pay any attention to what they say. And let me tell you, dear Vijay . . . that is exactly what they are doing themselves.'

Vijay waited for the smile that would score the irony, but none was apparent. Ranjit looked at him frankly and seemed quite sincere. With his dark-rimmed reading glasses, surrounded by dozens of paintings, statues and silk scrolls, he did indeed look different from the man Vijay had met in Bombay.

'My advice is to relax, be a thorough Hindu,' he added. 'Our forefathers never did anything else.'

'Isn't this thing you're holding in your hand a proof that they did?'

C

Ranjit laid the painting on the table. 'Art is relaxation, among other things.'

A servant appeared with a lighted hookah for his master and a casket of pan supari. Ranjit rose, took Vijay's arm and led him to a divan, saying:

'Let me tell you . . . this is the one thing I have against your student hotheads. In their shouting for home rule there is always a suggestion that the old is not nearly so good as the new.'

Vijay listened to the burbling of the water pipe and wondered if his visit had been one of the false starts engendered by a long depression. The gleam which he had once thought he detected in Ranjit was found at closer view to be a blurred one after all. He blamed it on the romantic nonsense which the family had for years bestowed on anything it could not classify. To his way of thinking, Ranjit was patently turning his back on everything that was necessary to most men. He would always be a charming host and a facile talker, but no pillar in a real difficulty.

Presently the room grew dark and Ranjit laid the pipe on its rack and patted his knee. 'And now, would you like a walk before supper? I feel I have enough of Indian art for one day.'

They went out of the house and into the garden where dusk had already united the trees in a realm of indigo. The front porch looked for all the world like the musty background of a Rajasthani miniature: slender and opalescent, the arches reflected the new moon on the outside, but their dark sides seemed to be an enduring part of the twilight. Did Ranjit's elusiveness spring from the fleeting character of the house, or was it he who enthralled the dwelling and held it captive for a purpose of his own? Vijay was not sure, and now the secret seemed to be no longer of any vital importance. Whatever it was, it made the sitar sound just right and it turned the flighty quarter tones of the vina into a trembling language of shadows.

On the lawn the host laughed softly, but failed to explain his amusement. In the depths of the garden a wildcat squealed, maybe a langur; then silence, a steady level all over. Night poured into the valley in the east, spread swiftly over the field and forest, then swamped the garden softly while a tuft of daylight still lingered over the Academy in the west. With it the moon came nearer and some of the gardenias on the fringe of the lawn moved into the picture with a tinselly suddenness. Vijay found it hard to remember that only a few miles away were the noisy bazaars of a town, where destinies were rehearsed in the usual manner.

'I can see that you are still shaken,' Ranjit said at length, entering a dark alley of litchis. 'You must have expected much more of us when you came back, did you not? I have been to Europe myself . . . I remember how appalled I was when I returned. Would you like to hear what I learned then?'

'Very much.' Vijay grabbed at the invisible cobweb he had just walked into, then wiped his face with his sleeve. Less and less he felt like calling his young uncle by the usual term of address: the small difference of age between them seemed to have vanished with daylight.

'I learned first of all that what I saw of Europe was her shop window,' Ranjit went on. 'Comparing that with our wretched India was not only unfair, but even quite silly.'

'That was not what let me down.'

'Maybe not, Vijay, but these impressions have a way of sticking. The second thing I learned concerns us as a people. I found out that we like having things done for us . . . and done on a pattern. You wonder why your patriotic idea was not understood? I shall tell you why. We think that patriotism is shouting slogans and voting for Congress . . . and sometimes going to jail for non-violent resistance. We often mistake the popular symbols for the real thing.'

'In my opinion, *that* is silly,' Vijay said.

'It is . . . but what is a single man to do? If you wish to serve the people, you must do it in a way they will recognize.' He, too, slashed at the gossamer under the branches before continuing. 'Listen, Vijay, this will show you what I mean. When I was in Lucknow last year a friend of mine took me to a new beggars' home. They were taking the riffraff from the streets and teaching them useful crafts. Well, what happened? The board of trustees had a hard time getting public support . . . and do you know why? A man was willing to give charity on a street corner, but not under any other heading. The idea of a redeemed beggar left him cold. And I must tell you that I understand him perfectly well. A destitute turned carpenter seemed somehow like the end of a custom. A look of pride on his face was something I was not accustomed to.'

'My idea of service was practical, even if it was novel.'

'I am just telling you, Vijay . . . not arguing. Only remember: These things make us Hindus. If there are paved roads, we follow them in preference to wild trails.'

'We need a little shaking, I am sure.'

'Maybe, Vijay. Maybe you and the others like you will give it to us.' He chortled again without warning. 'As for myself . . . quite frankly, I would hate to be shaken.' And, as Vijay stopped on the path to the cottage: 'Are you coming back to the house? Would you like to dine with me?'

'I must write letters before your guests arrive. May I stay here?'

'Of course, please yourself. You can do just as you wish.'

He scratched his knee vigorously and it was clear that he had made the invitation only from politeness.

'In that case I will stroll back and have a bath before supper. And tomorrow I shall let you know when the Prashads arrive.'

They parted with the customary blandishments and while his uncle walked briskly back to the house, Vijay went into the cottage, undressed and ate the supper which the old Jat had already brought in.

Owls and jackals were beginning to liven up the garden when he came out again. He sat in a chair on the lawn and watched the glistening roof o. the garden, wondering what had caused Ranjit's mirth a little earlier. The subject had been serious enough, even on the pompous side, and they had in true Hindu fashion covered a good deal of ground in a short space. Was Ranjit laughing at him or at some wraith from his own pastel land? Would he now go and read a book of gazals, as though the surface of life had not even been scratched? Vijay had to smile thinking of this. Two men had taken a walk on a lovely night, they had jabbed at the secret of their past and of themselves, and apparently the most exciting thing about it all had been the sound of their own voices. It had gone to their heads. They had spoken pregnant words and for a time enjoyed their revelation, and then they had gone to their quarters and stopped feeling elated about themselves, as though the sky and the night had yielded all they contained.

'Vau-u-ul' . . . said a jackal in the vicinity. Vijay thought the noise perfectly fitting. A wave of moonlit freshness cooled his head and limbs and he inhaled it for a long while. Then, as though wishing to remind him of something, a strain of instrumental music filtered through the trees and up to the cottage. He mused about the curious ways of his people and about his own sudden ability to see them thus, then he went in and sat down at the small teak desk. What had seemed so obvious all evening dwindled now to a mere nameless discomfort as soon as he tried to write it down.

Salim and I may be running a pace faster than some others, but at least we are going in the same direction. Ranjit refuses to budge altogether and seems to like it that way. What hope is there for a nation that hides such enormous caves of unconcern . . .?

The answer wouldn't come yet—perhaps because he had denied it in advance. He knew only one part of it: that it was not likely to lurk in the baffling personality of his host or the weird mesmerism of his garden.

2

NEXT morning the mail brought a letter from Salim.

Uncle Premchand's only comment about the Rajputana failure had been: 'I told you so!' and Salim's attempt at lightheartedness could not fool anyone; Jagnath did not understand why Vijay was wasting his time in the North when there was so much to do at home. Bombay was groaning in one of the hottest summers in living memory and everyone hoped the monsoon would not be too late. Depressed and restive, Vijay borrowed a car from Ranjit and drove to the botanical garden at Premnagar. The sky was white. A fierce sun brought back a recollection of the Rajputana wasteland so vivid that for a little while the immediate future appeared arid too. Up on the mountain, fluff stroked the ridges of Mussoorie; the houses of the hill station were minute and hazy. When he drove home in the early afternoon, the Prashads had arrived.

'They will not stay more than two days after all,' Ranjit told him in a disappointed voice. 'Rana Prashad is making a dash for Lucknow, to some conference or other. Instead of giving her a party on Saturday, I have had to make it to-night. Such a pity, Vijay . . . I was hoping to have you all much longer.' He threw his arms up in real resignation, which somehow increased Vijay's own glumness. 'But then, should not I consider it fortunate to have you at all?'

When Vijay admitted that he, too, was thinking of going back in a day or two, Ranjit took the news gallantly, as another man might receive the news of his bankruptcy.

'Nevertheless,' he said with a flourish of the hand, 'we shall not think of parting to-night. We are still together, are we not? We shall have music, maybe even dancing.' He smiled over his own encouragement. 'Might I suggest that you go and rest for an hour while you can? I will let you know when to come.'

So Vijay walked back to his cottage, spent a half-hour trapping a noisy horsefly in his bedroom, and later fell asleep. At a quarter-past seven in the evening Mrs. Prashad roused him by calling from the window.

'Ranjit was wondering what became of you, so I offered to come and see. What a time for a young man to be asleep!'

'Shreemati!' he exclaimed, jumping up. 'Where are you?'

'Waiting for you outside. Do hurry up, dear Vijay!'

He dressed, came out and found that she was not alone.

'Vijay, this is Hira, my younger daughter. I don't think you have ever seen her.'

Hira was fourteen and pretty like her sister Chanda, though not yet in the same coyly adolescent manner. She had flowers in her pigtails and wore the plain sari of a schoolgirl. After bowing to Vijay over her joined palms, she stuck close to her mother and faded again out of the picture altogether.

'How are you, Vijay?' Mrs. Prashad asked when he shepherded them into the litchi alley en route to the house.

'Hot and beaten down, Shreemati.'

'So Ranjit tells me.'

'It was time thrown out of the window.'

'I am sorry your Rajputs were not more understanding. The old loyalties of clan and race are dying out . . . only the show remains nowadays. How did they treat you?'

'Very well otherwise.'

'And your lecture tour?'

'Expired, as far as I can see.'

He sketched his disappointment and hinted that it might after all have been better if he had remained in England another year or two; she made little compassionate sounds of assent that caused him to wonder why all the people who thought as he did were invariably the ones who could never help him.

'We know what we once had, but we aren't at all clear about the future,' she summed it up for him. 'One is our strength, the other our weakness. We dash between these two all the time.' Then she made an effort to cheer him up. 'You should see my emancipated ladies sometime. They would make you wish we had never heard of progress.'

'But you've done all you wanted,' he said. 'Whenever I pick up a newspaper, I read about you.'

She sniffed modestly, picked a ripe litchi from a drooping branch, peeled it and gave it to her daughter. 'Mere sound and fury, my dear boy,' she said. 'Our men must be reminded that their women are up and about. They think that purdah is a godly invention and don't wish to disturb it. And would you believe it? Very often they are right and we women are wrong.'

'I thought men were always wrong.'

'Not always, but you are not to say I told you so. A woman coming out of purdah often barters her sense of belonging for an awful feeling of suspense . . . did you know that? Of course not, how could you? Have you ever felt that you do not fit into anything . . . that you are between heaven and earth and that nobody wants you?'

'I am feeling it right now,' he said, swallowing the crude definition as a part of his recuperative diet.

'Well, then,' she continued without force, but firmly and lucidly, he must know how a woman feels at the start of her emancipation, without the benefit of European tours and feminist meetings. Very rarely does such a woman manage to replace the old values with a new set, and when she does after a long struggle, it is always with a hundred reservations and compromises, for, naturally, she couldn't exist if she were to cut herself utterly adrift. Most women waste a lifetime in adjustment. Cut off from the petty chains of the household and laughed out of its soothing superstitions, they have to create a new rhythm for themselves. Inevitably, many of them stop the gap with greater extroversion, because, of course—did he not know that?—it is always an awful temptation for an iconoclast to mistake the noise of a new life for its real voice. They take to smoking, drinking and loud argument, anxious that their progress should be obvious at first acquaintance. So, it often happens unfortunately that the moral restraint comes undone too—oh yes, very gradually to be sure, but it comes all the same. She had watched it happen for years, she had seen the ravage; it was simpler to recoil from one 'don't' than to recognize another. And so the old-fashioned diehards who had nothing but contempt for the word emancipation were not so wrong after all. It was a sorry mix-up, all told. We might as well face the unpleasant truth: The 'modern' Indian woman, especially the rich one, is often a heartbreaking figure.

'But you're not giving her up,' he said. He saw two strange cars under the porch of Ranjit's house.

'I almost did, several times,' she said. 'Of course, it would not work. Giving her up would mean giving up myself.' She sniffed again, as if nettled once more by the relentless vision of work before her. 'If I didn't know that there is bound to be some change sooner or later, I could often cry.'

'There will be, Shreemati, I am sure,' he said.

They were on the round lawn. Lights were up on the arched verandah when they climbed it, and a liveried Punjabi servant waited for them; from the interior came strains of Indian music, but no voices. Mrs. Prashad shook the pebbles out of her sandals and pulled the sari closer around her face.

'By the way, where is Chanda?' Vijay said, as the servant began to lead the way.

'She was dressing when we went to call you.'

'How was Mussoorie?'

'Loud and sinful as usual. The roof of our bungalow fell in during a storm. We had a hard time repairing it. You must come up once, when we are there.'

He said he would.

They walked through a succession of halls and passages, all thickly carpeted and lighted through latticed skylights on the side, and he peeped through one and found that the light was a reflection from another source, itself invisible. An illuminated water basin? he thought with interest. It was not out of the question in this house. Furniture seemed to consist mostly of divans, screens inlaid with ivory and baroque-looking cupboards filled with statues of gods and women dancing. The ceiling of the last but one chamber rippled laxily, its twilight shot through with quivering rings of an intense white.

'Like the Hall of Mirrors in the Delhi Fort,' he said to Mrs. Prashad.

'Charming, is it not? You must not wonder why some people do not desire change.'

In the next room, which was another large and half-lit hall, four people

71

were to be distinguished on the plush couches—two ladies, another man, a Muslim, and Ranjit himself. All light was again artfully concealed.

'Rana, Vijay, at last! I have already given you up,' Ranjit said receiving them.

He presided over the introductions with the suave restraint of a host who is about to see his labours given full play. He had put on a dark-grey tunic and white churi-dar-pyjamas—narrow cotton trousers forming an effect of bangles just above the ankle, and named after them—which made him look very slender and seemed to tone down the last vestige of the Rajput in him. The other guests were Mrs. Prabha Devi and her young and attractive daughter Sita, and Mr. Haroun Syed Mehdi, a Muslim friend of Ranjit's, a lean unsmiling gentleman given to finger crackling and much pensive gazing past people's heads. Vijay sat on a floor cushion in one corner, next to a divan facing the door of the room, and crossed his legs comfortably.

Sinking back in his old place on another couch, which he shared with his Muslim friend, the host explained that the music they had been hearing was the complete recorded score from a recent Kathak dance performance in Old Delhi, in which Miss Sita Devi had taken part. He then switched on the electric gramophone by his side and pulled his silver-ringed hookah towards him.

As the music continued Vijay began to distinguish the faces around him and they seemed to match the scene admirably. The Muslim guest was Ranjit's age, though leaner and taller; his steady gaze dimmed after a time, so that his eyes began to look like charcoals about to gutter, and his long and tapered face acquired the thoughtful emaciation of a Muslim intellectual. His tunic was both darker and longer than Ranjit's; he kept time to the music with an expressive bony hand above which dangled a gold chain bracelet. Miss Devi was precious, and she sat strikingly upright on her folded knees and spread her embroidered skirt around her like a stiff silken doll; behind her, the mother reclined on one elbow and seemed to be counting and recounting her many bracelets. Ranjit hardly moved, save to draw softly on his hookah every now and then, with closed eyes. The gramophone worked quietly, its smooth husky voice seemingly attuned to the mood of the chamber. Batik and brocade spreads and old Tibetan scrolls covered the walls right up to the ceiling, from which hung a single screened lamp. No one spoke.

Servants came on soft catlike feet, lowering trays of sweets and curried relishes, and their shadowy flitting left the conjured assembly unruffled. The Muslim confined himself to rare muffled wah-wahs of approval, intended for the music, and did not stir. When the record-changer reached the bottom of the stack, Ranjit got up and replenished it. By and by, Vijay began to believe that if any of them had anything to say to the others, he was saving it for later. The waxing and heaving second half of the recital was marked only by a periodic exchange of stares between the host and Miss Devi on the divan, but deepening twilight grudged its content to the other guests. She sat erectly; only the dull gleam of her sari border kept her from fading into the spellbound background. Outside, the night set in— Vijay gathered from his watch—but the room seemed in no way related to it. What, he thought in growing wonder, was the secret of the builder of this mysterious home? Night and day flowed into one like two brooks in a legendary grove of heaven, and silence itself grew live and tepid, and a group of people sharing a common secret came to be transfixed in it. He glanced at Mrs. Prashad, but she, too, had been caught in her own webs.

Next: obeying a cabalistic hint from the host—or was it the melody, whose sinuous rhythm and weird groping of strings now waxed into a moan of hopeless yearning?—the young woman trembled visibly and slid to the floor in one liquid move. She quavered and rocked, and then it began to seem to Vijay that the purpose of her weaving arms was to coax the languor of the atmosphere into her own limbs and body, there to refine it into a drugging pure essence. He understood that it was a dance and that she was trying to tell them of things beyond the chamber, perhaps of another dusk and asok blossoms by a river, of an unkept tryst at the hour when daylight still lay on the roof of the forest but night had already moistened the grass beneath it, or of the sweet and heady layers of champa scent when someone slender and veiled had walked through it. He wondered and couldn't decide, even though the rustle of her flaring sari and the jingle of her anklets seemed to convey all that was necessary to Ranjit and his Muslim guest. The dim oval of Ranjit's face was now turned to the ceiling, while his friend had faded into his niche of darkness; the dancer's mother had covered her face with her hands. Then the upper end of the sari slipped from the young woman's head and shoulders and her bared arms recalled for Vijay the moonstruck branches of the eucalypti outside; by slow and inexorable stages, the room grew more restive and into it the dancer presently began to send nameless and wanton streams, and then the inexplicable scene came near to being a simple undisguised pulse of his own blood. He shut his eyes and tried to still it, but all in vain; when he opened them again, Chanda stood at the entrance of the room glancing from him and Ranjit to her mother.

Before he could motion her to the empty end of the divan next to him, she drifted across the space and became enmeshed in the waving and pulsing, and for a long and smouldering moment it made no difference to his tide who was who. He looked away ashamed of himself. Then she glided towards him in a faint churn of the dancer's scent, mingled with her own, and her soundless gait became indistinguishable from the other girl's. He rose, hot up to his ears.

'Is this a kind of temple worship?' she whispered. She sat on the edge of the divan and sidled a little in his direction. 'Have I missed very much?'

'Almost everything,' he told her.

She bent down to grope for her sandal in the billows of her skirt, and the rich-dry cloud shrouding her hair enveloped him too; he couldn't remember any scent ever rising so straight to his head; he shut his eyes again and cleared his throat, wanting her at that moment with all the clear and lascivious simplicity with which he used to think of Connie in the rare intervals of their separation. But she buckled the sandal at last, tossed her skirt over it and leaned back on her elbows. The unbelievable moment was over.

Miss Devi, too, was back on her couch, close to her mother, though the music went on and on as to a distant inaccessible cadence. A light came on in the next room, stamping the centre rug with a sharper and more intricate detail of itself, though not tainting the basic half-light. Ranjit and his friend had not moved either; they seemed bound together as before. The machine disposed discreetly of its fourth stack—even the click of the changer sounded more subdued.

At that stage it dawned on him that only loud and abrupt action would restore him to the world he knew, that Ranjit and his company were a new mystical sect and their stealthy intercourse a sublimation of everything that was forbidden between them. It was neither enlightening nor enjoyable in his sense; it simply disturbed him and made him restless. It revealed a new Ranjit who was a stranger—an upsetting find, for this new person seemed to exist side by side with the man who had talked so sincerely on the previous evening. Searching for an excuse that would stiffen his resolution, he rose gingerly and walked towards his uncle, only to discover that excuses were unnecessary. Ranjit let him go as he had received him, with a smile and a wave of the hookah tip. He turned at the door to look at Chanda, but she too had already grown into the gleaming and decorative pattern of the divan. The others were wraiths, herded together in a medium so subtle that they could even do away with the need of looking at one another.

At ten o'clock the dome of the night fell back behind a pale gauze that fogged the stars and also littered the floor of the garden in nets of shredded opalescence. As he walked down from the front verandah and on to the lawn, the boles of eucalypti looked like a row of flameless torches aspiring to the sky. The grove was now quiet, now secretively alive. When a breeze ravished the web, the sound flowed into the unseen levels of scent and the new substance nudged itself from shade to moon-slivers, from tree to bush, and then still farther and deeper into the shadows. He walked through cloud after cloud of clear fragrance and through distillations of many, and each fresh one sounded a different note in his mind. Then someone called, 'Who's that?' and he reeled around and recognized Chanda's anxious voice

'I thought you were a tiger . . . at least a leopard! You certainly walk like one.'

'What in the name of heaven are you doing here?'

'I should ask *you* that. The garden is neither yours nor mine.'

She came out from behind a tree and he saw her dimly outlined against the undergrowth. 'I was trying to walk, but you scared me. Where were you going?'

'Oh, anywhere. Can we walk together?'

'Why not!' she said. 'At least I will not jump at every sound.'

They strolled into a lane of mangoes on which the fruit already smelled faintly and came to a stone water tank sunk in the ground, where a gurgling cascade enriched the other furtive sounds of the garden. She said: 'Look!' and he followed her dim hand and saw jackals glowering at them from the other side. He found a stone and hurled it across, and the green stare went out instantly. 'They didn't expect us,' she said. 'It is a good sign. There are no tigers where there are jackals.'

'You don't really believe that, do you?' he asked.

'No,' she said, 'but it is good to think it all the same.'

They walked away and the bowl of the basin reproduced Vijay's sopping step with a ghostly sound.

Back in the grove she said: 'Now that you are not busy with interviews and invitations would you like to tell me about England and what you saw there?'

'Why not?' he said, echoing her own casual note; for a mere acquaintanceship it was an ideal subject. 'But wait first . . . I've got to empty my shoe of stones.' He stopped and sat down on the grass, while she stood close above him, a soft rustle and a streak of some unknown dry perfume. Then he rose, dusted his pyjamas, and they continued walking.

'It was a different England from the one you read about in our newspapers,' he said. 'I was very happy there. I made some good friends.'

'Why should you not! We are not savages.'

'Wait, Chanda,' he said. 'If you really want me to tell you, you must not fight me.'

'All right, I won't. Please go on.'

While the moon dived higher each time they glimpsed it, he recounted his flight to England, the highlights of his success there and his ambition to dedicate that experience to a better understanding between the two nations; he tried not to sound pompous. He didn't try to impress her either, because England and all it stood for were a tricky subject for any Indian, and because one's verdict of it often showed whether one's assimilative tract had been equal to the experience or become disrupted in the process.

He spoke of the English and the warmth of their reception with less and less restraint, at times even inspiredly. It wasn't their fault that their

75

friendliness now taxed his powers of readaptation; he could never again be deaf and blind to their better sides, as some people thought an Indian patriot should be. 'It is quite possible that I can never again be rabidly anti-British,' he told her. And did she see that? She did see, she said. Well then, that was how the plan of world lectures came to pass, and why he had been so keen on it; it was also the reason why his visit to Rajputana rankled so. 'They're biased because they're backward,' he said, borrowing from Ranjit. 'Inside they're still fast asleep. They think everything has been finally and eternally judged centuries ago . . . they don't even know the meaning of initiative. They're in a rut and love it.'

'I thought your uncle was going to help you.'

'This is now very doubtful,' he told her. 'No one really wants to do anything about it save myself, and that isn't enough.'

'It is a start, is it not?'

Fearing an innuendo, he watched out for the real colour of her voice, but there was none; her sympathy was quick and some echo in it reminded him of Mrs. Prashad. 'It is a start,' he said, 'but a very little one.'

'One of our teachers used to say that a handful of clay is to an artist what a whole claypit is to a bricklayer.'

'Schoolteachers don't know about flying.'

'Tell me about flying,' she then said. 'How is it different from this walk?'

He hedged, wishing she would not skim so. How was one to explain flying without sounding crass or making long metaphysical statements, even invoking death?

'In the beginning it was like nothing else before,' he said. 'Whenever I came down, I thought I would never again have the same experience. When it stopped, I had nothing to put in its place.' He glanced in her direction in the dark, fearing lest she think him too phrasy. 'It is really not at all easy to explain. First it was all excitement, later I used to sit back quietly and watch everything as if through a telescope. Does this sound silly . . .?'

'No . . . but neither is it clear.'

'I knew I could never tell you,' he said, realizing that words would never be anything more than a clumsy travesty of those lively flashes that made up imagination. How was he to explain something that had never been clear even to himself?

'All the same, I can see where it spoils you for other things,' she said when the pause grew too long.

'Yes, it does that,' he admitted. 'That is because it is all things in one, if you know what I mean. It can be a thrill, a job, a service . . . depending on how I do it.' His mind performed a prodigious leap into the past and pulled up before the body of his friend Nand. 'It can be life and death,' he said aloud, forgetting his earlier resolutions, 'all in the same minute, even the same second.' The memory now grew so vivid that it made him goosefleshy. 'You know, Chanda, I've just remembered something that is very much to the point . . . if you want to hear it.'

'Yes, I want to,' she said.

'I could tell you about Nand, a very good friend of mine. It might help you to understand.'

'Was he a flier?'

'Yes, a good one. We joined the Juhu club at the same time. He died in a stunt display in a flying meet three and a half years ago. Did you ever see a crash?'

'Never.'

'Let me tell you then. . . .'

He went on telling her, quickly and erratically, while the image still burned brightly, for it was an event he had never successfully recapitulated for himself. He no longer picked between what was suitable and unsuitable for a demure young girl. 'I hear the machine screaming to earth whenever I think of it,' he said, 'like something that has been falling since the birth of the gods.' The contact with the most impressionable phase of his youth was like a purge of everything that occurred afterwards; he continued without a trace of sophistication. 'I was at the lawn railing, I remember very well. There was a Maratha woman next to me, eating a piece of English cake. I wanted to watch, but she asked me foolish questions. Do you know what a flying gymkhana is?'

'Racing or something like that.'

'Yes, that is right. This was our first gymkhana . . . anyway, my first. There was a huge crowd on the field, I think over a thousand people. It was just before I got my A licence. I did a rope-picking item, then went back to the lawn to announce the rest of the programme. The last stunt was called "teacher and pupil." Nand was teacher, Salim was pupil.'

'Please explain.'

'It's an old meet stunt, as old as flying. "Teacher" does all kinds of aerobatics and "pupil" is supposed to follow him, then bungle each one at a crucial point and make it seem like a dangerous mistake. "Pupil" is usually the best flier in the team. Our best man was Salim, but Nand was very good too. He was supposed to make a loop and Salim was to go after him and stall at the top. Then something happened, nobody knows what. . . . Instead of levelling off at four thousand, Nand came straight down. I remember the Poona woman put the cake in her mouth and forgot to eat it. I ran out to the railing . . . I thought I could see right into Nand's mind. We both had the same idea and prayed for it. Someone said afterwards we even went through the same motions. But it wasn't fear . . . it was something else, I can't explain what.'

He shuddered. The recapture of that almost forgotten split second made him partake of his friend's death very poignantly. The memory did not descend on him benignly, as it had done before sometimes, but took sudden and powerful hold of him. Wording it lucidly was utterly beyond his powers, at this moment or any other.

'I was Nand, and he was me,' he said after a silence. 'I battered my head against the machine as if I were in it. When the plane hit the ground, everything became still . . . perfectly and absolutely still. I think he died in that stillness . . . I mean really died, because he was still breathing when we rushed him to a hospital in Bandra.

He said nothing more, but walked on faster for a time, not noticing that she struggled to keep in step with him.

Once more the main issues of his friend's death seemed to hover all around him, indistinguishable from the dark vaults of shadows and as baffling. Men's friendships were enduring parts of life to an oriental, the stuff of which the stars and the universe itself were compounded. They were better than Shahaja, romantic love, or, for that matter, any emotion between man and woman. A woman's love might change a man and lead him to great goals, but man's friendship was without motives or rewards, a thing for its own sake, which would sustain him when all else had passed. In resurrecting Nand for this girl walking beside him, he had therefore done more than restate his share of an early loyalty; he had reaffirmed his friendship with Nand in a way that was imperishable.

The moon now cleft the alley in a long and tapering gash of paleness in which all tinsel seemed to be lavished on the bushy crowns of the mangoes. They crossed a few watering ditches and drenched their sandals. and beyond the last one the ground became too soggy for walking. Still in silence, he took her hand and turned in at the first intersecting byway, hoping that it would take them back to the house. Before long the remembrance of his friend spent itself and blurred, and he began to feel clearer in the head and calmer.

'You would have liked him, Chanda,' he summed up confidently. 'The way I like him even now. Sometimes it seems he is still somewhere near, only I don't see him and can't speak to him.'

She sighed and recovered her hand, not certain whether a remark was called for. 'And sometimes you forget him,' she said all the same, 'because there are so many other things to remember too. I know how that happens.'

'Yes, quite true,' he said, 'but never for long. You should have stopped me when I started, Chanda. I didn't really want to talk about it at all.'

'Why not, Vijay?' she said with her old earnestness. 'I have always wanted to know what happens to Indians when they leave their cradle and go to Europe.'

'Well, now you know.'

'Now I know nothing. You have been talking to yourself all the time. But one day you will have to tell everything.' She laughed and shook her silver bangles, breaking the long spell. 'You may not think so, Vijay, but girls have minds too.'

'All right,' he said, stepping aside to avoid a dark sagging bough. 'This is not the last time we have met. Next time I'll remember what you said. Look, we are back.'

It was true. The byway had been a short cut to the servants' outhouses in the rear of Ranjit's home.

One of the numerous dogs prowling this part of the orchard sensed their approach and sent up a thin baleful yowl and the noise drowned the remote tolling of temple bells in Dehra Dun. An orange light marked the open space in front of the menials' quarters, outlining also a group of men squatted over their evening meal. Vijay threw a stone in the direction of the yowl, causing it merely to recede a little. The border between the orchard and the garden was still drawn in heavy lines of scent and they crossed it with a feeling of travellers exchanging one entranced land for another; the lawn again struck Vijay as a font of some ever-welling fragrance intended for the haughty noses of the eucalypti. Into it and over it Ranjit's current recapture of a bygone India poured a nostalgic melody of flutes and serangi, so airy that the garden had no difficulty in passing it on to the night as an aspect of its own swishing and stir.

'And now I think I'll go to sleep,' he said to her on the gravel drive. 'What about you?'

'I must go back in, or Ranjit will think I don't like his music.'

'And you're leaving in two days?'

'Mother says we must. She has been called to a conference, Hira and I must go back to school.' She went up the steps of the front verandah and on to the open carpeted entrance, leaving him in a small pond of her scent, now dampened with the breath of dew and night's humidity.

'Are your feet wet too?' she asked from the top. 'My toes are soaking.'

'Mine too. Chanda, how old are you?'

'Seventeen. Why?'

Her voice seemed to lose its pleasant overtone, and she turned her head away from the light. The brief hour of companionship was over.

'I want to take back everything I said about Indian girls back in Bombay,' he said.

'I don't remember what you said.'

'Then I take back all I thought about them. I'll explain next time we meet. Thank you for the nice walk. I hope you will come to Bombay again.'

'I hope so too. Good night, Vijay.'

She glided down the passage, a lithe and slender silhouette over the invisible light at the far end, and he wheeled around and walked back to his cottage. The moon's dross lay on the ground in more places than before. On the road side of the garden a slow breeze was beginning to rig up the lesser green craft; soon its backwash would roll up closer and create an illusion of coolness. He thought it would be restful to carry his bed out of the cottage and sleep under the open sky, and he did not think the mosquitoes would worry him. It was the last he would see of this garden for a long time and he might as well know it in all its hours.

At two in the morning he woke up from a stifling dream about Chanda and Constance in which the two girls became somehow identical, save that all the talking seemed to be done by Connie and all the love-making by the other—and he couldn't go back to sleep no matter how hard he tried. The breeze was still on, not much cooler than earlier in the evening, exploring the attics of the garden, gathering slumber and all rustle into a hoarse irresistible rhythm that seemed to chafe his innermost nerve. A strange bird called out above the cottage, once, twice, four times, ten times, its husky double note touching off a vaster restlessness in the night itself. He went into the house and tried reading, but the chaotic heat mounted higher and finally he couldn't separate it from the persistent hum in his ears and temples. He pulled a day shirt over his bed pyjamas and went strolling in the direction of Ranjit's house.

The reappearance of Connie brought with it a long train of intimate and frankly voluptuous images, all unbearable and rather regretful because of their practical distance; the more he dwelt on them, the more they seemed to taunt him, the less he wanted them. He began to walk faster and raised his head to the breeze; even his footsteps echoed with a thumping new hollowness. A bandicoot, maybe a mongoose, flurried across the path scattering shingle as it ran, and he kicked the ground after it viciously. He had not the faintest notion what he would do after he reached the main building, and for the moment it didn't seem to matter. The far-off laughter of jackals reminded him of the jungle at the end of the garden, and he thought vaguely that he might walk towards it and tire himself out and then go back and try once more to sleep.

He came round the lawn verandah and turned left, passing between orange bushes in full fruit, tied to one another by delicate scarves of gossamer, smelling of high summer. The house was quiet, its many cornices brooding stolidly just beneath the line of moonlight; there was no light in any of the windows. He faltered uncertainly, the humming back in his ears. A bed creaked somewhere, there was a sleepy long sigh, and he bated his breath until it died down and then recalled himself with the furious thought: Am I a thief that I should hide in the night? He strolled on more decisively and felt guilty all the same. Orange merged with gardenia, one scent flowed into another yet sweeter so naturally that he was not aware of the change until a flower grazed his cheek. The half-light took on a different character. A bulbul sang out in a tree nearby, but when he looked over his shoulder to find it, only a weak flutter of wings remained; this presently vanished among other unseen life. Now his eyes followed a capering firefly and came to rest on the dark oblong of an unsuspected entrance. With an involuntary heart leap, he saw the dim shape of a woman resting upon its step. Almost at once she spoke up and he recognized Sita Devi, the dancer.

'Is that you, Ranjit? How much longer am I to wait here and suffer these mosquitoes?'

He paused, swallowed, came a pace forward, then cleared his throat and gave his name. He saw her rise quickly and peer at him through the darkness; she was swathed in a long shawl of a light colour and her hair seemed to be hanging loose over her shoulders.

'What are you doing here? How did you know I was here?'

'I didn't. I couldn't sleep and took a walk,' he said soothingly. 'I didn't even know there was a door on this side until I came to it just now.' A sudden wave of relief and laughter bubbled up inside him and he had to keep it back with the utmost restraint. 'It seems I am not the only one who does not think of sleep in this house.'

'Has anyone seen you come?'

'No one.'

'That is something, anyhow.' She stepped down from the entrance and came forward, draping the covering around her head as she went; close to him she stopped. 'It is strange that I, too, should have thought of it a little while ago,' she said, giggling. 'A truly peculiar house . . . in daytime it sleeps, at night it lies awake. It forgets to keep one promise, then it makes another. Anything is better than sleep or mosquitoes. How far did you walk?'

'Up to here. But the paths on the other side are better.'

'I know,' she said. 'We once put up in your cottage.'

She went slowly up the narrow path that led to the front drive, and he came behind her and took her arm silently; he was no longer amused; now his blood pumped away with the same deafening echo that had made him get up from bed and seek calm in the garden. They walked across the luminous lawn and came crunching upon the path to the cottage. Tatters of moonlight lay on the gravel, like seaweed on a phosphorescent surf.

'Why did you walk out after my dance this evening?' she said when the mangoes closed over the path.

He groped for the hand under her shawl and drew her to him. The garment fell open, emitting a warm musky perfume.

'It put unspeakable thoughts into my head,' he said into the hair around her neck.

'Then it is fated.'

'It must be.'

She wore only a sleeping bodice and a short skirt underneath, and those he loosened easily; his hands closed over her bare buttocks as if in a slow cramp.

'Not here,' she said. 'Are you not alone in the cottage?'

'Quite alone.'

He took her there, sat her on his bed on the lawn and took off all her clothes.

From the spasmodic exchange of information during the following hours he gathered that she was a professional dancer, that her mother was really a combination of stepmother and manager, that she and Ranjit had had an argument earlier in the evening, that she was therefore leaving the next day, but that she would nevertheless think fondly of this full moon in Dehra Dun.

3

NEXT day Ranjit's Muslim friend threw a party in town, but Vijay excused himself and slept all morning instead. In the evening he went to the flying field and checked over his machine, setting at the same time a date for his departure. He got home late, ate by himself and went to bed. Late on the following morning, the Jat bearer brought him a note from Chanda; to it was attached a newspaper cutting.

> *You said people did not understand your ideas. How about putting these on an airplane? Everyone in the country would know what that means. Good-bye—you seem determined to spend the day in bed.*
>
> *Sincerely*
> *Chanda*

Almost all of the clipping was a picture of pilgrims on their way to holy Badrinath in the Himalayas. As Indian newspaper photographs went, it was nothing out of the usual: There were nine Hindu pilgrims, four in palanquins, two on ponies, three on foot, all rather tired and shabby. The caption said 'Third day uphill,' and it was easy to imagine how much shabbier they would look at the end of the seventh and eighth days—for this was the average duration of the holy trek from Hardwar to Badrinath, from the spot where the Ganges flowed into the plains to its source almost on the frontier of Tibet.

As was the way of ideas, this one gripped his mind and set fire to it all at once, and the red-hot gist of it was: pilgrim air service! He dressed in a hurry, strode off into the garden and gave himself up to its heat. Despite all past experience he could not manage to be half-hearted about such a vision;

82

it was a thrilling one the kind which forced one to sleep, talk and sit with it at an unwavering pitch. The more he toyed with it, the larger it loomed.

To sacred Badrinath the valley of five Bhadris and the Vishnu temple said to have been built by the ascetic philosopher Shankara himself, pilgrims from all parts of India climbed every spring and summer. They made the journey from the Ganges at Hardwar, one of the seven holy cities of India, and over the scree-covered foothills of the Himalayas in any manner befitting their place in the community, some riding, some in dandies, the local version of palanquins, and the great majority simply marching. Above all other pilgrimages this one exacted their utmost devotion and grit, and its completion was said to confer purity on the soul and blessings on the individual; the valley was a gate to Mount Kailas, the old abode of Lord Shiva, and a bath in the hot cistern of the temple at Badrinath ranked higher than a similar dip in the muddy Ganges at Benares.

Along the writhing path uphill were villages, food stalls and dharmsalas —charitable lodging-houses—and dak bungalows built by the government for the use of the wealthier pilgrims, but all this was insufficient during the peak summer months when great droves of pious Hindus began to converge on Hardwar from all corners of India. This devotion of one kind of people was good for another kind, the families of hillmen living along the hallowed route, to whom the prosaic fundamentals of faith on the move were bread and butter. The poor bought their victuals where they could; the rich carted it with them, in copper and brass vessels. The poor had all the time in the world; the rich were in a hurry, for they had stinted the trekking time to some business transaction or some shareholder. In that case why not a pilgrims' airline . . .?

An exciting vista, this—in the direct line of descent from electricity and motor car, perhaps even more momentous; in the forward spirit, too, for it would open up the godforsaken hill tracts, expose them to modern influences and push India's upper borders a little farther north. It would serve the most cherished need of the people, observance of religious custom, and strengthen the fame of the shrine and induce the lazy to come and pay their homage. Chanda was right: It would be practical and valuable. Priests, patriots, businessmen, moneylenders—none would quarrel with such an interpretation of service. Nationalists like Premchand would welcome it; Jagnath would have the satisfaction that his heir had firmly planted his feet on the soil of India. He himself would be engrossed once more. Deciding to go and see Ranjit at once, he thought with pleasure that his guess of Chanda's imagination had been a good one after all; the girl thought amazingly like a man, her visions were like a man's.

Ranjit was having tea on the lawn when he finally ran him to ground. He greeted him with the news that the Prashads had left by the afternoon train and that he had taken the liberty of wishing them good-bye on Vijay's behalf. 'And by the way, Chanda left you a note . . . I can't think where I put it. They said they might see you in Bombay this autumn.'

'The letter was in my room,' Vijay said, unfolding it for his uncle. 'Please read it . . . I should very much like to talk to you about it.'

The host read it with raised eyebrows and not a little amusement. 'What of it?' he said mildly.

'Don't you see . . .? Flying pilgrims . . . thousands and thousands of them. The greatest aerial idea of the last ten years . . .!'

'You sound excited.'

'Excited . . .! Just listen to this, please!'

He made a swift and tumbling attempt to impart to him some of his own effervescence, adding inspired flourishes and using better and more flamboyant colour as he went along. Even the way the picture spread out was beautiful in itself. Like a young and athletic body after a first stretch in the morning, when blood began to flow more triumphantly and each new swing of the arms brought a livelier and better sense of power and balance, it grew and frisked and its giddy caper became giddier every minute. 'Just you try and imagine it!' he said. 'No one's ever thought of it in the whole country. Just try to picture it!'

'I am. My hair stands on end.'

'And why not, tell me!' He pegged his pitch a note higher. 'Badrinath Air Service Limited, think of it! Or even better . . . Pilgrim Air Service Limited . . .!' Forgotten was the unpleasant odour of Kathiawar and Rajputana and the recent slough of despond. 'And here's an argument you won't be able to answer . . . or I don't know the meaning of reason. They've flown over Mount Everest and the whole world said it was a brilliant idea. They've flown over Tibet from sheer curiosity. Here is a practical idea and that's the only difference I can see.'

'Most unusual,' Ranjit commented.

'Most simple and realistic. There is no other name for it. Instead of dying from hunger and exhaustion, they can fly there and pray ten times as long. Can you give me one good reason why not . . .?'

'Kindly stop asking that question. I have not denied anything.'

'You don't understand, Ranjit,' he said more patiently, for when something was so close to reality as this vision of his, it was easy to forgive dullness in others. 'Think for a moment of the Marwari bankers who make the pilgrimage once a year in a dandy. Have you ever seen them? They're either too fat or too asthmatic to walk . . . they get bored and listless. All they ever want is to get to Badrinath as soon as possible, bathe in the tank and make their gift to the temple. That's simple, isn't it?' He leaned towards his host and made the next point hard and clear: 'Do you mean to say that they would not fly if that were possible . . .?'

'Not owning a bank, I would not know.'

84

'Well, I do. I know that they would welcome it, just as they welcomed the railway when it first came. You think our grandfathers would not have gone to Puri or Konarak if there'd been a train to take them? But there wasn't, Ranjit . . . so they went to a local shrine instead. Their children had the railway and used it. And now everyone who can buy a third-class ticket can be a pilgrim. He can go to any place he wants to because it's so easy. I should like to make Badrinath so easy every good Hindu will want to visit it at least once a year. And I think I can.'

'Good luck, Vijay. When will you start?'

He didn't have to ponder an answer; it was plain and arrayed in his mind. That, he thought, remembering the weeks at Delhi, was another blessing of action. One flash set off another; before you could say Rajagopalachariar, the blaze was high and bright.

A little more calmly he said to his uncle:

'I can start to-morrow. I have my plane here and Hardwar is only forty miles away. I'll fly there to-morrow morning and explore the country.'

'And then?'

'I must talk to the local people and see what they think. I've got to write to Bombay and find out what our banyas will think about it.'

'Most necessary.' Ranjit took Vijay's arm and led him to the house. 'You propose to increase the cost of their religion and they may not like it.'

'They will. I'm not worried about that. My friend Salim Haq can find out for me. I must also know how Premchand will take it . . . he has the only money in the family.'

'I thought you had given him up?'

'I have, but now I can go and see him again . . . with a real plan. I want to give him such a good report he won't have a chance to argue.' And here the voice of caution twitted at the back of his head and he thought it good to add: 'I want to ask you a favour, Ranjit . . . not to discuss it with any-body until I am back. Not even your best friends, please.'

'You may be sure of that.'

'I can already see Premchand's face when I surprise him with it.'

'I can too,' Ranjit said, staging an elaborate shudder. 'Your coming to this house was fortunate after all?'

'Oh yes, very fortunate.' He slapped his back warmly, forgetting all the depression and goings-on of the past three weeks. 'You were a most patient host. I am really very grateful.'

'Happy to hear it, Vijay. So Rana Prashad was right about you.'

'In what way?'

'She said that you were your own best tonic.'

He took the compliment in his stride—who could pause now to weigh the meaning of remarks! There was so much to be done in no time at all—he had to get ready for to-morrow, write to Salim, send a note to Chanda, thanking her for the idea, send telegrams to the chief officials at Hardwar, announcing his call, pack, make a list of things to be accomplished and so forth; even the thought of it gave him a tingle. He told Ranjit he would try to spend another day with him on his way back to Bombay, monsoon permitting. 'But if I don't,' he added in afterthought, 'what would you like me to tell them in Bombay?'

'That I think of them fondly.' Ranjit steered him into his rug-smothered bedroom. 'And while I remember, Vijay, there is something I want to give you.' He burrowed in a camphor chest and held up a gold-embroidered shirt of fine white muslin. 'We call this a mirzai in these parts. You may wear it, if you wish . . . but I would not advise it. It is over a hundred years old. I cannot finance your noble schemes, but this home will always be open if you should happen to pass by.'

Vijay shook his frail hand and was again disarmed by his smile. He promised to join him at supper and take proper leave.

'I shall look forward to it,' Ranjit said. 'As for my friends in Bombay, give them my respects . . . especially to your parents. You asked me for a message. Tell them this, if they should be curious enough . . . that the rogue steadfastly refuses to reform.'

He waved his hand deprecatingly and strolled back to the door.

Vijay took with him a characteristic impression of eyelids languidly drooping on a face that still smiled, as though curtaining off a greater confidence, and of the relaxed and graceful posture which the conjured unreality of this house seemed to confer upon the inmates.

Kinship and ordinary gratitude excepted, he did not think he owed him anything else. If there was anything to learn from Ranjit, it was that pleasure by itself was not sufficient for full Hindu dharma, and this after all was something he had known before he came.

4

THE official map of Garhwal was more up to date than his own and the recent improvements in the pilgrim route were marked on it in pencil. The engineer of the Public Works Department was a sombre lower-caste Hindu who had done the trek several times and knew the mountainous regions like his own office.

It was odd to find him in the orthodox holy of holies, even if his public activity was confined to advice of the most technical sort, for Hardwar was a citadel of the Brahmans and other twice-born castes and subcastes, and the pilgrim traffic and fairs were in the hands of a municipal board, watched over by a Pilgrim Commission, both wholly high caste and strict.

No one knew how this had happened; it was one of those things which like the first scab over a sore of long standing, was then beginning to form on the caste epidermis of India. He well knew about the pitfalls of his position and held severely aloof from local squabbles, but among the Brahmans of the town his climbs to Badrinath and Kedarnath were common gossip, and not entirely without credit. There were good signs in this for the future, if one only had time to give them; Vijay had none. His mind now ran on a single track, in one direction, at high speed.

The engineer thought that everything would depend on the way it was handled; the religious feelings of the upper classes were not always to be relied upon. He agreed to fly the route with Vijay and help with his knowledge of the territory. More could not be expected for the time being, 'lest certain elements in town accuse me of forcing new ideas on an unwilling community.'

The town board named a caucus, but the latter, true to custom, divided itself on the issue. Vijay listened to the grave Brahman chairman and compared him to the engineer; comparison was hardly fair. The engineer looked for benefits, the Brahman for trouble; well might the engineer think the time was ripe for a little streamlining of an old institution—it was not his. The Brahman saw it from inside, with a great deal of inborn canniness.

'First and foremost, we should look at it economically,' he opened smartly, so that no one could later accuse him of caste bias. 'The service would cater only to the rich and I don't see how it would improve the normal traffic.' What was more, it was bound to divert rich travel from the mountain populace who needed it very badly indeed, whereas the company would have no real stake in the district. They would just mulct it, to put it plainly. 'I say that the orthodox will resent it.' He made the point in a level voice; he was not to be counted among them. The municipality was always ready to make an experiment in the name of progress but they would not be drawn into any controversy. Then, the local capital would have to be given a share, as otherwise concession might be withheld. This was universal language; no English periodical could later tear the remark from the context and write: Another diehard stops the wheel of progress!

Then other comment gushed forth and Vijay grappled with it patiently and tactfully. They gave him a list of the town dignitaries and told him to sound them. Privately, they were of the opinion that the matter was entirely outside the sphere of the Public Works Department and that the engineer's profusion of good will was neither here nor there. He watched them scurry off in their tongas and rikshas and wondered whether the meeting had been a victory or a defeat.

Two days later he set off to make the trek on a pony. The ranges looked deceptively brittle in the humid sky which heralded the monsoon, and the forests were full of birds and butterflies. He made it in five days. The bridle path wove laboriously first through white forest, then fir, and it rarely strayed more than a hearing distance from the young Ganges. The dak bungalows were clean and well kept, as were the better dharmsalas. Villages huddled on the steep slopes and were an appalling mixture of filth and devout fervour; sadhus, coolies, children, pack animals, their half-Tibetan drivers, food vendors, were all thrown together with utter disregard for comfort and well-being; temple and shrine flags flapped in the wind at every turn. He met whole families on their way back, men marching, wives swinging awkwardly in dandies, small boys on the backs of sweating hillmen, the strain of the march plain in their faces. Rich Punjabi Hindus dozed in their palanquins, or chewed pan, or contemplated the scenery and the lower life behind their dark sunglasses; mendicants and sannyasis, dressed and ash-smeared, fingered their beads and muttered to themselves, staring at him as though he were a foreigner, because of his European tweeds. And still he passed party after party on the way up.

He made a record of the fields which might serve for emergency landings. At Badre itself the valley was tortuous, but one mile below it there was a terrace of pulse fields which, with some ingenuity, might be broadened and levelled out to make a minimum strip. He lounged at the small stone tank in the Vishnu temple and watched men, women and babies splash in the warm waters; their baths were brisk affairs, enriched by much loud breathing, rubbing and mumbling of runes; they paid scant attention to one another. Prayers over, they dressed quickly and returned to the village with the nimble gait of people who no longer had to fear the imponderable. He mused on faith in its pure state; there seemed to be truth in the contention that drugging oneself was the line of least resistance. The other fact was more obvious: For these people other methods did not exist, for they did not know them. At what point was their spiritual stature enhanced by merit . . .?

He descended to Hardwar in forced stages and took a day to rest. The engineer listened to his account and did not comment. His only remark concerned the municipal members, on whose opinions, he thought, it would not be safe to rely excessively; they seldom knew what they wanted, and almost never how to go about it; contrary to what they said, concession was a matter of sound argument and some influence, not necessarily local.

Then both took off in the plane and surveyed the landscape from the air. In the gorges the quicksilver glittered like nothing the engineer had ever seen; the flooded rice fields heliographed merrily; the snowed-up ranges shone in a tier of waves. The flight took two hours one way, one and a half on the return trip—the man was awed. All had been amazingly simple, ruggedly lovely and he had not even been sick; he felt he could never again traipse up and down the trail either on foot or in any other fashion without some impatience. Such was the impact of flying on earthly plodding.

The next ten days were given to the notables of the town; three he persuaded to fly; two were violently ill all the way, the third admitted he liked the experience but felt he hadn't really been to Badrinath, only peeked at it; the flight was far removed from the leisurely satisfaction they had been able to extract from the soothing swing of a palanquin and the moaning chant of coolies. They talked airily of the benefits of an air service and did not venture into particulars for, naturally, they stood to lose nothing. But—and this at the tail end of a long harangue—if the government backed the plan with a subsidy, they would gladly reconsider.

As he was ready to leave, Salim's first letter arrived.

Only by wilful optimism could he convince himself that things were moving. Salim had gone to Premchand and broached the idea anonymously. The uncle had maintained that the plan was 'interesting, but difficult,' and that the same time and money might just as well be used on some other part of the country 'where the need is more legitimate.' He was curious about the instigators, whose names Salim had not disclosed, of course, and he did not think that he himself would fly for a purely spiritual purpose; it was not the same as flying in a hurry or on business.

The other people Salim had seen were of a like frame of mind. The adjectives ran from 'original' to 'foolish' and the common tenor was polite incredulity. Good and imaginative enterprise was in order, but flying pilgrims . . .! Salim's careful abstention from any advice made it rather clear that if he didn't hold the general opinion of the people he had sounded out, he had come to the same ineluctable conclusion about the pilgrim scheme. He had, in fact, taken time to sober down, as always. 'I want to hear *your* news,' he wrote, but this was another way of saying,

'Wind up and get home.'

On the last day but one he went down to the bathing ghats on the river. No visit to Hardwar would be complete without the famous Harki-Charan, the ghat said to bear a footprint of Vishnu's. It was evening. There seemed to be nothing more to do; he had seen and talked to everyone, collected all his data and photographed everything between Badrinath and the plains. Aside from the footprints, this was also the locale of Kumbh Mela, the greatest of all devotional fairs, which Hindus from everywhere celebrated in a mammoth gathering every twelve years.

A thin crowd of bathers splashed at the edge of the river—naked, purposeful blobs against a sheet of restless glimmer. One sat on a wooden platform just above the water and his long hair fell about his head as if after a wash. He spoke without turning.

'I take a much better picture in front. I shall require baksheesh . . .'

'Uday . . .!'

'Vijay Ramsingh! What are you doing in Harki-Charan with a camera?'

89

He joined him on the dais and sat down. Uday was naked except for a very brief loincloth and his hair had again grown ascetically long; he was thinner than usual.

'I didn't recognize you. I thought . . . we all thought you were at Benares.'

'I have been and returned. Yesterday I came back from Kedarnath in the mountains.'

'And I've just been to Badrinath.'

'Arre!' Uday said, smiling at last. 'What is this . . . a sudden urge to penance?'

'To business, Udayji. I walked and flew there, both. It is for an airline to Badrinath . . . my own idea.'

Uday parted his wet hair and peered at his nephew. 'Airline . . .? Of such a thing I should like to hear.'

He listened quietly while Vijay unfolded his ideas. From time to time he wrung and shook his wet plaits or combed his crispy beard, and at one stage he simply gazed across the river.

All along the wooden embankments men and women worshipped the Mother of Rivers in suppliant attitudes, sometimes scooping a potful of it and pouring it back over a mumbled prayer, then wading in chin deep and hanging on to the chain which a thoughtful Pilgrim Board provided against the swift current, often just squatting and flinging morsels of food to the fat and tame salmon in which the offshore abounded. Tired old men and clean-shaved widows in white saris dozed on broad platforms, and here and there an ash-matted holy man sat on his deerskin, facing the sun with closed eyes. At the upper end, a group of dark-brown boys fed the sacred fish in the inner sanctum of the ghat, a round little cove tucked in under the very abutments of the town, separated from the main stream by an under-water fence and an arched wooden bridge that might have come straight from the heart of China. Over it and away from it, the town rose in roughly parallel tiers of houses, each one a little higher and more jagged, which might appear distinctive at close quarters but which, from this distance, the sun merely herded together in a gaudy brotherhood of advertising signs. A few Congress and temple flags shivered in the breeze.

Hemmed by the ghat and the tall bank of reed on the other side, the river rushed past in full view of the sun; kingfishers hurtled out of their perches and nibbled at the restless shimmer in a vain effort to pierce it. Ganges in her youth! After bolting from the rocky Himalayan defiles it seemed delighted to find so much elbow room; it basked under an open and hot sun, still clear and exuberant, not yet the father and mother of all rivers nor feeder of swarming millions along its lower course. Allahabad, Benares and Patna had not yet emptied their sewage into it, neither had their miles of bathing ghats given it a soul which it did not possess or burdened it with a dignity which it did not know how to wear. It was still a gamin, cool and fresh from its shaded romps, playfully veering into the plains. Bathing on its banks was closer to an outdoor sport than religious oblation.

But Uday's first comment was hesitant; he made it in a lazy singsong that was devoid both of elation and of irony.

'A great innovation. I do not know if the pilgrims will like it.'

'And you yourself, Udayji?'

'Not interested, Vijay. Firstly, because I cannot afford it. Secondly, because ours is meant to be a hard, repentant life. Flying sadhus would be the end of Hinduism.'

'Now why should you say a thing like that? Gas, railway, electricity . . . were they an end of Hinduism?'

Uday went on with his toilet, and Vijay lighted a cigarette and had to wait.

This second young uncle of his was not a professional mendicant who scaled the mountains as a part of a planned territorial coverage. He had turned sadhu accidentally, or so the family had always believed, and his notions of holy life could hardly be said to stand in the popular tradition; but for that accident in his youth, still a deep mystery to all who knew him, he might have been just another man of the family. He had been to college; there was a time in his youth when he drove a car, wore European clothes and talked to pretty girls. Behind his restrained bearing was a fairly extensive knowledge of life—an anathema so dear to the hearts of mediocre introverts—which he did not hesitate to show if the occasion called for it. In this he was a modern sadhu. To Vijay he was a bewildering blend of philosopher, spiritual man, crackpot relative and fickle friend.

'Now you are talking like a man born a hundred years ago,' he told him reproachfully. 'All I want is to shorten a pilgrimage, so that even the old and the weak can make it.'

'I can believe that,' Uday said. 'Perhaps our feelings are the only problem. A pilgrim must have time to prepare himself.'

'He will have some. Not very much, but quite enough.'

'Not nearly enough, Vijay. Let me explain . . . it is very important. Take this river, if you wish. Look . . . I only have to drop my hand to reach the water. If I were to meditate upon the meaning of water I would at this moment be too near it . . . but not so if you forced me to reach it through jungle and desert. A man dying of thirst knows the meaning of water not only with his brain but with his whole being. A pilgrim is like that. It took me ten days to go up to Kedarnath and in that time I had the opportunity to get ready. The joy of arrival gave me a feeling of realization. An hour of flying would never give me that.'

'Then the old and tried way is the only one? You're either very lazy or very stubborn.'

91

'Neither, dear nephew. If one way is good enough, what is the use of designing another?'

'Then it is laziness, Udayji!'

The sadhu laughed—a dry little echo from the outer fringes of a more esoteric amusement. He said: 'There are many names for it.'

When the hair was dry he began to twine it first into separate braids, then into a knot on top of his head. In contrast to his lean body, his voice and movements were faintly effeminate; the voice which proclaimed beliefs at such a remove from life at large came from a girlishly pouting mouth. His whole manner was haughty in an entirely worldly way, rather than humble. Where but among us, Vijay thought, would this man be taken to belong to the general scheme of things?

'If you cannot take action out of our lives,' he then began, trying another tack, 'and you certainly cannot, sadhuji, no matter what you say . . . then we should be able to find fulfilment in action. No less than in your yoga trances. If you deny this, you are very stubborn.'

'I do not say yes or no,' Uday said, smoothing out his beard and whiskers. 'Mine is the way of peace. I do not know enough about the other to make a stand. There was a European in the last century who condemned our waste with some eloquence. He thought like you . . . that men should not seek peace, but increase their activity. His ideal human was a veritable dynamo, a kind of intelligent and efficient machine. He called him superman. Perhaps you have heard of him?'

'I haven't.'

'It does not matter. I have often compared this superman with our sannyasi, and now it appears that they are merely two ends of an arrow . . . an arrow streaming towards fulfilment.' He paused delicately, to enable the other to see the image, then proceeded in a slow, tutorly fashion: 'The sannyasi is the original attitude . . . the superman a powerfully motored version . . . as they say of the cars nowadays. We teach: That man who lives free from longing and desires, abandoning the sense of I and mine, he attains to peace in this life. On the other hand, a superman is expected to be cold, philosophic, sensitive to beauty, farseeing but hard, not through lack of feeling but because he is a master of his emotions . . . and he must be overflowing with generosity and vitality. Our sannyasi denies crude life . . . the superman is a triumph of it. The one is the world of senses, the will to power . . . the other a slow retreat from it. The one is your Westerner expressing himself through action . . . the other our Indian yogi and sannyasi . . . myself, if you wish The two choices each of us has. I have made mine, you are about to make yours. Who am I to say that the active way is not right?'

'The difference may be temperamental,' Vijay said. 'It may be in the climate too.'

'It is possible. The man I was just quoting also said that Buddhism was most natural to exhausted peoples. It is my impression that he must have meant Hinduism too.' He smiled and his look was at once personal and bemused. Eels of light from the river trembled on his hairless chest. 'For that reason, dear nephew,' he concluded, 'one's own way is the best. You are a Rajput, of the warrior caste. Your solution may be in action . . . I would not be surprised. It is your dharma after all. It will remain your dharma even if you should make a mess of it. "Better is one's own dharma, even if not well performed, than the dharma of another." A most sensible safety valve, I have no doubt.'

Vijay threw his cigarette into the river; the surface boiled up at once as the fish rushed to it.

'My ideas may be new, but is that the reason why they should be laughed at?'

'The answer to that question,' Uday said thoughtfully, 'may contain your personal fulfilment. If I knew it, I would be solving your dharma instead of my own.'

'Very clever, Udayji. That is all I ever get!'

'Then let me tell you differently. We are a large, slow river. A tributary makes no impression on us, but as we swallow one after another, they start to change our colour and size. So far we have swallowed the Buddhists, Muslims, Christians and all the foreigners down the ages and, naturally, we have become bigger and different ourselves. That is just how we are . . . and it is not for you or me to question it. We have the choice of swimming in a tributary or in the main stream. Speaking for myself, the stream has all I need.'

'It is not what I meant . . . but never mind.'

There was so much more he had wanted to say, but after all was there any point in saying it? Arguing was for all the world like the revolutions of a prayer wheel. There was no comfort in words; was the final meaning a segment discernible only after the waves of commotion had passed over it? That smacked of the moment before death. His instinct rebelled against it. And how did one, beginning with practical things, invariably come to discuss right and wrong . . .?

He gathered up his camera and screwed his eyes at the sky. The sun had almost set; long, whittled replicas of the ghat towers lay on the ground and across them the bathers now moved towards the exits—too late for photographs. A cloud of pigeons wheeled around a deep orange sky, a temple drum throbbed somewhere in quiet and dedicated frenzy, a child cried into the wet folds of his mother's sari. Beyond the stream, the first range began to have a fuzzy mauve look. He rose unwillingly and stood above his uncle.

'Tell me about your own plans.'

The sadhu stroked his knuckles, still gazing across the river. Now the hair lay combed and twined on top of his head, baring his clean scrawny neck and a string of coral and moonstone beads In his lap his hands lay on top of each other, seemingly listless; his folded legs seemed to be a part of a shining bronze statue that might come to life if the right word were uttered.

'You could hardly call it a plan,' he said softly. 'I am still endeavouring . . . if that is what you wish to know. I may be wasteful, but I am the way of Asia. I say that in all humility. According to one science, I am less fitted to survive than you . . . but then, survival is not all.'

'I'm going back to town,' Vijay said irreverently. 'Will you come with me?'

'No, Vijay.'

'I may not see you again. I am flying to Bombay to-morrow morning.'

'Still no. I have not yet meditated, or prayed. I was going to . . . . after my bath.'

'Then I must take my leave now. I hope you will find your peace.'

'And I wish you success.'

'Do you think I shall get it?'

'No, Vijay.' He turned around and smiled almost apologetically. 'Still, this will not stop you. You are different from the rest of us in the family . . . you pry and press . . . and push. Opinions do not matter. Perhaps one day you shall push far enough for yourself.'

'Will you be seeing us again this year?'

'It is possible. I do not know yet. If I do, we must have a long talk . . . after I have washed my hair.'

'Yes, we must, Udayji. Now good-bye, and don't catch your death from cold out here.'

'Good-bye, Vijay. And good luck.'

He stirred at last and walked away.

At the top of the ghat, on the stairway above the holy pool of Harki-Charan, he turned to wave once more, but the sadhu was already a dim bundle on the shore of the greying river, a rather helpless and forlorn little bundle, apparently welded to the square wooden dais on which he sat.

Fourth Chapter

1

OVER the ghats on the way to Bombay the air currents were more turbulent than before and the atmosphere seemed to be all pockets—the vanguard of the monsoon. He landed at Juhu, saw his machine packed away in the club's hangar and left orders to have it stored for the rainy season. Villa Ram was back at full strength. His parents and sisters had spent the last ten days at the hill resort of Mahableshwar, and he found them more animated than he expected. Kandubai's eyes seemed a little less deep set and her cheeks fuller; her son's return even flushed them noticeably.

All told, Jagnath sounded comforted. He knew nothing yet of the Hardwar and Badrinath explorations, but he seemed to sense that the lecture tour, at any rate, was safely and finally buried; he had looked upon it as a wild-goose chase from the outset, and its demise struck him as a hopeful sign. The celebrated realism of Hindu parenthood was reaching the stage of near-equanimity in his person; there was so much a young man of Vijay's talents and accomplishment could do, provided he could be nagged into doing it, that it was often a good policy to give the youngster a discreet length of rope. He was reasonably sure that the flop of the Rajputana visit could not fail to have taught his son the value of parental advice.

Providentially, too, Bombay gasped in the last pre-monsoon hush, which made any great zeal or singleness of thought hard of practice; bickering had to await the break of the rains. A universe smashed into yellowish dust came to hover above the city and above the flats of Juhu, and all dwellings seemed to huddle hot and lonely in the sun; on the beach behind the club bathers drowsed at all hours or waded into the sea and cooled themselves. The reef in the bay shimmered without respite of an afternoon, and the land stretched its wasted, dry limbs far out into the water as if to slake the long fever. At dusk, some of the swimmers drove over to the club and lingered over their drinks and admired his plane with flaccid enthusiasm. Their airs were distrait, like his own.

He went and saw Uncle Premchand several times and each time the talks were on an evener keel. Like Jagnath, the uncle was still in the dark about his nephew's doings at Hardwar. He had lost some face with the two princes to whom he had written letters of introduction, but the damage was not great; his vitality, too, flagged in the broiling swelter. Vijay's rancour towards the princes was genuine enough even to infect him slightly for, when all was said and done, it was deplorable that so few rich Indians used their money for the right causes and that, when they were willing to spend at all, they usually backed the wrong horse; the Hindu invariably seemed to spend against the Muslim, the maharaja against the Congress, the landlord against the Finance Department, and so on *ad nauseam*, and it was really small wonder that the country was a hotchpotch of foreign exploitation. Such a view enabled Premchand to place his nephew among the wrongfully persecuted. The youngster's first misadventure was now behind him, and the uncle could pore over its finer points with a detached kind of compassion and feel responsible for the young fellow, even patronizing in a benign kind of way. Premchand remained a potential ally, and Vijay set out to remove the sting from his failure before pursuing his Hardwar goal any further.

All publicity and travesties of value were over, and that was something to be thankful for. Now that the upheaval was at an end, family life rallied again. He found that there was a lot to be said for the obtuseness with which the Hindus chewed a great event to solid and unexciting cud before dispatching it for ever. It was in a sense the way of all flesh, and remarkably effective at that. Multiplied over and over, it was the way in which the cataclysmic advent of the Aryans had been pared down to a feeble *fait accompli*, in which the Mogul invaders had been reduced to small fry that devoured one another. It was no accident the cow was the popular symbol of Hindu India. History was an interminable hour of digestion, cud-chewing its only hope; if the look on the face of the Indian cow was that of supreme callousness, the wondering observer might remember that it is an old, old look, much older than his wonder, and he might also reflect upon the proposition that few things in the world managed to withstand the relentless four stomachs of the cow—as, Uncle Premchand might have added, the lofty British were about to learn to their cost.

At last the monsoon broke at the end of July with the customary glitter and crash. The club closed down for three months, as it did every year. On the rocks of Bombay the wind pounded the surf into fine spray and the boom became an aspect of the coast. All over the islands the soil went through a swift change of colour, from arid ochre to dark brown, then to apple green with streaks of verdigris, and the hills waxed more darkly each day. Urchins drew weird shapes in the silt, low-caste men slung their shoes over their shoulders and waded to work, water buffaloes reeled in the pools of mud and their purple skins gleamed dully. Streets had a tidy, laundered air. In defiance of the calendar, one year came to an end and another was ushered in, smelling of wet grass and leaves fallen to the ground, full of ozone and the miracle of germination. Water flowed everywhere, swift and elfin, a mirror in which the city saw itself once a year, vainly, in grateful relief; when it stopped falling, it strung lurid sunsets and cloudy piles all over the town; of an evening the sky became a huge glowing underwater cave, with the source of light itself hidden away at the far end. Remembering the pale performance of the English skies, Vijay found his own breath-taking. They struck him as a reckless and rather characteristic gesture for all that his country had so far failed to give him.

He plunged into a different kind of life, pleasant and sure for a change. While rain fell there was nothing much to do, and the city stayed indoors and tried to amuse itself; it took up startling hobbies and renewed its social bonds. 'If you are free on Saturday,' people often said to him, 'come and see us'—and there it was, he didn't for the moment have anything better to do. They liked him well enough despite his earnestness. This was an India into which he felt he fitted better than any other for the present, one admittedly self-centred and rather unpredictable, but one which was nevertheless the spearhead of other Indias, the numerical ones. The souls of Salim Haq and many others like him, whose company he now sought, were no less redeemable because of their occasional precocity; their monsoon sprees might be dismissed as deplorable lapses of restraint, but that would not make them any less Indian; the British themselves were wont to remark with an odd resentment, that an Indian remained an Indian whether he drove a motor car in a dinner jacket or joggled along in a bullock cart in a simple loincloth. Vijay averred these truths in his own vengeful way. He had wanted to work and be of use, but he had been snubbed; now he was going to play for a change. This India of prodigals, rakes and disenchantment was not the Bharat Mata of the versifier, but it would pamper him and make him forget; it would amuse him and make up for the time lost in Kathiawar and Rajputana: with it he would mix and laugh until the rains were over, until it was time to think of the next move. And if anyone dared to suggest that his post was elsewhere, he would point out to him that this circle was the crust of the nation, from which emerged saints and leaders alike, the lava at the top of a volcano, the yeast without which no bread, no matter how large, would ever rise and amount to anything—and he would quote chapter and verse to prove it even to his own temporary satisfaction.

2

AUGUST was almost gone when he got round to seeing Uncle Premchand in real earnest.

The busy newspaper magnate had moved out to his other house on the Juhu beach and was living virtually on conferences. Juhu was a suburb of Bombay, lately become a vogueish residential section for those who laid store by seclusion and beach life and did not mind the distance from town. It lay hidden in a dense palm grove skirting a wide stretch of sand between the Indo-Christian suburb of Bandra and the fishing village of Versova, overlooking the bay of Juhu and the ocean on the western side, the Flying Club, the fallow marshland and the village of Andheri on the eastern side. The rains had glossed over the long rib of palmland, and from a distance the white and cream villas of the wealthy seemed like so many rabbits lost in high grass. A sea breeze was puffing the crowns of the grove and sprinkling the sun this way and that, its whirring no longer dry or agonized, and Vijay was reminded of a European acquaintance who had once described it as the most conventionally tropical scene in all India. Remembering it, Vijay emitted a small involuntary snort. The lovely ridge was currently one of the sharpest real-estate offerings in all Bombay, and what little romance it might have possessed was already being brought up to date by the residents themselves, for their radios blared forth shrilly at all times of the day and night and the exhausts of their large cars were often stronger than the scent of the shrubbery. And higher up the beach towards Versova in the creek, these same palms bestowed their impartial rustle on chatai huts of fisherfolk and even on a leper or two. An invisible but categorical boundary marked the two sections, and no one upheld it more jealously than the residents of the fashionable one. The dead, too, must have finally learned it, since a surburban by-law had the burning ghat moved to the end of the beach where the charnel odours would be blown over the sea in fitting isolation. Tropical idyl my foot! Vijay thought, as his car lurched between two cement posts and into the narrow, well-kept drive of Uncle Premchand's house. Now his mind sheered back to the business at hand and he shuddered nervously; the impartial observer of Juhu gave place, suddenly and rather sickeningly, to the first goblin of diffidence.

A servant showed him in, salaaming respectfully. He said 'Jee-huhn,' gave him a chair and went to announce him. The large cool-looking house seemed quiet.

It was a modern dwelling, well placed to overlook the ocean and a wide expanse of beach, and its garden was one of the lushest and biggest in the neighbourhood. On its flat roof terrace, almost directly under the palm tops and their clusters of coconuts many a foreign journalist, too, had been initiated into the maze of Indian politics. In the days when the Congress flag had been illegal and its display a punishable offence, little orange and white and green stickers on the staircase and upper walls used to remind the visitor that an Indian, like his ruler the Briton, was king of his own home even though not of his own country. Lately, the restriction had been allowed to die a quiet death and a gay new flag fluttered continuously from a pole on the roof.

The uncle came out almost at once—hospitable and a little baffled. He took his nephew to a long and airy room on the upper floor where two strangers rose silently to greet the newcomer, then backed out into the next room and shut the door. The blandishments over, he listened attentively to Vijay's long preamble and played with his gold pencil; his raised eyebrows gradually descended and his stare intensified without becoming more revealing. He nodded a good deal, too, and shook his knees with a rapid small tremble—the popular Indian sign of good listening.

'And so you are behind it after all,' he cut short his nephew's explanations. 'I ought to have guessed it from Salim's great partiality. Why did you not speak to me first?'

'I wanted to, uncle, but I had to prepare maps and estimates before coming. I will show them to you after I have explained.'

Premchand pulled up his homespun dhoti and tucked it under his knees, in order to shake them more freely; he also reached for the silver box of betel-nut condiments at his side.

'Dear boy,' he said weightily, 'I could listen to you until next week if I knew that it would change my opinion. First of all . . . I do not agree that the plan of flying pilgrims is a good one. I do not think that the time-honoured practice of our devotion needs any such revolutionary improvement. I should certainly not like it for myself . . . and I could well do with more religion. Such old customs are best left to themselves.'

'But listen kindly to the end,' Vijay said, forgetting his diplomatic intentions and plunging into it rather more passionately than was wise. 'Please.'

As he went on, his uncle's eyes sat on him unflinchingly, only now their directness seemed a makeshift for the decision hardening behind them.

Premchand seemed to have become a different man in the last few months, but while the change might have been summed up in the thinner face, the shrunken potbelly and a new gravity, the other deeper change was for the moment much more elusive. Did his heightened pace of public life have anything to do with it . . .? Vijay imagined that even his tummy sagged between his crossed legs with a curious new dignity—a pertinent point this, for when a man turned an essential indignity into an ornament, that was the time to suspect him of achieving a certain inner harmony. For Vijay this was a burning question. So he wound up his brief with a scarcely controlled breath and took out his carefully drawn-up estimates, hoping that the other man's look might clear presently.

'Vijay, there is something I have to tell you. Will you follow me carefully?'

'Yes, uncle, of course.'

Premchand seemed to contemplate him with the mind of another person, one unweighted by any concern for family or relationship, as he said: 'I talked with your father while you were in the North. Did he tell you?'

'No.'

'We both thought the testing time for our young men is here and now. India is at long last getting a measure of freedom with this Act of 1935 . . . not a large measure, but a measure all the same. The day of complete freedom seems not to be far off, and this I should very much like to impress on you: What we do now . . . at this time . . . will either keep that day away from us or bring it nearer. I know that you have been busy and may have overlooked the fact, but I want to tell you that our community has a long memory.'

'The community didn't give me a fair chance.'

'I am only thinking of the time . . . very close now, almost at hand . . . when the community will start remembering . . . Your father and I should very much like to see you among those gratefully remembered.'

'But I want to work, this very moment, if you will let me!' Vijay said with unintentional heat.

Premchand bent over the arm of the chair to reach for the cuspidor; he spat into it deftly, then shifted the betel nut to one side of his palate in order to speak without hindrance.

'Our people will not put up with anyone who has sat on the fence during the struggle.'

The brutal phrase brought Vijay up short. Had his father conspired with the uncle behind his back? If so, it was unfair—and at the thought of that his annoyance swelled up suddenly.

'A kind of reign of terror, uncle . . .?'

'That would be an exaggeration Sometimes people want to distinguish between friends and drones.'

'But I'm not sitting on the fence. I thought you would understand, because you have always preached progress. You're saying that the majority have the corner on all action . . . that I must pay my rupee in their own currency. It is blindness, don't you see . . .?'

'That may be so, dear boy. The truth is that if you do not enter the movement at this stage, you will remain outside for ever. All great struggle is like that. We cannot twiddle our thumbs at a distance and remain convincing.'

'Help me then. I have a plan here . . .'

'It is what I am trying to do,' the older man said with hard precision. 'It is the only help you need. Stop wasting time on foolish schemes and start being practical. You are no longer a college boy . . . you are a man. Come down from the clouds and attend to your obligations.'

The telephone rang out on a teapoy nearby; Premchand reached for the receiver without moving out of his chair.

So much arbitrariness! Now he was so roused he could barely hold himself. What had come over his uncle, over everyone? Had they all banded together simply to foil him? Was it possible that this smug new uncle would rather see him join a street demonstration and go to jail than do the kind of work he was best suited for? It was regimentation, that's what it was, under the banner of patriotism, and they were even losing their subtlety! He didn't interfere with them, how dared they dictate to him!

He had known for some time that there was fresh brewing behind the scenes and that Congress had decided to go to the polls that winter, to prove its strength once and for all.

The masses would never understand any but the most immediate issues, Vijay thought, but in actual practice this would matter very little. The events of the late twenties had proved that if a struggle was initiated by the intelligentsia the masses would follow sheepishly enough. That backward, long-suffering, dimly seen backbone of India, the Indian peasant, drew his spiritual strength not only from religion but also from the higher castes who dispensed it—and if one educated Indian whom the people had met on their hearth matting condemned another whom the people had not met, the latter could go and hide himself. Almost any of the men filing in and out of Premchand's house might be such a condemning type, and that at any rate was a safe guess. While Vijay was willing to grant importance and good faith to their missions, he did not care for their tense air of fanaticism; a good many struck him as the kind of people who would keep all opinions save their own in endless abeyance; who, moreover, might loudly deny his view that all Indians had the right to choose the kind of work they were most clever at, for these khaddar-clad busybodies were plainly cold to all contributions not their own. In this sense, but only in this one, Premchand was probably right.

Now the uncle put the receiver down and pressed his eyeballs, and his knees began to shake again. 'Where were we?' he said.

'You were saying you wanted to help me. I don't think you meant it at all.'

'Yes, I remember. . . .' He picked up the hem of his shirt and wiped his glasses, not ceasing to shake.

'Please believe me, uncle, I do not wish to be obstinate,' Vijay attempted once more, with all the restraint he was capable of, because the door had to

101

be left ajar even if this meeting achieved nothing else. 'I just don't care to be yoked into anything simply because it is customary. Right now I do not care for politics either . . . there must be thousands of people who are much better at it than I could ever be. Let them do it. I can do other things which they cannot.'

The look of the host cleared, as though the vision he had been training it on had drifted closer.

'Vijay, my dear boy,' he said, 'you talk so big . . . but what is it you want after all? Fly around the world and have a good time . . . on other people's money? Become the managing director of an airline from one day to another? Who of us would not like the same thing! Wake up and stop dreaming!'

'I have, this very moment.' He rose and felt flushed.

'Have you?'

'Yes, uncle. I'm not a Congress or Muslim League volunteer . . . you can't drill me like a boy of twelve!' he said, not caring any more. 'I came to you for help and you talk of movements and communities. Let me tell you one thing . . . the community needs a kick in their dhoties . . .!' His anger waxed prophetic. 'We use the words of free people, but look . . . our actions are slavish. The British have known that all the time, and that is why we still have them. And as long as we think like slaves we don't deserve anything better than we get.'

Premchand nodded gravely. 'One reason why discipline is so necessary!'

Vijay started for the door, tripping over a set of carved Kashmiri teapoys all neatly stacked on top of one another.

'And if you're not going to help me, I'll have to go to someone else, that is all! There must be people in this country who can talk of the future without insults!' Remembering his papers, he came back, slapped them together and thrust them in his pocket angrily. 'And I shall not bother you again . . . this is the last time! A day will come when I shall prove you wrong . . . so wrong that you will be ashamed!'

'We should keep our tempers to ourselves,' Premchand said evenly.

'We should, but sometimes we can't. Sometimes the provocation is too great!'

At the door he remembered to make a quick half-obeisance towards the munching uncle, who made no move. Then he ran downstairs and out of the house.

It was dusk. The first weak trail of electric lights hung in the grove like a listless spirit. He drove out and along the main road, furious with himself, with Premchand, with his family and with the entire brood of Hindus. That it should have fallen to his uncle to accuse him of uselessness was the crudest accident; what rankled much more was that the accusation flaunted him from the heap of the last six months, a time crammed with failure and misunderstanding, and that it was the flower of that sapping attrition which was so hard to separate from sheer bad luck. And of course he was furious too at the claim of the group to have limitless power over the individual, all the more as he was now convinced that his own group was half a century behind him. Worse luck, the door was slammed shut now and the break was in the kind of dramatic tradition of which he had never suspected himself.

Driving unhappily along through the congealing dusk, of which palm trunks leaning at crazy angles were already a part, he sank in a daze. It was a feeling at once blighting and heroic—heroic because, for better or worse, he had at last voiced his protest and the act seemed to wipe out a good deal of his debt to himself, and blighting because it was quite plain to him that in quarrelling with his uncle he had, for all immediate purposes, thrown away the baby with the bath water. With his uncle out of the running, the pilgrim plan would have to go a-begging once more. New contacts would have to be made and tried, more arguments thought of, more time wasted —how much? If he could only know that, everything would be so much easier.

And then he found himself at the southern end of the grove, facing the open garden gate of the Morrisons—a Eurasian family he had got to know lately via his friend Salim Haq—whom, he decided quickly, it would be easier to face in his present frame of mind than returning home to face his parents and sisters.

3

'MR. RAMSINGH, how very nice to see you again. . . . Do come in, it is so damp here in the garden,' said the perfectly oval shape of Mrs. Morrison as it waddled up the porch steps and waved him on hospitably. 'We didn't think we would see you again so soon . . . certainly not in this little jungle retreat.'

'I was driving past and I thought . . .'

'But yes, yes, dear me, I would never have forgiven you if you had not looked us up. Do come upstairs, please. I know Thelma will be as happy as I am. . . .'

She began to tackle the steep staircase and here the strenuous labour of ascension cut her short. To Vijay, she had appeared formidable in a chair before, but at this moment, heaving herself upward step by step with a series of desperate wrenches that involved every last part of her rotundity, gasping busily and leaning on each knee to shift the fiendish centre of gravity ever forward and ever higher, and this by sheer co-ordination of a dauntless will and a body past all tricks of the usual locomotion—now she commanded respect and admiration.

She was fortyish and short, wore a simple afternoon dress of black silk and was ingratiating with a wealth of gesture and singsong which a half-caste instinctively called into play in the presence of races purer than himself. When Vijay had first met her in the flat of his friend about a month ago, Salim was unable to explain her background beyond saying that she was a widow and an amiable soul and seemed to be kept by an elderly ruling prince from Central India, and that the ostensible purpose of this arrangement was to give her daughter Thelma enough leisure to study dramatic art and eventually become a film actress; privately, Salim had looked upon it as a cozy seraglio set-up and all his curiosity had been centred on whether the ruler's affections were in the ransom of the mother or the daughter. Vijay paid no attention to this. He rather liked the fat Mrs. Morrison, her inexhaustible store of Anglo-Indian anecdotes and the soundless droll quake of her laughter; her happy-go-lucky Eurasian ways were such a relief after the attrition of his home life, and there was no doubt that Thelma Morrison, her daughter, was a provocative example of the much maligned Eurasian womanhood and that she might in due course lend colour to Salim's belief that bed was the natural goal of all Eurasian girls after fourteen. Indeed Salim was not alone in such attitude; most Indian boys were brought up in the belief that the Eurasian males were either policemen or railwaymen, and that their women habitually sought romance where they could find it. Climbing behind Mrs. Morrison, Vijay thought that this was making mountains out of molehills and that the probable truth lay somewhere between Salim's malice and Mrs. Morrison's laughing refusal to take life at its dreary face value.

'This way, Mr. Ramsingh,' she gasped on the landing of the upper floor. 'I was just going to town when you came. I know Thelma will be glad of company . . . she has been in all day, and such a lovely day too.'

She led him to the drawing-room and bade him sit down; for his suggestion that he might come at another more convenient time she had only a quick and skittish flip of the hand. She called an Indo-Christian servant and was on the point of ordering tea when Vijay said that he had already had it at his uncle's place; they compromised on some freshly cooked relishes and a glass of brandy. Vijay drank seldom and was not very good at it, but now Premchand's infamy seemed like an occasion to break the rule.

'You know, we've been hearing processions all morning,' she said, clearing the round teatable of film periodicals and brass knick-knacks. 'It is Ganpati down on the beach . . . so many people must have thrown their little dolls of Ganesh into the sea. Even my servants took the morning off. Cook came back only an hour ago . . . smelling of toddy, I'm afraid. We had an awful row. I am telling you, Mr. Ramsingh, if he didn't make such heavenly curries I should have fired him long ago.'

She went to the window and studied the sky for a moment. Down over the sea heliotrope flashes signalled another squall. She shut all but one window, then dusted her hands and hobbled towards the next room.

'More rain, oh dear,' she said cheerfully. 'Now I must really run. You will excuse me, won't you? Do make yourself comfortable while I call Thelma.'

'Thank you,' Vijay said.

While she was gone the servant brought a large platter of sandwiches, spiced kevabs and Indian sweets, and a tray of brandy and sodas; he poured out a drink and swizzled it club-fashion. Vijay gulped it rather rashly.

The room was crammed with the sort of furniture which a Central Indian raja might consider exquisitely modern—an English couch covered with a pink brocade-like material, a matching suite of upholstered armchairs done in a darker use and a great many chromium-plated side tables; on them reposed the unavoidable Anglo-Indian bric-a-brac: brass monkeys and hooded cobras, caskets of inlaid bronze and carved Kashmir walnut, book-ends without books and long-necked herons whose open bills served as receptacles for unpaid bills and, on occasions, a stem of tuberose. By the couch was a toy-size airplane which, by a manipulation of levers, became a winged bar, disclosing a cocktail shaker and a set of glasses. Vijay was trying to make it work when a rumpus next door announced the entry of Thelma Morrison.

'Vijay, what a nice surprise! Just when I was getting so bored!' She shook his hand and smiled delightedly. 'Mother says you were seeing your uncle up the grove. How have you been? Is Salim with you?'

'He couldn't come,' he lied. 'He sends his regards, though.'

'Thank you. I haven't seen either of you since that last party in his flat. Come to think of it, I haven't seen anyone for the last two weeks. We're leading such a dull life up here. But do sit down and tell me about Bombay.'

He re-sat himself then, while she sank down on the couch and drew her legs under her.

She was twenty and fair complexioned, in contrast to Mrs. Morrison. Wavy black hair, parted in the middle and swept down over each temple to cover up the high cheekbones, those telling brands of a Eurasian; a low forehead, a pair of oily black eyes, short upturned nose with the nostrils flattened ever so little; a round, thickly painted mouth over a small and pointed chin; disproportionately large breasts stuffed into a bodice so tight that it must have hampered her breathing; a close-fitting dress of white crepe designed not only to offset those but also to show the rest of her to the best plastic advantage—these were Thelma at first sight. To Vijay, for that matter, they were the hallmarks of any Eurasian girl. In ten years

Thelma's figure would be sacrificed to a lazy life and too long a diet of curry rice, and she would take to wearing roomier dresses and more sensible shoes, but now she was still young and conscious of her value. Where Mrs. Morrison had no more qualms about singsong and accent, Thelma took deliberate care to modulate her voice and flip her fingers as little as possible. She had nice regular teeth and flashed them readily.

He hinted at the unpleasant encounter in Uncle Premchand's villa, but didn't go into details. He added that he was not sure if he did well in coming back to India.

'Poor you,' she said at once. 'You have all my sympathy. I'd give anything in this world to be home myself right now.'

He winced privately. This mania of the Eurasians to talk of England as 'home' was actually amusing after a time; it was the fetish of the entire Anglo-India, a reminder that they were here only by the grace of their better selves, that they should do what was required of them with good cheer and aloofness, bracing themselves against the bland ways of the country and people alike. To hear it from the lips of a half-caste, whose mingled roots went deep into the soil of India and were practically of it, was a constant source of merriment to the Indians.

She gave him another drink, then settled back on the couch and told him of the small part she had recently been given in a Hindi-Mahrati film called *Draupadi*. Did he know the story of Draupadi, the wife of the five Pandu princes in the epic Mahabharata?

'Oh yes. Who doesn't know it,' he said, sipping again unwisely.

'Well, it's my first part in any film,' she said with more animation. 'I am so thrilled, Vijay, I have no peace any more. I stand before the mirror and rehearse all day. I even dream about it. There's a scene in the film where Princess Draupadi is condemned for marrying all five Pandu brothers at once . . . imagine, five of them! . . . and then the king asks the maids to strip her right there and then, in front of the whole court. Then the maids . . . by the way, I am one of them, it's really quite an interesting part, but a small one, of course . . . then the maids start undraping the sari of the princess and, just imagine, they can't take it off because a miracle happens. The sari becomes an endless piece of silk. They pull and pull at it, but there's always more coming. Of course, it's a trick of the gods, you see? because they've known all along that she was a virtuous woman, even if she did marry five boys all at once, and they don't want her to lose her womanly honour. I think it is a charming idea, don't you?'

'Very nice,' he said. 'What happens then?'

'Of course the king realizes he should never have done anything so awful, and he stops the whole thing. Well, I was going to say we . . . the maids, that is . . . start to dance as we pull the sari off the princess. The dance is supposed to show how full of grief we are. Then the miracle becomes clear to us and we start dancing for joy. I know it sounds terrible when I tell you, but it's a very effective scene really. I've had to learn dancing to do it . . . three week's practice for that one scene, would you believe it? I never thought I could do it. So many incredible movements of the hands and fingers . . . so much body control, it made me quite dizzy. You just can't imagine.'

'I can, Thelma. I've seen it very often,' he said, infected by her enthusiasm.

He knew little about the dance of his people beyond what was normally to be seen in India films or sometimes at private parties, but among the educated Hindus the opinion was prevalent that the Indian technique surpassed the European ones by much intricacy and finesse. The thought also flitted through his head that the prohibition of liquor by the Brahmans was another sample of the traditional Indian unreason. The stuff he had swallowed was anything but evil.

'I'll tell you what, Vijay . . . I'll show you the costume I'm wearing for the scene. It's an absolute riot, really it is. You've never seen such colours. I shan't be a moment,' and she leaped from the couch and dashed into the next room.

He heard the wardrobes bang and scrape furiously, then there was a tinkle of silver and then silence. A gust of expectancy all but wafted Uncle Premchand to the outer frontiers of memory. He made himself more comfortable on the couch; Salim's aspersions on the Eurasian breed came back to him, sharpened now with a sense of adventure and sex. He wondered, too, whether Mrs. Morrison had gone yet, and if so, whether she would be back soon. His head swam pleasantly. Then Thelma came back and all his guessing faded away magically. It was as though a legendary king's daughter had stepped on to the palace balcony.

'I haven't bothered to put it on properly,' she said. 'But this is it, Vijay. I wear three muslin veils over my head . . . in different colours . . . and throw them off as I dance. Don't you think it's a riot?'

'My goodness, I wouldn't have recognized you!' he said.

She described the models from which it had been copied—an ancient fresco from a place in Ceylon, a cave or something like that—and used old Sanskrit names for the different parts of it, names he had never heard but which sounded funny on her lips. The rustle of the heavy, garishly woven silk became more personal as she flounced this way and that; the massive silver clasps on her ankles jingled with real abandon. The classical conventions required a bare midriff; each time she came close to him her white waist gleamed a little less awesomely.

'How can you dance in this?' he asked with scheme.

'Oh, quite easily. It's not nearly so heavy as it looks, see . . .?' and she swirled about several times, so that the hem of the skirt all but grazed his chin.

107

'That's not dancing, Thelma. Show me what you do in the film.'

'Would you like me to, truly?'

'Truly.'

'All right, here we go.'

She stood still for a moment, got into her pose and began to sway. Vijay sat back and relaxed. One didn't have to be an expert to realize at once that she was a dilettante and that the classical school had indeed been too much for her. The dance was a three-cornered marriage of Kathak, European ballet and hula, and although she put much pain into the rasas of her face and the mudras of her hands, only the hips responded with anything like true fluency. He knew that she couldn't help herself. Just as a European's rhythm was in his legs and feet and an Indian's in his face and hands, a Eurasion's lay somewhere in between, for he was a fusion of both. Vijay smiled at her and said 'Shabash!' by way of appreciation, and then he found himself ogling her frankly and without any compunction. A good-looking half-caste entertaining a Rajput—the scene even had a befuddled kind of fitness about it.

Then she threw up her arms, stamped her foot finally and came back to the couch and called for her drink. He gave it to her, held her head as she drank and afterwards kissed her. This led to so swift an exchange of caresses that he would later wonder why such elaborate preliminaries had been necessary.

'Wait here,' she said at length and left him to go to the other room. He gulped down some neat brandy and closed the other door. She came back wearing a white satin dressing-gown, a little box under her arm. 'Aren't you hot in this suit?' she said, flipping the gown off her legs as she lay down. 'I'm so hot I can't breathe. My, that costume was warm after all.'

'What about Mrs. Morrison?' he said. 'And the servants?'

'They're all in the kitchen. Mother won't be back for a couple of hours.'

Her fingers explored him thoroughly, first with a fumble, then more surely. Salim had not been far wrong: She didn't know the meaning of reticence; things were as they were and she made no attempt to gloss them over. Then it transpired that she wore nothing at all under the coat and that she liked roughness.

'Half a mo', dear. Give me that box.'

He did. However, when she was done with it, he found he only wanted to lie and smoke a cigarette. He even turned away from her.

'Never you mind, dear,' she said sympathetically. 'Don't let it upset you. You've probably had too much to drink. You people don't stand it as well as we do. Just lie back and take it easy.'

'What do you mean "you people"?' he snapped. 'Weren't *you* born here?'

'Sure, dear, sure . . . it's only a way of speaking. I didn't mean it like that at all. Forget it, please.'

He said nothing, and she wriggled closer and took a puff from his cigarette; she watched him with half-shut eyes for a little while, then tucked his loose hair behind his ear and sighed. 'Are you a Kashmiri Brahman?' she asked at length.

'Rajput.'

'Of course, I should have known it. My, you're too handsome for a Brahman, even a Brahman from Kashmir. Where do you come from?'

He told her.

'You know, dear,' she said cajolingly, 'your English is absolutely amazing. You mustn't mind if I say so. If I heard you over the phone, I'd swear my life you'd been to Oxford.' And, as he began to squirm: 'Now, don't jump up all at once. I mean it as a compliment. After all, it's not your language, is it? I know a lot of people who've spent all their lives in England and don't speak it nearly as well as you. I think that's wonderful. If anyone said that to me I'd be very happy.'

At that, his resentment began to strike him as rather foolish and he rolled over on his back and gave her a cigarette all to herself. Then he dressed, listening to her small talk; it was impossible not to marvel at her complete naturalness. She told him her father had run away when she was a baby; he was in the merchant marine, and so they never saw him again; her mother had run a dance school for years, but had to give it up when she fell ill during one cholera epidemic; since then they had made some good friends and were having much less trouble; her mother wanted her to marry, but she preferred an acting career. Anyhow, what was the good of marrying if one did not love the man. 'You know, dear,' she said, moving the box out of sight, 'you're the first one I really like. I liked your friend Salim, too, but not in the same way. He knows too much about women. Sometimes he's just a little bit too cheeky, if you know what I mean.'

He sat back next to her and had to laugh. 'What do you mean?'

'Ah, you know very well. Sometimes he looks at me so insolently I think he can read my mind. And I'm sure he can. It's not nice when you can't have any secrets before a man.'

'Well, whose fault is it?' he said with a wave at the hidden box.

She pulled the gown over her and seemed ruffled for the first time; he even thought that her face flushed a little.

'Yes, I know, dear, I shouldn't have let you see it. I won't ever again, I'm very sorry. I always thought men found these things exciting. Well, it just goes to show . . .'

'Never mind,' he said. 'We can still be friends.'

Turning round then she curled up once more and let out a long and luxuriant sigh. 'I would like that,' she said. 'I've never had a Rajput friend. I hope you'll come more often. We'll go down to the beach and swim . . . I get so bored all by myself. One day . . . when I'm not such a coward

. . . we'll go to the club and you'll take me up in your airplane. I've never flown yet. I don't think I'll be afraid after the first time. I never am afterwards. Mother used to say I wasn't even afraid of ghosts as a baby. . . . She thinks it's not decent for a girl not to be afraid. Poor mum, what's there to be afraid of once you know where you stand . . .? D'you know, dear, I like your nose . . . it's so strong . . . your mouth too. I wonder how you kiss, when you really set your mind to it. Well, next time . . . I simply must close my eyes for a moment.'

A minute later she was asleep, and he got up uncertainly.

The liquor mist was beginning to lift somewhat, revealing the latent threat of Uncle Premchand, the now forlorn hope of his Hardwar plan and Salim's uncanny sense of timing—for it was now plain why the Muslim had introduced him to the Morrisons. In many ways Salim and Thelma saw things in pretty much the same rugged light. He remembered Salim's words a few weeks back, when he told him he was going to see Uncle Premchand about the pilgrims and confessed his nervousness.

'Bhai, I have been watching you,' Salim had said in the tone of an elder brother. 'You are becoming more neurotic every day. You can't even amuse yourself any longer.'

'You Muslims always could,' he had answered him. 'That's why you lost India to the British.'

'Not lost, dear fellow . . . we became India. Would you like to know why?'

'Why?'

'Because we do not fret over our misfortunes. You do not find neurotics among us. When we are sad, we blame the Hindus. When that helps no more, we go to a woman and demand songs. And that is what you will need after you have seen your uncle. Take it from Salim, bhai. . . .'

And now that was just what he had done, and it was certainly better than carrying Premchand's rudeness in his head and moping around unhappily.

He left the house as quietly as he could and drove home. He rang up Thelma the next day and took her to the cinema in Salim's car. They got on much better after that. She was even more accommodating than Connie, and much less of a strain. He took her driving, swimming and dancing, often in defiance of all proper custom, and she was complaisant throughout. He could behave as badly as he wanted, and it was never more or less than she expected; in domineering and maltreating her he retained, too, a vestige of his jealousy of Constance, for Thelma was just as white as she had been. But where Connie never suspected this streak in him, Thelma knew it from an old instinct and pandered to it with a disarming frankness. Sure, dear, take it if it helps you, her look seemed to say after each time. I may be a half-caste and you a pure Rajput, but I'm fairer than you anyhow.

It was degrading, of course, and at the back of his mind the thought was ever present that he was perhaps relinquishing more than he was getting, yet he couldn't tear himself away. The infamy itself became curiously indispensable. After a time they had not a secret between them and although they never quite confessed their real thoughts each could anticipate the other's weaknesses without visible embarrassment. Thus the blackest aspect of the affair turned out for him to be the most convenient too.

Thelma became a symbol of all he might have become but hadn't, of all he might have done but had failed to do. Her presence and ultimate inconsequence fitted well into the void which was then beginning to grow wider and deeper all around him.

4

BY THE end of the month of Bhadon—August-September—the south-west monsoon veered in its tracks and the fragmentation of a grey sky into woolly white fluff, that forever scurried south-east, brought sunshine to a city grown pale and weary of half-light. The grass on the hillsides and in the parks encompassed all the known shades of green, and the downpours which had shaken down the blossoms of the asoks now healed the ravage with a glossy rash of new green. The breath of the asphalt, too, condensed of a morning and men gadded on their errands through rising layers of vapour and their dhoties were no longer tucked in at the waist but fell jauntily and spotlessly to their ankles; their faces wore a collective expression of relief and a new alertness.

A festive month throughout Western India for its holiday of Ganesh Chaturti, Bhadon was important in the Ramsingh household because both Jagnath and his wife devoted the punultimate day to the remembrance of their ancestors—the ceremony of sraddha. This was an eminently Rajput rite. In doing his sraddha year in and year out, a man sped the souls of his patriarchs to final and complete bliss and earned lasting credit for himself. The uncertain zones between past, present and future were thus ranked in a hopeful sequence and the lambent wicks of prayer somehow bared them of all menace. In making her preparations Kandubai also reaffirmed the ritual supremacy of Hindu womanhood.

On the morning of the sraddha she personally roused everyone and bade them dress and get ready. The buzz drifting up from the kitchen was already formidable, as the servants had got up several hours before sunrise to cook the food which would be given away to the purohit—the family priest—or eaten by the family later in the day. The information was communicated to Vijay by Rajuram the Elder, the first servant in the household, when he brought the morning tea.

'If one were a good Hindu, one might have risen earlier and worshipped the new sun,' he said righteously, for he had scolded Vijay as a small boy and was not above a reprimand even these days.

'One might have, if one had a reliable servant,' Vijay said. 'But one is allowed to sleep, while the servant gossips away in the kitchen.'

'Nai-ji, the truth is quite otherwise. You came home late last night and did not speak to me. How is one to know without an order?'

'By thinking.' Vijay tapped his temple firmly.

'Even if I had roused you, you would not have prayed. Young Rajputs are no longer as their fathers used to be. I thought it better not to wake you.'

Such twisted reasoning enabled Rajuram to cope with the many adverse situations of his daily round, a round doubly weighty because of his singular prestige. A Rajput himself, he had grown up with Jagnath and served him ever since, taking only a rare leave to visit one relative or bury another. Not only that, but when his oldest son came of serving age he trained him to be a bearer and, later in Bombay, put him through a driving course so that he could drive the Ramsingh car if the need arose; thereafter, the son came to be known in the family as Rajuram the Younger.

Now the old man gathered the tea things and his dark and earnest old face wrinkled up apprehensively.

'You must dress and come down quickly, or lalaji will blame me.'

'Now I should break my neck because you have been lazy,' Vijay said from the bathroom door. 'Put out my clothes and tell lalaji I am coming.'

'Lalaji' was the term of respect which the servants used of Jagnath.

'Jee-huhn.'

Rajuram crossed over to the almirah and rummaged on its shelves. So the morning of the sraddha began.

It was a fine and promising morning. The first puffs of steam were still on the horizon in the north-east, but the sun had already risen above the rocky thrust of Worli and flooded the offshore and the offing with a clean and great brilliance. Villa Ram, looking down upon the sea road, found it pure and shiny, while beyond it the pounding of the breakers sounded as though the erstwhile fury had gone out of them. Around the house, the smell of peat sent up by the garden acquired almost the redolence of the effluvial Indian earth—after dry dust the true, true breath of her soil.

The dining-room had been cleared of smaller furniture and over the carpet had been laid a matting of clean white sheets. In the centre Kandubai and the servants had erected a kind of dais on kush grass, on which the family putra had been enthroned; this was a brass image of a warring ancestor of Kandubai's who was alleged to have met violent death in battle, one Kishore Singh on the maternal side of her family. Around it were the usual bowls for worship, a tray of fruit for the departed ones, a wicker bowl of flowers, an assortment of cereals and some clarified butter; on the cupboard, the statue of Radha and Krishna had also been remembered with a drape and garland. Chalked swastikas adorned all thresholds. When Vijay came down in a pair of white pyjamas and a white cotton shirt, his mother gave him an approving look—only the simplest Indian attire would befit the solemn occasion. She herself had followed the all-but-forgotten Rajput tradition down to a detail, with a heavy pleated silk skirt, a matching bodice-blouse and dopatta, a voluminous scarf which she used as head covering and general outer raiment. The grave moment did not blanch her flush or dim the thrill in her eyes; anyone watching her fuss would have known that this was life as she conceived it.

'Where are your sisters?' she asked Vijay. 'They are not ready . . . it is a bad habit. Only once was I late for my parents' sraddha and I still feel the shame of it But we did not go to college and political meetings. . . .'

She lighted the oil lamp to be used in the ceremony, and this caused her to squat down vigorously, perhaps even too vigorously, for Vijay knew that she hadn't been fit lately.

'My brothers did not drive cars,' she went on. 'They rode horseback and hunted with my father from the time they were boys. They got up with the sun and went to bed after dark. They worshipped on Nag Panchami and Nawratri. . . . Dasara was a joyful day for them. They grew up a fine Rajput lot. I am still proud of them.'

'Should I call Tara and Munu?' Vijay said, preparing himself for a long wait.

'Let them be, son. If they are not down presently, I shall go up and speak to them myself.'

Rajuram the Elder burst in with trays of rice balls and other dry sweets, and she arranged these around the putra, got up and threw the silk scarf over her head. While the servant moved away, she stopped in front of her son and smoothed out the sleeves of his shirt. 'What was I speaking of? There is much I had been meaning to tell you lately, yet the time never seems to be sufficient. . . .'

'Your family feasts,' he said. 'You were telling me about them.'

'Ah yes, truly. . . . There were so many of them each month. We lived in the country, nearer to God and true law.' She clasped her hands at the waist. 'I remember the gulmohars in the spring . . . the jasmines and silk-cotton trees. When the festival of bracelets started, there was always great rejoicing. No man in the house had any other engagement on that day. If my brothers were away, they came back.'

This was an allusion to his absence in Dehra Dun during the last rakhi festival. 'We are in a new century, ama,' he said softly. 'Feasts are not

113

everything. If I could have been here the month before last, you know I would have.'

'Would you, for truth . . .?'

'Of course, ama,' he lied. 'I even observed it in a manner. I gave a rakhi to Chanda Prashad and received one from her.'

'You have not told me.'

'I didn't think it was important enough. But now you know.'

A rakhi was an amulet or silk or gold thread or wire which women tied to the wrists of their men on the annual festival of the same name. It was for good luck and protection from evil. To Kandubai it was a living thing. Surprise and curiosity flitted over her face and for one uncertain moment she did not try to hide them.

'I am very pleased. It is good that the daughter of so modern a mother should follow in the Hindu path.'

'I found her an odd girl. I don't yet know what to make of her.'

A bustle from the upper floor intimated the imminent descent of the sisters. Outside, a car horn sounded.

'The priest . . .!' she exclaimed, the organizer's zeal quickening her movements. 'He has arrived! I told the driver to warn us when they should come. Son, go and call your sisters!' She started for the kitchen passage, but stopped before it as if in sudden recollection. 'Son,' she said, 'if you were to meet more people of your own caste and belief . . . many things would be less odd to you. Indian girls are like all others. There are clever and stupid ones among them, as in all other countries. I pray that you should marry a clever one before long.'

She went out, pulling the veil lower over her face. There were only the voices in the hall and an upsurge of hum in the servants' quarters and a considerable clatter on the stairs.

Halfway to the first floor he met his father and sisters, these last freshly anointed and bubbling over. He pulled Tara's tresses, illustrating her mother's displeasure at all this tarrying, but Tara had a ready alibi: the shower in the girls' bathroom had gone out of commission.

'Admit that you overslept,' he said.

'Certainly not! But you did,' she told him. 'I know all about it.'

They clattered down all together and found the priest already in the dining-room. He was a cool and middle-aged little Brahman of the professional clan of purohits, a frequent presider over the Ramsingh rituals. They squatted down opposite him, Vijay in front, beside his father, Kandubai and her daughters in a row behind them.

Presently the ghosts of Jaswant Ramsingh, Kishore Singh and one dozen generations on each side received the annual tribute, and the smell of simmering butter, baked rice and pulse rose up to the ceiling to sate their assumed hunger. Petals of pink rose and jasmine fell on the brass image

114

and the supple fingers of the Brahman gave the shower a transcendent meaning. The embattled warriors—who had lived and died true Rajputs, thus accomplishing their dharmas—did not need the offering for themselves; their virtues had placed them beyond any rebirth. Now the brass countenance of one of them personified all those males of the family who might have been wholly virtuous had they not been a little weak. To them the devotion of the living went, to them the fragrance of flowers and solemn incantation, to them, too, the earnest hope of Jagnath and his wife that the drawn-out discomforts of the hell of Put be spared to all, for now and ever after. Even though he was the king of death and hell, Yama's power was not really assessable, nor were the reaches of his domain simple to imagine; the chant of mantras, the falling of petals, the sacrificial food bowls, these might in time dispose him well towards the departed.

And sunlight slid into the room through the open window and built a bridge to that other region, and its trail seemed afire with minute stars of this earth. Uninvited, a garden beetle stormed into it, zoomed madly for a while, then dropped off and took dazed stock of itself on the bronze head of Krishna on the cupboard. The bridge sparkled a while longer and its burnish tapered off towards zenith, and at the other end the phantom clan must surely have been appreciative. Perhaps even Siva the terrible, and Krishna, the piper of flutes, sitting in rarefied isolation far above all, nodded approval. The reflections of one sceptic at the sraddha did not blemish its overall aim. Vijay found himself pleasantly lulled by the oil in the priest's voice.

'We will first feed the purohit and give him a present,' Jagnath said at the close of the worship. 'Then we shall eat ourselves. Then I should like to have a talk, Vijay. I myself would prefer to have it walking.'

'As you wish, pitaji,' Vijay said.

Not looking at her, he yet felt his mother's searching glance for one uncommonly long moment.

The road on the sea face was forlorn as they came down to it from the rocky slope. Yellow monsoon seas still boomed over the reef and at a few places against the parapet, and their spray kept a part of the wall in a varying state of polish. Up on the hill the shrine hut of the old hermit blended into the verdure much better than the rows of pseudo-modern houses below it. The contrast was thoroughly Indian; none but a foreigner would have given it more than a cursory thought.

'Let us walk before the wind,' Jagnath suggested.

In the gutters, the remnant of the last shower had changed to puddles of black silt. Strolling along Jagnath took out his betel-nut caddy and put a roll in his mouth, then offered one to his son. They munched thoughtfully for some time and Vijay wondered anew what other subjects his parent would wish to air beside the everlasting ones of job and marriage.

Jagnath's long pale-brown face, usually so mellow that people often mistook him for a soft-humoured emigrant from the eastern provinces, had been showing concern for some days. Now this concern slowly congealed into an air of vague malcontent and the ends of his full mouth grew more pointed. His hooked Rajput nose began to jut out unmistakably and a trifle incongruously.

'Son, who is Miss Morrison and how much do you see of her?' he said at last.

'She is a friend of Salim's,' Vijay said after the first surprise. 'I met them last month. They're Anglo-Indians and live at Juhu.'

'What do they live from?'

'I don't know. They seem to be well to do.'

'You go to their house often?'

Vijay baulked, not from embarrassment, but from a desire to save his father a lengthy preamble. 'Yes, quite often,' he admitted.

'You have taken Miss Morrison to the cinema and to some clubs?'

'I have.'

'You do not know, then, what many others seem to know . . . that the house in which they live belongs to a ruler from Central India . . . an old reprobate raja . . . and that he pays all their bills?'

'It is of no concern to me, father.'

'But it should be . . . it is to me. The young men of my time took good care to keep their vagaries well concealed. They minded the good name of the family. This is a progressive age . . . family does not count . . . upright living is too much to ask . . . the barriers have been pulled down. The young Hindu of to-day does not marry . . . or employ himself usefully. His friends are not even caste men, but Eurasians, Muslims, foreigners. It must not be said that he is not emancipated. The country owes him a large debt. . . .'

He stopped and waited for Vijay's interruption, though none came. He gazed at the sea with screwed-up eyes and the bareness of the horizon seemed to distract him. He might have been sorry to have ventured outdoors; such a talk went with twilight in a closed room, with reminders of one's authority placed within familiar reach.

'Vijay, I am not easy. . . .' He could only think of his unhappiness, not its presentation. 'I am worried, and there is no denying it. I should like to . . .' A car suddenly raced up from behind them spurting mud, and he lunged aside and said instead: 'How inconsiderate!'

If truth were known, he probably welcomed the pause. It procured for him a few more seconds in which, now that he was forced to extemporize,

116

he could do so with dignity. Thoughtfully, he bit his thick lower lip and made another gingerly attempt.

'I cannot regulate your friends . . . but I can and must think of your future. This question of marriage has been put off long enough. When are you going to decide? Whom have you in mind, if anyone . . .?'

'I have not thought about it,' Vijay said.

'You are twenty-five, are you not? Long past the common marriageable age?'

'Those are old rules, pitaji. In Europe a man does not marry until he is quite ready.'

'Ready . . .? Arre, who is talking about Europe!' Injury glazed over his eyes, usually so mild. 'We hear of nothing else since you are back! Vijay, this is your own country . . . we are your own people. We marry early and beget families. A couple of ideas from the West cannot change a whole system from one day to another. We want progress . . . but not at the expense of all that has been built. I am a government official . . . I drive a car and wear these unnatural clothes . . . but this does not make me a European.'

He peered ahead and the breeze ruffled his grey hair. To anticipate his fervent appeal by an ill-considered answer would have upset him even more, and so Vijay remained silent.

'I think you will agree that we are a liberal family. We live in the spirit of the times, within reason . . . and decency. Your mother is old-fashioned, but no enemy of real progress. Your sisters are often hard to manage, and still she is very patient with them.' He glanced up and down the road for a possible focus, then spat the remnant of the betel-nut juice into the gutter. 'I am not certain that if the last few years had happened to me, they would not have changed me in some way or other. All this publicity . . . these empty friendships . . . I think they may have made you believe that the rewards of life come easily. The fact is you are losing yourself with each new day. . . .'

'I want to do what would please you, pitaji, but I'm not ready to marry.'

'I am sure that marriage would be a solid start. You are in a good age. A wife would be a great encouragement.'

'Yes, I believe that. I have not yet looked for one, that is all.'

The gaudy mansion at the end of the road belonged to a Marwari mill-owner. Through the windows on the first floor a radio crackled forth under a clumsy hand. Crackle, crackle . . . 'and now we take you to Delhi to hear . .' a long whistle, a gale of Western music . . . silence.

Jagnath said: 'Let us go back,' and his distress sounded less poignant.

Musing about the talk, Vijay could not distinguish where his father's worries ended and the clammy threads of a Hindu family took up; the two probably mingled and bound each other. This was the pressure he had lived with ever since coming back from England, and now it was beginning to tell. Was this legacy of a coarser social system a good thing for India's future? So far he had given it little attention, but now it struck him as a prime question. At a mixed gathering in the Juhu club someone had recently remarked that mankind was abandoning the collectivism of the family for one of the state, and that this was the main event of the century. If that was true, India's pretensions to the twentieth century were sham; she still lived and felt in terms of blood groups.

'Do kindly understand that I am not choosing for you,' Jagnath said more calmly. 'There is at least one girl of my acquaintance who would be a most suitable match.'

'Who?'

'Chandraleika, the elder daughter of Rana Prashad.'

'That feminist . . .?' He was so amused he forgot his deferential manner. 'I should have known that Mrs. Prashad's last visit was not only political. Father, has this been discussed behind my back from the beginning?'

'It was, it was . . . the parents still have that right.' He faced his son in a self-conscious challenge.

'She paints her nails. We quarrel every time we meet.'

'But she is accomplished . . . and beautiful.'

'Arre, father, you wouldn't want me to marry a girl who only talks female suffrage.'

An unkind thing to say, but a sop to his father's conservatism. There had to be some common ground between them; the narrow male view of marriage would be proof, more than all the protests, that Vijay was all right inside. He didn't even feel guilty; between Hindus it was the stratagems that counted, not the argument itself. And his father confirmed his hope—he stopped being uncertain of himself. This was the core of the whole problem, his ideas on it were well formed, putting them in words was comparatively simple.

'She will change, I have no doubt,' he said. 'Girls grow up like boys. She will come out of college next year. I am told that some of the most eligible young men of Lucknow are quite taken up with her.'

'Yes, pitaji, I can believe that.'

'Anyhow, son, I should like you to make one promise. That you will think of her as a possible choice.'

'I can promise that, certainly.'

'I will not drive you into anything you do not desire.'

Now the circle was joined; there wasn't much more which his parent would consider of first importance.

It was the circle Vijay had wanted to step out of, for the sake of a greater vision, but now it was tightening round him and he couldn't even think of a trapdoor. Yet, he was still fool enough to hope that he would somehow escape the dutiful Hindu grind. And even though his essays in independence had already grown their crop of frustration, what remained beckoned him on still. This point he would never satisfactorily explain to Jagnath, no matter how hard he tried, for it represented the whole difference in their outlook, the difference in their language, the whole gap between them. It was really formidable.

Where the road snugged the curve of the promontory and the sea rushed over the wall, a rainbow quivered in the spray for a split second. Villa Ram basked in the fulgence of the early afternoon, already flanked by the first cloudy pile. They left the promenade, to branch off for home.

'I did not wish to harp, believe me,' Jagnath said. 'I thought you should learn to lean on another person. But it is also your own problem . . . you should know best.'

'I am very grateful, pitaji.'

'As for Salim Haq, I do not like his cynicism. Our younger men have yet to earn the right to condemn. One cannot be frivolous and constructive.'

'He is a good friend. You don't know him.'

'Maybe not. You have changed since you knew him.'

'Was it not important that I should?'

'There are changes and changes.'

They were silent all the way up to the house. Then Vijay pushed the garden gate open and held it for him.

'Please don't worry about me,' he said. 'Soon one or the other of my plans will come off and I will settle down to real work.'

Jagnath sifted his son's look and the intentness of the effort made him frown. Then he passed through the garden gate, up the paved path to the entrance of the house, and his shoulders evened up gradually. Seen from the rear, his faltering progress reminded Vijay of a person bemused by the morning's purchases.

5

Aswin—September-October—the brightest and noisiest of months, brought along the festival of Nine Nights, devoted to Lord Siva, and Dasara, the most gala annual occasion for every Rajput, and then Divali, the Hindu New Year; this last would be greeted with firecrackers and a myriad oil lamps in the whole of Hindustan. All that could walk and claim a title to Hinduism would mill about in a haze of bliss utterly incomprehensible to a non-Hindu. Husbands would pray for the fertility of their wives, wives for the potency and long life of their husbands. Sons would pay homage to the sires, fathers-to-be would ask for sons. Females would fawn on the deities presiding over marital fidelity, early conception, infant mortality, smallpox, careers of offspring, evil eye and other more specific complaints of a family. Children would furnish the din and get indigestion from the edible symbols of the splurge. Night would become day so that neither Muslims nor Europeans nor any other 'minority' would be able to sleep save in snatches, and drums and bells would throb in the shrines at twilight, and above it would be laughter and delight so effervescent that sociologists would lag aside their columns of per-capita income and maybe even nurture a fresh hope. Mist and smoke would lie over vast stretches of the country. A powerful, as yet uninvented, receiving device might rake the ether above India and decode a gigantic dispatch of messages on their way to nether-most regions, but the task would call for an inspired editor indeed. In this apparent exclusiveness of prayer lay the brightest attraction of Hinduism A man might address himself to any part of space in the glowing assurance that it was peopled by so Many that One would certainly hear it and not have to divide His attention.

The Ramsinghs were forced to park the car a quarter of a mile from the Maha Lakshmi temple, behind a solid line of other cars, and the family had to get down and walk. It was late evening, the first day of Dasara. Past the holy precincts swept a steady flood of wheeled traffic, to and from Worli. Crows and vultures hovered above the crossroads—an air umbrella inseparable from Indian mass assemblies. The other kerb was blocked by *gharries*, Bombay version of victorias, scores of them, all manned by Muslims and all black, for this local trade had been a Muslim province since time immemorial.

The lane up to the temple became a riot, and they had to close their ranks in order to advance together. Hot, redolent, rustling, sweating, but bent on fun, the multitude eddied seemingly towards the shrine, yet it also swirled in the other direction and around itself, and in the midst of it stagnant pools had already formed around the roasted-gram and sweet-meat stalls. Toymakers' wares dangled from the outer wall of the temple, even on the part of the pipal tree that overhung the land.

'I doubt if we shall ever get through,' Jagnath said. He seemed to give up suddenly; he had wormed his way to the wall, almost stepping on a beggar, and now eyed the crush with misgiving. 'Such a crowd . . .'

'It is not as though we were keeping an appointment,' Kandubai said. 'There is no hurry. If only it were less hot. . . .' She was out of breath and looked faint.

'You are not feeling well?' Jagnath inquired. 'We should not have come.'

She braced herself and smiled. 'Arre, what talk is that! It is Dasara, is it not? It is not the first time we have gone to a temple.'

'I should not have listened to you,' Jagnath said, making another attempt to advance.

120

'Let me, pitaji!'

Vijay squeezed ahead and the family re-formed behind him. He bored, wedged and elbowed, and Tara, slipping deftly into the gap, maintained it for her mother and younger sister.

From the gate a stairway forced the hubbub to eddy faster and then debouch into channels around the water tank. They paused on a high vantage point and surveyed the scene; the rout was crumbling into scents, colours, piety, grace and motion. Like irises in a bed of narcissi, the saris of Maratha women rippled in the sacred pool; other reflections brimmed through them and beside them. Charily, Vijay observed the wriggling buttocks of these Maratha ladies, their peculiar way of tucking the sari between their legs, the rows of new jasmine in their hair buns; how much better they looked than their Gujarati sisters! But in the shrine the big drum suddenly beat out a plangent call and all the pigeons of the neighbourhood took off with a pelting flutter.

'We must make our obeisance,' Kandubai said, stepping back into the cloud of sandal and kusha.

The percussion mounted towards the louder drone, making it at once deeper and more nondescript. On the nearest telephone pole a pair of crows fought over a piece of scran. The noise waxed more evenly now, became a cupola, then a dome, and the tough outer surface of it repulsed all would-be comers of sound, such as the traffic jam on the road and all the human hubbub beyond the walls.

'We are almost there, thank God!' Tara said from behind. 'Ama should rest as soon as possible.'

He pressed forward with renewed energy, overhauling the banya and his wife, and then spoke privately to his sister.

'You were at home the last time the doctor came. How is she now?'

'He said better, but I do not agree. She cannot sleep and tires easily. Often I think she is in pain . . . but she will not admit it.'

'She won't tell me either,' he said. 'Is that all you know?'

'All, bhai.' Tara sounded cross, wiping the perspiration off her face. 'It is the same old trouble. Where is the need to hush it up like this? If she is ill, she should not strain herself.'

'Well, you know ama, she's always stubborn. Who treated her when I was away?'

'Some homeopath . . . I can't think of his name. She would not go and see a proper doctor.'

She tossed her plaits huffily and her pretty face darkened all of a sudden. The notion that in this enlightened era a person should seek and follow the advice of a quack was more than she could stomach. Also, she had been upbraided for rising late that morning and had, in the afternoon, quarrelled with the gardener for his selection of votive flowers. Aside from that, the strange aloofness of her brother was beginning to vex her.

'He must have given her herb potions . . . and for sick kidneys! What does a homeopath know about the human body . . .? Are you surprised that we don't live longer?'

'Never mind the nation,' Vijay said. 'We must get another doctor. I'll talk to father this evening.'

'You will talk!' she sniffed. 'You will go to Salim or to that Anglo-Indian and think of something else. It is a wonder you come home at all!'

That was on the steps of the shrine. He waited until his parents caught up with him, then climbed up and inside. The earsplitting frenzy of the drum became almost too much. The naked attendant who beat it looked as if he had dozed off and his raving hands lived on separately.

'Come!' Jagnath said to his children. 'Let us pay our homage and then sit down and rest.'

In a black stone enclosure the great goddess of wealth, Maha Lakshmi, reclined between two white elephants and her robe of yellow brocade seemed to be on fire. Her face was gem studded, but glassy and disappointing to Vijay. Kandubai placed a token of moistened rice and coconut at her feet and Jagnath added a silver rupee; then both the parents touched the pedestal and their own foreheads and bowed reverently, and Vijay and the girls followed in their wake; for one fleeting second the family was alone with the gilded idol in a hushed kind of unity; then another couple pressed into the crypt and room had to be made for them. The drum went into another dither, the bells clanged more startlingly as the Ramsinghs emerged from the shrine and narrowed their eyes at the remainder of daylight.

On the ghat of the bathing tank Kandubai took off her sandals and leaned on her younger daughter; Jagnath came after them, more anxious to stand guard than pray. She gathered the skirt of her sari, crouched, splashed a little with her free hand, then made her oblation. The face she raised to the hidden sun and her closed eyes spoke for themselves, and Vijay, waiting on the uppermost step, mused uncertainly whether a change of physicians was what she needed most.

'Look, she'll drench her clothes and feet and get a chill,' he said to Tara. 'How can anyone take care of her if she won't do it herself?'

Now the parents stood shoulder to shoulder and the pose was like the reverent illustration in a sacred old book. Vijay watched them until Jagnath turned and signed to him. Then he moved down a step and gave his hand to mother; she patted it, but didn't take it. Sighing loudly, she came up the steps and sat down on the stone pavement.

'Let the girls go and call the driver,' she said to Jagnath. 'It will be some time before he can bring the car to the gate.'

For a while after Tara and Munu had gone Vijay and his parents sat silently and watched the milling on the other side of the tank. For an indefinite moment it seemed to them that time had not really rushed forward in the last ten years but had stood perfectly still. Behind the temple and the pipals the sun was slipping into the watery slot and only a small part of the sky saw it off faithfully; the eastern portion already cringed to the dark new regime. Bells and noise notwithstanding, pigeons began to settle on the roof of the fane and their loud rutting enriched the drone. Flags drooped resignedly. At the tank itself piety became tinged with little practical impulses.

'They could not have been married more than a few weeks,' Kandubai said, gazing at a young couple on the steps.

A young Gujarati in a long clean dhoti washed his wife's hands at the edge of the pool. He scooped water from the tank, poured it over her fingers and rubbed them with his own; she then passed her wet palms over his forehead. They prayed standing upright and afterwards he said something to her that made her smile.

'I did that to you when you could neither walk nor speak,' Kandubai said to her son, sighing demurely. 'In those days it was easy to get you into a temple, and hard to get you out. I remember how you paddled in the tank of Sri Narayen at Indore. You were only five, but the priest thought you much older.'

'Truly, you were a big boy for your age,' Jagnath said.

Kandubai had gone back so compellingly that both Jagnath and Vijay wandered quietly after her.

'We found a teacher for you, I remember,' she said. 'It was a Dasara day, like now. He was a learned Brahman and he spoke Sanskrit as well as we speak Hindi. We worshipped Goddess Sarasvati and the priest blessed your new books together with all the family papers. Then we gave a feast and fed the beggars . . . and watched the court procession from the windows. I prayed for more sons, but you came to be the only one. . . .'

'It seems like yesterday,' Jagnath added.

'Not to me, pitaji,' Vijay said. 'It seems time moves very slowly when one is young. Indore to me is like another Maha Yug, another era. I remember everything, but it is as though it had happened to someone else.'

'I know,' Jagnath said. 'We all know and feel it.'

Now the couple came up the steps and passed them snickering. The young woman walked with a bowed head after her husband, but her front of coyness could not fool anyone; her slippered heels had marks of henna on them, and she smelled of newly bought clothes and soap. The last reminded Vijay of the years when temple visits were an essay in the sharp tingle of incense and perfumes, when he was still intrigued by the bare calves of worshipping girls and by their teasing and giggles. Henna had then been a mark of beauty; now it appeared to him as a simple ginger-hued stain whose æsthetic purpose was a little difficult to appreciate. Had he already gone so far in forgetting that even such little things spoke to him no more . . .? Didn't someone write that sensual memory was more constant than all the others? But thinking about it merely resolved into images of Connie and Thelma and the answer seemed to fade before the unadorned whiteness of their bodies. Thelma's brightly painted toenails were in a class with henna stains, yet he rather liked them. Why was that? When did his idea of Indian girls and their beauty develop this critical bend?

But Kandubai put on her sandals with a deliberate fuss.

'A few years should not make a Maha Yug,' she said decisively. 'Some things continue longer than others. They are, because they have always been. This place, son'—she drew her hand in a half-circle—'may not have been always, but the people were . . . and their prayers were . . . the souls for whom they prayed also were. Worship is as old as we are. You and I and your father will go, but worship will remain.'

'Maybe, ama,' he said, giving way. 'We are slaves to our customs. We cannot forget our old habits.'

'Laws, son . . . not habits. In these laws we are, in them we endure. If you will have a sraddha-worship done for yourself, you must have a son. Friends cannot make sraddha for you. If you are to have a son, you must marry . . . so the marriage is law, too. What is this talk of habits? If you forget your laws, you shall forget to be a Hindu.'

'Customs or law, what does it matter, ama, how you call them? The main thing is that they should suit one. If they should be stunting, one must avoid them.'

'And bring hardship and injury on himself?' Jagnath asked with raised eyebrows. 'Arre, Vijay, sometimes you talk like a boy who has been forbidden to play with a kerosene lamp. How can you call them stunting? Have your mother and I become stunted because we follow custom? Where would India be without her caste and law?'

'Cowards talk like that too,' Kandubai said. 'Sometimes it is more pleasurable to disobey than to obey.' She watched the first lamp reflections on the other side and looked as though she wished to develop the thought; then she righted the sari border over her hair and took both the men aback by remembering an all-but-forgotten subject. 'When you came back from Europe I asked you to perform ablutions for your return,' she went on. 'You said not to rush you, but later you forgot it completely. If I had asked you to take a simple bath, you would have done it. Why is the one so easy, and the other so hard?'

'I will tell you, ama,' Vijay said. 'One is a sensible suggestion, the other meant that I would be bad if I didn't do it.'

'What is the difference? When we do something it is either to please ourselves or someone else. These customs of ours are not politics . . . one does not lose face in observing them.'

'Yes, that is well said,' Jagnath put in. 'You took part in the Dasara worship this morning, did that make you any less modern?'

'No, pitaji, but . . .'

'There is no South without North, no Jain without a Hindu,' Kandubai broke in, propping herself on her husband's knee and rising with an effort. 'One cannot hope without remembering . . . and remembering is the past. Man does not exist without woman, and he does not remember as much as woman . . . that is why she is necessary for his complete success. These are not habits, son. They are the laws because they are the truth. It is just that you have become a foreigner and do not see them any more. Lately I have been asking myself, How much does Vijay still remember? It seems now he remembers almost nothing.'

'It is not true, ama,' he said.

But she only tightened her bracelets and glanced towards the exit. 'It seems even the time for explanation is past. I do not know what has come over us. It seems Bombay has become the undoing of the Ramsinghs.' She put her hand on her husband's patting fingers and sighed in profound disappointment. 'Arre, let us go. Tara and Munu must be waiting at the gate.'

'Yes, let us,' Jagnath said placatingly. 'It is quite late.'

They went along the steps of the tank, in the direction of a side exit, and Vijay walked after them saying nothing more. He felt aching and restive. His earlier concern for his mother's health acquired now a dull edge of displeasure and hurt, for she had obviously meant so well, and understood him so little.

And the drum had ceased throbbing in the shrine and the tumult began to look as though it were slowing down. Lights came on transforming the temple dome into a tall river craft, afloat on the waters but not sailing anywhere; beyond it the trees no longer stood out against orange streaks in the west, but their jagged outline became a part of the twilight. And the sky soon deepened to a dark purple in which it was easier to see the stars than the space between them, and ravens alighted in the neighbouring gardens and joined their raucous wrangle anew, and vultures wheeled away towards the Parsi Tower of Silence on Malabar Hill as if renewing a broken bond. The buttocks of the Maratha ladies bobbed less; musky scents commingled with the spreading smell of joss sticks; dolls swayed from the lines of toymakers, shrieks of praise mounted from the throats of sundry vendors. The hum and commotion went on emptying itself into the endless ceiling of Bombay and the heart of mankind grew perceptibly lighter. The air was full of magic and the magic was timeless. It was India's most bewitching hour.

'Mind the step!' Jagnath warned his wife at the gate.

From the road, the sparkling roof of the temple seemed to rise more resolutely into the night, and Vijay glanced at it with a vaguely envious eye. Ranjit had said that most men worked and lived on inherited formulas and that that was the line of least resistance and therefore of most contentment. At this moment he seemed to be almost right. One had only to splash in a pool of hallowed water, touch a particular piece of marble or stone, answer the drum at a certain hour—it all brought credit in one cause or another. Gods, half-gods, quarter-gods; Pitris, avatars, Brahma, Atmans, it didn't matter what the cause was, for one continually bumped into thousands of people doing the same things. Who shall say that they didn't serve their purpose, at least in blurring loneliness and the sense of insecurity . . .?

6

Two days later he arrived at Salim's flat on Marine Drive just as the phone rang in the living-room.

'Your father,' Salim said, thrusting the receiver into his hand. 'He has been asking about you for the last hour.'

Vijay drew a deep breath, and spoke into the telephone.

'Son, a most terrible thing has occurred,' Jagnath said in an ominously low voice. 'I would like that you should see me here in the office right away. It is a matter of the utmost importance.'

He knew that when his father's syntax broke down, his agitation was very great. He said: 'What has happened, pitaji?'

'I cannot speak now. It is concerning your sister Tara. You must come and see me immediately.'

'Where is she?'

'That I shall tell you when you come. Please hurry! Walk straight into my office . . . I have informed the peon.'

'All right, I'm coming now.'

They hung up at the same instant, and Vijay got up in a slight daze.

He told Salim of the summons, borrowed his car keys and said he would return them later. The Muslim took him to the landing and pressed the lift button for him. He hoped that Tara had not gone and insulted the king-emperor, which misdemeanour the British punished nearly the same as murder, and he asked his friend to let him know immediately in case she had, after all. He would give her such a rousing boost in his Marut's Hour that the police would be sorry they ever meddled. Vijay barely heard him.

He drove off to the secretariat just as the sun veered over the Backbay Reclamation and the palms along the oval maidan threw the first thin shadows eastward. The austere, quasi-Gothic mansion was next to the university building; above the high line of its trees fluttered a new Union Jack; the garden drive underneath was full of the officials' cars and the liveried drivers sat on their haunches in the shady spots, smoking and swapping gossip. He parked on the main road and went in. Jagnath was in the wing of the meeting chamber in a flimsily-partitioned cubicle which one reached through a labyrinth of lesser offices, filing shelves and cramped-looking desks, for the new ideas of working space were still unknown to the bureaucracy.

Jagnath received him in his cubicle, then shut the door. All traces of poise faded from his face. He shuffled behind the desk, slumped down and leaned forward; a moment of vacancy visited his features, but failed to soften them.

'Vijay, your sister Tara was arrested this morning,' he began at last. 'I don't know what she has done and it is no use asking me. The inspector from the Tardeo chowki rang me up an hour ago to say that she was detained there.' He clenched his fingers over the ink blotter. 'Son, your sister is in jail . . . the second time in a few years. It is a great blow to me. I could not tell you over the telephone . . . these walls here are made of paper.'

'Does anybody know?'

'No, nobody knows, unless . . . but no, that would be too much . . .!' He shut his eyes hard and wrestled, Vijay imagined, with the woebegone surmise of Indian officials that all wires were tapped by the ever-vigilant Criminal Investigation Department. 'I cannot think of your mother hearing such news,' he went on. 'Such an unsavoury development . . . on the eve of Divali of all times! Why is my name besmirched in this fashion, why . . .? Why does my daughter break the law when there is so much else to accomplish?'

'Surely we can bail her out, pitaji.'

'Yes, yes, but a formal application must be made to the magistrate. Now it is past the court hour. Do you know what that means?'

'She'll spend the night in jail. It won't do her any harm.'

'That is not all, Vijay. How callous you are . . .! It is not enough that you do not care for your sister, but you forget everybody else too. Day after to-morrow we begin our Divali celebrations at home. A priest has already been engaged, food has been prepared. Can you not think what this will mean to your mother?'

'We'll get her out before then. Should we not talk to a lawyer at once?'

Jagnath raised his face in an attitude of anguish. 'Son, you are not paying attention to what I say. I told you I cannot trust this telephone. I cannot go to the police station, nor can I telephone. That is the reason I called you.'

'You mustn't worry so much,' Vijay said soothingly. 'No one can blame you for what Tara did . . . whatever that may be.'

His father gave him a long and searching look, then pressed his lip in exasperation. 'That is hardly the point,' he said. 'Do you not understand? If my daughter chooses to waste her good education on such extra-curricular activities, I cannot help it. I cannot keep her locked in the house. But I have responsibilities of which you do not know. Vijay, it is no use pretending.' He slid again forward and couldn't look at him. 'If I were to be dismissed, your sisters might not be able to complete their schooling . . . our house might have to be sold, servants discharged . . . so many things might happen. We are not as well-to-do as we once were. Your mother's treatment has been going on for many months. I told you the other night that I had to engage one specialist after another . . . there have been long tests, consultations, photographs, I have spared no expense. Only last June I was forced to sell another portion of our Indore estate . . .'

'Pitaji, I want to know. Is she being cured?'

'She is getting better all the time, that is the main thing.' He cleared the space in front of him and took a pencil and a slip of paper. 'It is an obstinate ailment and the treatment is a matter of months. I told you the other night, when you asked me, that everything necessary is being done. You can rest assured of that. But she must have quiet . . . no upsets of any kind. *That* is most important. She must not be told on the eve of Divali that her daughter is in jail just like a hooligan. That would spoil the cure of many weeks, I simply cannot permit it.'

'No, of course not,' Vijay said, feeling strongly that his father had again evaded the issue, and deciding to go into the question more fully at the first opportunity. Now the time was too short. He said: 'If Tara is to remain in jail to-night, mother must have a good explanation.'

'I have thought of that,' Jagnath said. 'I will tell her that you and she are spending the night with the Premchands. This I can arrange safely. Then to-morrow morning you will return home with her. In this way no one will know. And now you must go to our lawyer, Mr. Mehta, and have an application drawn up. In the morning you will appear before the magis-trate and pay the bail. I can only hope that it will be granted. The inspector told me there had been quite a disturbance. One policeman was injured with a brickbat . . . this is the kind of patriotism your sister is devoting her time to. Is it any wonder that people can no longer tell students from street ruffians?'

'And if bail is not granted?'

'It will be . . . Mr. Mehta must see to that. You must make him see. Tara must be warned not to aggravate the position with any new foolish-ness. You will request him to go and see her right away. I want to give you a cheque for the bail.'

He wrote it out with an unsteady hand, then pushed his chair back and rose. He had regained some of his outward composure, but his mind was plainly full of the event's reverberations. Vijay realized for the first time since his return what the officialdom had done to his parent.

'Five hundred rupees, son!' he said. 'Do not lose it, for goodness' sake. We could ill spare it at this time. I hope it will be enough.'

'It must be, pitaji. No policeman's head is worth that much.'

'All right then. You must hurry. You can telephone me from the lawyer's office. Be careful of how you speak to me.'

'Don't worry. I will be.'

They went out of the cubicle and walked through the outer offices where several typists looked up curiously. On the corridor Jagnath took his arm and led him to the staircase, lowering his voice confidentially.

'How I wish we had never left Indore. You would never have taken up flying . . . there would never have been any Europe, or politics . . . or trouble. We might have lived so quietly.'

'Pitaji, when we talked about my plans the other day, you never told me all this. If you had I might have looked for a job . . . or saved the last of my prize money.'

Jagnath glanced away and let go of his arm. He waved to a colleague crossing the corridor at the other end, then reached in his pocket for his handkerchief; this he passed over his face quite needlessly.

'Telling you of these things would have been the same as compulsion,' he said. 'I do not believe in compulsion. You were to see the problem as it affected you . . . in your own interests. Force cannot accomplish that. You said we were old-fashioned. I had thought to prove it to myself that we were not. Now you had better hurry along. Do not forget to telephone . . . !'

And he strode back to his office before Vijay could think of an answer. In the arched and now dusky corridor he looked fully the frail embodiment of parental care that Vijay had always supposed him to be. Then his stooping silhouette vanished in the passageway.

Although Mr. Mehta had bidden him to be in court not later than eleven, he himself was already half an hour overdue.

All benches, chairs and railings overflowed with people; in the rear more than four dozen visitors squatted on the floor, and beyond them the barred prisoners' dock was like a cage without roof, with the birds sandwiched on top of one another. If he craned his neck he could just get a glimpse of his sister—a bright speck of white in a mottled group. He had waved to her on arrival and she had waved back, and the act had aroused much curiosity in the crowd and an equal amount of whispered and guffawed comment. He had never been so ill at ease. The idea that Tara had been thrown together with all the riffraff of the city poured irritation on his distress and he even sympathized with his father for not wishing to bail his daughter out in person. He also made up his mind to have a firm talk with Tara on their way home; it was one thing to indulge in a little private rowdyism and quite another to justify it in so sordid an atmosphere.

When the magistrate walked in and the entire room rose as one, Mr. Mehta also shambled along; he peered hard through his gold pince-nez, discovered Vijay at his elbow and bent down confidentially.

'Ah, Mr. Ramsingh, how punctual you are! We were held up in the advocates' chamber by all kinds of things . . . mostly downright stupid chitchat. . . . But we are in time, I am glad to say.'

He was a stocky little gentleman, more like a Parsi than a Hindu, and his moist eyes had almost the sheen of his heavily plastered hair. His black cape was slung casually over his shoulders; his eyes staggered over the hall when he spoke, as though mounted on stilts.

'Now we shall see . . . we shall soon know. . . .'

'Is everything all right?' Vijay asked him.

'Sure, there is not a thing to worry about. We saw Miss Ramsingh last evening. It was far from easy, but we did manage somehow. She wasn't anywhere close to the constable when he was injured . . . anyone might have done it . . . there is absolutely no evidence. But we are likely to be delayed somewhat. A busy morning, if I know anything of this court. ... Wait, don't move from here.'

He drifted away nimbly, sweeping his cape over the heads of the people, making murmured apologies, and Vijay next saw him under the high podium of the magistrate, bending discreetly, advancing on the court's clerk. The pates of the two men came together and the clerk shuffled through the papers piled up in front of him, then smiled at Mr. Mehta. The lawyer edged his way back in the same deferential but riotous fashion.

'Dear, dear, Mr. Ramsingh, I am afraid we're going to have to wait longer than I expected. It is the last day before the holidays. At least one dozen stabbings, thefts, burglaries, demonstrators. But our application has now been placed higher up, thank heavens. It will be called in about an hour or so. . . .'

'Where are you going, Mr. Mehta?'

The advocate stopped in his tracks. 'I shall be gone for ten, twenty minutes at the most. Must call on a colleague, here in the building, Mr. Ramsingh. I shall be back in a jiffy.' And off he was again, this time towards the corridor nearby, with a fling of his robe and an air of great concentration.

Vijay sat on broodingly and tried to attend to the florid exchanges at the podium, but he was too remote, the hall was too spacious, the hum of small talk too intrusive. The audience were middle-class Hindus in European clothes, bored with the current case; Parsis dressed in traditional long coats and odd hats of tubular shape, their bulbous noses and receding chins such a contrast to all the other races; Muslims in blood-red fezes, somewhat shabby by comparison. Up in front was a solid phalanx of the legal profession, brightened here and there by a shiny top. In the witness box a man expostulated with the counsel of his plaintiffs; he used his hands and face so tellingly that the magistrate could not take his eyes off him. On the verandah outside a fir tree trembled silently, filtering sunshine and the heated breezes that had travelled all the way from the ocean.

So this is the famous British justice at work, Vijay thought curiously, not having encountered it before—that well-touted system of dispensations said to be above board and above the Indian communal prejudice! It certainly was awesome. There was no denying that the British had nibbled their way into every corner of national life save the purely private and that one came up against them sooner or later, often without having to meet them face to face. He thought how even at Villa Ram, and in other Indian homes which they had scrupulously refrained from invading, they yet lurked in the minds of the people—now less, now more clearly. Yet they were strangers; their home and loyalties were elsewhere. Unlike the Moguls who became Indians after the first hundred years of domicile, the British showed no such inclination even after almost two hundred. Would they leave a mark comparable to the Moguls? He was sure that they would, a permanent one very likely, but he did not feel like taking his casual reflection that far. He was too hot and expectant. He closed and pressed his eyes, then turned towards the rear. Tara was waving and the signal plainly meant: Come!

He got up and went along the verandah to spare himself the pushing, and re-entered at the last door. He waded through the humble squatting humanity and neared the cage unobserved by the guards.

'Have you any money?' Tara said. 'A boy here would not be able to pay if they fine him. He can't eat the jail food.'

'Only some,' he told her. 'Our lawyer has the rest.'

He emptied his wallet into her cupped hands—thirty rupees. She placed it in her lap and smiled at him, a pretty and unabashed white smile that was such a contrast to her appearance. She had combed her hair that morning and washed her face and hands, but her sari was bedraggled and there were purple bruises on her forearms. He saw some of the ruffians behind her in the cage and a strong wave of outrage rose within him.

'How could you allow them to touch you? If you could only see yourself!'

'They don't ask one's permission, bhai. You really have no more with you?'

'Not an anna.'

'What newfangled goings-on are these?' one of the guards said, stepping between him and the cage. 'Passing money, maybe a bribe for silence . . .? Give me that!' He plunged his hand through the bars and caught Tara's wrist. She gave an involuntary cry.

'Unnameable son of filth!' Vijay cried and leapt on him.

A fracas issued in which he managed to pull the man away from the bars and hit him in the stomach. Other guards swooped on him from behind and a lathi flashed briefly. He went down on his knees, picked himself up again, only to be clutched at the elbows and pressed down relentlessly. Such a thing hadn't happened to him since he was a boy.

'Jackals, murderers!' Tara screamed.

'Give him from all of us!' a tousled male prisoner said.

'Arre, you shall pay for this!' the guard said who held him. 'Violence in court, bhai, what next . . .!'

'Let me go or I'll kick you to small pieces.'

'Just you try. . . .'

The grip proved to be too powerful and the other constables formed a threatening ring around him, and after a while he gave up the futile struggle. Excitement rumbled up the hall, enveloping the pleaders' row and the podium, and a part of the crowd stood up to see better. At the door nearest to the magistrate's bench Mr. Mehta stood on a chair and shaded his glasses with his hand. The court's clerk came along and spoke to the senior guard.

'This untouchable tried to maul my sister,' Vijay explained in gasps. 'I stopped him, that was all.'

'Stopped me indeed! They were passing money!' The guard gave a short and factual description and the clerk nodded gravely. He turned to Vijay:

'Talking to a prisoner of the court is not permitted . . . even if you are related. What was the money for?'

'She asked for it.'

'Against the law, I cannot help it. The judge would like to know about it. If you promise not to run away, I shall instruct the constable not to hold you. Otherwise it will . . .'

'Dear, dear, what have we done now!' Mr. Mehta piped breathlessly. Having fought through the tumult and relinquished his cape somewhere in the process, he finally made his way through the ring of uniforms; his was a model forensic blandness. 'I see that we have not heeded the good counsel, Mr. Ramsingh. What a sad sight to see you so constrained. What is it all about, perhaps you will tell me?'

Vijay repeated what he had told the clerk, while all present eavesdropped with much interest; the lawyer cocked his head low and then spoke to the clerk, with one arm on his shoulder. The huddle broke up with the clerk ordering Vijay's captor at ease, and by his own return to his desk. The other constabulary dispersed according to their earlier posting and the magistrate's mallet recalled the last avid spectators. An aftermath of hush filled the hall so that the proceedings up in front began to interest some people once more.

'Really, Mr. Ramsingh, was there any good reason why we should have gone and shown contempt of court? Such a needless aggravation . . . now, I am afraid, a fine will have to be paid, even though it is our fortune to have an ex-colleague as judge. The dignity of the court must be upheld at all costs.'

'And these aborigines in uniform can be as rough as they please?'

'Now, now, my friend. The aborigines are here to keep order! Which reminds me . . . the application is likely to be called at any moment. Come, and we had better look as penitent as we can. My honourable friend is something of a stickler for order in court.'

They elbowed and sidled along the inner side of the hall, advancing on the witness dock, and many a pair of eyes accompanied them with lingering fascination. Then, as they came abreast of the pleaders' row the case was called, and Mr. Mehta squeezed Vijay's hand comfortingly and surged forward, polishing his glasses as he went. A legal apprentice with the pale features of a Parsi made room on his bench and beckoned Vijay to sit down. On to the stand stepped Tara, while behind her a long line of youthful patriots stopped for a long wait. Everyone looked up at the pretty young girl, whose sari showed signs of violence; much of the staring was in open admiration.

'Your wife?' the apprentice said.

'My sister.'

'She is not frightened. More Indian girls should be like her.'

Higher up, Mr. Mehta did his job like a beautifully greased robot, declaiming one part of his application and chanting the other in mellifluous tones, flourishing his glasses as a woman flourishes her scarf, then subsiding again with dignity and respect. Even the inspector who had preferred the charge for the Crown had to smile, though testily; to him the judgment was a foregone conclusion. Presently the bail of one hundred rupees was allowed and Mr. Mehta went on to deal with the other charge, that against the brother. Dwelling on the latter's affectionate nature, on a well-known Rajput temper and touchiness with regard to the ladies and on many other qualities of his client, he sent a high tremor of mirth through the court. The magistrate hid himself behind a bright blue kerchief; the police inspector smirked helplessly; at least one colleague of Mr. Mehta's looked up in approval. The judge ordered a fine of fifty rupees and coupled it with a warning against similar infractions in the future; then the clock chimed out the first hour of the afternoon and he rose for the recess. Mr. Mehta paid up at the court cashier's.

Outside, the clerk ran after Vijay and tugged his sleeve.

'His Honour would like to see you in the chamber, if you don't mind.'

'What for?'

'We had better go, Mr. Ramsingh . . . all three of us. One does not ask the reason when a judge requests our presence.'

They were taken to a musty chamber behind the courtroom and found the magistrate reaching into his lunch basket. Across the wide table, peering myopically above a dish of dark brown vegetable stew, wearing a high starched collar several sizes too large, he struck Vijay as another of those anæmic and stunted Gujaratis of whom Bombay was too full.

'I took the liberty of telephoning your father this morning,' he said to Tara. 'He sounded most grieved. He assured me that you got into the scuffle by accident . . . and that you would take greater care in the future.'

'I went there of my own free will,' Tara said.

'It was a private ceremony on private grounds,' Vijay said. 'The police had no call to interfere.'

'Dear, dear, we have covered all that just now, have we not?' Mr. Mehta stepped on Vijay's foot under the table, adding eagerly: 'Sir, my clients understand perfectly.'

'And as for fisticuffs in the middle of a session, Mr Ramsingh, that is normally a very grave offence. It was really on account of Mr. Ramsingh the elder . . .'

'Father had nothing to do with it!' Vijay stood up, obeying a fierce impulse.

'There we fly again, like real Rajputs. . . .' This from Mr. Mehta.

'You would have allowed bail to a beggar,' Vijay said. 'It's what you're supposed to do under the law. We've paid the dues now . . . why don't you leave us in peace?'

Tara got up, too, rather flushed. 'When we need a lecture, we shall go to one,' she said.

'Dear children . . .' Mr. Mehta began haplessly.

By then Vijay had grabbed his sister's arm and dragged her off to the door, where the clerk stepped aside just in time; he had been following the developments from a safe distance. Before leaving, Vijay wheeled round once more.

'In England, sir, where this ridiculous version of justice comes from, everyone is responsible for his own acts. They don't molest anyone who is not a witness. They do not worry the parents or relatives of the accused. It is only here that private lives are anyone's game . . . anyone, that is, who has power. It so happens that I'm neither guilty nor frightened. Good morning!'

He towed Tara through the door and pushed the sepoy out of the way; he could only remember to find the staircase and mind the steps. Half a flight behind them Mr. Mehta held his glasses high above his head and his anguish was so real that only the words 'Dear, dear' could give it full expression.

'Well done, bhai!' Tara said in the car, 'I didn't know you until to-day.'

'I was a fool and it's all your fault.'

'You might have fought better, but you fought all the same.'

'You dare even to talk!'

He gave the taxi driver the address at Worli, then lighted a cigarette with trembling fingers. The maidan slipped past in a halo of dust and daze, then the melting circle of Dhobi Talao, and then the Irani driver swerved into New Queen's Road with rakish abandon, and his stomach rolled over in a welcome and distracting heave. The ghastly cinema billboards on the right kerb streaked past like a battened rainbow and the heat of noon flowed into the car powerfully, a gaseous elemental bore. He was angry with Tara and angry at his own lapse, and yet his resentment went beyond all obvious provocations of that morning. He thought; I'm feeling anti-something, what is it . . .? That uniformed son of a Mahar pawing at his sister was only a pebble that set the avalanche going; everything had just about teetered in the last few days.

'You are to tell mother we were with Uncle Premchand for a day,' he said after a lengthy silence. 'It's been arranged like that. And to-morrow you're to try and be a real old-fashioned daughter for a change. This must be the best Divali we've ever had.'

'Lucky you got me out to-day. I would have starved in that jail until the holidays were over.'

'And get this into your revolutionary head: You've cost the family a hundred and fifty rupees so far. And that's only the bail.'

'Fifty was your chivalry.'

'Stupidity, you mean. That you're not ashamed to be herded together with a lot of thieves and assassins!'

'Five other students were in the same court. Vijay. You can't be an Indian until you've been to jail a few times.'

'Well, I'm going to have a good try, just you wait and see! I'm sick of such politics!'

He shut up, narrowing his eyes before the swaying haze of asphalt on Sandhurst Bridge. He made an attempt to marshal all common sense on the side of his statement, but everything that was awake in his mind continued to produce pictures—Tara on the stand, approving looks of the people, the goggled admission of the apprentice. Her flush was a familiar sensation to him; it was like his own tautness when he stood before the adventures of Rajputana and Hardwar; it was why, at this stage, he thought that they had actually swapped rôles.

'I wish you had been with me,' she said more calmly. 'When you are in the middle of it, it turns out to be very simple. Never for a second did I think myself a martyr.'

'It's schoolboys' play, that's what it is,' he said. 'What does it amount to in the end?'

135

'Nothing much, bhai. You don't stop to give it much thought. Once it is a flag, another time a speech . . . all small things, true.'

'It helps no one. Nobody ever learns anything from it.'

'Not all at once, Vijay. There has to be a lot of repetition, and that's true. But you forget them very soon. I had seen the man we were commemorating yesterday . . . a Congressman from Rajkot. They had beaten him to death in a riot when I was still Munu's age. I only remember a thin face and a wart on the chin. But yesterday, in Mr. Sundaram's garden in Dadar, someone mentioned his part in the riots and we pulled the flag up and sang *Bande Mataram* and the wart never even occurred to me. Then a friend said, "Think, if he had only wanted to look after himself, he would have been alive to see his country finally freed." You know, I felt like crying then.'

She snuggled against the window in a wistful, faraway posture. Shots of sunlight alternately healed her bruises and made them a deeper mauve.

'Go on,' he said.

'Nothing more, bhai . until that imbecile yellowcap started bea ing on the door. You were quite right, he had no call to break into a private yard.'

'Why did you let him in?'

'No one did, what do you imagine? Sundaram's father refused to open and then the fool climbed over the wall and that was the end of the ceremony. You don't know the Sundarams . . . they're Brahmans from Madras, very strict about caste and formality. And you know these Mahars, the lowest of the low, really. At first it was only funny. Sundaram's father said it was a private compound and the policeman said that was all right but the flag could be seen from the street and it was therefore against the law. He wanted all the time to pull it down and the old gentleman wouldn't let him touch it. The boy Sundaram tried to push him out of the yard and they started to wrestle. Then the ladies came out and raised a hue and cry . . . then the man whistled.'

'If you had gone into the house, it wouldn't have cost us all this money.'

'How could I, bhai?' She faced him on the seat now and the old blaze kindled her eyes anew. 'Before I knew what was happening the yard was full of people. They pushed and shouted . . . "Gandhi-ki-jai," "*Inquilab zindabad*," oh, anything they could think of. One of the boys went on singing *Bande Mataram*. All of a sudden there were so many policemen . . . sticks came down on our heads, then stones, bricks, all kinds of things . . . I got very excited. Then one idiot yellowcap tried to pull me away from the pole and I scratched him and he bent my arms and I screamed from pain. I couldn't have gone away if I'd wanted to . . . such a riot . . .! I can only remember someone pushing me into the police van . . . also full of people. Brother, I haven't been so pushed in all my life. The things these yellowcaps say would be too much even for a sweeper. . . .'

136

'You don't have to be so happy about it,' he said. 'All you can show for it are two days in jail and a rumpus in court. It is no victory.'

'I wasn't thinking of victories. I was thinking of you.'

'You don't have to,' he said tersely. 'I have all I need.'

He sat back to gaze at the shimmer in the Hornby Vellard inlet. The mosque on the reef seemed to float on a lake of ruffled white gold. A smell of seaweed and brine flooded the car suddenly, reminding him of the air of Worli and the open windows of Villa Ram. He harked back to that walk with his father and this brought back the memory of their recent talk in the office. He tried to fight his irritation and make his voice sound as reasonable as he could.

'You must make no more trouble, Tara,' he said. 'Father was terribly upset. We must all behave better and give him no more trouble. And I am speaking of myself, too.'

'How will you do that?'

'I don't know yet. I might find a job and go into an office. And maybe one of my plans will come through. . . .'

'A job? Have you already lost heart, Vijay?'

'What do you mean, lost heart?'

'You know well what I mean. I mean giving up. Bhai, have you grown tired of everything?'

'You talk just like some of the fools I know,' he said crossly.

He said nothing more until they came to Worli Road.

Soon the glare became more intense and the sight of home pressed heavily down on his spirits. He had not thought of any stories to tell his mother, if she should ask him about the Premchands, and he had forgotten to phone his father at the office before leaving court, as he had promised to; he would have to remember to do it when Kandubai lay down in the afternoon. Above all, Tara would have to be smuggled upstairs before anyone had a glimpse of her state.

'You had better go and change quickly, while I talk to mother,' he said when the taxi swerved up the rock road. 'You are quite something to look at, let me tell you.'

'Clean clothes are not everything.'

'Maybe not, but try to explain that to mother. In the old days our girls went off to wars on horseback, but now they toss about with a lot of reeking policemen.'

'Bhai, I have thought the same about you. You looked more like a Rajput fighting that guard than you ever would sitting in an office.'

Then the driver pulled up at the garden of Villa Ram and he helped her out. The sari looked worse than it had in the court.

'You had better scrub yourself too. Some of your fellow prisoners looked as though they had come through an epidemic of plague.'

❦❦❦❦❦❦❦❦❦❦❦❦❦❦❦❦❦❦❦❦❦❦❦❦

1

BEYOND the low-slung offices and hangars of Tata Airlines the crust of the village betokened an evening of inland India, a time of bluish smoke palls and smouldering cakes of cow dung on the open hearths of village huts, and of sparrows screeching in the neem crowns nearby. In mid-distance the main Juhu road strung a random line of lamp-posts above the landscape, so that its destination seemed like a self-illusion. Where the club's private road fused with it, the funnel of dust had taken on the colour of twilight; somewhere in it the red light of the departing car gleamed faintly. He ordered another brandy, held it in his lap and gave himself up to a fresh wave of gloom.

'Sahib does not come so often any more,' the white-clad waiter said.

'No, I do not,' he told him. 'And from now on I shall come even less.'

He watched the dust settle to a streak of haze above the road—well, that was that. The bloated rajkumar who had bought his machine was at this moment on his way to town; it had been so simple, and yet so momentous. Here he sat on the lawn of the club and gazed at the lonely field and felt his sense of belonging weaken as in a swoon; the thought made him even gloomier. Now his status in this place had been reduced to a visitor's—the past notwithstanding. It was like a door shut and bolted on a whole era. In the repair shed the last strident sounds of a lathe escaped into the open. Someone on the radio in the restaurant shack. The tune quavered, then steadied; a demure little air, exquisitely suited to a single serangi and drum.

He had received a cheque for fifteen thousand rupees, less than he had hoped for, and the money had failed to bolster up his security. He had made no plans for its use and had only thought vaguely of giving one half to his father, without explanation, and keeping the other against the remote day when the pilgrim venture might be revived. Now he could only liken himself to someone whose sacrificial expectations had not been fulfilled.

Divali had come and gone. There had been the usual decorations and worship, and Jagnath had taken his family to an English cinema and been especially kind to his wife. Heaps of food and sweets had first tickled, then jaded the palates. Kandubai had drawn the Divali symbols at the entrance of the house and waved a cup of water and rice around her husband's face to ward off the evil eye. Vijay had floated around half-soothed and half-alert for a miracle, but the feasts had drawn to an end and the jasmine had rusted and his boyhood had not spoken to him beyond a few coarse whispers.

' 'nudder brandy,' the waiter echoed. The lathe was dead. Several members and guests had walked into the club and begun to amuse themselves.

As if the strain of the holiday season had not been sufficient, Salim Haq had wormed Tara's story out of her and made a gleeful splash in Marut's Hour. *The spirit of Rajput gallantry was revived last week in the second court of the presidency magistrate when a taunted brother rose to the defence of his sister.* . . . Salim's style had reached new poetic heights, because he was at heart a sentimental Muslim of the old order and could not remain deaf to the ancient Indian virtues. Premchand had been terribly upset—as who would not be?—and had reprimanded Salim severely, and Salim had walked out of his office in a huff and later out of Marut's Hour altogether, vowing not to touch a newspaper again until his novel was completely written and ready to be published. Having lately acquired a wealthy Parsi widow as mistress, he would anyhow rewrite the existing material and shift the accent from the Parsi community on to some other, perhaps even his own, the Khoja Muslims. And the magistrate had phoned Jagnath at the secretariat and blamed him for the gossip and hinted at the need for a maximum fine when Tara's case came up for hearing. Remembering it all, Vijay squirmed. His father had not blamed anyone, but the shock had taken him unaware; the effects of it would ripple on through the family life for months; he had refused to go to the office for several days and his pained silences had been hard to bear. Kandubai had said nothing either, but her glassy look and frequent retreats to her room were a withering comment on the whole thing; she seemed sallower and more tired. Now everyone was unhappy. And evening lay on the field with that blend of September's aftermath and October's wetness that proclaimed the passing of the rains and the sultry pause before the next change of seasons.

'In a statement to the press this afternoon,' the radio said aloud, 'the president of the Congress Working Committee declared that his party would enter and contest the elections to the best of their ability. . . .'

And this was the broader canvas beyond the field and family—tha tense and for the most part bewildering sequence of bravado, scramble for advantages and internecine tug-o'-wars of which he knew only the barest outline, but which had been looming sharper and more real of late. So now we'll know how we stand! he thought vaguely, though the reflection had no immediate significance. He knew that in Premchand's circle it was a time of decision; the uncle was toeing the party line and playing safe. Congress had not recognized the 1935 Act of the British, had in fact rejected it, but they were all for elections now in order to prove their strength. Premchand would now almost certainly be elected to the Bombay assembly. His two important newspapers had revived Mr. Gandhi's old pet project—prohibition of intoxicants; they were also wont to poke fun at the leaders of the Muslim League, Mr. Jinnah among them. Vijay would not have been surprised if Salim's disgust and resignation had not sprung from that, even though he would not admit it. New camps were being pitched, fresh enemies and friends being discovered on all sides. A time of decision it certainly was.

He gulped the remainder of his drink, coughing violently afterwards; a fine mist drifted low over his thinking. The prize money, the world tour, flying pilgrims and now his machine, everything on which his hope and security had rested, were gone. In a short time, he mused, I'll get a job, then very likely marry some dumb girl and lie fallow to the end of my days. The thistle will float back to the soil. In time I shall be quite content with Dasara and Holi and the songs of the priests. It was the way of thistles, and Hinduism brought them back to earth just a little sooner. And all round it would sprout once more the stubborn and perennial life of a whole continent and none would have noticed his short absence; for their reckoning was in hundreds of years and their cycles were never ending.

Turning about to call the waiter, he saw Thelma coming down the verandah of the bar, led by the very man he wanted to call. He made a move to slink away, but it was too late; she bore down on him swaying a little, her light summer dress strangely luminous in the dusk. He was to have picked her up at her house over an hour ago and they were to go to town, but he had tarried too long and finally forgotten all about it. Now the fuzziness of his head would not volunteer a single convincing excuse.

'You might at least have phoned and told me,' she said, coming up. 'Anyone with any sense of decency would have done at least that. I told you I was meeting a girl friend after the cinema. Now you've gone and made me look a fool.'

'No need to scream,' he said coolly. 'I forgot, that's all.'

'It is not all and you know it. One doesn't make promises and then forget them!'

She flung herself into the wicker chair and threw her bag on the table, upsetting his glass and the ashtray. Loss of temper did two things to Thelma, and neither gave her fury the compelling ring of urgency so necessary for utter conviction: It played havoc with her carefully modulated speech and caused the tight seams of her dress to chafe her. Plucking at her shoulder straps and armlets, crossing her bare knees with unaccustomed force, she went on in a singsong that resembled her mother's:

'And what about Mr. Varma? What's he going to think of me if we don't turn up at all? This is the second time you have promised to take me to him, and you've broken your word. You can't treat me like that, Vijay! I won't allow you!'

'If you don't quiet down,' he said, 'I shall get up and go away.'

'You will, will you? Why don't you answer my question?'

'We will meet him another time. Mr. Varma is in mourning. His son died the other day.'

'That's a lie, and you know it!'

'Then why do you ask?'

She half rose, glowering at him across the table, and couldn't speak for a moment; then she sank back and made a last effort to restrain herself. He heard her tug and tweak at her waist and bodice, and all the usual slurs upon Anglo-Indian womanhood flocked to his mind only too readily; he had always believed most of them, but now they gave him a confused personal offence.

Mr. Varma was a friend of his father's, a Vedic scholar and a luminary in the recently formed literary circle of Bombay, from whom Vijay had learned all he knew of the classical history of his race, mostly in the days when Villa Ram was still being built. Now the amiable old philosopher had been caught in the cultural revival of the Bombay province and he sat on many unusual committees, among then the Friends of Indian Cultural Heritage, to which the more conscientious film studios were beginning to look in behalf of their mythological productions; he therefore had many friends and some influence in the Bombay film colony. Meeting him was a roundabout and rather tedious way of self-improvement for Thelma, but it was the only one she knew for the present; as long as there was an even chance of making the grade, she could not lose her temper altogether.

So when Vijay lumbered slowly out of his chair and made for the parking shed, unsure of his immediate intentions, she came after him and took his elbow hesitantly.

'I can't quarrel with you,' she said, trying to sound calmer. 'Not when I've just had a row with mother. Drop me home. We are too late for everything anyhow.'

He tripped over a wooden peg in the grass and swore instead of answering. The merest stir of alcohol sickness made him conscious of his stomach, but he decided to ignore it by thinking of other things. He found the car and got into it, waiting until she settled on the other side of the seat; then he drove out towards the palm grove, into smoke and the smell of freshly laid tar. It was almost night. The loud roosting of crows and other birds seemed to be floundering in the greater murmur of the darkness. An inexplicable sadness began to shroud his gloom and he even felt a small comfort at her presence.

'Why did you quarrel with your mother?' he asked her when they gained the main Juhu road in the heart of the grove.

'Oh, it's a long story,' she said. 'Mother is trying to boss me just a little too much. She thinks I ought to marry a rich man and go and live in the hills. She gets like that once every six months and then we have an awful row. Now she's gone to town and won't be back for a few days. She can't see that I want to go home and become somebody.'

'Home? What, again?' He snorted without wanting to.

'You needn't be offensive about it,' she said, snorting back, 'my father was Welsh. I've wanted to go there ever since I was that big.'

'Why don't you? No one is begging you to stay in India.'

'Because it's not easy. You'll never understand that.' She trailed off in sudden embarrassment, looked away wringing her fingers, then collected herself and came back without any pretence. 'If father had stayed with us it might have been different. Now mother wants to stay here . . . and make me stay . . . and I'm afraid. This isn't my country no matter what I do to make it. And it won't be ever, even if I die in it. I can't help it if I feel like that. . . .'

Honesty on this point was so rare among the half-castes that it was worth listening to; before this stripped Thelma he had no fear of humbling himself. He loitered on at low speed, and the soft outer crust of his sadness became almost sympathy. A car passed down the road and he dimmed his lights automatically.

'A year ago I'd have been happy to marry an Englishman and ask nothing more,' she continued. 'I almost did, too, but he turned out to be an awful snob about his complexion. After that I lost interest. I'd best like to go far away and be left all to myself. I'm sick and tired of insults.'

'Your raja friend might help you, if you ask him.'

'He . . .? Don't make me laugh, Vijay! He's sweet on me . . . he'd build a cage and put me in it if he could. Not that he doesn't try either. . . . Last time he was here I used a new perfume and he wanted to know who gave it to me. Mother nearly died of fright.'

'What kind of man is he? Old . . . middle-aged?'

She paused, balancing the virtue of honesty against its cost in impression; she tossed her hair and decided to come clean and square.

'Fifty . . . maybe more, though he doesn't look it. You never saw anyone so conceited about himself. Back in Kandra he's supposed to have four dozen mistresses. Mother and I go there twice a year, so I can tell you. He keeps them in a house in the bazaar . . . they're not allowed to go into the street without his permission.'

142

'I know these lewd old pigs,' he said. 'I wouldn't live in one of their places for anything in the world.'

'Neither would I. But mother doesn't see it that way . . . she's blind. She thinks he might marry me one of these days . . . just to make quite sure I don't see another man. But I want to meet other people. I want to have friends who won't only think how soon they can undress me.'

He said nothing, but pulled up by the side of her garden gate and switched off the motor. Now that everything was out and she had not attempted to whitewash herself, he found he had nothing against her. He didn't even feel repelled. Seeing a member of another race so starkly meant seeing her safely and without commitment. He might even have tried to say something compassionate and heartening if the hint of sickness in his stomach had not now turned into a clearer and ominous tide. He belched helplessly, covering his mouth with a kerchief.

'You wretched boy, how many of those did you put away before I came? You know you can't stand it!' Reaching across his lap, she opened the door at his side and nudged him out gently. 'Better run in quickly and get it off your chest. I'll make you a cup of tea.'

After some hesitation he got out and walked into the house and upstairs, and she ran after him. He wanted to say, 'I'll speak to Mr. Varma when I see him again,' and thought of making other amends, but none could divert his mind from the sickness, now rising to his throat and head. He made for the bathroom on the first floor and doubled over the toilet like a boy who had eaten too many plantains, vowing, between spasms, never again to touch brandy. When it was all over, he washed himself, tidied the bathroom and came into the living-room.

'My, you do look green around the gills,' she said through the open door of the bedroom. 'Lie down on the couch and rest yourself. Tea will be here in a minute.'

Then she closed the door and left him alone for a quarter of an hour, in which he lay still and felt the blood ooze back to his cheeks; he even shut his eyes and dozed off for a few minutes. When he sat up again, the mist was gone and his depression had returned. Thelma was in an armchair, turning the spoon in a piping hot cup of tea; she had somehow found time to change into a dressing-gown and more comfortable slippers; her hair was combed back behind her ears, exposing her high round cheekbones.

'Drink this down, dear, and you'll be the same as ever.'

'I am the same as ever,' he said.

She brought it to him, however, and insisted, and he took the cup and blew at it. Sipping it he couldn't look at her. The incident had given her an intangible edge; his shame and anger at having once again made a fool of himself made it worse. Gone was her fluster and pathos; it was as though the change from street clothes to a negligee had shrunk the area of her uncertainty.

'You need looking after, dear. Maybe one day you'll know your friends and stop hurting them. What was the matter with you, anyhow?'

He looked at her obliquely, then stood up feeling for the car keys in his pocket.

'Don't go yet,' she said. 'I mean that, Vijay. What's come over you lately? You act as if you'd lost something. You're always thinking of other things when we're together. Is anything the matter? Is there another girl . . .? If there is, you'd better come right out with it. I've played fair and square with you and I expect to be treated in the same way.'

'There is no one else. You talk too much.'

'All right, no need to growl. I have a right to know.' She struck a familiar pose against one arm of the chair, though unconsciously; a wheedling new note crept into her voice. 'You know, Vijay, I've tried so hard to understand us two and I don't seem to be getting anywhere. Must we always growl and scratch? Don't I go against my own mother just to please you? Have I ever refused anything you asked me? Why can't we be friends like other normal people?'

'I don't know,' he said. 'Anyway, I must go now.'

She stood up, too, retying her waistband.

'I think I know. I suppose in any other country we might have really got together. Not here though.'

It was the truth—indeed gallingly evident from the beginning of their relationship—but now it bruised and angered him; no Indian would have taken it lamely from one who was neither privileged nor truly sympathetic. As he strode out to the landing and began to totter down the unlighted staircase, his old contempt for the half-caste revived turbulently.

'Oh, come off that high horse of yours, Vijay, will you!' she said after him.

He was halfway to the ground floor when the telephone rang out. He stopped and heard her walk to it and snatch the earpiece violently.

'Yes, he is here . . . just leaving . . . shall I call him?'

He climbed back, while she called him loudly, and re-entered to hear her say: 'The least you can do is to return the courtesy and tell me who you are . . .'

'Give me that!' he said.

'I will not. What does she take me for! This is my house and my telephone, in case you don't remember!' Her singsong returned with a vengeance.

He wrested it from her with difficulty and pushed her away. There were several voices at the other end and they spoke in a rapid Hindi that made no sense for a moment or two. Then Tara came through perfectly clearly and her tone cut towards his heart with a fateful suddenness.

144

'I have tried to reach you everywhere for the last hour. Just now Salim gave me this number. Are you still at Juhu?'

'Yes. I was just going home.'

'Vijay, bhai, you're to come home at once . . . mother collapsed this evening. She is still unconscious. Two doctors are here . . . they want to take her to the hospital . . .' Her voice broke and she rallied only with a great effort, so that he grew limp and weak all at once. 'It is very serious . . . you must hurry, please!'

'What is it, tell me!'

'I don't know, bhai . . . nobody knows yet. She fell down in the kitchen . . . we had to carry her to her room. Wait, wait, the doctor is coming down just now. I will ask him . . . no, it is Rajuram. I can't tell you more . . . I must go up now. Please hurry! Father is asking for you. . . .'

'All right,' he said. 'I'm going this moment.'

He put the receiver down, missing the hook. His ears pounded and perspiration broke out on his forehead and in his armpits; a parching dryness settled on his tongue.

He frowned at Thelma, trying to grasp the meaning of her movements; she had walked to the door and flung the curtain aside with such force that several rings broke off the rod at the top. His mind refused to congeal.

'You told her you were going,' she said trembling. 'Go then, and good riddance! And you can tell your little Indian trollop to give her name next time she wants you so badly!'

Glaring at her, while the import of the words seeped through the waste in his head, he forgot to move, forgot almost to breathe. Then life flooded back all at once. He swung out with his open palm and caught her cheek full and hard. The sound had a clear, shocking resonance. She stepped back and found herself wedged between the couch and one of the tea-tables; she kicked the table scattering all the brass and magazines on the carpet.

'You wretch, you black wretch . . . how dare you!'

He went on slapping her and couldn't stop, and each burning smack relieved a little of the pressure in his head. It seemed to him he had been slapping her for years, so easy it became after the first shock; it also seemed he had never hated anyone so much in all his life. She grabbed at his face and screamed; then caught his hand and bit it fiercely. They wrestled in a moment's gasping confusion, broke off and faced each other glowering.

'Now go back home!' he said, beside himself. 'No one is keeping you here. We can live without you!'

He grabbed the lapels of her gown, pushed her back to the couch and sent her sprawling on her back. Then he dashed out of the room and stumbled down the black stairway, tripping several times and almost falling headlong over the porch doormat.

2

VILLA RAM was in a state of barely restrained suspense when he reached it after a mad ride. All lights were on; with the collapse of the lady of the house, the household restraints had broken down too, and the servants huddled in the corners and halls of the ground floor and listened wide-eyed to Rajuram's whispered bulletins. Tara sat on a divan in the living-room and held Munu's head in her lap; both had been crying.

'They have taken her just now in the car. Tata hospital. Lalaji went with them. She was unconscious . . . they had to carry her out. Vijay, bhai, she looked so pale I was afraid. I thought . . .'

She burst into sobs and Munu, who was already thoroughly terrified, buried her face in her hands and cried out loud. He had to help them up and soothe them before Tara would continue. Rajuram came to furnish the details, of which she knew nothing, for she had not been present.

It had all occurred very suddenly. Kandubai had come into the kitchen, as she always did in the early evening, to see to the family's dinner and prepare her own dietary dishes, and she had not seemed different from any other time. She complained of a headache and the old Rajuram administered the usual aspirins; then she sat on a stool against the kitchen wall and apparently went to sleep; next she toppled over and seemed to stop breathing. The ensuing alarm, the fearful scramble up to her room on the first floor, Jagnath's dismayed pleas, all failed to stir her. When he came, the doctor's expression did not give any clue; he looked grave and spoke only to the head of the family, in hushed flurry. Now she was gone and they were to follow her to the hospital as soon as Vijay arrived. A taxi had already been ordered.

'Let us go then!' he said, trying in vain to hide his shock. Worry, guilt, shame all came together to make this the most bewildering night of his life.

They drove off and he held his arms around his sisters and made a pitiful effort to quiet them. Munu wept with a child's abandon, but Tara's grief was of many parts, some of which were like his own. They had both taken a good deal for granted lately; many a thing they had got into the habit of accepting as permanent was now shown to be brittle, almost perishable. They were scared, too, without realizing it, lest no time be left to make up for it—and made up it had to be. They would not admit it to themselves, but from this moment on they would meet each other halfway and their sense of guilt would be shaped into a tacit solidarity which no rational appeal from outside could have moulded.

At the large modern hospital in the heart of the industrial district Jagnath was not to be recognized. His eyes were puffed up and their look was haunted; the lines of age, miraculously latent all these years, were breaking to the surface, almost by the minute; his dishevelled grey hair seemed in some dark way to speed up the gallop. He received his children listlessly, with a few shakes of his head and a tired wave; the girls, who had wanted to sit close and be comforted by him, edged away and sank into other chairs by themselves.

'Pitaji, tell us . . .!' Vijay said.

'She had an attack,' he began. 'Nephritis . . . complications. The doctor has not yet told me. It was so sudden, we never expected it.'

He stood up and walked to the door as if he had thought of going up-stairs, then faltered on the threshold. He was still in his lounging clothes; his fingers tore at the hem of his loose shirt and there seemed to be very little blood in them.

'The truth, pitaji, please. Is she very bad?'

He came back and his bearing was that of a prisoner whose hope of an open window had been dashed. 'I cannot say. The time has been so short. It is an old illness. . . .' He sank down in the steel chair, propped his elbows on his knees and hid his face in his hands. 'She has had it for over a year. . . . We thought it was getting better.'

'Why did you not tell us?'

'She forbade me to.'

'How could she! What good could that do?' Tara said.

'She forbade. That was how she wanted it.' His frame seemed to sag; he wiped his face with his sleeve, something he did only rarely.

A time bell chimed in the interior, echoing through a hundred rooms and passages, filtering down to the mezzanine and vanishing into the yard through the broad and open entrance. They sat on for half an hour, glancing first at one another, then past each other, as though afraid of further questioning. The cool, sparsely furnished waiting-hall seemed hostile to weaknesses. The girls stopped weeping; Munu dabbed her eyes only every now and then. In the night just beyond the windowsill buses con-tinued to grind to a stop, a seller of medical roots went on crying his wares in a doleful and creaking tremolo; sweating humanity tore along between high embankments, bent on fun and a good time. At this hour of the evening the swarm of cells which was India under the thick lens of the ethnologist banded together with a light heart to form a rude and compact organism; its contours were those of a single giant, pressing onward and backward with an old but vital instinct. But inside here one such cell seemed suddenly not to belong to anyone. It was of the giant, but much more of itself. To the man who placed community above individuals, this cell said, I am in danger, leave me alone!

At length the doctor came down and they read the decision on his face before he spoke of it. He was a sallow, hulking Parsi and quite the best physician in the hospital; he beckoned the father into the passage and murmured low and fervently; Vijay only heard: 'Rest assured that I will keep you informed,' and 'Mr. Ramsingh, you had better get some rest yourself.'

'We are not needed, let us go home,' Jagnath said, re-entering with him.

'You must not worry until I start worrying,' the Parsi added. 'I shall remain here all night. I am on duty.'

They drove back home and the short trip took on the aspect of a long voyage. Worli struck them as being more isolated than before. The tide had gone out and the surf had been stilled, and from the long exposed spine of the reef silence welled inshore like a delayed primeval phenomenon. Servants gathered in the dining-room once more, but Rajuram the Elder dispatched them softly; he stayed back to serve hot tea with turmeric and scan the countenance of his masters. Then Tara took Munu to bed and failed to return. Father and son kept up the watch for one more hour, then went upstairs too, each to his own room. Rajuram brought his bedding roll from the outhouse and spread it under the telephone in the hall, but the precaution was unnecessary; the house had grown so quiet and alert that a ring would be heard all the way up to the terrace.

Vijay slept like the dead and woke up early, to find that Tara and his father had gone to the hospital once more. He waited for them to call, but Premchand, then his wife Radabai, then Salim Haq and many other friends called up first to ask for news; he could give them none. He rang up the hospital several times and finally reached his father. Jagnath sounded exhausted. Kandubai had come to once and he had been permitted to see her for a few moments; dropsy had set in and vision had been badly deranged; the doctor could not be moved to prognosticate. 'If she passes, there will be nothing to live for,' Jagnath said tiredly, and his son's heart dwindled for an awful moment.

'Pitaji, I'm coming with Munu, right away.'

'No, don't. I would have called you if it were any use. We are returning ourselves. The doctor says we help no one by being here . . . and the waiting is too much.'

Vijay roused himself from stupor. 'I want to wait. We can take it in turns.'

'Dr. Duggan said not to. They are watching her all the time. We are not likely to know for a day or two. . . .'

He hung up as if suddenly losing interest.

But the doctor turned out to be right.

Kandubai wavered between consciousness and coma during the rest of that day and all of the following, and the family continued with their alternate watch between the hospital and Worli. Their hope ebbed with each new relay. On the fourth day Ranjit arrived by plane and two of Kandubai's brothers, Ajit Singhs, came from Indore. Mrs. Prashad sent a long and warm telegram from Lucknow, which Jagnath took to read to his wife—a needless gesture of bravado. Hydrotherapy and treatment had enabled her to see better and speak almost coherently, but could not help her otherwise. The Parsi diagnostician spoke of uræmia and endocarditis and some unexplained, treacherous danger to the lungs; Kandubai asked to be returned home, and he complied with resignation. He had tried to cure many of these elderly Hindu ladies and always they had known the truth before he would even face it in his own mind; quietly but resolutely they took their fate out of his hands and made their own arrangements. Who indeed would cling with any certainty to that flimsy line between a doctor's duty and a patient's right to plan his own end?

So she was returned to Villa Ram; an Indian nurse was engaged. The living-room was taken apart to make a sickroom, at her own insistent wish, for it was on the ground floor and nearer to earth. The wish begloomed everyone save Kandubai; earth was the place a dying man lay on in the hour of his return to it. Her equanimity remained the same as ever. If she had called for more and better medical treatment and demanded assurance and courage, her people might have borne it more easily; as it was, she settled back on her cot with a feeble, apologetic smile and met their concern with a humble self-possession.

Several times a day on that Friday and Saturday the screen was removed from her bed and the family gathered to pay their respects, often to be twitted for their long and bleary faces. How well did she see them? Vijay wondered about that with growing anguish and fear. Apparently well enough to recognize each one. Her breath was a rasp, her pallor more transparent each time. The nurse often changed her into a white sleeping-robe that concealed all but a small part of her neck and lower arms; these were swollen and blanched.

It was kind of you to go to Hardwar at my request,' she told Ranjit when he joined them.

'You are not to give me undeserved praise, Shreemati,' he said quietly. The respectful appellative rose to his lips with a sombre new poignancy. 'I drove there because I had to anyhow . . . and from there to Delhi, almost without getting out of the car. I was on the Willingdon Airport half an hour before the plane took off. It was very easy. I could have brought you other things, if you had only remembered to ask.

'It was all I wanted.'

'And you are to start thinking of the day when you will get up and bring order back to this house. When you will travel to Hardwar yourself and be my guest afterwards. And maybe we shall all take Uday Ramsingh's advice and climb up to Badrinath, for once in our lives.'

'Where is it?' she asked, smiling faintly.

'Here, by your bed, Shreemati.'

'I put it there as soon as you came home,' Jagnath said.

She made as if to rise on her elbows, but the nurse patted her hand and admonished firmly. Ranjit reached under the bed and held up a container at her eye level; it was a vessel of baked clay in a sack of raffia netting, and it contained the water of the Ganges. Vijay was to learn later that it was one of the first requests she had made to her husband after prostration and that he had conveyed it to Ranjit in an urgent telegram. But watching the scene now he divined the meaning nevertheless; it made his heart heavy with care and foreboding, for the water of the Ganges was used in the last rites.

'I cannot tell you of my gratitude,' she said to Ranjit.

Ranjit was about to protest when the nurse made a warning sign. He smiled instead, made an obeisance and bowed out of the room.

Then it was the turn of the Premchands. Radabai Premchand, walking before her solemn husband and foster-son Lakshman, touched the patient's hands, feet and her own forehead, all in one gesture of respect. Younger than Kandubai by a few years, she was seldom seen at family gatherings; delicate and shy, towered over by her unsmiling husband and flanked by a son who, though gaunt, was as tall as his foster-father, she did almost explain her obscurity. She told the patient that she was praying for a speedy recovery, paused awkwardly, offered to come again in the evening if her help should be needed, then subsided in embarrassed silence.

'Care should be repaid with care,' Premchand said, stepping into the breach. 'You looked after her four years ago when she was ill, now it is for her to do it.'

'We must all see that you do not lack anything,' Radabai said.

'I do not, but your presence will make me happy.'

The invitation was a pregnant one to all present. Women were getting together; they did that only in times of stress; there were errands in the life of a Hindu matron which could not be delegated either to the males or to professional nurses.

'I shall bring her myself,' Premchand promised.

He, too, made an obeisance and retreated, and his wife and son followed him. Jagnath saw them out of the house. When he returned Kandubai was tired out; she could not lie comfortably in any position and her breath was faster and hotter. It was getting close to the doctor's visit. The nurse motioned Jagnath to end the conversation and he signed to Vijay and the girls.

'Let only Tara and Munu go,' Kandubai said. 'I wish to ask something.'

'I wish to ask for a promise,' she amplified laboriously when the sisters had withdrawn. 'I would have asked even without the illness, had I but been better prepared.'

'Speak, ama,' Jagnath said.

All three waited while the nurse mopped her face.

'I have been praying that I should be awake to speak of this. Hari has been complaisant. . . .' She beckoned them closer with her finger; Jagnath sat on the edge of the bed, Vijay moved to the foot of it, where she could see him without budging. 'I must not squander the time given me, or deceive myself. . . . You should not do it, either. I have asked the good doctor to tell me . . . and he told me.' Shutting her eyes she came to the point so simply that both recognized her conviction to be stronger than their hope. 'Do not say that I should have taken better care of myself. Perhaps I ought to have . . . but if I had done, so much that was important would have remained undone. What good would have been six more months . . . or a year . . . if I had felt useless . . . if the house had gone untended . . . ?'

'We need you more than the house,' Vijay said.

'Son, I am the house. I was the house. . . . But it is not what I wished to ask.'

A grating of motor car brakes came into the room with a gust of breeze. The nurse tiptoed to the window and drew the curtains, then went out into the hall. The sudden shade made purple little pools of Kandubai's eye sockets, but it blurred the tortured corners of her mouth; perspiration glistened on her upper lip and her forehead.

'You should see that all . . . all the rites . . . are held for me. I have been mindful of the true way all my life . . . with all my errors and failings. Now that should be completed . . . I do not ask more or less than it has been set down. This little you should promise.'

'I promise,' Jagnath said with difficulty.

'I too, ama,' Vijay said. 'Please try to think of recovery, and of us.'

'It is not a matter of thinking . . . rather of knowing. The hour is set for all things.'

'Priyaji, my loved one, what are you saying!' Jagnath still fought his tears, but his voice was past all restraint.

Dr. Duggan appeared at the door, with the nurse behind him; she carried his bag and a small clean towel. Jagnath rose and did not attempt to hide his face.

'Remember,' Kandubai whispered. 'Do not forget. You made a promise.'

Vijay took her hand with both his and pressed it to his forehead. Then he followed his father out of the room. Jagnath crossed the hall towards his study and shut the door behind him; there was a sound of nose blowing and of a falling chair, and then Vijay heard his father sob out loud. This was not to be listened to. He strode out to the lawn and walked across it and there, belatedly but with a troughing force just the same, the tension burst out of him in one wave after another. He shook violently for a while and only remembered to muffle the sound in the sleeve of his shirt.

'Sometimes I think our women know the whole truth,' Ranjit spoke presently, stepping forth from the bushes. 'They are the only yogis. I think that is because they get to know about everything without meditation.'

He took Vijay's arm and led him to the hedge near the road, where they both halted to look down on the sea face. It was still early afternoon. The offing was brightly blue against the seesaw black of the reef; half a dozen dhows crossed it in mid-distance. It seemed to them that the glare was greater than it should have been and that it came over from the seething cauldron of land behind them and merely hovered thus above the water to cool itself. There was in it a feel of surging flames and cracked earth and a consumption not to be halted by the puny denials of mortal mind.

By the evening of the next day death lay unmistakably over the Ramsingh household, stopping all but the long and eerie vigil. Jagnath, Vijay, Tara and Radabai Premchand took turns sitting in the living-room and helping the nurse to minister the prescribed comforts, but each new relief took place amidst silence and haunted glances, and each new watcher prayed more fervently that there should be another after him. They walked about on bare feet and sought each other in their rooms, as if waiting together might somehow head off the calamity. If Vijay thought at all in those hours, it was to search his conscience and trace all retribution to its likely cause; now his reason could neither soothe nor convince him. In the unearthly hush of Villa Ram, the boyhood teachings of karma seemed to flock back in an altogether different and more fateful light. Now he began to feel that his callousness of the last few months had somehow sped on the present misfortune and that his guilt was proved by his recurring fear. He had neglected his mother and family and gone to seed in all other ways; now there was Nemesis, in a shape more stupefying than he was prepared for. There was no getting away from it. It was idle to call it superstition. It sat heavily upon his shoulders and did not let up even in pain or tears. Worst of all, he could not talk about it to anyone.

An hour after sunset his father met him on the landing of the upper floor and he looked tenser than before.

'Come with me at once. She has asked to speak to you.'

'How is she, pitaji?'

'Bad, son . . . very bad. I am terribly afraid. There is no time at all.'

He followed him with a pounding heart. The doctor had just finished examining her, Jagnath told him. Coma was expected at any moment, lungs and heart were giving out; she could not see any more, or speak for that matter. It is the end, son,' he said hopelessly, for he had sat up with her all night, reading and ministering, and carried out her last wishes throughout the morning. Now he was near breakdown himself. He strayed off into Hindi and muttered a childhood prayer to Hari.

The sisters waited at the foot of the stairs.

'The doctor must see you at once,' Tara said.

'I am coming.'

He led Vijay through the hall, where Ranjit, the Premchands and the Ajit uncles from Indore had already huddled, and from there to the sickroom. An oil dipam had been lighted; the vessel of Ganges water had replaced the tray of medicaments on the small table. The matting of darbha grass which they had prepared that morning with Radabai Premchand's help was covered with a clean new cloth. Three Brahman priests squatted next to it, chanting in unison and mixing the offerings for the ritual of 'perfect expiation'; a silver salver of coins and another of sandalwood paste and pavitram amulets stood in their midst; incense mingled with the smell of priestly potions.

'Speak loud and short, for she cannot hear much,' Jagnath said. 'First we must place her down here, she wishes you to assist in this.'

The physician and the nurse gave them a hand. They raised her out of the cot and lowered her on to the matting with great care; then Tara and Radabai swathed her in another clean sheet. Wrapped thus and lying very straight and flat, the dying matriarch of the Ramsinghs looked no bigger than a child. Vijay knelt and stroked her cheeks; they were turgid, but cooler than before. The story of Emperor Humayun circling the sickbed of his son Akbar came to his mind compellingly and he wished for one stricken moment that he could do likewise and take all her ills upon himself.

'Vijay . . .?'

But the sound seemed to battle its way upwards from a part of her which neither death nor fear could touch, and it was dry, as though it had passed over a hot brazier; the eyelids batted a little, steadied, gave up in defeat.

'Not here, in the next room,' Dr. Duggan said to Jagnath, and they tiptoed through the door. Then the nurse folded the screen and put it away altogether. The Brahmans stopped chanting and only their lips twitched on in a silent enunciation of the same Sanskrit prayer. Vijay squatted by her side and took her hand, squeezing it gently.

'Here somewhere,' she said with a gasp 'Look . . . read it to me.'

The nurse handed him two books from the other side. 'Mrs. Premchand and I had been reading it to her last night and this morning,' she said. 'We marked some pages at her wish. Yes, those with bits of newspaper in them.' She opened the first volume and gave it to him with her finger on the passage.

'Read,' Kandubai said.

'But ama . . . dearest ama, let me talk to you,' he said.

Kandubai's mouth trembled soundlessly.

'You had better read,' the nurse said. 'She had it marked so that you will read it to her.'

He looked from the nurse to his mother, but Kandubai lay quite still and seemed to be waiting; he raised the book and found it was a Hindi text; there was a pencil mark against the passage from the Laws of Manu.

' "To be mothers were women sent forth, to be fathers men," ' he read slowly, raising his voice at a sign from the nurse. ' "Begetting a virtuous son a man will save himself, and also the seven preceding and seven following generations. . . ." '

He glanced at the cover and had difficulty in deciphering the besmudged title, *Right Outlook*, an anthology of quotations from old Hindu sources.

'Go on, son. . . .'

' "The begetting of children," ' he continued, ' "the nurture of those born and the daily life of men, of such things is woman the visible cause.

' "For without offspring no door of heaven is known or named. . . . I have not paid the debt to my forbears, and this is a torment. When my life is at an end, then, too, is the end of my fathers. Men are born unto earth with four duties: towards the forefathers, towards the gods, the *rishis* and mankind, and to them all debt must be discharged as the law enjoins.

' "To worship gods and give alms and read the scriptures and offer plentiful sacrifice, none is worth the sixteenth part of an offspring. I, a childless man, shall not reach the pure and fair worlds.

' "Let man wed and beget sons, for they are boons greater than all others. A son is as one's very self . . ."

'I will read it later, ama. I promise,' he said.

'Now, not later.' She pressed his hand feebly and wet her lips. 'One more, at the end. . . .'

'Do as she asks. She must not be upset,' the nurse said.

He found the underscored page at the end of the volume and read in growing confusion. In the hall beyond the door, the relations were beginning to shed their footwear preparatory to entering. The Ajit Singhs, her brothers, came in at the head of the group and they seemed worn and dazed; after touching her hands and feet, they squatted behind Vijay and began to pray.

' "There is no kinsman like one's wife," ' he read on erratically. ' "In this world wherein we must seek pious merit, there is no comrade like the wife. The home of him without a sweet-spoken wife is like a wild and lonely forest. . . . Even when man betakes himself to another birth, when he dies, hurrying along paths alone, the faithful mate hastens ever after him . . . and if she should have gone away before him, she will await him unfailingly. Hence it comes that a man will marry, that a master will have a wife in this world and the other. The self begotten by the self is by the wise called 'son.'

' "Women must be honoured and cherished, for when they are, the gods are gladdened. And where they are not, all devotion is barren of fruit. And offspring indeed is the abiding place in this world. He that partakes of the fruit of sons is not cast down from the heavens, nor does he go to hell like the sonless. . . ." '

'Better stop,' the doctor said softly, laying his hand on the book. 'I doubt if she can hear you.'

Jagnath and the girls joined him on the floor and Munu could muffle her sobbing only by a desperate effort. Some paces away Radabai Premchand raised a kerchief to her face, while the others peered at the bed or watched the mournful shifting of the Brahmans. Vijay freed his hand from his mother's to enable his father to hold it. He brushed the hair which had fallen over her forehead in the moving.

'Vijay. . . .' She tried to focus him, batting her eyelids and frowning strenuously, but did not seem equal to it any more; night must have been growing impenetrable for her. 'Yes, I can hear,' she said. 'Read, read. . . . It is what I have tried to tell you, but could not. It is all written down. . . .'

'I will ama. Rest a little now.'

'Man and woman are a godly pair . . . remember always.'

Tara put her arms around her younger sister and began to rock her. They sobbed into their saris.

A little later Kandubai made another painful and panting effort.

'I wanted one more son . . . it was not granted. Now you are the one and only. . . .'

Bending low over her, the doctor felt her pulse and looked at her pupils with a small torchlight. 'She is holding back very obstinately,' he said. 'I never saw anything like it.'

'Priyaji, my beloved, light of my eyes!' Jagnath said, swaying from the waist upwards.

'Dear ama, don't go!' Tara cried.

Vijay bit his lips and grew rigid; in the pit of his stomach a fresh swirl seemed to lower the floor under him.

'I cannot take more than a promise with me,' Kandubai said fitfully. 'Make it, son. . . .'

'I promise, ama.'

'Now . . . water.'

Tara reached for the earthen vessel and passed it to her brother, from whose hands Jagnath took it without pausing to sway. He scooped some in the palm of his hand and poured it through her swollen lips, muttering, 'Drink, munuji, drink. . . .' She swallowed what she could; the rest trickled down her chin and into the collar of her white shirt. Then Vijay

155

moistened his fingers and drew them over her eyes. It was the best they could make of their undertaking to her; had there been time, they would have done it on the banks of a holy stream and let her eyes rest on the darkening but eternal sun.

'How many are here . . .?'

The family spoke up all at once, heeding no rule of precedence.

'In the old days it was like this . . . I am content. . . . Read the Bhagavata.'

This time the head of the family read. The stress of doing it and the failing light gave his recital a soft quality out of this world. The younger of the priests put a ladleful of clarified butter into the sacred fire and began to rake it with a subdued, almost pensive air.

' "It is better that one should do his own task as he may," ' Jagnath read slowly in Hindi, ' "even though he fail, than do tasks not his own, though they seem good. To die performing duty is no ill; but who seeks other paths shall wander still." '

'True . . . true,' she whispered.

' "Mourn not for those who live, nor those who die. Neither I, nor thou, nor any one of these ever was not, nor ever will not be, for ever and for ever afterwards. All that doth live, lives always. . . ." '

He broke down and gave the book to Vijay.

' "And whoso loveth Me, cometh to Me. Whoso in faith and love shall offer me a leaf, a flower, a fruit, water poured forth, that offering I accept. . . . So wilt thou free thyself from Karma, the chain that holdeth men to good and evil issue. Safe shalt thou come to Me, when thou are quit of flesh, by faith and abdication joined to Me.

' "Of that which is born, death is certain; of that which is dead, rebirth is certain. Therefore do not grieve over destiny. . . ." '

He passed it on to his elder sister, and she read from another chapter holding herself with all her strength. The doctor bent down to look at the eyes once more; his flashlight flickered, lingered lightly and weirdly for a short while, then went out.

' "Nay, but as one layeth his worn-out robes away
    and taking new ones sayeth, 'These will I wear to-day,'
    so layeth by the spirit its garb of flesh
    and passeth to inherit a residence afresh. . . ." '

'You can read on, but she can't hear you,' the doctor said.

There was a pause in which even the Brahmans stopped chanting.

'She is unconscious. I doubt if she will ever hear you again.'

In the next room, leaning on the jamb of the door, the old Rajuram slumped involuntarily and slid his elbow over the light switch. A sheet of light fell over the lower half of the white wrapping on the floor. The father, the son and the daughters looked at one another in dumb disbelief.

156

The coma took altogether seven hours to run its course. First the family and after them the relations and friends sprinkled the Ganges water over her mouth and face. The chief priest applied the unguents from time to time, never ceasing to intone. Smells of incense, ghee, flowers and fruit receded before the pungent fumes of ampoules which the nurse handed to the doctor every now and again. Night came on in real earnest, refreshed by a south-easterly breeze from the ocean which the garden received with a lively rustle. In the house of a neighbour a radio sent out the electioneering address by a Parsi candidate, while lower down the late promenaders sat on the sea wall and spat betel-nut juice over their dangling feet. The surf lapped patiently, everlastingly, in another tongue. The thickly flowing, never covered sewers of northern Worli wafted their message high and wide on the range, so that only the stronger wafting of the priestly sacrifice saved the watch at Villa Ram from profanation.

The company wept in fits and starts and shuffled about desultorily. Utterly exhausted, Jagnath dozed off twice and was awakened by one or the other of his children. Vijay either wept or took turns with Tara in reading the Bhagavad-Gita. The rings of darbha grass, called pavitrams, were distributed by the elder priest to the inner family, and by them to everyone else; the wearing of them would shield Kandubai's soul against evil spirits, and she would find it easier to battle her way to freedom. A steady relay of servants came from the outhouses and paused in the frame of the room door, performing obeisances towards the dying one, beating their chests and giving vent to the grief. In the kitchen, all to himself, a Nai barber smoked one country cigarette after another. He had been engaged by the priests to shave and clean the body when the time came.

At two in the morning Dr. Duggan thrust his stethoscope in his pocket and nodded for the last time. Those who happened to be in the room cried out anew, and some said, 'Hari-bol! Hari-bol!' The women tied Kandubai's toes and thumbs together with small pieces of cloth, for that was how she had wanted it. Then the second part of the last rites began.

Jagnath and his children went to bathe ceremonially in accordance with tradition, and the rest of the weeping company herded out into the hall and sat down to wait. Unassisted but deft, the Nai unfolded the screen in front of the body and quietly went to work.

157

3

IN THE lore of Lord Yama, the sovereign of deathdom and hell, there was one legend which had fascinated Vijay as a small boy, and it had been told him by the old Mr. Varma, the family's good friend. In the later hubbub of adolescence it had gone down in his mind and lain there like a snared firefly until now, when the violent shaking of those depths set it free and soaring to the surface as bright and beguiling as ever.

It was said in the Katha Upanishad—from which Mr. Varma had digested the story in a manner suitable for a child—that Yama once received a most unusual visitor. He was a Brahman boy called Nachiketas, whom his father had sacrificed to the god of death in a fit of temper. It so happened that Yama was away on other business when the boy reached his kingdom, and the latter had to wait three days for his return. To keep a Brahman waiting and unfed was bad form even for a god, according to the sacred books, and Yama offered three boons to Nachiketas, one for each day of waiting. The first was a promise of safe return to earth and appeasement of the father's wrath; the second, a revelation of the sacred fire by which men could win heaven; the third caused the god many scruples and a headache, because the boy wanted to learn the meaning of death and be allowed to take it back with him. 'It is so subtle a matter,' Yama declared, 'that even some of the gods of old could not grasp it.' But Nachiketas was stubborn, and the ruler of death finally launched on a long and involved exposé of the soul's immortality, epitomized in the verse: 'Unborn, constant, eternal, primeval, the soul is not slain when the body is slain, and those who who would try to glimpse that soul on this earth, are those who are likely to escape the rigmarole of outward death.' And after this Nachiketas went back to earth resolved to discover his soul and become a yogi, and tried so hard and so long that in the end he did glimpse it and so became free from death. Unfortunately, he was never able to convey the secret to anyone who did not strive for it in exactly the same fashion. Mr. Varma didn't know it either, because his interest in the subject was purely intellectual, but he later tried to redeem himself by a verse from the book of Bhagavad-Gita, which said that a thorough discharge of one's duties assured a man an elevated rebirth and eventual union with the universal spirit, thus reducing his fear of death at the same time. He also stressed the importance of this idea to a Rajput, for Rajputs were Kshatriyas, the active and warring caste of Hinduism, and it was really for them that this Gita had come to be preached.

It seemed to Vijay on that Monday morning, as he marched behind his mother's litter and pall, echoing the cries of mourning—'Hari-bol!'—and also breathing the dust and brine cloud of that meandering road in Mahim, that the boy Nachiketas was either a being of exceptional gifts or, as Salim Haq would have said, a village oaf. For having learned the secret of death he had already placed himself beyond it, and had therefore no need of returning to earth. If he had gone back, as might be supposed, to share his secret with his parents and all his people, his adventure might have made sense. But he was unable to convey it to his fellow humans beyond the uncertain exhortation: Become an ascetic as I have become. He made the journey twice, instead of only once, as all the god's creatures did. He came back with the simple aim of proving to himself what everyone knew already —that the soul never perished. As for death itself, that last curtain on the last act of the last day of the last performance, he had learned nothing save that he must not fear it. He knew nothing more than Vijay did when Nand gave up the ghost in that hospital at Bandra or when Kandubai crossed the nethermost boundary of her long coma. For all the deft words of priest-philosophers, death still was what it always had been—a sallow corpse, a jasmine garland rusting in the sun, a cry of 'Hari-bol!' and a vast, sleepy vacuum in one's head. And dogs and crows, of course.

These had to be shooed out of the way or scared off with waving scarves, for they might be the roving messengers of Yama come to claim the soul for their sovereign, or evil spirits bent on similar mischief. The way these outcasts sensed the body of a dead person was uncanny; they slunk out of holes in chatai hutting and out of doorways and unlikely-looking under-growth, or swooped down from the sparse green roof which the palms rigged over the village of Mahim, and circled the procession both on the ground and from the air, as though showing the way. Premchand, his son Lakshman, Ranjit, Jagnath, the Ajit brothers, Mr. Varma, even Vijay himself, all waved at one time or another, although none really believed in spirits any more. And sunlight, shredded by the grove's roof, dappled the bier without pause and gave Kandubai's face the kind of flitting, deceitful life which a picture-frame sometimes gives in brilliant light. In those moments her necklace and ear-rings would light up distressingly and the brocade of her sari would seem to glitter with a sheen altogether ghostly. She had been decked in her best, as befitted a believer of the old ways, but all of it would not follow her into the flames. Jagnath would take off the jewels at the appointed hour and they would be placed in her room at home and left intact for a whole year.

'Hari-bol! Hari-bol!'

They halted in an open patch of wasteland and Jagnath put a few grains of dry and wet rice in her mouth, to assuage her thirst and hunger. This, too, he would not have done had she not wished it. It was the belief of the humble classes that the emissaries of the other world sometimes contended for the soul of the dead and that therefore time must be allowed for the correction of any possible error in the rival claims; hence the stops. But it was a widespread custom, and custom had been three-fourths of her forty-seven years. To tired Vijay, the halt was simply an agonizing delay in an already torturous journey.

' "I am the road of the good; the comforter; creator; witness; resting place; asylum; and friend. I am birth and dissolution, repository of all things and the inexhaustible soul of all nature." '

The Brahman intoned with a throaty depth that seemed to flout the morning sun and the whirring of palm leaves. Once more Jagnath crouched by the bier with his cupful of rice. He was an old man now, with an old man's features and movements.

That was how he had appeared downstairs after the first funereal oblation, and how his scion would see him from this day onward; a man passing from outward middle age to inner petrifaction reminiscent of octogenarians, robbed of sensibility and the power to love; fumbling and unsure of himself. This marriage had been all that a mild-tempered Hindu could hope for in this life; it had given him passion with compassion, trust with realism, and sustenance with a complete give-and-take; it had made him understand, in a way all his own, the interdependence of personal fates—a clean enough slate for any ancestor. And now the habit—for that was what it had become—was at an end and the future would be filled with familiar debris and a storehouse of pictures which he would be unable to adapt or exchange. To his son, dully observing the ritual shuffling of his parent, it seemed unfair that a relationship so well fulfilled should cost so much.

After the Nai had done his work, the women had bathed the body once more to remove his defilement, because a Nai, with all his usefulness, was after all the lowest of the low. They had dressed her in a brocade sari from the heirlooms in her camphor chests and hung her with the better jewels from her collection; Jagnath's last Divali present was given a place of honour. While the priests stirred the mixture of pancha-gavia—five products of a cow—and the women lamented, Jagnath had put the ring of darbha grass on his finger and performed the sacrificial worship. Then coloured rice was placed on her forehead and garlands around her neck and the rite went on through the night, so that in the small hours of the morning many a neighbour on the rock appeared in his window and bowed his head in the direction of Villa Ram. Dawn had come at last out of a cool sky, painting the assembled family ash-grey, one after another, finding some asleep, some still muttering. Lord Yama and his rout had been warded off so far—the Brahmans made sure of that. Then, as the first sparrow twittered under the windows and the last garden mouse scuttled for its hideout, they had gone to sleep for a couple of hours in order to be wakeful for the march to the Mahim cremation grounds. The younger priest took over from his elder; the fire must not cease for a moment, lest Kandubai's struggle for liberation receive a setback. Vijay dropped off as soon as he lay down, but the waking brought him no strength or consolation, only a throbbing headache and a flailed feeling.

And now, as Jagnath fell back wiping his eyes, Ranjit turned to Tara and asked:

'How many more stops?'

'This is the second and the last,' Tara replied.

'You look awfully tired. Did you sleep at all?'

'One hour, maybe.'

She was in plain white, like Munu, like the rest of the subdued company. Her eyelids drooped. She seemed to have matured overnight, with all the awkward tangibles of too sudden a growth, and little Munu could not be persuaded to leave her side for a second.

' "Obeisance to Thee, O moon-coloured One; obeisance to Thee, O Lord of Universe; obeisance to Thee, O Divine Shape; show us the path to bliss!" '

'Kaman, kaman!'

'Hari-bol . . .!'

They moved on, into the grove once again, into the smell of seaweed which now met them more strongly. New pariah dogs crept out of the refuse heaps and scattered at their threats. Tara sobbed, blew her nose, clutched her younger sister with an air of despair and protection. The litter bearers changed several times. An old fisherwoman came out of her hut and touched the pole of the litter with deep reverence. Vijay's migraine pulsed up anew and he took up the chant in order to forget it; by then he had trained himself not to look at the face on the bier, even though the sun continued to animate it. His pain, too, had somehow been taken from him and strewn all over, and little separate tongues of it seemed to flutter through the air above the procession and way ahead of it, so that it was hard to guess if they would ever again reassemble and reside in him and give him the kind of blunt, all-displacing pang which the catastrophe called for. 'Read, read!' said one recent picture, 'Promise me!' said another. They soared up and sped away, each in its own callous manner, and none had any bearing whatever on the swollen eyes of Tara or the ravages of Jagnath's face or the baleful slump of Ranjit.

The woods parted to disclose the calm surface of the Mahim cove, and they arrived at the burning ghat. More priests stepped forth from the lime-washed, two-storied mandir by the side of the ghat; they were anointed and ash-smeared. The pyre, too, was ready; stealthy, efficient-looking attendants stood by it, ready to spring at the priests' bidding. A basket of fresh flowers, a pot of water, a length of fibre rope, an urn—these had been set in one corner; ash heaps of a previous fire in another.

'This was how I left my own mother,' Ranjit said at his elbow. 'I was younger than you, only a boy. I did not believe I would laugh ever again.'

'I feel like that,' Vijay said.

'May they both be blessed. Kandubai was a true Rajput. I wish now I had known her better.'

' "I am death and immortality; I am never-failing time; the preserver whose face is turned to all sides; I am the revival and destination of the dead. . . ." '

'I wish that our priestly class spoke a purer Sanskrit,' Ranjit said, suddenly vexed. 'This slurring is an insult to the dead.'

Vijay detached himself, to complete the semicircle of inner family which the officiating Brahman indicated with his hand. As the prayers, invoked over the logs to consecrate them, were being pronounced, the other priests sprinkled holy water upon them and the mourners cast silver coins at their base. This done, Jagnath divested his dead wife of jewels and the women burst into tears. The sight was poignant and somehow supernaturally exposed, as no other had been so far, and still Vijay awaited the oncoming rush of despair. Perhaps this was the arid waste of the night before, when pain had coursed through him like a mortal fever and anguish had sat on his mind like a tightly-fitting millstone. Yet despair and a stubborn disbelief there was, caused, as he would remember afterwards, by the spectral figure of his father denuding his one companion of the glittering tokens of his affection. It was done in silence. One heard the click of the clasps as they came asunder, the swish of the brocade, and his sobs; one feared that he would not dare to rise and endure the rest. But Tara stepped forward quickly and took his arm and helped him up. Vijay held him from the other side. ' "This is the time to give to him who deserves Your gifts. It is for you to give, O Compassionate One; with this I will be content." '

The body was lifted to the pile and secured with rope. Jagnath stumbled three times around it and the oldest Brahman spread the paste of panchagavia over the logs. Each member of the family placed a grain of rice in the body's mouth and said a prayer over it. Then all was ready. A helper brought the lighted torch to the Brahman, who gave it to Jagnath.

' "I see You crowned with a diadem, armed with a mace and shield, a blaze of effulgence on all sides, difficult to look upon, more resplendent than a thousand suns, and more inscrutable. . . ." '

His lips twitching, his whole frame weighed down by the crushing and wordless burden, Jagnath raised the torch.

'Hari-bol . . . farewell. . . .'

The fire caught on; the breeze wafting over the low walls of the ghat fanned it to little vortexes of flame, and these spurred one another to yellow leaps of frenzy. Ghee simmered, garlands shrivelled and darkened; incense burned with a tang. Poking here and adding there, the charnel helpers nursed it and guided it. Above the snapping brushwood and hissing logs the chant rose an octave higher and the many dirges commingled in one long lamentation. Jagnath stepped back, into the arms of his son and elder daughter.

' "Obeisance to You, Vasudev, in whom all beings abide; obeisance to you, Lord of our faculties!" '

'It is done. Go back now!' Radabai Premchand said. 'Now it is up to the Brahmans. . . .'

'Hari-bol! Hari-bol!'

'It is done!'

'Kaman! Kaman!'

' "I am the birth and dissolution, the hope and repository. . . ." '

Soon the fire ranged all over the litter, puffing and billowing into live grey fumes; the edges of the pall curled up and caught on too. Aghast, Vijay saw the black tendrils grope across each other, then twine swiftly and race over the white expanse; a black column seethed up inside the grey one, a chrysalis leaving the cocoon, and the uneasy air coiled, battened and ginned it. Streaks pregnant with the odour of matter drifted inside the courtyard for a while, causing the youngest Ramsingh to cough through her tears. Then a new gust cleared all but the obstinate heart of the conflagration.

'Come, Tara, it is finished,' Radabai said hoarsely. She took the girls by the shoulders and pushed them towards the exit. The mourners fell in a double file to let them pass.

'Munuji, the peerless one . . .!'

Jagnath offered no resistance when his son gripped his elbow and led him away.

' ". . . hope and repository . . ." '

' ". . . from this birth to the next and last one . . ." '

Some villagers and their children had gathered beyond the waiting cars on the street, but, like the usual Indian crowd, they lingered at a safe distance and did not speak. They stared at the shaking sisters and the elderly lady consorting them, and at the stricken old gentleman who could see so little that he had to be guided to the car by his son, and at the rest of the people filing out of the gate in two's and three's. One small boy clapped his naked belly and sang out for baksheesh. To the astonishment of his parents, this was readily tossed by at least two men in the company.

4

'AND now what?' Ranjit asked when the Punjab Mail groaned over the last hump in the Western Ghats and heaved on to the plain of inland India. 'I mean, when you go back to Bombay . . .?'

'I don't know yet. Probably some kind of job. I hope with flying in it.'

'Then it is good-bye to the pilgrims?'

'For the time being, yes.'

'I am very sorry, Vijay. You have had many misfortunes since you returned from Europe. It was the same with me, many years ago. Home is never the same if you leave it for any length of time.'

'Yes, that's true.'

On the plateau, the ribbing of earth and rock ran altogether northward, as though a slighted god had tugged at it from one end of the basin, and the view was unlovely save for the blue rivers of shadow flanking each rib. Villages clung to the railway lines and to the main roads like colonies of microbes, and the roads themselves, crossing the blurred region to and fro, held the landscape in a languid truss and kept it from fading altogether. Here and there was a flattened trail of smoke, a smouldering haystack in a field, maybe another train . . .? Night was not far off. Soon it would arrive and blanket the plain with no regard for past or future, caste or creed, loss or redemption.

Ranjit went on remembering—it was the blue hour. He had shed everything but a featherweight muslin shirt and his sleeping pyjamas. His face, too, bore an air of nights without sleep.

'It is not that the land and the people have forgotten one. They are so terribly slow with their recognition. When I came back eight years ago . . .'

Vijay listened on with half an ear.

His mind still tarried over Ranjit's mention of home. He thought that 'home,' too, had ceased to be the stable and rock-like thing it had once been.

Every time one changed, it changed. When one accepted it, it accepted one. When one needed it badly, it became patronizing. And if one resisted it—why, it simply left a man to his own poor devices. His thoughts harked back to the funeral and the first ten days of mourning, and he came to the conclusion that home for him was a stalemate. He had done everything demanded of him, and more from his own impulse, and now there was nothing more he could do that would in any way lighten or gloss the picture. For all immediate purposes, his land and people had at last reclaimed him—but not fruitfully. His cocksureness was gone and his conviction of superiority was gone, as though he had never possessed them. Plans had been shelved, ambition had gone by default—replaced by uncertainty and a desire to create no trouble; he was on the crossroads, with no bridge behind him and no materials to build another in front of him. 'What you need is a synthesis of the old and new'—but the venerable Mr. Varma had said that with averted eyes, as if he doubted that there was any hope for it.

'I remember how shocked I was to find a cow in the Victoria Terminus after ten months of Europe,' Ranjit was saying.

Synthesis indeed! He, too, remembered a couple of cows grazing away peacefully in the middle of the Juhu flying field. Could anyone synthesize them with an airplane trying to take off at the same time, in the same place? The India of the airplane was not the same as the India of the cow, but they insisted on rubbing elbows; and rubbing elbows was not the same as synthesis. This Mr. Varma did not know because he had never lived outside his own country, and perhaps that was the cause of his complacency. And at the viceregal lodge in New Delhi the splendidly caparisoned guard was often nuzzled by a castaway Brahmany bull; roaming chickens thwarted the dignity of peacocks in the courtyards of maharajas; straw huts adjoined some of the most up-to-date hospitals in India. That was how synthesis looked from outside. The old for ever shadowed the new and neither failed to swallow the other completely. This was the face India turned to the world at first acquaintance, and very often at the second and third and fourth—a face both humble and grotesque, engaging and disenchanted. He remembered how strongly this had impressed him on his return last January and how soon the impression had been watered down in a sea of general unconcern, in spite of his deeper knowledge.

'And look at me to-day. I have a cow in my own garden and do not even see it. . . .'

That was true also, but it was no synthesis. Variety and garishness blunted the human capacity for perception quite as much as a lack of them. The newcomer, recoiling in horror before his first riksha, used one without a qualm six months later. Another, who stared at the wooden plough of the peasant, took artistic photographs of it in a year's time. Acceptance of the situation brought about a new viewpoint; new viewpoint meant a change of the original conscience. Thus neither a foreigner nor an Indian of the old dozing school would ever feel acutely about India's wretchedness; he only paid it lip service. Only a man with two kinds of experience, egged on by the devil of discontent in him, could go on feeling strongly about this country, and he should by preference be young and anti-synthesis; he should definitely not be religious, because too rigid a faith was likely to immobilize his other urge and defeat whatever good intentions he might have had. Yes, a cow did have a whale of a lot to do with this business of synthesis, only that it couldn't be synthetized itself. That was why, among other things, the stalemate seemed so absolute for the time being and why Mr. Varma's kindly meant warning was no help really.

But some of the others seemed to be faring much better.

'I had a note from Uday lately,' Ranjit said. 'He is at Benares. It seems his kind of life is beginning to pay dividends. He tells me he has reached a higher form of samadhi.'

'I am very glad for him.'

'Here likewise. He fasted and prayed and mortified himself so much.'

'But he succeeded, that's the main thing. Home to him is in a trance, and he wishes for nothing better.'

'I didn't think he would.'

And there was Salim Haq, too, although he could hardly be said to come under 'Hindu Endeavour.' He had gone over to the Tata Airlines at Juhu and taken a job in their office, a part-time jobber and part-time novelist. Salim did not particularly care what his land and people thought of him, and perhaps that was because he was a Muslim and a fatalist, and because India had not been the same to him since the passing of the Moguls; and perhaps he just aimed lower and chose his targets more wisely; perhaps being cynical about things made everything less painful. It was hard to know with one so artful and so bland. But he had finally parted company with that wretched Parsi widow of his and the new freedom was having a wonderful effect on his writing. 'Now I can do the two things I like best,' he had told Vijay on the terrace of Villa Ram on the second night of mourning. There was no hint of adjustment, no urge for introspection, no good or evil about it. He had simply swapped jobs, thrown out a nuisance and heaved a sigh of relief.

Then there was Tara—a most unexpected surprise, if one were to judge from past history.

'She was really a wonder,' he told Ranjit during the first pause in the reminiscences.

'Who, Vijay?'

'Tara. It was not to be believed that only a month before she was a rebel in a court of law.'

'Was she in court? How splendid of the girl. There goes another true Rajput.'

On the way home from the funeral he had recalled a promise he once made to his mother, that he would undergo a purification rite soon after his return from overseas; he had put it out of his mind and done nothing about it for many months. It had not been an excessive debt, nor had she spoken of it again until recently, but the recollection on that particular morning had given him such an overpowering sense of guilt that he decided to do it forthwith. It was something, he felt, that might be suitably given back right away, in partial reparation of everything which he could have, but had not, done for his mother. But Tara had stopped him on the staircase.

'Not now, Vijay,' she had said. 'First the room must be cleaned and shut, and afterwards we will all bathe and eat.'

'I'm not hungry.'

'Neither am I, but the others must be fed. They're in our house and care. And it is the way to do it.'

He demurred a little at the new note of authority in her voice, but bowed to it eventually. She had stopped crying and was temporarily beset with duties. When Rajuram the Elder and the cook came forward to receive their orders for the day, it was clear that a complete shift of responsibility had quietly taken place from one week to another. The change came to the servants quite naturally; to them the traditions of household were immutable, and Tara was their present heir.

'The pandal is ready,' Rajuram reported.

'Food, too,' the cook said.

'Good. Bring out the betel nut.'

She was a revelation, even in the dark mood of the day.

And while the mourners went to wash their hands in token of a more thorough oblation, she helped Radabai Premchand and Jagnath to clean up the living-room. They removed the grass matting from the floor and threw a clean sheet over the cot, but did not touch the two books or the vessel of Ganges water. The priest placed a new water urn on the bedside table and hung a grass thread above it—enabling the departed one to climb down and quench her thirst in the first ten days of mourning. They echoed several prayers after the priest and set up two large screens in front of the cot; this was an adaptation of the old practice of locking the death-room for a whole year. Tara helped Rajuram to pass out the betel nut, and later took everyone upstairs for the ritual bath of cleansing.

'Keep your clothes on while you're in the shower,' she admonished her brother. 'Otherwise the oblation would be for nothing. Change when you come out.'

It did not occur to him to question this sudden zeal for orthodoxy and he merely thought that she had been moved to it by something like his own feeling of past inadequacy. He stood in his bath fully dressed and performed a greatly simplified prayashitta ablution, feeling that he was doing the right thing. This bath used to be the first ritual a Hindu returning from overseas had to undertake, but his act was a mere token version and the delay did not strike him either as an outrage of his reason, as he once supposed it might do, or as a trite superstition. The water did cool his mind as well as his body. At one point, too, the flow seemed to melt and

167

wash away the reek of the last two months and also his sense of guilt. He came out of it feeling that his mother and Tara had not been far wrong, and that he had fulfilled the only promise for which it was not too late. He had made a gesture, and as such it would be accepted.

And downstairs Tara presided over the large and silent meal, coaxing her parent to eat in an unconscious manner of equality. She pushed the tray towards him time and again, saying, 'Eat, pitaji, eat; you have not touched any food for five days.'

She saw to the service and to the guests and still managed to stand guard over her father and take a protective interest in little Munu. When the post-funeral ancestor worship was resumed, she sat down in front of the ladies and pronounced the prayers more gravely than many a male relative. And in the ten days in which the proper remembrance of Kandubai was continued, in which her spirit was said to linger around the house and soar above it, as though unwilling to depart altogether, in which countless gruels were mixed and numberless flowers and all kinds of fruit offered, Tara remained steadfast and a comfort to everybody. She spoke more softly and cried no more; what she said seemed always to be on the side of discretion and common sense. The child demonstrator and college rebel were no longer; the fiery glance and impetuous shake of the tresses had been distilled in a purposeful look that seemed to enjoin: Help me to carry on.

'Are you asleep?' Ranjit said from his bunk.

'Not yet.'

'Thinking?'

'Yes, Ranjit.'

'I meant to have asked you before. Whose notion was it to take the ashes to the Ganges?'

'Mine.'

Ranjit tossed over restlessly and turned out the light. The full moon looked into the compartment with a bloated yellow face so near that they could read it from their pillows. A Central Indian moon, like no other in all the world.

'You loved her very much, did you not?'

'Yes.'

'And now everything is upside down . . . like this compartment, when I switch off the light?'

'Yes. We're again single persons, not a family.'

'How well I know the feeling! It was the same with me when father and I remained alone. We were thrown upon each other and we branched out independently. But I had no sisters. They should make a difference.'

'I hope so. Just at the moment I don't know anything.'

Ranjit pondered, watching the moon sway from side to side, then: 'Vijay,

I will tell you something. I have decided to accompany you to Hardwar. I, too, threw some ashes into the river in front of Harki-Charan Ghat. I was younger than you. Will you suffer my company?'

'Of course, dear Ranjit.'

'And afterwards I shall go home, to my paintings and records, and perhaps you shall come with me?'

'I would, but I'm supposed to be in Delhi at the end of this week. It is an old engagement.'

'What a pity, truly. Then we shall have to part at Hardwar. Still, we shall have two days together. Where do you think we are now?'

'Nearing Bhusaval, most probably.'

'It is a very hot night, is it not? I think I shall go to sleep, or try to. Good night, Vijay.'

'Good night, Ranjit.'

Up ahead, in the pale shroud that bound this many-headed land once a month, and with more forgiveness than any emperor or politician could have done, the shriek of the engineer's whistle rent the air at short intervals. The pitch never varied; it tore into the night curdling the earth and staggering the dreams of peasantry on both sides, then darted over the plain and spent its impatience over the jheels and forest. Faster and huskier the engine seemed to pant in its wake.

'Do you know, Vijay,' Ranjit said from the dark, 'I am reminded of our little talk a few nights ago. I liked your old friend, Mr. Varma, very much, but I do not think I see eye to eye with him. Who is he, by the way?'

'An old friend of ours. Used to be a journalist, but does everything nowadays. Now he works for Congress.'

'I enjoyed his version of the Gita, and one especially "He that abstains to help the rolling wheels of this great world, lives a lost life " I couldn't go to sleep listening to the wheels directly beneath us.'

'But it's true, isn't it?'

'I do not believe it is.' He lit a cigarette, in a mellow mood. 'This whole country denies the statement. The villager who paints the linga Siva-red denies it. I deny it each time I dig out an old Rajasthani miniature. We want no wheels and don't wish to hear them rolling. We want our hookahs and our women, both suitably scented to be sure . . . so that we can lie back and dream. Our holy men want the same thing, only without sex. Do you know why?'

'Tell me.'

'Because we are not like the others. No, I am not being a racial snob either. Listen to me, Vijay. Mr. Varma may know his Gita, but I know *him* and other thousands like him. We don't wish to be awake, if there is a chance to sleep. I have thought about it ever since you left Dehra Dun. It is a great force in our lives . . . this desire to daydream, stagnate, sleep . . .

169

and we like it. Europeans want to be up and about all the time. We only want a corner where we can lie down and moon.'

'You're making too much of it. I don't want to sleep if I can help it.'

'Something you picked up in Europe, no doubt. But it is only in your brain. Not in your blood.'

'In my blood, too, I am sure.'

He propped himself on the pillow in order to see the moon better and be reassured by the snort of the train's head. The whistle seemed to be mocking Ranjit.

'I don't think about it often,' he told him, 'but when I do it is very clear. Like just now, for example.' He raked his memory for the other highlights of that discussion with Mr. Varma. 'I think him right and you wrong,' he went on. 'There was another line I remember. "For the upholding of thy kind, action thou shouldst embrace." That's how I think and how I feel.'

Ranjit drew a leisurely reddish circle with the ember of his cigarette.

'For that matter, dear Vijay, I could quote you more than one-half of it,' he said. 'All would prove nothing more than that the man who wrote the Bhagavad-Gita thought action a lot of hocus-pocus. Dust to be thrown in the eyes of those who did not like a society composed entirely of priests and yogis. He, too, wanted to sleep, but the hand that fed him had to be justified. So he made it into a stand for his nobility. Listen: "Therefore do thou always perform actions which are obligatory, but without attachment." Do you detect the cunning . . .?' He gurgled lightly to emphasize the question, then added: 'Continue to feed me, he says to the hand, but do not expect anything in return. And lest the hand begin to falter, he puts in quickly: "By performing such actions thou wilt attain the Highest." My dear Vijay, this is all the action he would have you indulge in. Nothing more and nothing less. If you like wakefulness better than sleep, Gita is simply not your book.'

'There are so many like me, not wishing to sleep.'

'It is possible, Vijay. But those who do wish are many more.'

'I can't believe it.'

Now the long line of coaches thundered through a station siding and the clatter seemed to bring down the sky and rub it against the earth. He felt himself hurled through chaos and obstacles, always forward, always on and higher, and the shriek at the head of the train seemed to point the way without divulging the goal.

'I can't believe it,' he repeated. 'If that were true, all life would be a cheat.'

'Does it not look like that?' Ranjit said.

Vijay did not answer. He remembered the long evenings with his father and Mr. Varma, in the days when he was only a stripling on the verge of perception, when the Gita was still no more than a melody of sound and metric perfection. While the two men waded through the verses and pored over the hidden messages, tasting here and rejecting there, he just sat in one corner and drank their simple beauty. Half-hints, doors firmly barred on meaning, sudden soarings towards sun and song, twitchings under the ribs, eyes brimming with such happiness that tears were often a part of it—this was the impact of the Gita on a mind that had not yet limbered up. But that couldn't remain so for ever, of course. He grew up. He began to discern. While never losing the ear for the sheer music of that book, he began to see it with other eyes and grasp it with another mind. The beauty of it, people said, lay in its unfathomable depths; like a piece of difficult South Indian music, it would yield new joys at each new rendering. As long as he lived, they said, he would be tied by those early revelations and the bond itself would be worked upon by that legion of influences that pass under the sketchy title 'school of life.' He would think of the Gita at all vital moments of his life, but in a steadily changing frame of mind.

Renouncing all action to Me, with mind centred on the Self, cleansing yourself of hope and selfishness—free your mind from fever!

And now Ranjit's version suddenly sounded so watertight that it left him a little breathless. Which was right then? Sleep or wakefulness? Should one perform or renounce? Should one fold into oneself, like his ascetic Uncle Uday, or retire with one's past, like his father Jagnath, whose personal incentive to wakefulness had been gutted as late as a week ago? Was one to erase the obvious from one's life simply because it was the line of least resistance and because some beautifully spun words claimed that it was the meritorious thing to do . . .?

He turned the idea over in his mind and made an honest attempt to see himself.

I am weak, he said to himself, and undecided. I do not think clearly. I just swarm with all sorts of attachments. I am a hybrid in the prime of my career. My attachments are so many that life without them would not be worth the bother. But should that bar me from the rewards of an upright existence? How can I perform actions and renounce them at the same time: How can anyone?

No longer concerned with the music of the verses, he delved into them for the last time, with all the frank clearheadedness which the train wheels would permit him. Performance of duty—duty by any definition, Gita or otherwise—was action itself. This was plain to him. Sifting the personal motive from action—another name for attachment—meant reducing that action to a mystical freak for its own sake. If that was the highest in existence, as the priests would have it, it was a starved, mathematical state, without particular attraction. This, too, was clear now. Then what remained? *That* wasn't clear at all.

His family remained, among other things, with Tara as a temporary stop-gap in a great void, with his father needing solicitude and support. Villa Ram remained, for they would now not dream of letting it go. Then the ash-urn—which he would presently empty into the Ganges and then break into a hundred pieces. Then Ranjit—who would have you believe that he was really not there. Then the train—which itself bore him onward. And later: The flying meet at Delhi, return to Bombay, maybe a post with Tata Air-lines, buckling down to a job of work, another bright plan, another Anglo-Indian, and then, who knows! maybe marriage and a new outlook. All that was there, if one didn't go to sleep. It was not a synthesis, but it was no daydream, either. It was action of one kind or another—Ranjit and his fancies notwithstanding!

Action is an aspect of me! he thought. If it were not, there would be no karma either!

He began to feel less humble about himself. The longer he saw himself in this light, the better he felt. I am a man of action, he reflected, not of meditation. The affirmation sent a warm glow through him—the reflexive counterpart of rational independence. All explanations of life and mankind were a matter of temperament at bottom. Some condemned, others upheld. He simply went on. Blundering on and on in a stream of one's deeds might conceivably turn out to be a one-way passage, but its mere momentum was hope. He believed fervently that somewhere at the far end of this hope was hope's fulfilment, even if partial. To try and anticipate it seemed eminently worth his while.

'Good night, Vijay,' Ranjit said again. 'Try to get some sleep.'

'Good night, Ranjit.'

Harking back to the recent years he realized that it couldn't have been otherwise. Activity was a wave—a crest and a slough at the same time. If one performed it, one was equally performed upon. One stumbled from exhilaration to the dumps, from loveliness to monsters, from dismay to hope, from meanness to value—growing in breadth and stature. To arrest that stream at any stage was to justify the past and qualify for the future; the willing of it was personal fulfilment in cameo. A man of action fulfilled himself as often as he glanced over his shoulders, and he could do that once or a hundred times or never—it was up to him.

Crashing through the night and through siding after siding, whipping up invisible funnels of dust, rocking the villages and hillocks to their foundations, the Punjab Mail sounded as though it were hammering away at the same point.

Sixth Chapter

✿✿✿✿✿✿✿✿✿✿✿✿✿✿✿✿✿✿✿✿✿✿✿✿✿✿✿✿

1

THE first spring festival, Vasant Panchami, had set the pace for men and women alike. They had gone to the temples in joyful droves and prayed to Goddess Sarasvati and made their offerings; women had dodged their husbands' advances for one day. A good time was had by all, save perhaps the Muslims, whose sad month of Muharram was about to begin. Now Holi was around the corner—the second and still greater holiday of spring, in which bonfires would blaze from one end of Hindustan to the other and each caste would burn an effigy of its own. Already advance parties of merrymakers strolled the streets, throwing coloured dust and singing bawdy couplets to Holika, the giant she-demon whom Lord Krishna slew at the dawn of history; the boisterous spirit swept village after village, town after town, fusing irresistibly with another release of spirit, even more triumphant than the first. Foreigners shook their heads and said, 'How these blighters manage to mix religion with politics!' and the accusation had only a limited hearing in the clubs. 'What have demons to do with elections!' they said, huffed. What indeed!

In the early months of 1937 the provincial elections had brought the Hindus their greatest victory of the century—that was all. They had won seven provinces out of eleven and the event had flushed even the bleakest doubter. It did not matter that the victory nominally belonged to Congress, beyond doubt the largest and most disciplined party in India. It was the heyday of Hinduism and Bharat Mata, the era of Vikramaditya and Ram come to life in a modern setting. The peasant would now get his steel plough-share, his land debt would be remitted and his children would go to school at the government's expense. Indians would run their own lives, at any rate in the provinces. The British, they said, had given them the Act of 1935 in the hope that it would send them squabbling among themselves, perhaps to forget their dreams of freedom; but they had seen through the guile and come out on top; they had refashioned the trap into a master weapon against bureaucracy; they said, 'We have won the elections to prove our strength, and now we shall need more than your tricky Act.' The law-makers in Delhi wondered where all this would stop. And then, suddenly, it was again spring and the gulmohars hung out those flaming red bracelets and girls began to walk to the wells with teasing step and their bodices seemed too tight all of a sudden; Lord Krishna lurked in every tree and his flute could be heard over the hills and plains. It was a way life had with religion, and religion with men's minds, and men's minds with unwanted Acts.

By a margin narrower than he would care to remember, Baboo Ravi Premchand squeezed into the assembly, past a popular rival of the Congress left wing. He would not go into office until the party signal had been given; this would take some time, for they now refused to work the Act. Mean-while, his knowledge of publicity was needed in the campaign of recrimina-tion against the Act now afoot; he would probably go to Delhi for the meeting of the All-India Congress Committee, there to get his orders. Already his newspapers screamed defiance. The house at Juhu overflowed with fellow damners and well-wishers of all ranks, especially after the last visit of Mr. Gandhi. This skinny little saint had spent one week in a thatched hut in Premchand's palm garden, and the two men had been seen walking the sands in the evenings and saying prayers together; afterwards no one was surprised at the growth of Premchand's political stature. Now Radabai Premchand and her son Lakshman had difficulty in sorting out the callers and brewing tea for all of them. One thing with another, it had been a good season and everyone felt that being born Indian had acquired a fresh significance.

Everyone, that is, save Salim Haq. His promotion to superintendent in the Tata office at Juhu had been followed by the publication of his novel. The book had caused a stir. The story was frankly autobiographical, and readily understood by his few friends, but he had not been able to resist stocking it with a good deal of caustic sentiment on the subject of Muslims and Parsis generally. Muslims felt aggrieved because he was their co-religionist and because his railings against Islam's old guard ran counter to the illusion that all Islamis were brothers. Parsis rose up in arms because the picture of their licentiousness was accurate. He received calm notices in the British-owned periodicals, but all other reviewing denominations took him apart. The Parsi panchayat met formally to express chagrin; an angry society of Muslim young men challenged him to an open-air discus-sion, a challenge he ignored wisely; women eyed him curiously and men rolled their eyes to heaven if they happened to pass him in a public place. He had to explain himself before the managing board of his company, a Parsi enterprise, and was saved only by the memory of his pioneer flying work. And the widow, Mrs. Dastoor, who had so trifled with his affection realized the enormity of her mistake and made an overture for peace,

174

embodied in a beautifully carved cigarette case of solid gold, which he had the presence of mind to keep without acknowledging. Invigorated by it all, Salim went his own way and made no plans for the future. The rash presently died down in the high places and became endemic in its proper sphere—salons of the intelligentsia and women's minds—and Vijay learned once more that in his country one upheaval did not preclude another, and that his people lavished their best hours on tragedy and comedy alike and that there was enough time for everything at all times.

His father was bearing up better than they had dared to expect. He had lost much weight and become almost gaunt, and there came to linger about his face an uncertain cloud of distress which somehow blurred his age but gave his look a hunted, searching quality that made his children, after these many years, behave in his presence and choose their words more carefully than before. By and large he fulfilled their hope and did not pine away. The general exultation of the country barely ruffled him; he went to his office and remained a dutiful official. The economy of Villa Ram had been curbed severely and the task had not been pleasant; there had been a reshuffling of the staff and retrenchment had been carried to the minutest corners, and Tara had picked up the threads of the household with noble zeal. A quiet, thought-provoking nostalgia settled on the home, in which life proceeded apace with fewer mishaps and greater resignation.

Vijay looked for a job. He saw the heads of large concerns and some bank managers, but all was not as simple as he had imagined. 'Yes, yes, isn't it splendid!' they exclaimed, looking at his scrapbooks; the more they read the clearer became their resolution not to have any such violent talents in their offices. Flying was fine, but what about desk experience? And then Holi was only a couple of days ahead and time had to be given to the family and the customary preparations. Everything possible was to be done to distract Jagnath. And then a telegram arrived from Delhi, putting a new slant on all plans.

HAVE BEEN CALLED TO BOMBAY—Mrs. Prashad wired—LOOKING FOR-WARD SEEING YOU STOP CAN YOU ACCOMMODATE THREE OF US. LOVE.

It was typical of her not to indicate the date of their arrival, but since the message came express, Jagnath assumed that they were already on the train and might knock on the door of Villa Ram at any moment.

'Who is the third?' he asked Tara.

'Chanda's sister Hira. She is now fifteen.'

'Hira . . .? Ah, yes, yes! So she is already fifteen? How the time flies!' He scowled a little and scratched his wrist. 'Then the girls shall have the room next to mine. Rana Prashad can occupy mother's.'

'I am so pleased,' Tara said, glancing at her brother.

But Jagnath had gone shuffling into his study—daftar, he called it—and from there into the kitchen and back. This was a habit he had acquired lately. They didn't see him for an hour and had already thrashed out the news among themselves when he returned. His forehead was puckered and he strummed his lower lip with the knuckle of his finger. 'Vijay, I want to talk to you,' he said. He led his son into the daftar and spent the first five minutes gazing out of the window.

'Son, this visit is a greater honour than in the past. Nowadays Rana Prashad is a famous person. We should all do our best to make them comfortable. . . .'

He gazed again, and his son waited respectfully.

'Mrs. Prashad is sure to have a lot of meetings to attend. Perhaps some will be out in the district. If she goes, Chanda and Hira will stay at home. I should like that you and our girls keep them good company. I don't remember how well they know this town, perhaps not well enough. They will want to see it. . . . I suggest that you show it to them. The Victoria gardens, museum, other worthwhile sights.'

'We'll be glad to, pitaji,' Vijay said.

'And I would like to remind you of the promise you made me last year . . . concerning Chanda . . . do you still remember? I cannot help feeling that she would make a most suitable match for you.'

'Wait, please!' Vijay said, pulling abreast of his leaping parent. 'I remember the promise, but it had nothing to do with marriage. You asked me to think about it and I did. I don't want to marry Chanda or anyone else.'

'She is like one of us . . . a good Rajput, even though they come from the hills.'

'That may be so, pitaji. I don't dispute it. I will see that she is happy here, and I would have done it anyhow. I would have done it for her mother too. I like them very much. But please don't ask me to promise more.'

'All right, son. Please do your utmost.' He walked away from the window and paused at the door. 'What was I going to say . . .?'

'I don't know.'

'Ah yes, I remember. You must know your own feelings . . . only the time has come to think about it soberly. If you do not marry her, some other young man will. . . .' He looked into Vijay's face for a sign of impression but none was apparent. 'It would be a shame,' he said, shuffling off again. 'A double shame . . . a fine and beautiful virgin gone and not another opportunity in sight. But as you wish. I was in duty bound to bring it to your notice.'

He went back to the girls in order to plan the domestic dispositions, and Vijay climbed to his room.

So there it was—a really crowded spring, all told.

176

2

LATER that week he made this entry in the old logbook:

The Prashad clan is here. It is good to have guests again. Rana is thinner and better looking than ever, also grander and surer of herself. Hira is a lovely romantic child, such a contrast to out little Munu. Chanda has grown up—too early to say in how many ways. Father dabbling in politics again, under Rana's influence thank God! Hardwar Pilgrim Board is 'awaiting further developments with interest.' Can't say I am. Transport Department officials in Delhi are having 'the matter of your application under active consideration'—can imagine how active! Holi is here! Too many young friends of Rana Prashad are waiting just a little too much on her daughter!

But it was only a sketch, drawn in a hurry, before the holiday hurly-burly caught up with him in earnest.

The first three days were a traditional round. On the day of full moon the girls dug a hole in the garden and planted a castor plant in it, and the family sat around it that night throwing red dust at each other and remembering demon Holika in song and verse. Next day they built a bonfire and Tara improvised a martial dance which was supposed to com-memorate the family virs, men who fell in battle. This amused everyone and moved Vijay to some merciless ragging. Tara retired to the kitchen, vowing never again to show initiative. A dol-swing was hung from the still blooming temple tree by the side of the house, intended for a breather for Lord Krishna after his exertions with a she-demon, and to it a rather stagy puja was offered in due course. Cakes and sweetmeats circulated freely. It was the death of one season, the birth of another. The wheat harvest was in the saturnalia were a short pause before the strenuous tasks of spring. The myths of Holi were many and varied and each part of India remembered only those of their own preference, but whether it was the death of Kama, the god of love, which they remembered, or the death of the giantess Holika, or Krishna's amorous dalliances with the milkmaids of Brindaban, the main idea in remembering them was the same everywhere—to have a good time. It was one of a number of consolation prizes which house-holders received from a religion that put a premium on absolute forbearance —inviting more than comparison with the icy scraps of divine condescen-sion among the Christians. It was Hinduism's most eloquent argument in its own flock. How, Vijay asked himself, could a Hindu peasant ever succumb to foreign missionaries? Before ever staking a claim to his flighty soul, they would first have to double his inalienable quota of laughter and

177

good cheer; they would have to invent a more delightful folklore and learn to caper and make music *and* preside over the lot with a smile, not a hatchet countenance. This the missionaries seemed incapable of doing.

'I haven't had such a lively Holi for donkey's years,' Chanda told him during the festival, borrowing an expression of her mother's.

And that was true of him too.

Then, regretfully, Mrs. Prashad had to begin paying her ladies more attention and this started a series of lengthy daily absences. Sometimes her daughters went with her, sometimes not. She lectured to the local Women's Association, went to meetings and teas in her honour. Once she took Jagnath, Vijay and Tara to a luncheon in town, at which she talked of the unfairness of the '35 Act to Indian womanhood.

There were only four men in the large crowd of ladies. Vijay sat at a U-shaped table, sandwiched between Chanda and a tinkling Parsi matron, and felt very awed. It was his first look at a purely zenana gathering, the articulate vanguard of female India—Hindu, Muslim, Parsi and even Indo-Christian. They seemed to do all the things men did on such occasions, from heckling to loud shabashes and chain-smoking. Far from glancing away coyly when he looked at them, they sized him up with a level gaze, and he thought that there was much defiance in their eyes. They painted their faces and nails, and talked a good deal in a shrill mixture of political jargon and normal gossip; on the whole the gossip was quite frank. Chanda talked with her other neighbour as if determined not to come to his rescue; she laughed often and shook her wrists when the bangles slipped too low, but did not smoke; for no sensible reason at all, this seemed to relieve him Jagnath toyed with his food, attentive and calm on the surface, but Vijay suspected him of being full of regrets. Until the end of the proceedings neither received any enlightenment from the occasion, and Vijay took Chanda to a cinema afterwards wondering if he would be asked again.

When Mrs. Prashad took her first train to Poona, her daughters stayed home—as Jagnath had predicted. This caused only a mild flutter, for the girls were used to their mother's crowded schedules and could well look after themselves. Tara and Munu got on famously with them. From his room on the first floor, he could hear them giggling all day and often well into the night. Jagnath was calmed; he had had fears about Tara, who would be very busy in the kitchen and might show her resentment, and about Munu, who seldom, if ever, left her side. But everything went well and even the friends of Chanda's who came calling in the mornings failed to jar the harmony. These last often drove up in their gleaming American cars and took Chanda walking along the sea wall; one was the son of a rich millowner from Ahmedabad; he later became awkward in Vijay's presence.

Vijay dutifully met all strangers and kept his word to Jagnath. He took

Chanda around and showed her everything he could think of: the view from the terrace gardens of Malabar Hill, the Tower of Silence of the Parsis, where the dead were given over to the birds, the sheen and cobweb of the incomparable Bombay stream—this from the uppermost gallery of the Rajabhai Clocktower. They walked through the Fort and assorted bazaars and later saw the mill quarter. She was a comfortable tourist and gave him as much fun as she received. Then she felt she wanted to see all of it from the air once more, and he drove her out to Juhu, deciding to see Salim about a job at the same time. That was one evening. He took her up in a club machine and flew her over the suburbs and lakeland of Salsette Island, then gave her a cup of tea on the club lawn and asked her to wait while he walked across to look in on his Muslim friend.

'Don't tell me he is still with those Parsis?' she said in surprise.

'Oh yes, and why not? He is the best man they have yet had.'

'I thought his book had made him a gentleman of leisure,' she said.

'Hardly that,' he told her; he went on to explain that the sale had been under two thousand copies and that this wouldn't even pay for Salim's cigarettes. Moreover, the job was a kind of insurance for the continuation of his feud with Premchand; as long as he held on to it, Premchand would regret his rashness. Then he explained why he was going to see Salim.

'Oh, this is good news, Vijay,' she said with real warmth. 'Your father was saying only the other day what a pity it was that you had nothing steady to do. I tried to defend you, but he said I didn't know you as well as he did . . . and that you had changed.'

'Have I, Chanda?'

She sipped her tea and thought. 'Yes, you have, Vijay,' she said. 'I haven't seen you for almost a year and you are a different person already.'

'You too. A different girl. We have all changed.' He signed the tea chit, drank his own cup to the end and got up. 'You, your mother, I, Tara and Munu . . . we're all different. . . . Well, I'll be back in half an hour, Chanda. Ask for more tea if you should want it. Then I'll show you the beach and Uncle Premchand's house.'

Striding across the already damp field towards the offices of Tata Airlines, kicking the lumps of earth which the plane wheels had dislodged in landing, he thought that her observation was quite acute. They had all grown up a little, learned a little, forgotten a little. One might almost say we're meeting for the first time, he mused, thinking of her and her mother. And because of the freshness of discovery and the change in himself, he now saw them less sentimentally and more clearly.

Now he saw more in Mrs. Prashad than an iconoclast after his own likeness. Refutal of purdah must be justified, and she had done that well and conspicuously. Unlike himself, she seemed already to have won full absolution in the field of patriotism, so that now her smoking was more

179

often forgiven than tolerated. Her public life was not what an old-fashioned parent, say, Jagnath, might hold up to his daughters, but it commanded respect and was admirable in many ways; it took courage and often sacrifice; it brought her many snubs and hardships, a high price in any sphere of life. That she came from a good family helped her, because among her ladies wealth was a sign of strength and righteousness, and not of weakness, and her call would therefore be heard where some other might be hushed up. Lately even her widowhood was no longer a handicap.

And for Chanda, to be spared the usual abashment of the term 'modern girl,' it was apparently quite enough to be her mother's daughter. They had a strong affection for each other, deepened perhaps by their isolation in a society of so close a texture. Chanda was not beautiful in the same sense as her mother. When Vijay tried to find out why the fact was not important, he tangled himself in speculation; beauty was a radiation of inner serenity, and for this she was too young. Yet she was most effective— something he had learned soon after their arrival. While Mrs. Prashad's good looks seemed to rest in the immaculate symmetry of her features, Chanda's handsomeness was as yet only frail and promising; though bodily mature, she was still young enough to make her face a playground of her moods; of these an inquisitive zest and sudden relapses into woolgathering were the most frequent. When alert, she bubbled over with an infectious kind of vitality which she also managed to pour into her movements, looks and words, and even leave behind her as a strong whiff; with all his cautious detachment, Vijay found himself a tool of it time and again. In moments of reverie her face would soften in a demure loveliness, rare in one so young, unconnected with serenity. He would often think that there were two of her, an adolescent basking placidly in the effulgence of her mother, and a whimsical child with grown-up ideas and too much knowledge, but the moods would interplay quickly and give him a sense of natural, if not easy, continuity.

When she was in the room, the gamin would seem to multiply and visit the faces of all present, even if she sat quite still; when she talked and the subject happened to be one of her causes, the spirit would dance in and out of her voice like a fugue. Jagnath, who had never quite learned how to talk to his own daughters, talked to Chanda for hours and with apparent enjoyment. She wore her hair in two shiny plaits braided with the flowers of the season, and sported no jewellery other than a row of plain silver bangles on her left arm. Her saris were plainer than her mother's, and she wore them with a light abandon which made up for their lack of colour. As far as it was possible to separate her figure from the usual flattery of a sari, her body seemed fully developed and not without a disturbing attraction. She had her mother's fair and clear complexion, supple and expressive hands and a sprightly way of moving. One thing with another, it was easy to see why the young clods of Lucknow and Bombay paid court with such fervour.

At the other side of the field mechanics were wheeling a passenger plane into the hangar. They pushed, presumably with all their strength, along the broad carpet of light that unrolled itself deep into the dusk of the interior, and the fuselage shimmered on the bright side like the veins of mother-of-pearl. They nudged one another with shouts and groans, and the majestic bird sank slowly into the twilight and lost its shimmer. Then they gathered under the tail and began to talk in their natural voices—that is, still very loud. Seeing him pass, they touched their peaked caps and one of them jettisoned his cigarette behind him; smoking in the hangars was not permitted.

Inside the main office the air was stale. Salim's air-conditioned cubicle was built into the far corner of the building, but the apparatus was out of order and the room smelled stuffier than the rest of the office; the air was tinged with a faint odour of enamel paint. At his desk, Salim looked up with large bloodshot eyes.

'Arre, Vijay bhai! What brings you here?'

'A little plan in which your help is needed.'

'Another pilgrim foolishness?'

'No, Salim. I want a job. In this office.'

The Muslim lurched forward and planted his folded elbows heavily on the edge of the desk.

'Brother, you're better off as you are now,' he said. 'Working for these Parsi slave-drivers is the same as working for your unnameable uncle. If I had any choice in the matter I should walk out at this moment and never come back. But sit down, bhai. Have a cup of tea.'

'Thank you. Chanda is waiting for me over at the club. I came to ask you that one thing. I should like again to fly under you.'

'Pilots are terribly underpaid.'

'Even so, it's more of a principle.'

'There may not be a vacancy.'

'Then a job in the workshop. I don't care what it is, Salim.'

'Ai, ai, so it has come to that!' Salim said.

He leaned back again and locked his long arms behind his head; his eyes, framed in inverted purple crescents, went over Vijay in disbelief. His copious black mane all but hid the little Hindu boy in the picture of the company's wall calendar. The last of the sun, filling the window luminously, divided his thick face into light and dark parts. One of his eyes glittered for a moment; the other, screwed up until it was barely open, faded into the shade and ceased to be present. In the old days this unconscious mannerism had often been a prelude to some personal confidence which, together with

181

the gusty fortunes of the club, had taken their friendship from strength to strength—but now Salim merely blew through his closed lips and sank slowly forward. 'Bhai, it is the wrong thing for you,' he said. 'Terribly wrong. Are you not happy as you are . . .?'

'No.'

'There was a time you were after big things. What happened to them?'

'Nothing, as you know. I am tired of waiting. I don't like being tired.'

A pause, then a knock at the door. A peon thrust his head in and with him came the hum of the departing staff. 'Ready, sir,' he said.

Salim struggled to his feet, gathered the papers on his desk and straightened his uniform in front and at the back. 'Come with me,' he said. 'We can talk while I do my rounds. I shall draw up an application and arrrange an interview. Interviews are the chief difficulty. You will have to behave with enthusiasm.'

'I shall be most eager.'

They walked out of the office in silence. Near the main hangar men were testing a single-engine plane, one at the controls and a second at the propeller, and Salim talked to them and later climbed into the cabin. After a time the engine spluttered and the man near the propeller stepped back and waved to the man at the controls; a rose sheet of flame spouted from the exhausts, lengthening and becoming bright orange as the engine roared more loudly; a loose pane of glass jingled somewhere behind the hangar door. Then Salim came back and took Vijay's arm sociably. He tossed his head at the other side of the field and enounced the words 'Walk back with you' with the gross mouthing of a deaf-mute.

When they were some distance from the roar Vijay said: 'By the way, are you and Uncle Premchand completely finished?'

'We are, bhai. Political differences. Do not be shocked.' Salim stopped, searching the face of his friend; his look was no longer veiled, and the pure air of the evening had smoothed some of the tiredness back into the skin of his face. 'You're surprised, my friend? You think Salim has after all chosen the path of patriotism? In the face of his bitter experience?' And before Vijay could frame a suitable answer: 'Well, it is not so. There must be a limit to forgiveness, even in a broad-minded Muslim like myself.'

Down at the bottom of the field a procession of private cars traversed the open salt flat; the spiralling cloud of dust which they raised marked the boundary of the residential area. Beyond, the bungalows and gardens seemed already very much dimmer.

'It may be a surprise to you,' Salim continued with more feeling, 'but I have accomplished much thinking in recent months. We Muslims have been living in a fool's paradise, as the British say. We thought we were Indians first and Islamis only afterwards. We spoke and dreamed of freedom, the same as you Hindus. We thought we had no other problems. But look, bhai, the elections told us that when the freedom came it would all go to the Hindus.'

'What has that to do with Uncle Premchand, Salim?'

'Plenty, my friend.' In spite of his obvious attempt to sound casual, he couldn't altogether suppress a dire note. 'When your uncle wrote of freedom, he meant a Congress freedom. I was in his office when they prepared the election propaganda. Brother, no Muslim, even a very sleepy one, could have swallowed it. They went out to the villages and said to the Muslims, "Vote Congress and you shall be safe." Then they came back and laughed and said how terrible it was that the Muslim was still free to butcher a cow, such a sacred animal. . . . They talked of putting a stop to it when they came into government. They said . . .'

'Surely that could not upset you?' Vijay said, remembering Salim's various sins against the Prophet.

'They said . . .' He narrowed his eyes and frowned mightily. 'What a coincidence that you should say that! It is just what they said, too . . . even Premchand. "Salim is one of us," he said in a conference. "Salim is an educated Muslim." And they went on abusing the Muslim League and other Muslim bodies as before. And then your uncle called me in one day and said, "Salim, we are at an important stage of our history; you must show that in Marut's Hour." And when I asked him what he meant, he said, "Nowadays every column of my newspapers must be behind the editorial policy." After that, bhai, I could forget my history no longer. I am very tolerant, but this was too much.'

'Tell me one thing, Salim. Are you quite serious?'

'Listen, Vijay, my friend. If I were not serious, I would not be telling you. I don't mind being a bad Muslim before myself, but I do not like your uncle to remind me of it. I do not care for politics any more than you do. I want to be called an Indian, not a minority. I like all meat, and beef especially. I do not like to hear that it makes other people sick . . . or that I should speak Hindi because it is a national language. I love my Urdu . . . it is a language of great beauty. Some of the greatest Indian poetry was written in Urdu. I think these are serious reasons, do you not agree?'

'But this sudden passion?' Vijay said in wonder. 'You were Muslim and I was Hindu when we first met. We have known it all along. Is it not too late for us to be passionate about it?'

A confounded look opened Salim's eyes wide. 'Passionate . . .? Have I spoken passionately?'

'You did, Salim. It is all very new between us. You taught me to fly, remember? Nand was a good friend to both of us. There has never been any difference between us two, except your filthy private life. Why should you suddenly make so much of being a Muslim?'

He meant it, too, for he was finding the drift of the talk quite incongruous.

He stopped and gave Salim a cigarette from his case. He lighted it for him and glanced across the field: they were more than halfway to the club lawn. He said, 'I wonder how late it is?' and looked at his watch and then at Salim. A small, so far never experienced twinge around his heart made him suddenly sad and thoughtful, as though a secret buried away under layers of other memories had been dragged to the surface for an utterly wanton reason. So this was 'communalism,' of which there had been so much glib talk of late? Instead of clasping hands in the sight of freedom and forgetting things that had been, and instead of being generous towards each other, the Hindu and Muslim now searched one another more awkwardly. There was a reason in his sadness too. Only men who had been blessed with the ability to see India as the birds saw it—as they, too, had looked upon it—could feel that sadness and share it, for to them Bharat Mata was one and indivisible. Salim was not sad; his emotion was of a different cast. It was this that made the twinge all the keener.

'What is this country coming to,' he said sincerely, 'if two friends like us start discovering that they have been divided by some politician in Allahabad? What do I care what flesh you eat! We ate the same food in Rajputana, and from the same table. Why should the nonsense of my uncle upset you so?'

Salim ran his fingers through his overflowing hair; one of his eyebrows curved up and remained there.

'I don't know why. Maybe because he and the people like him are now in the saddle.'

'What is that to you?'

'Nothing, brother. Only they will now be saying those same things over and over again, because it will be easy. We have not heard the end of it.'

He stopped with a snort of finality; a slight change for the better came over his drawn features. He, too, pinched his sleeve and read the time carefully.

'So now you see,' he said. 'It is a disease and your people are spreading it. Unfortunately, one cannot go and see a doctor about it.'

'We've got to be our own doctors, Salim.'

One corner of Salim's mouth now twitched almost quizzically. 'And now, my friend, I must go back. Do you really wish to work for these bloodsuckers?'

'It would keep me occupied.'

'Then I shall arrange everything. How is your esteemed father? Your sisters?'

'Much better now. You must come and visit us again.'

'I shall, bhai. I shall.'

This seemed to exhaust the subject for the time being. Vijay promised to call on his friend in a few days' time, to learn of his success with the company; Salim renewed his assurances; his big face relaxed and broke into the old grin. They shook hands English fashion and walked off each towards his own side of the field.

In the hundred-odd yards that separated him from the club, Vijay made half-hearted amends for his terseness by averring his loyalty to Salim Haq despite all outward silliness, and by vowing never to think of him as a Muslim, no matter what happened. He realized that Salim's quandary was awful enough as it was. After all these years of aimless buffeting he seemed to have manœuvered himself out of every shelter his country could have given him, and he had done so in the fond belief that he was avoiding labels. He had got into the hair of more people than might have been wise even for a man of wealth. Now the Parsis, Muslims, Hindus all wanted his skin. Plainly, India liked her men labelled, and Salim couldn't escape it any more than the others. It was bad luck indeed for Salim to start entertaining 'communal' feelings just at a time when all conscious Muslims refused to have any truck with him. Vijay felt sorry about this. The repulsive truth was that there really didn't seem to be any such thing as an 'Indian first'; there were only Hindus, Muslims, Parsis, Sikhs, Jains, Buddhists and Eurasians. Plainly, too, the only people who thought of India as one were the British and their reason was easy to see.

'Have you forgotten me?' Chanda said from her chair. 'Look, it is almost night.'

3

THE hills of Salsette had blued, greyed and finally vanished in the great Indian darkness; the shaded lights of the Tata offices ate into the night steadily, like some famished celestial rodents. In the grass an unknown number of crickets bestirred themselves.

'Let's walk to the beach,' he said, gathering Chanda's things. 'You must see the surf on a dark night like this.'

As they walked, the palm grove rose like a mute wall around them, full of faint life and unspoken memories. Almost at once the gleaming road flowed into the black floor of the forest, though he saw it accurately in his mind— a long tapering corridor of leaning trunks on which the leaves would grate and creak at the slightest breath from the ocean, a rough patch of potholes and loose gravel and then again asphalt for a few hundred yards until it broke off on the ridge of the beach itself. He liked this part of Juhu more than any other; it was more truly Indian. There were little chatai huts in it, exuding smoke and tangy clouds of spices, and its small sounds harked back to the age of Asoka and Vikram, when all India was one and the galaxy of gods was great enough to go round and make everyone contented. It was chastening, too, with its airs of mystery and faith, and also comparatively safe; no tipsy laughter or gale of radio noise would burst upon you when you least expected it; you just walked on and felt that being an Indian was a part of something enduring—sounds, smells and all—which no one, no matter how sophisticated, could ever take away from you. The tapping of Chanda's sandals seemed somehow to belong to it, as did the rustle of her sari. In the end he took her hand and led her along naturally. Her step was so light that he pictured her for one improbable moment floating beside him in the air, a half-materialized bundle of flesh, silk and swishing.

'Salim thinks it can be done,' he said after a time, thinking of his last talk. He already caught himself passing from a sense of assurance to one of absolute certainty.

She understood at once. 'I am very happy for you,' she said.

'He also thinks I am mad. The salary is insulting.'

'Never mind the salary, Vijay. It is a start, that is important.'

'Yes, I told him.'

He adumbrated Salim's spiritual conflict in brief, careless strokes which drew a picture not of Salim but of the hapless background of his loss of faith. Before he realized what he was saying, the wraith of communal unhappiness which he had denied before his friend rose up before his eyes and sharpened into a huge and true picture. He tried to laugh it off, but it would not go. Did she think, he asked of her, that there was anything serious in the Hindu-Muslim cleavage, beyond a few political tricks? Was she a nationalist first and a Hindu only afterwards?

'I don't know enough about it,' she said. 'Salim is probably just a little too vain. Good friends should not allow such things to spoil their friendship.'

'They don't as yet.'

'So why do you worry? Don't talk about it and you won't think about it.'

'There's a lot in that,' he said.

They weathered the potholes, but she lost a sandal; he found it for her with the aid of a match. Then they went off into a lane, bounded by high hedges, which would presently take them to the beach; there was thick dust in the ruts and they flopped through it holding their noses and occasionally coughing.

'I was a little like Salim last year,' he told her when the dust thinned out. 'I mean, cut off from everybody . . . completely alone. I needed the people, but couldn't make myself go to them. I just stood around and waited.'

'You did not give that impression.'

'I was angry most of the time.'

'But no more . . .?'

'No, it's finished. I compromise more easily. I ought to be ashamed of myself, but I am not. I should be doing something worthwhile . . . like that pilgrim idea of yours, but I'm going to be a pilot for a very rich Parsi firm.'

Then the lane steepened and they slowed down unconsciously.

'Wait, Vijay,' she said. 'When there is an Indian government, somebody will do something about it.'

'I very much hope so. Well, here we are. This is the beach.'

The ruts petered out in grass and the lane left them to their own devices. He took her down the creeper-covered escarpment, still warm from the afternoon sun, and to the soft sand where she lurched a little and clung to his hand more firmly.

'That shining line there. That's the sea.'

They walked towards it and the change from night in the grove to night under the open sky was very great. Visibility improved. Dimly, the sands ran south and north in a broad monotone ribbon. The water front of Bandra twinkled in one part of the blackness; in the other Versova was going to bed, its minute cinders guttering one by one. It was fresher, too. Night was like a female giant with a black sheet over her shoulders but with a bared breast—and he remembered the cholis of Bikaneri women when they walked home after dark, their full breasts bouncing, the glass insets of their bodices sparkling in the reflected fires of their homes.

'Nice, isn't it?' he said.

Now that the ground sank softly and the lapping of the surf joined the whirring of the palms, and the yowling pye-dogs merely gave an Indian meaning to the night, he felt freer and better. He thought Rama of the old epic must have felt like that, pacing up and down the beach at Lanka; all surfs were approaches to the unknown, all open skies spoke of infinity.

At the edge of the water Chanda stopped and bent down; next, she splashed in the water beside him. He took off his shoes, too, and they trod the wavy line of sea foam just barely on the inside, and the water was tepid and the sand in it harder than on the shore.

She said: 'I don't know anything about Islam, Vijay, but I like their idea of feet washing before prayers. Water is lovely for the soul.'

'Yes, it is.'

'Our Brahmans must have thought the same thing when they invented our worship. They spend a lifetime in the bath.'

He grinned in the dark; her tone implied a return to impishness. It was true that one couldn't waddle in the sea and remain loftily reflective. He said, 'What a big splash you do make!' and rolled up his trouser legs; he was sure that she had done the same thing with her sari, was probably holding it high above the water, and he wondered if her legs were thin and bent. Europeans were always saying that Indian women had the worst legs in the world.

'You must come out one Sunday and watch the English on these sands. I think they leave their souls at home.'

'What are they like? I mean, without clothes?'

'Very funny . . . not like rulers at all.' And he told her how the European women gadded about in their passive, shameless fashion and how ungainly most of them looked, and how they always seemed to be wearing borrowed swimming suits, many sizes too large; how fat some of them were and how foolishly complacent about it; how the appalling sight had shocked him deeply in the beginning, as impersonal nakedness was bound to, and how he had got used to it with time. And once in a while, which was very rare, a pretty one used to saunter down the beach and atone, at least temporarily, for the importunities of her kind. He told her this with frank malice, and Chanda laughed delightedly. What he didn't tell her was that the Juhu nudity was functional and that it wasn't meant to please. Like most Indians, he was distressed by its casualness, and then contemptuous. Nudity was an intimate thing, to be discovered privately and kept away from strong light for a good legitimate purpose. He knew that if Chanda had walked like that in a two-piece suit in broad daylight, and he had happened to see her, he would have had no respect for her. The reason for that was even less clear than the reason why, now that she was fully dressed, he was guessing the shape of her legs with instinctive if not pronounced interest. Anyhow, he concluded aloud, it was impossible to connect these lobster-pink limbs with the idea of rulers. They were funny more than anything else.

They ambled half a mile up the surf, laughing and being catty. The line of the grove rose up on a crest of sounds that prowled the night and later straggled over the sea. Mongrels howled in the undergrowth, on the ridge and the ends of the bay. Then Chanda gasped and leaped out of the water.

'I stepped on something!'

'Let me see.' He went after her and lighted a match between cupped hands. 'I hope it wasn't a Portuguese man-o'-war.'

'What is that?'

'A kind of floating sea bee that stings. It isn't their time though.'

She wiped her big toe with the handkerchief he gave her. 'I don't think it was that . . . it is a small cut. Maybe a broken shell.'

'Maybe,' he said. 'All the same, you'd better get back into your sandals. We have roughed it enough for one night.'

'And I was on the point of loving it.'

'You still think water is good for the soul?'

'Yes, I do.'

They sat down. The cool moisture seeped through the seat of his trousers and made him shudder pleasurably; he had forgotten everything except how nice it could be out in the open. He raised his arm and squinted at the ember of his cigarette; it was redder, but not brighter, than the nearest star. He dropped it and the ember seared the sky.

'Have you ever seen a meteor, Chanda?'

'Only once. But never in my life did I see a Portuguese man-o'-war.' She giggled a little. 'Why not a British man-o'-war?'

'I told you what I knew. It is not funny when it stings you.'

'I suppose not. I never was stung.'

'You might be one of these days. Splashing up the ocean like that!'

His contentment was only partly of the night; the other part was brought on by Chanda and her flair for lightness when lightness was suitable. She skimmed from attentiveness to flippancy so smoothly that she disarmed him in advance. Two weeks ago he had found it bewildering; now he liked it. Then the inane urge which he had restrained only a little while ago returned once more and he virtually let it choose its own words.

'Chanda, what sort of legs have you?'

She laughed; he thought she had thrown her head back and was laughing at the stars.

'Is it a request or a command?'

'Don't be a Marwari! They never answer a question except with another question.'

'They are fat, like pameloo fruit.' The laugh diminished to a snicker, then to small throaty noises. 'Hairy in the middle.'

'All right,' he said. 'Truth will out sooner or later.'

Lying so calmly he thought that relaxation, the lowest of states among the holy men, had more to commend it than they were prepared to admit. He thought of the women he had known since he left college; with the possible exception of Thelma, none had allowed him to be himself; always they had imposed on him and made him squirm and given him a sense of obligation which even the ultimate pleasure could not remove. And here was Chanda, the youngest of them all, who made no demand on him; and still, if he shut his eyes, the air fairly sparkled with her presence.

Some yards away the surf swished gently; the sound was highly suggestive, like the rustle of a book in the next room. For some minutes he had been aware of its invitation; now it spoke to him so plainly that he felt he had to obey it at once. He rose abruptly, not quite knowing what to say.

'Are you frightened of the dark?'

'No, why?'

'Then stay where you are. I'll be back in a few minutes.'

There was no need to go very far to become invisible. He stripped quickly, dashed into the sea, shivered, threw himself flat in. The bottom sloped off very gradualy and he went some distance before the water came up to his chest. The surface was tepid, but around his feet it was cooler. Presently the bottom gave out and he began to stroke slowly and powerfully, and the wake behind him came to life with a shimmer.

Swimming in total darkness was much like flying in total darkness, save that now the unknown slithered on and around his body. He derived great satisfaction from his strength. He stopped once to catch his breath; floating on his back he saw the stars directly above him and thought: There is Sirius, almost in the Milky Way; he said it aloud several times and even sang it. Nothing meant very much just then and the sound of his own voice was an echo of the nothingness. Then he turned over and swam back lazily, until his feet scraped the bottom once more. He stood up, breathing hard and loud, and splashed the water with his hands. The noise went only a little distance, then recoiled strangely; he splashed again, straining to listen above his breath.

'Stay where you are!' Chanda said from the dark.

'Where are you?'

'In the water. Up to my shoulders.'

'In the sari . . .?'

'Don't be silly. How would I go home?'

'Chanda, how can you!'

'You did, didn't you? Who is a prig now?'

'I am different.'

'I don't see how. Women have all the rights, or have you forgotten?'

The first shock passed quickly and he thought, Why shouldn't she swim if she felt like it? Had he not known that she was 'modern'? And anyway, standing up to his neck in water and wrestling with prudery would have been against anyone's nature. He simply had to get used to the idea that a Hindu girl had all the impulses of a European girl, and sometimes even her daring. Nevertheless, he thought again, how full of surprises she was and how the last one had a clear pagan flavour. He heard her splash and gasp and thought that he saw her move—a luminous shadow in a whirl of liquid silver.

'If only your mother were here now!'

'She is not always as dignified as you think. There is a gypsy streak in our family.'

'I can believe it. Where did you leave your clothes?'

'In charge of the Portuguese admiral.'

He chortled helplessly. 'Portuguese man-o'-war. Yes, I can see the streak.'

'I knew you would. They also said you were intelligent.'

He beat the sea savagely, creating a wild, loud eddy. When his eyes began to smart he stopped, out of breath again. Close by, in a darkness that seemed suddenly to have a life all its own, she churned too, like a vicious catch nearing the end of the line.

'Chanda, you must have been a boy before this birth.'

190

'Not likely, my dear friend. See,

"My hidden beauty grows—
  I'm born in every note showering from the bulbul's throat,
  I dwell in ev'ry starry spark and laugh alike in light and dark!" '

'You wouldn't if a cur chewed up your clothes!' he said.

They laughed together. Far off, the lights of Bandra were fewer, like the slags shed by a planet of another age; they faded and brightened in a slowing rhythm and each glow seemed remoter. The grove, too, was turning in; its lights went out in silent order, as though quenched by a methodical ghost. Once a car beam swept the palms and the sky, with rays out of a child's drawings, and afterwards the grove was many shades darker; laughter and voices sprinkled the underlying silence from afar.

'Enough! You must go out now and dress. And shout when you're finished.'

'Must we . . .?'

But he heard her float away and wash her feet in the surf, and he wondered how Salim would have behaved. To Salim, the removal of one barrier meant a downing of all others; he would have waded over to her, on a pretext of teaching her to swim, no doubt, and made love to her as naturally as he did everything else. That was why he envied him so often. Then, 'Ready!' she called from the shore, and he went out to his pile of clothes and dressed quickly. It was still getting fresher and cooler, and the shirt clung to his back and enveloped him in a delicious cloud of chill, making him thoroughly supple and alive. He walked over to where she sat and lay down beside her.

'How did you dry yourself?'

'With my bodice. You?'

'I just rubbed the water off and put on a shirt. With a little practice you could do it too.'

'And you have had so much. With all those good-looking Eurasians.'

He ignored the gibe. 'Let me tell you how it is done.' He sat upright and drew his palm down the side of his arm, forgetting that she could not see him. 'You wipe it down like this several times. Rubbing makes the skin warm. This helps evaporation. . . .' As he said it, the word 'bodice' fell into the appointed place in his mind and he grew suddenly hot. 'Did you say you used the bodice?' 'Yes, why?'

'Where is it now?'

'Here!' She flourished the bundle before his face. 'Do you need it?'

'No, no. . . .'

The mood changed instantly. If she didn't wear the bodice, she must be naked under the loose drape of the sari; if a wind blew at this moment she would have to hold the end in her hand, so flimsy it was. He remembered

191

her leaning over his chair one evening at home, this same garment rounded out by her full breasts, and the image produced a strong reflex. He said, 'You'll catch a terrible cold like this,' and felt her bare arms and shoulders. 'You shouldn't do it.'

'No, don't,' she said, backing a little.

'But you are still wet.'

Almost before he thought of doing it, his hand slid around her shoulders and down her moist back, functionally and yet in some kind of trepidation, and then, as his sense of wonder grew more heady, faltered at the waist and groped upwards again. Here the possessive habits of the past came back to him with a vivid and natural ease; he cupped her breast, vaguely aware that it was both smaller and more alive than the last one he had held. But she edged away with a gasp, then got up and threw the loose end of the sari over her naked shoulder. Her voice quaked; it seemed to crash on him from a great height and take him defenceless.

'Do you think I am one of your Anglo-Indians . . .? What has come over you?'

She picked up the bodice and shook the sand out of it violently; then she quailed, anger changing to sobs. 'I want to go home. It is very late.'

'Yes, yes,' he said dazedly, getting up. 'Let's go.'

Walking fast across the beach they had no time to speak. He woke up completely, with an onrush of annoyance and a sense of foolishness. They climbed the ridge and went up the lane by which they had come, then stopped on the main road to shake the sand out of their clothes, and there she went behind a palm to put on her bodice. She cried no more and felt well enough to remark on the blackness of the forest. Then a faint gust wheezed through the foliage and a mongrel woke up nearby to yap at their passage.

'It's like a jungle,' she said. 'I should be afraid to walk alone.'

After a while the lights of the field twinkled through the trees and a glow spread through the sky, as though mirroring a far forest fire; the mast lights of the radio station hung over it like a vigilant spirit. Up and down the arterial road beyond Tata's, sharp beams probed the glare and beyond them was Bombay, the vast, fallow source of the glare itself. He was now quite dry and warm. They marched into the club grounds and looked for the car in the parking shed; he helped her in and waited until she was settled. He said:

'Please forgive me, Chanda. I am sorry for what happened.'

'Let us forget it,' she said.

On the main road the traffic became more brisk and he didn't speak at once. After a while his self-consciousness passed. They drove through Vera Cruz and Bandra, skirting large groups of Indo-Christians on their way back from church, and he became a guide once more and explained how the Bombay suburbs were full of Indians who had intermarried with the original Portuguese and had kept Christianity up to this day, how their names were Portuguese and their society was set apart from the rest of India. She listened and asked questions. Friendship was re-formed even though on a changed keel. He now took her as an equal and his words betrayed a new, still unconscious respect; added to his memory of her smooth warm body, this feeling made a curious kind of mixture and tinged their talk in a number of small ways.

'I wanted to show you Uncle Premchand's house,' he said when they crossed the causeway at Bandra. 'Why didn't you remind me of it?'

'I forgot. You will show it to me next time.'

'Next time when?'

'Oh, maybe later this summer, when I am through with college. Mother says there might be a Congress session in Bombay. I would come down with her, of course.'

'What will you do after graduation?'

She wound the sari leisurely over her head. 'I don't know. I haven't thought about it.' Some vague regret softened her voice. 'I suppose I shall marry and have a home of my own and lots of lazy servants.'

He entered the broad highway of North Mahim, and speeded up. 'I want to tell you a secret,' he said at length. 'Father wants me to marry you. They all think we'd make a good match.'

'Yes, I know. Mother told me.'

'What! You knew it when you came down?'

'Yes.'

'Well . . .!' he said. 'A fine thing!'

He felt nettled. The discovery would not have been important had it not once more shown up the uncomfortable amount of intrigue at the back of his life. What a muddled family they were after all! Hindus trying to live like liberals—it was really piteous; no wonder reformers threw up their hands in despair. Jagnath plotting the moves of his young, then deluding himself that the first step was up to them; then, with that logical mind of his, going and telling the young they were being plotted upon!

'You know,' he said, 'I was sure only my parents and I knew about it. I told you just to amuse you. If I had known that you had been told, everything might have been quite different.'

'In what way?'

'For one thing, I would have told you right away I didn't want to marry. Marrying from custom is not my idea of marriage. I like you very much, of course, but this wouldn't be enough. I mean to cast no aspersions, you understand?'

'I understand,' she said curtly. 'Let's talk about something else.'

But, of course, this kind of situation was no good either, and he restrained his impatience and made up his mind to make a clean and honest breast of it.

'You mustn't get me wrong though,' he said. 'I want to tell you what I mean. Then we can forget it.'

He made a sincere try to sum it up first in his own mind, then word it appropriately. 'It's like this, Chanda,' he said. 'You can't be modern and a slave of custom at the same time. My father thinks you can be . . . that's where all the muddle comes from.'

'Everyone knows that. It is nothing new.'

'No, naturally, but listen all the same. He gave me a Western education and it has made us strangers. He realized it when I came back from England, and now he would like to undo the whole thing. But it is too late. Like a good old Hindu, he thinks that marriage is a sober arrangement and he forgets that I might have new ideas on the subject. As a matter of fact, I have. So we can never agree. Are you listening?'

'Yes, Vijay. What *do* you expect of marriage?'

'Oh, that is a long story.'

'Tell me.'

'It is not easy to explain,' he said, carefully steering through a crowd of Holi celebrants. 'Fifty years ago I would have married because I wanted a woman in bed and a mother for my children . . . maybe also someone to wave me off to a battle. I believe Rajput women did that. Now I'm not a warrior and I don't want any children just yet. If I marry, I should like to have the feeling that I don't need another woman for the rest of my life. Otherwise, why marry at all?'

'So far so good.'

'I should like . . .'—pausing to soften the effect of his confession, but achieving the opposite—'I should like to start with love and end up with companionship . . . not the other way round. With us Hindus everything seems to be done for convenience. There is one thing I learned in Europe which is quite true . . . you cannot mix convenience and love.'

Chanda jingled her bracelets impatiently; she ceased being stand-offish and became interested.

'Rubbish, Vijay! You do use such long words for very simple things. Love is to be desired. Let us leave it at that.'

'All right, let us.'

He didn't wish to argue, but he knew that he was right, even if words were long and unwieldy. Had he fallen in love with Chanda, this might have lighted up a whole lifetime; marrying her then would have thrown open a whole new panorama for exploration together. He thought that love was in many ways comparable to the beam of this car, now ranging over the wide road and the dwellings lining it; it picked out all the windows on both sides and saved the houses from darkness and oblivion, whereas all

194

the combined lightpower of the latter would not have made the beam. The beam was supreme, that was its secret; that, he mused, clutching the wheel with a firmer purpose, was how sensitive people saw life. Teaching the value of the beam—as his education had done—and then trying to swap it for a substitute would be unthinkable, and damaging besides. It would be an admission that life was dull and middling at the best of times, not noble or exciting. It would be sowing weariness under the banner of happiness— the worst of grafting one outlook on another. It was the reason why Jagnath and Hindus like him usually fell between two stools, and why he himself wanted to avoid it.

'Now you know, and we can forget the whole thing,' he said. 'I didn't want you to have a wrong picture of me, that was all.'

She was involved only obliquely anyhow. It didn't change her as a human being or make her less interesting. He thought that he had got to know her as well as it would ever be possible to know another person without some kind of surrender. He had heard her talk and laugh and she had been very real for him, even though the unabashed intimacies of Connie and Thelma did rather injure his enthusiasm for demure Indian maidenhood. Now there could be no more illusion between them, and perhaps that was a good thing. Illusion was difficult in a room where the roof, doors and windows had been removed. 'Now we can be brother and sister,' he said sincerely. 'We can give each other amulets every year and be good friends.'

'If I do give you one and make you my brother, you will have to behave like one.'

'I will. I promise.'

They wavered a little between embarrassment and a desire to be generous, then smiled at each other. This broke the long spell.

They rode the rest of the way almost without a care. The bazaars of Mahim grew scarcer and more bedraggled and then the palm forest closed in for a moment and parted for the last time. At the foot of the Worli cliff he left the main road and veered right towards the sea. A smell of brine and seaweed blew through the car, a reminder that home was near. When they climbed the road to Villa Ram, Chanda said:

'Will you laugh if I tell you something?'

'Do you want me to?'

'Oh no, please! It is nothing to laugh at. I have just remembered a stanza from the drama *Shakuntala*. It goes something like this:

    "Wilt thou have charms and delight,
      wilt thou have strength and support,
      wilt thou with one short word encompass the earth and heavens?
    All is said if I name only thee, Shakuntala."

'Very nice,' he said, turning into the garage way. 'What made you remember?'

'You said something about wanting all or nothing. My mother would tell you that nobody has the right to ask for everything at once. She thinks I am like that, but I think you are much worse. She once told me that there is a magnolia for every earthquake . . . a bulbul for every flood . . . a perfume for every pestilence . . . a rainbow for every death.'

'That may be so,' he said. 'But what am I to do if the rainbows and bulbuls don't satisfy?'

'You should take them until the other things come along.'

'Do you take them?'

'No, but I try.' She was quiet for a moment, frowning and tugging her bracelets. 'That was how I thought of the stanza. It is supposed to mean that you can see a big thing through a small one sometimes. Neither you nor I seem to be very good at it. We both want everything at once. I wonder if that is really a mistake or not?'

He said nothing.

He parked the car and stared into the beam, waiting for the words to speak to him more clearly; they promised a theme and a rhythm. Now if the engine didn't have this absurd power of jogging his mind up and down in its obstinate beat, he might perhaps have understood them. But stopping it would have meant moving, an end of magic. He sat still for a while and realized regretfully that this time the meaning would not come. He twisted the ignition key and put on the handbrake, saying in all sincerity:

'I wonder, too, Chanda. I hope we won't be disappointed.'

4

On the day of the Prashads' departure he was apt to loiter about the house and put his nose into things that didn't concern him. Tara was in the kitchen, watching the packing of the guests' viands. A brass food carrier lay on the table, waiting to be filled with curry and vegetable balls, purattas and curd sweets; oranges, bananas and chikoos had already been packed into a basket; the earthen waterpot which high-caste Hindus used in their travelling had only to be filled and corked.

'Oh, Vijay bhai, will this be enough?' she asked him, glancing doubtfully at her handiwork.

'Enough? Have you forgotten that they are going by train, not by coach? Who is going to eat it all?'

'They will, I am sure. Whenever I go on a train I think of food all the time.'

'But it's too much!'

'You can think all you want,' she said, flouncing away from him. 'It has nothing to do with you. Now kindly leave the kitchen.'

He laughed and wandered into the living-room. From the ayah's bower just behind it came a fast warble, then giggles. He thrust his head through the door and discovered Hira and Munu exchanging souvenirs; Munu had given Hira an illustrated copy of the Ramayana in return for twelve bangles, one silver and lapis lazuli necklace and a Panjabi silk veil, and she was still rummaging in Hira's walnut casket for one other object. He walked in, moved by an instinct for justice.

'Hira is our dear guest,' he told Munu good-humouredly, though firmly. 'It is customary to offer gifts to a departing guest as a sign of our pleasure. It is ungracious to ask for anything in return.'

'She wanted the book, which was not mine. Then she said I could have anything I wanted from her.'

'It is true,' Hira said. 'I wanted the book very much.'

'I had to give it,' Munu said. She could not brook any shadow cast upon her integrity of conduct, even though she believed that a bargain was a bargain.

'Certainly you could not refuse, Munu.' He took the book and looked inside the cover. 'Anyhow, it is mine. See, I give it to her with our love and best wishes. Take it, Hira, it is yours.'

Hira held it to her chest and her long eyelashes closed down on a strong flow of emotion. She was a little older than Munu, but already set apart from her playmates by the special brand of the Prashad handsomeness. She was less assertive and dreamier than her older sister, and the wonders of the Ramayana plainly meant more to her than all the frippery of her casket. 'I will never let it go from me,' she said in a whisper, 'never till I die.'

'We won't think of dying yet,' he said. 'Munu and I had much happiness from your company. The book will remind you of us. That is so, Munu, is it not?'

'It is so,' Munu said, vanquishing her sense of realism with a brave front.

He pinched their cheeks and went out unsteadily.

On the first floor Rajuram the Elder was helping Chanda and her mother to pack; sounds of the ladies' chatter and scraping chairs and creaking wardrobe doors drifted down to him in a muffled cloud; a thin, male voice drifted after it. This was Lakshman Premchand, the younger and foster-son of Uncle Premchand, a frequent guest in Villa Ram of late. Vijay paused at the foot of the landing, then strolled out to the garden and the garage, to see if Rajuram the Younger had washed the car and made it ready.

Chanda had carried her many belongings from her own room into her mother's, and these now drooped from beds and door handles and overflowed from the suitcases on to the floor. She folded the saris one by one and laid them in the cases, talking simultaneously to her mother and Lakshman. Like her mother, she did the chore with that half-present, half-gone expression which envelops the parting ones.

To Lakshman, riding the only vacant chair in a corner, they seemed already to have gone beyond the possibility of communication or real understanding. He recited his last poem, rocking in his chair, tilting forward at the end of each quatrain; it was called 'Forever Is the Sun Faded' and he was doing it at Chanda's request. He would never have done it, for he was shy and tight-lipped, if Rana Prashad had not added that she would take it very much amiss if she were to leave Bombay without hearing it. He spoke the whole thing from memory and betrayed a burning, unsuspected fervour which was in sharp contrast to his lean frame and haggard face.

He was nineteen, a college graduate, a shade darker than his foster-father or Vijay; his bony, intelligent face was apt to seem haunted or mournful, but it was more Rajput than the Premchands'. He came from line of Ramsinghs so distant that they were virtually extinct, a line, moreover, in which exogamy had further weakened their claim to Ramsingh kinship. Orphaned as a small boy, he had been adopted by Premchand at the age of six. It had been hoped in the Premchand household that he would grow up a Jain and imbibe some of the family's practical hard-headedness, but somehow neither of these hopes had been fulfilled. Lakshman was increasingly given to poetry, reading, and the tenuous but engrossing game of words for their own sake. He was shy before the easy worldliness of the younger Ramsinghs—all save Tara—and nearly awed by Rana Prashad and her sophisticated elder daughter. Seeing these last in the present fit of packing, listening to their uninhibited chitchat, was like a sudden revelation, so that he avoided looking at them and strained with all his will to keep a casual front and manner. Then, mercifully, the declamation of his poem took him away from suitcases and boudoir matter-of-factness, and for a brief spell he felt bolder and more like himself. He ranged far and wide, in a clear and ringing voice, and did not remember anything save the lines of the poem—not even Tara. When he finished, he sat back, coughed dryly into his clenched fist and closed his eyes.

'Beautiful . . . beautiful . . .' murmured Rana Prashad, gathering the cosmetics from the dressing-table as though they were the winnings of a card game. 'Chanda, did you again borrow my kohl?'

'No, ama.'

Kohl was the black stuff which women used to outline their eyes, to make their gaze more bewitching and less dependable, Lakshman kept his eyes shut, pervaded by a feeling of shame not on his behalf.

'Just imagine, here it is!' Rana Prashad said with a sigh of relief. 'Everything is in such a mess! That was a beautiful poem, Lakshman.' She emptied her hands over an inlaid enamel box and dropped the entire thing into the nearest suitcase.

'Very lovely,' Chanda said. 'Can you write it down for me?'

'There is no time left,' Lakshman said, looking out of the window, wondering whether or not to tell them that the poem belonged to Tara, that he had written it for her alone.

'There is, bhai, there is. You are saying that because you are lazy. Please do it for me.'

Lakshman said, 'Very well, if you wish,' and drew himself up with a mild crackle of his stooping shoulders. He faltered at the door to look at them, then moved away soundlessly.

'Tell Vijay I should like to see him,' Rana Prashad called after him.

'I like Lakshman. You can see he has never been out of India,' Chanda said.

'Strange that there should be a poet among the Premchands,' her mother said. 'They are Jains . . . such a humourless lot. . . .'

Then they packed away in a silent, methodical frenzy, forgetful of all save the slowly diminishing clothes heaps, and Rajuram did his best to get out of their way and help them at the same time. Afterwards Vijay came up, trailed by Lakshman, and he stopped at the door, appalled by the desolation that met him.

'How good you came, we are almost finished!' Mrs. Prashad exclaimed. 'I was looking for the envelope which you said yesterday you would give me. I cannot find it anywhere.'

'I told you, ama,' Chanda said. 'I have already packed it in.'

'You did? I don't remember. Are you quite certain?' When Chanda nodded, she smiled at Vijay, walked over to the bed and flopped down exhausted. 'Did you make sure you gave me everything?'

'Quite sure, Shreemati.' He enumerated the maps, estimates and copies of letters which he had sealed in the envelope; it was all the information he had gathered with so much pain for his scheme of flying pilgrims. She had asked for it because she felt that she might be able to push the plan with the government of the United Provinces. But now he was doubtful and said so openly.

'Wait, we shall see!' she said, trying to sound encouraging in spite of her fatigue. 'One never knows with these officials. Besides, we have won the elections and they are sure to show more interest from now on.'

'I hope you are right, Shreemati.'

'What is more,' she sighed, rising again, 'one of these days we might be the government. I always say, Try anything once. I will let you know what happens.' Then, as he began to thank her for the time she was devoting to so small a matter 'Rubbish, Vijay, it is nothing. I am thankful for every-

thing you have done for us. You have given Chanda a splendid holiday.'
She placed the last stack of her clothing in the case.

They exchanged other words of praise and raised their joined fingers to one another. The code of parting was carried out; they basked briefly in the warm glow of their friendship, feeling that it would outlast all distances and separation. Then Tara called from downstairs announcing that lunch was ready, and Hira appeared in the door, hugging her new possession. Vijay went to his room, saying that he would see them downstairs.

A little later, as he was about to close the door of his room, Chanda came in dressed and ready for the journey.

'Vijay, I know these station good-byes,' she said. 'I should like to take my leave now.'

'I had the same thought, Chanda.' Flourishing a small packet from behind his back, he held it before her. 'I didn't know what to give you,' he said uncertainly. 'I hope you will like this. . . . You are to pack it away and look at it only when you're out of Bombay.'

'Oh, and I have nothing for you.' She took the little bundle, probed it with a finger, then blushed.

Standing so close to her, smelling the tuberose in her tresses, watching her long black eyelashes screen and accentuate her fluster at the same time, he recaptured for a moment the fine friendliness of their evening at Juhu.

'Never mind about me. It is you who are the guest,' he said, pressing her hand downward, familiarly, as though his intimate memory of her were a mutual bond. 'We're now brother and sister, remember?'

'I couldn't find a rakhi amulet anywhere, Vijay.'

'You can send me one.'

'I will. I promise. You have been a marvellous host.'

At another shout from Tara, she sidled away and began to walk down the stairs. 'Let us write to one another. You can tell me about the happenings in Bombay, and I will tell you about Mussoorie,' she said, recovering herself. 'All right,' he said and followed her. 'I do envy your going to fly again,' she said, and he answered, 'Nothing to envy, it'll be commercial flying, no pleasure at all.' 'I will envy you all the same,' she said, tossing her bangles and landing on the ground floor.

'Dalpuries will be cold if you don't hurry!' Tara said in the dining-room. They sat down with the others.

There was a royal pile on the table—vegetable dishes, cooked cereals, curried eggs, sweets, purattas, and some left-overs from Holi—but they were too animated to eat as Tara would have wanted them to. They talked loudly about the parting and the journey to Delhi, and Rana Prashad revived somewhat after her exertions.

'This dreadful life of trains and conferences!' she said wearily, wondering in the same breath if life would be quite the same without them. How cruel it was to have a family and spend so little time with them, she thought. Her mind wheeled back to Bareilly, her home town, where a lovely ancestral house resounded to nothing more than the shouts of servants and an occasional rattle of the windows. Her face grew sad; food lost its flavour. She remembered the years of long ago when Professor Prashad was still alive, when being a doting mother and mistress of a sprawling household seemed to be the height of a womanly calling. How far gone all that seemed at this moment! Now she served a greater cause with much less dignity or peace of mind. Her girls were scattered in hill schools, her home was gathering dust, her love was being squandered on a lot of ungrateful strangers. Well-meaning folks called it a life of dedication. 'What do they know of such a life!' she asked of the youngsters seated around her and, when they waited respectfully, without much appreciation of the real point, drew her own conclusions. People said things simply because that was easier than understanding them! People were sillier than children sometimes! And then, conciliated by her own clear vision, she felt somehow unburdened. She nodded across the table at Tara and Vijay, liking their attentiveness, and rewarded them with a smile. 'Such a luxurious meal, Tara dear! Some day you shall make an excellent wife to some boastful Rajput!'

'I will not marry anyone boastful,' Tara said, flushing.

At that moment Rajuram the Elder burst in from the kitchen, wiping his hands on his shirt, his old face deeply furrowed and scared. He spoke to Vijay, as though the others were not present:

'Sadhuji has arrived!'

'Sadhuji who?'

'Uday sadhu . . . fallen dead in the garden!' His eyes shot around the assembly, satisfied that his words had taken effect.

'Impossible, how can that be?' Vijay said, leaping up from the table. 'What are you saying, Rajuram?'

'Dead in the garden, truly! Out on the grass!' Rajuram averred.

'Goodness gracious! Get a doctor at once!' Rana Prashad exclaimed, paling a shade.

They all jumped up and dashed out after Rajuram.

It was almost true. Uday Ramsingh was attempting to get up when they found him. He wore a faded, soiled swami cloak and his head was clean-shaven, highlighting his dreadful emaciation; his face was all bone and muscle, his hands wasted like the limbs of a faster at the end of a long and sapping vow. He allowed them to stand him up, but waved them away when they tried to walk him to the house. Shivering and tripping, he made the last seven steps all by himself, only to give out again at the steps of the porch.

'I have not eaten, that is all,' he told them feebly.

'Whether it is or not, you are going straight to bed!' Vijay said sharply. 'And you're going to eat as never before. Just look at you!'

'He had better!' Rana Prashad said. 'You can't have an uncle expiring on your doorstep.'

'There is a bed in ayah's room,' Tara said. 'Let us put him on it until he is well enough to be taken upstairs.'

So they hustled him into the small room in the rear of the dining-room, and Rajuram brought a large glass of milk, which they forced him to sip while they held his head. Children were shooed away and told to finish their meal alone and quietly. Servants came from their quarters murmuring, 'Arre, baba, look at sadhuji!' Vijay sat by and watched him come round slowly, while Tara phoned the doctor. Half an hour passed, then an hour, in which he stared at the ceiling and at each one of them in turn; from their deep, darkly bronzed recesses, his eyes shone more and more burningly. Then the doctor came, poked him up, questioned, and lost patience. He was a Parsi with Western degrees and robustly materialistic views.

'Plain case of suicide!' he clucked angrily. 'If he were a son of mine I would know how to treat him! If he is fed up with life, I could have told him half a dozen pleasant ways of putting an end to it. Starvation for what . . . for a ghost . . .? Cluck. Cluck. He ought to be ashamed of himself!'

Uday shut his eyes in mute sufferance.

They were to feed him little at a time, the doctor said—milk and fruit juices first, then soups, broths and boiled vegetables. 'Don't stand for any yoga nonsense!' he admonished Vijay before he snorted and clucked himself away. 'A law should provide against such wantonness!' And still Uday said nothing, but lay quietly and refused to open his eyes.

In the early afternoon he fell asleep. They put a jug of milk and some fruit juice on his bedside table, let the shutters down and tiptoed out of the room. Tara offered to stand guard and call the doctor if there should be any need. Then the two Rajurams brought down the luggage of the Prashads and Vijay got the car out.

'A terrible time to leave you, dearest children,' Rana Prashad said, 'but we really shall miss the train if we don't hurry.'

They took leave of Tara and Munu, and Mrs. Prashad phoned Jagnath at the office to say good-bye once more and to mention Uday's appearance. Then Rajuram and his son put the cases in the car and roped the surplus to the rack in the rear. They were all subdued; too much had happened in one short morning, too much in the brief and breathless fortnight. Life suddenly seemed to go up in flying particles, more ephemeral and puzzling than anyone would have thought. This India of theirs, which the outside world saw as a tawdry and sometimes glamorous belle of Asia, this swarming, milling, starving, scheming, pushing, noisy Bharat Mata, was not one spirit, but millions of them. It was theirs all right, and would remain theirs for ever and ever, yet how baffling and strange its manifold tongue could be! How difficult to know just what it was saying!

'It is not that we lack courage,' Rana Prashad told her silent audience as the car sped towards Bombay Central. 'It is that we put it to such odd uses.' Vijay agreed heartily.

He remembered the bloodless fingers of his uncle, and the lissomeness of body and movement, his uncle's only Rajput heritage, which now seemed to have frittered away in some unexplainable stress. Even now those emasculated fingers looked as though they might snap knuckle by knuckle if he moved them at all energetically. Was that determination gone astray, as Rana Prashad would have it? He thought that all the signs pointed to it. Uday's calm was impressive, but also terrifyingly unreal. It was like an aftermath not only of starvation but of something that lay beyond it, beyond reason or understanding, something that flowed on without a ripple even when all the streams of perception and will had been sucked up by the sands.

5

THEY were not to find out what it was for some days.

He had come from the Deccan and was on his way north. The delay at Bombay was unexpected and against his will. That was all they could learn without prying; prying would not have done with so earnest a sadhu, so ill a guest. Instead, they took good care to follow the doctor's orders; they moved him to the spare room on the first floor and made him comfortable without fuss. Tara saw to it that he was kept in milk and soft foods, and that he drank them, while Rajuram the Elder stood by to help him in other ways. Uday submitted in silence for the most part; the one sociable exception was a request to Jagnath and Vijay that they stop worrying over him so much. He slept almost continuously in the beginning and, when the doctor held forth on his negligence, kept his eyes closed and appeared to mumble a prayer. At the end of the first week he was able to sit up without sickness and walk to the bathroom by himself. Once Tara took up the food and found him sitting cross-legged on the floor, deaf to her urging. They decided that he had fallen into a samadhi trance, and must therefore still be very weak; they ordered quiet throughout the house and consulted the doctor, who was of the opinion that noise should be continued and, if possible, increased. 'Do not let him moon about,' he admonished sternly.

By and by the sadhu began to emerge and mingle with them in the evenings. They were all carefully casual; the girls studied, Jagnath retired to his daftar, Vijay read the newspaper or wrote in his logbook. At length the skin over his cheekbones relaxed somewhat and colour returned to his thin hands and the veins on them began to throb less conspicuously. He essayed a walk or two in the garden, then a longer amble down to the sea wall, from which he returned rasping a little. Finally he took a bus trip to town, which they attempted to foil but did not succeed.

'We are glad to see you feeling so much better,' Vijay told him later that day. 'I've never seen anyone so close to death and so far from it, all in a few days.'

'Death is reluctant when you are not curious about her.'

'We thought you were, Udayji.'

'Nothing like that, believe me. Hinduism does not approve of suicide. It was a simple vow.'

Vijay waited, but the sadhu was not in a confiding mood.

He spent the following day washing his cloak and dyeing it fresh ochre. When he put it on in the evening he looked as though he had lately come out of a monastery; he had shaved himself anew, rubbed his scalp with coconut oil and hung a cowrie-shell necklace on his chest; he had the air of a priest getting ready for a ritual event. Vijay was dressing to go out and see Salim, when he walked into the room holding a piece of paper.

'Vijay, I have been looking for a book of Kabir's, but I have not got it so far,' he said. 'Somewhere in the Thieves' Market there is supposed to be a Muslim bookshop and they are supposed to have it. I should like to ask you to help me find it. I went there yesterday, but lost my way.'

'I shall be happy, Udayji,' Vijay said. 'Only I must tell you that there has been some rioting in that part of the town. It may not be safe.'

'Who would molest a penniless sadhu?'

'One never knows with these ruffians.'

'What were the riots for?'

Vijay had to smile at the unearthliness. 'I cannot tell you,' he said. 'They start like a match strike and spread just like fire. A few people are stabbed, a few shops looted . . . then there is a curfew and all is quiet. Afterwards the Muslims blame the Hindus, and we blame the Muslims. Nobody is any the wiser.'

They took a bus to Crawford Market, just as the evening crowds poured out into the street. It had been a hot day; the spring was beginning to feel as though it would turn into summer any day. There was humidity in the air instead of the usual March freshness, and Salim Haq, whom Vijay had phoned before leaving the house, had said that the planes crossing Rajputana from Delhi reported strong heat currents and frequent air pockets over the Western Ghats. Peasants in the interior of India sniffed the air in the morning and cast troubled eyes on their dwindling reserves of grain.

'I wish you'd been here for Holi,' Vijay said, making conversation in the crowded and reeking bus. 'We had the Prashads for a fortnight.'

'Interesting family,' Uday said. 'I hear you are marrying Chanda.'

'Who told you?'

'Your father.'

Vijay looked at him and saw that he was earnest. 'That is not exact,' he said. 'He merely desires that I should do so.'

He said nothing more until they alighted on Carnac Road and walked up Sheik Memon Street. A dense crowd of shoppers, loungers and beggars began to jostle them rudely. The sight of a swami accompanied by a well-dressed young Hindu drew a number of curious glances from the white-clad Gujarati and Marwari silk mercers on both sides of the hot street. Hawkers with portable and wheeled stands shoved along the kerbs uttering ear-piercing cries; most were Muslims, wearing rakishly slanted fezzes and sporting dyed beards and bright waistcoats.

'I also hear that you are taking business employment,' Uday said after a time. 'Very good in your case . . . interesting work together with marriage. You should not complain any more.'

'Wait, Uday! You seem to know such a lot! Work, yes, but the other thing . . .'

He gave up, centering all his attention on their physical progress. It was not only that Uday listened with half an ear, but he was also a jaywalker. He would make an uninformed remark and then sheer off into the middle of the narrow street as if the carriage traffic were not his concern; he would waddle along in his flowing robe and raise his staff at the oncoming gharries as though they were the trespassers. And, more often than not, the gharry-wallahs would rein in and let him pass with a look of amazement.

'Dear Uday, this is a big city, full of dangers,' he finally had to warn him. 'You've lived alone for so long that you've forgotten it.' He steered him back to the pavement and took the outer position. 'And anyway, this is where we turn off.'

The alley was like a dark canyon inhabited by a furtive race. Dhoties, saris, counterpanes and mattresses dangled from the open windows, and on the higher balconies half-naked boys tried to launch their kites in the breeze. In murky doorways, banyas quarrelled with customers and their cackling made any attempt at concentration a wan hope.

Vijay fingered the Tata letter in his pocket—he had had a vague intention of telling his young uncle about it. He had made his application to the company and they had interviewed him; the letter, making him a pilot on probation, had arrived only that morning. Jagnath and his sisters already knew about it and seemed overjoyed. He himself should have been glad, but was not. Writhing about the bed during the previous night he had felt again strangely unquiet: visions of things started and unfinished, promised and unfilled, had crowded his mind and kept him awake for hours. It was all very illogical, but it was there: the letter had stunned him a little, but not soothed. And here Uday, whose advice might have been helpful, careered along in this absent way of his and seemed not to care.

'We've had much excitement since your last visit,' he tried again, pointing to a tattered election poster on a wall, on which one eye of the candidate had been gouged by an unknown hand. 'Politics are back in the running.'

'I heard,' Uday said. 'Excitement should be pleasing to a Kshatriya. Public events are a part of his destiny.'

'They are, Uday, but sometimes they are confusing.' He thought a little, then added, 'When your destiny swoons in my garden, it is hard to know which is which. I want to say, Welcome! but still it is confusing.'

Uday smiled civilly for the first time; he included Vijay in a gleaning look that took in the far end of the canyon and the uneven row of groceries tapering towards it.

'I have not thought of it in that way,' he said. 'Forgive me, I did not mean to be rude. I have talked to your father about it. My guru ordered me to go on the road for three months as a preliminary to my training. I was to beg for food, visit certain holy places and make due penance. It so happened that on my return I walked through wild country where I could not beg. I became hungry and weak. I had no money for a ticket to North India and had to get some. Your father was most kind . . . I cannot thank him enough.' He grew pensive again, but there was no sadness in it. 'There is no more to tell. Doctors,' he added slowly, as though formulating a long-delayed judgment, 'make the mistake of thinking that their knowledge of flesh and guts gives them the mastery over men's minds. According to my experience, one should disregard them on these subjects.'

'Was the penance successful?'

'Only partly.'

'What are you after?'

'Freedom.'

'That's very loose, Udayji. You are free now. Can you explain?'

'No, Vijay. Can you explain your being a flier?'

'I think so. It wouldn't mean anything to you, though.'

'That,' Uday said, swerving out of the way of a group of children, 'is the main difficulty, always. Our reasons are not to be explained, because they do not explain.'

'But they must sometimes.'

'Rarely. When two people have the same reason, a little might be mutually explained . . . otherwise not. When I was in Satara a soldier came to me saying that his wife had slept with another while he was away. He wanted to know if he should cut off her nose, which used to be the custom in the Deccan, or merely beat her and throw her out of the house . . .

206

which would have been weak but more in accord with his feelings towards her. Not being married or a soldier, I told him I did not know. He abused me coarsely, for he believed that a sadhu should know everything. For that reason, try to meddle in the cause of another, and you are meddling with the divine dharma.'

'You must tell me more later,' Vijay said, stopping and catching his cloak. 'This is the Thieves' Market. What was the name of your shop?'

Uday fumbled in the pocket of his robe and read the address from a piece of paper. Vijay took his bearings and chose a dusky-looking short cut to the nearest small square.

'It seems that I am to answer questions every time we meet,' Uday said 'Why is that, Vijay? Are you not settled in yourself?'

'I don't know,' Vijay said honestly. 'They all say that I try to do everything at once. Sometimes I think that Europe has done that to me, and then again I am convinced that it is good that it did.' He strove hard to compress his innermost anxiety in a few sentences, but whatever came through struck him as either trivial or inaccurate. 'You know, Uday,' he said with a little puff of defeat, 'right now I feel very much like your soldier. I think a sadhu should be able to answer such questions, even if we cannot. After all, he spends a lot of time thinking of them. We householders do not. Is life to go on as if you had not come?'

'We live alone,' Uday said. 'My coming and going could make no difference.'

They reached the square just then and Vijay stopped a man to ask about the shop. It appeared they were standing right in front of it; they had not noticed it because the entrance was hung with fezes and black caps, like a hatter's. They went in and Uday named the book he was looking for.

'It might be in this row,' the proprietor said indifferently. 'Look for yourself!' He was an elderly, bearded Muslim, with a white band around his fez to show that he had been to Mecca and was a hadji.

Uday rummaged the shelf with mounting disappointment. 'They are all Urdu,' he said, 'and I want a Hindi or English edition.'

'You have come to the wrong place,' the Muslim said, eyeing him coldly.

Uday ransacked all the shelves, but in vain. The old man shook his head, repeating what he had already said; his manner became openly wrathful for some reason. Perhaps Uday's irreverent handling of the sacred Islamic texts made him hostile; perhaps the recent turbulence suddenly made him remember. When the sadhu suggested that the volume might be elsewhere in the shop, he sat down on his dais and, fingering his string of beads, refused to be drawn out any further. Vijay was swayed into remarking that rudeness was not what they had come for.

'You are free to leave the shop,' the Muslim said, with a vulgar flip of the fingers.

Two young men slunk out of the dark nooks in the rear and stood behind him without a word. They glowered. A strange, unprovoked hatred made their silence more menacing than any words.

'Come, Uday,' Vijay said, taking his uncle's arm. 'We are plainly not wanted.'

'This address was given. . . .'

'Never mind the address!' He pushed him out into the street, angry and baffled over the snub. Communal passions had always aroused his impatience, because he himself was free from them, but he saw now that they must mean very much to simple people. He had been in the habit of shrugging them off as the sinister mongering of a few hoodlums, probably paid to incite violence for some tactical advantage of a politician, but now he realized that the passion went deeper, much deeper, apparently. No one could stare like that unless he felt it too.

Strolling down the street again, Uday said: 'Kabir had a message for Hindu and Muslim alike.'

'That may be so,' Vijay answered. 'I wish that men who stab and loot would read him. I told you it was too soon after the riots. In this part alone there were eight killed and I don't know how many wounded.'

'On second thought,' Uday said calmly, 'I might just as well get the book in Delhi.'

They came out on Mohammad Ali Road and headed back for the Crawford Market. They walked in silence, busy with the pavement crowds and their own thoughts. Over the sea, the sun must have set completely, because its bright train was burning out in the sky and the moon had become clearly visible. A creeping greyness reset the streets and rebuilt the houses after its own hankering; the dark overtook the light, they mixed and lost character; the mixture poured westward so swiftly that men called it dusk at one end of the town and night at the other. Birds, seeing both, soared lower and settled on rooftops. Then the street lamps came on unveiling all mystery, giving each shape a look of fixed wonder. Hushed in the heat of daytime and glaring sun, the small voice of spring rallied again and piped forth. At first it could not surmount the town's deep rumble, but then it grew and sallied and finally commingled with the rumble itself, giving it a new and more rousing pitch. Walking silently into it, Vijay heard it distinctly and his thoughts straggled again.

There was so much he would have liked telling his sadhu uncle, not only because Uday might have offered an answer but also because talking would have made it easier in itself. Now the moment seemed to have gone, between piddling generalities and ill-advised passion, and it might never return again. Aloofness in a holy man was seemingly all-exclusive; if he didn't care for the world, he cared still less for the people in it. Yet Vijay had the feeling that somewhere beneath the thick film of Uday's platitudes was a partial truth—not a very practical truth, but an acceptable one. It was that man and his dharma were alone before divinity. It was true of both the ascetic and the householder. The importance of others was measurable only in the light of self; self was the goal, the sab-chiz, all of it, as the Anglo-Indians would say. A man trying to save others before he saved himself was un-Hindu and a fool; his first duty was to make order in his own dharma, a design out of his own confusion and insecurity, minding the well-being of his fellows at the same time. It was sensible and not really selfish, if you thought it right out to the end. *Better is one's own dharma than that of another*. . . . Now he understood why the Bhagavad-Gita was held to be so sacred. Ordering one's life was a whole-time job, and if men gave it all their attention they would keep out of mischief, and to keep out of mischief was the same as saving oneself. Explained like that, Uday was right in saying that his coming or going made little difference. If it did, minds would be interchangeable and happiness would be so cheap that no one would ever go after it.

And now spring made everything only brittler and sharper. His lungs tingled with more things than dust and the smell of joss sticks. He looked at the sky, breathing faster; the night was spacious, much more spacious than any of the restive stirrings so audible in his head. He touched the letter in his pocket and looked at Uday; the sadhu marched long in a web of his own. He thought of Chanda and her warm taut skin, and of Ranjit in a cloud of hookah smoke, and of Thelma's small belly wriggling close to his face, and he shuddered expectantly. Perhaps everything could be talked away as a chemical reaction; he had read that somewhere; perhaps this was simply the fretful natural pause before another spurt of action. Perhaps—but here was Crawford Market, where he would leave Uday and take a bus to Salim's place.

Uday came to a slow, hesitant stop, tearing the piece of paper with the address. The bright lights of the square danced in his eyes, not kindling them but simply mirrored.

'I have not taken leave of your father and I should like you to give him my respects,' he said moodily. 'Tell him that I shall pray for him. And my greetings to Tara for all her care and help.'

'What do you mean, Udayji?'

'I am taking the first train to Delhi. There may not be time to go back to Worli.'

'You are leaving us just like this . . .?' He glared into the set, thin face and couldn't believe what he heard; he patted his hand gently, as if to waken him. 'Listen to me, Udayji. You are not well enough to travel just yet. You need a little more rest. What would father say if I told him you left me in the middle of the road and went to Delhi? Are you joking?'

'I joke rarely, Vijay. It is time for me to go.'

They gazed at each other, Vijay dumbfounded, his uncle with a steady unflinching look. Then Uday finished tearing the paper and threw the bits sideways. A Gujarati couple passing by at that moment received the shower in their faces; the man reeled round to protest, but seeing the ochre robe restrained himself.

'All I can say is that you have become very strange,' Vijay said. 'I will take your message home.'

'Thank you, Vijay. Farewell and blessings for the future.'

'Farewell, Udayji.'

The sadhu shambled off stiffly, like a colt after long lying.

While he still stared after him, the bus came along and its wheels ground to a screeching stop. He got in and climbed to the upper deck in order to see the street better, but Uday had already vanished in the crowd.

Dropping into the seat he felt curiously spent, as if Uday's disappearance had taken away his own energy. The bus joggled close to the pavement, close to the trees, so that he could smell their dusty dryness and feel the cool breath which they exuded. The leaves rustled in gusts. Their theme was one of the bus engine and voices floating out of the open windows and of the ocean murmuring softly at the other end of the town. All was one and yet so varied. He wondered if he would ever learn why it was varied and how it came to be one. And what did the ocean think of it? He could hear it wallowing everlastingly between the first æon and the last, lolling to an age of its own, full of wisdom and sympathy, and then a Bengali song came to his mind and the words struck him as very apt. *This day will surely pass, this day will pass. . . .*

What did the ocean think of that? Was this suspense to go on and on without let-up, like some elemental prank obeying no rules save its own, like light, for instance, which was intermittent in its smallest particles and yet never stopped going once it started, although men of science were beginning to have new thoughts on the score? What was the hope of the Hindu who had lost his simple faith but none of the faith's burden . . .? He clambered out at the Marine Drive station wondering also why, whenever things grew specifically vexing, he chose to wrestle with them in a general and unwieldy lump.

210

❀❀❀❀❀❀❀❀❀❀❀❀❀❀❀❀❀❀❀❀❀❀❀❀❀❀❀❀

1

'A MOST auspicious event,' Jagnath said warmly when his son returned from the offices of Tata Airlines and confirmed his appointment as pilot. 'I am very happy, son, not only for myself, but for you too. Now we must find out whether April fifteenth is auspicious too. It is only fitting that your new life should start on an appropriate day.'

'You are joking, pitaji?'

'I am not, Vijay. It is a serious matter.'

On that date he was to report for duty, but his father decided that it was up to the astrologer to pronounce it either lucky or unlucky. This was a new trait in Jagnath. Nothing could be left to man's decision alone, but stars and numbers had the last word; endeavour was still expected of everyone, to be sure, but in itself it was no assurance of the future. 'One might as well be thorough on such an important occasion,' Jagnath said with the merest trace of flurry.

They went and saw the pundit who used to advise Kandubai and the learned fellow heard them out earnestly and wrote down all the interesting particulars. He would work out the horoscope and let them know in a few days; the young man's zodiac was most promising—most exceptionally so, he said—and they could rest easy during the interval.

'If he says I should put off my joining, what then?' Vijay asked his father.

'Then you shall postpone it, naturally.'

'But this is witchcraft . . . it's like a story from the Mahabharata. I thought we educated Indians had done with it for ever.'

'That is probably at the root of our many troubles,' Jagnath said stolidly. 'Do not forget, Vijay, that our history started in the stars. Our ancestors did all their hunting and fighting with the help of the stars.' A little cloud of nostalgia drifted over his face and he turned away abruptly. 'Your good mother knew that very well. I know that if she were here she would have wanted me to observe it.'

When the pundit's report came it was a great success. The date was auspicious and the presages were of the best. Jagnath went around the house cracking his knuckles—a sign of pleasure—patting his son's back whenever they met in the hall or in a room. He spoke more affectionately to Tara and Munu and called for a statement of the kitchen expenses, something he had not done for months. 'There is nothing to worry about now,' he said to Vijay with a shy smile that lighted up his face and ironed out some of its ravages. 'All being equal,' he said another time, 'you should go far in your new career.' Later that evening he sat down in the garden and read aloud from the Bhagavad-Gita, while crows and sparrows circled his head thinking that the papers he had spread on the grass were food. His handsome grey crown reminded Vijay of a lotus bud swaying on the surface of a quiet pond.

Tata's had taken him on probation, but soon after he joined up at Juhu they shortened the period to sixty days and assigned him to the Bombay-Trivandrum route. Salim took him through the offices, workshops and hangars with the patience of one who was above human folly. He also flew him down the coast once and broke him in dutifully. 'It is no doubt splendid to have you here with me,' he told him, frowning massively, 'but, brother, it is the wrong thing for *you*.' When pressed for an explanation, he waved his long arm in several directions: 'If you do not see yourself, I cannot make you see.' But he added that he would help wherever necessary. 'It is my job,' he relented towards the end, 'and, apart from that, you are my favourite Hindu. It shall not be said of Salim that he is a petty communalist.'

The flying personnel seemed pleased to have him. Most of them were his own age. They were Parsis, with a sprinkling of high-caste Hindus, and they came from all provinces, so that the small fraternity was more representative of India than many a patriotic organization with a like claim. Vijay was touched by their friendliness. The flight route, too, grew to be a pleasant surprise. All flying was done in daytime; passengers and mail were light, because the service was a recent addition to Tata's all-India network. The long line of surf, jagged here and there by islands that were emerald in colour and by frothy little inlets and glimmering coves in which a million palms threw their shadows across the cream of the beaches; the shiny carpet of verdure that lay like wainscoting against the rib of the Western Ghats; the Ghats themselves, dipping a little here, swelling rough and bluff-bowed there, a long, straight furrow turned up by a ploughshare at the end of the last Maha Yuga but healed since under a lush graft of forest—these were gifts of beauty which he had not expected, for which he was now grateful. They showed him that the hardships of mind were not all. He thought that some day the beauty of his new job would out-distance its duller aspects and that he would then begin to see other things through it, as Chanda had said it might be possible.

And then Chanda wrote from Mussoorie in reply to his first letter:

I was so happy to hear that it is better than you had hoped. I looked up my atlas to see where you might be, but maps are such impossible things! I try to imagine myself nosing down on some fishermen and their nets in the early morning, and I envy you from the bottom of my heart. Why do men have all the luck in India? One day when I am an old lady and you have cast a cobweb of services all over the country, you shall take me flying round India beach by beach, delta by delta . . .!

He smiled as he read it, remembering the time he flew her over the islands of Bombay and Salsette and the way her face glowed with the thrill. The letter cheered him quite unexpectedly. He smelled it and tried to peer through it against strong light, but did not read it at once; he wanted to find out just how curious he was. It turned out he was quite unduly eager. It was nine closely written pages, in a neat hand which was such a contrast to the vivacity of the writer.

I can imagine full well what this must mean to Mr. Ramsingh, your father [she went on]. *He was complaining only recently that our young men waste more time talking about the future than working on it. There should now be an end to this argument. You are doing what you know best, and you seem to like it too.*

As guesses went, this was a shrewd one for a young girl. Not only was she right, but he was glad that she was. The rest of the letter showed her animated as usual.

Here is the promised rakhi, which you should wear like a real amulet-brother, which is a poor return for your own lovely gift—she wrote next, thanking him for the silver plane model which he had given her at the time of her departure from Bombay—*Now we are brother and sister according to the old Rajput custom. If I am ever in distress, I will let you know and you will ride in on your white Arab and come to my rescue! I wish you could rescue me right now, with my senior Cambridge coming up in May! I am supposed to be studying hard and thinking of the exams, but all I do is stare out of the window and watch the white clouds over Dehra Dun in the valley. Hira, who is living with me, says they are the souls of Aryan princesses seeking another incarnation, but I think they are too haughty for that. They have brought spring to these hills and then lost all interest, and now they seem to be on their way to new countries, and here we are left with pools of buttercups and bright red rhododendron and blossoming plum trees which never stop waving right through the day.*
And yet everything seems to be happening at the other end of the world. Mother has been to Delhi, Lucknow and Patna; now back at Delhi. She writes little, because she is a likely future minister and because these people are not supposed to have any family or feelings! Premchand is

there too. I know about it from the newspapers! Isn't that awful? Every-one is wrought up over the coming Congress session in your city. I wish I were there instead of here! If they decide to make peace with the Viceroy and then take office, we shall have an Indian raj before the plums under my window are ripe. Wouldn't that be heavenly! Mother, your Uncle Premchand, your dad, they would all be ministers. They would pass a bill for your Hardwar airline without any delay and maybe even put you in charge of civil aviation. Why shouldn't they? They are all so keen to show the British how this country should be run. By the by, you will see mother in Bombay before long. I know she has been singing your praises in official circles.

What a queer person Udayji must have become, leaving you like that in the middle of the road. Ranjit wrote the other day that he had passed through Dehra Dun and borrowed some money for a trip to Kedarnath, in these hills here. He must have become very holy with all those terrible austerities, don't you think? I was wondering why we never hear of his mother who is supposed to be leading a quiet widow's life in Calcutta, but Ranjit says there has been much unhappiness in that family and that that was the reason why he left the world and became a sannyasi. I think this is true, because Ranjit is very fond of Uday and wouldn't lie about it for anything in the world. Ranjit will be up here in May. If Mother can tear herself away for a week, she will come up also. I only hope I will pass, so that she can really enjoy her rest.

This is all for now, dear friend and brother, and don't forget to wear the amulet. It is to guard you from bad luck. My love to Tara and Munu and all my respects to your father. I will write again when I hear from you.

Yours

Chanda

Soaring contentedly over the west coast two days later he took the rakhi out of the envelope and tied it to his wrist. It was of gold thread twisted around many times to resemble a filigree chain, and still smelled faintly of Chanda or perhaps the chest in which she had kept it. Now the lie he had told Kandubai last year was redeemed; he had accepted a bond which the Rajput legend valued more highly than anything else between men and women, save maybe the duty to one's father and forbears. He surprised himself feeling even a little sentimental over it. It was pleasant to think that he had become the protector of a girl who needed no protection, and that the status gave him all the right of an intimate relationship without any of the serious responsibilities.

With the logbook on his knees he began to draft her another chatty letter.

But the family truce soon received a severe test. One morning, after he had gone to the secretariat, Jagnath phoned home and asked for his son.

'Vijay, come here this evening and we shall go home together,' he said.

Vijay promised. At five—for it was his free day in the week—he climbed the dusky staircase to his father's office and announced himself through the peon. Jagnath seemed worn out by the day's work and his cotton suit sagged limply, but his eyes brightened somewhat as he rose to greet him. He went to wash his hands at once and came back rubbing them briskly and officiously.

'Now we can talk and nobody will disturb,' he said. 'It has occurred to me that I have never thanked you for being so helpful to our guests last March. I mean the Prashads, of course,' he added, observing Vijay's wonder. 'You thought I had forgotten . . .? Well, I did not. I know that if it had not been for your very courteous attention, they might have thought me a poor host.'

'I liked them very much, pitaji, so it wasn't hard to be nice to them.'

'I am pleased to hear it, son. And now you and Chanda are writing to one another. Rana Prashad says that she will probably study law when she comes out of college . . . they still cannot decide between Allahabad and Bombay. I think Bombay would be much better . . . our law school is supposed to be the best in India. You know that Chanda was going to America once upon a time, but the government withdrew the permit. She needs to live in a big city for a year or two. It is good for a girl of her talents, don't you think?'

'Very good, father.'

Drifting towards the bookshelf, he was not sure for a moment whether to acknowledge Jagnath's feelers or not. It was true that Chanda's letters had sent his mind wandering along new paths, but not in the way his father expected. Why could they not leave it at that?

'Law studies are not everything, son.'

'What do you mean, pitaji?'

'I mean that Rana Prashad is not an old-fashioned woman, but she must sometimes bow to tradition all the same. It is not good to have a grown-up daughter who is not even betrothed.' He walked up to the window and the end of his jacket fluttered in the air stream; he clasped and unclasped his hands across his back. 'I did not tell you before,' he said haplessly, 'because you seemed not to care. Mrs. Prashad has had several firm proposals in Bareilly alone. She has managed to stay them so far . . . I must tell you now . . . at my request. She cannot do it for ever. She has a right to know; her last letter was on that subject. If I write that you have not decided, Chanda will be married off by the end of this year.'

'It might even be better for everyone.' Vijay uttered the words as gently as he could.

Jagnath came back and began to tidy up the desk in his old distraint way. He looked upset, and Vijay had to restrain a pang of compassion; he felt sorry and coarse.

'We can go now. I have to make a call on the way,' Jagnath said.

He took the topee off the rack and crossed the office slowly, bent forward as if braving inclement weather. In the open door his grey hair lightened against the dingy outer office.

'I can only say that I regret it very much indeed,' he said in a hushed sadness. 'Chanda would have made you a lovely wife, I am sure of that. We are all very fond of her. I feel as if I am losing my own daughter . . . but I tell myself that it is your life after all and that you must know what you are doing.'

'Yes, I do know, pitaji.'

They walked along the tomblike corridor and down to the ground floor. Rajuram the Younger brought the car round and stood by while they settled in the back seat. Jagnath gave him an unfamiliar address, and the car swerved out of the broad drive and came into the road. A fine spray of pollen, as tangy as the dust of the street, blew off the trees and teased their nostrils delicately.

'Then again, it is not only you who must think about it,' Jagnath said, going after the subtler implications. 'It is also myself. I am on the retired list for next year and I was hoping that maybe your marriage would be arranged by then. This would have left only Tara for the time being. My pension would not suffice for two weddings one after another.'

'Mine can wait, father,' Vijay said.

'How can it?' He gave him a vexed and questioning look. 'Have you forgotten that the older must marry before the younger? What would our Indore relations say if Tara were married before you?'

'They would get used to it, I am sure. Nobody follows that rule any more.'

Jagnath said nothing for a few minutes, and when he spoke again it was clear that patience and the resolution to be discreet had won the day over his emotions.

'The question of precedence is not all either,' he said slowly. 'It is also a matter of propriety and . . . belief. It is not good for an old man to know that he has not done his duty . . . that he has failed before himself, before the community . . . and God also. Your dear mother understood that all the time, but I learned it only lately.'

'What can I do, pitaji?' If I felt even a little like marrying, I would do it only to please you. But I do not, believe me.'

He and Tara had been privately wondering whether Jagnath's loneliness of recent months was beginning to pale, and had come to the conclusion that it was. Everything seemed to point to it. But brace himself as he might,

216

a Hindu at the porch of old age would miss a woman of his own, and this was what they were afraid of. They had wondered if their father would follow the old custom of marrying a second time; the idea was repugnant, but they had to admit that it was fairness itself. Vijay had detected no undertone in his father's last remark. The name of his dead wife sounded as though it were still culled from the large and rich store of their life together.

'I remember,' Jagnath went on, 'I remember when the roof was put on our house many, many years ago. Your mother and I stood on the first floor with the contractor's plan in our hands. It was a great moment, how well do I still recall it! We marked each room for one or the other of us . . and we gave them each a name. . . .' He stared out of the window, watching the buildings on the street as if comparing them. 'I remember telling her how the house was built so that the rear could be extended at any time. You must have noticed it . . . our conduit pipe enters the wall from the east. She cried, poor ama . . . she was so happy. It was our first thought of the day when you, and your family, would need more space. Dearest ama . . . she was not to see another plan made in her lifetime.'

Vijay took his hand and pressed it fondly. 'Please, father,' he said coaxingly. 'We will build another wing one of these days. If not for me, then for Tara.

'No, son,' Jagnath said, returning the clasp though not looking at him. 'I am finished with plans. Also with bricks and mortar. Now it is up to you. . . .'

Then Rajuram drew up before a cream-coloured building in Kalbadevi, and Jagnath took his hand back. There was bunting of the Congress tri-colour on the upper balconies, and above them a long flag of orange, white and green; the walls were full of election posters as high as a person could reach. Men and women in khaddar streamed through the arched gateway and they were mostly Hindus. Jagnath scrambled out of the car, not taking his white topee.

'Wait for me. I shall be back in five minutes.'

Vijay lighted a cigarette—something he had forborne doing in the presence of his father—and settled back to wait.

'Congress headquarters,' the young Rajuram said obligingly, for he was certain that Vijay would not know it otherwise. 'We were here last week.'

Vijay said 'Huhn' and did not inquire further. He felt distressed. It had not been a simple thing to shatter his father's illusion, and he had not done it as tactfully as might have been possible. The good work of the recent weeks had been somehow tarnished—not much, but enough to intrude on the pleasant and carefree harmony of life at home. Regretting this perhaps more than the other sides of the problem, he also wondered if he had behaved selfishly in the filial sense. The duties of being a good Hindu and a good Hindu son were often conflicting; one either sacrificed in order to please, or stuck to one's guns and felt sorry long afterwards.

But Jagnath no longer wore his liberalism like a new suit of clothes, and this, anyhow, was a small gain. He was laying it aside. He was falling back on tradition not from a mere instinct but with a seemingly renewed conviction. In all the years since Vijay could remember, his father's modernity had not meant more than an occasional grant of reason to things which mattered very little anyway; his concessions to the spirit of the times were always rather grudging; lately he seemed to have made up his mind that they were altogether superfluous. This would only comfort him in the future. At the end of middle age, a Rajput of old used to hang up his weapons and pension his concubines, but Jagnath marked the withdrawal in his own fashion. The hopeful thing about it was—to Vijay's mind at any rate—that he would be less and less torn between what was good in the time-honoured sense and what the reformers said ought to be done. And when he retired from service and all his children did finally marry, he might become a very contented man indeed.

He was startled by Rajuram leaping out of his seat and grabbing the other door handle.

'Worli!' Jagnath said, sinking down beside his son. 'I was not too long, was I?'

'Not at all, father.' He threw his cigarette out of the window.

The car surged up the street, scattering people with a shrill and loud note of its horn. In the driver's mirror, the face of Rajuram fell into its usual fiendish mould.

'I met our friend Mr. Varma,' Jagnath said after a time. 'I am to give you his warmest regards.'

'That was nice of him. How was he, father?'

'Very busy and very philosophical, as always.' Jagnath was feeling much better after his visit; he tapped his breast pocket and took out an open envelope, which he held up to Vijay almost shyly. 'Look what he gave me . . . go on, open it. Mr. Varma said it will surprise you more than it did him.'

Vijay took the envelope and emptied it. A Congress membership card came to light. On the dotted line above the local secretary's signature was Jagnath's full name in red block letters.

'Arre, father, is this true? I can't believe my eyes!' he gasped.

'You must, you must, son.' Jagnath beamed more expansively. 'These are new times and every Indian is in the front ranks. How can this country ever be free if we don't think of the future now. And, by the way, Mr. Varma expressed the hope that you will also come for such a card one of these days. . . .'

2

IN MAY the sky stretched higher and the funnels of heat that made it ree l seemed to gush not from the sun, which had soared into the limbo and was diffused by its own hazes and distance, but from a stewing crater in the earth close by.

Life fagged in the hours of daylight, recouped itself after sunset, pulsed vengefully for a brief spell and then folded back until the next lull. Trembling in the uneven temper of the season, men nursed their grievances with a petty love that would have been untrue at any other time. Dust crept into their throats and noses and made it all worse—dust as fine as air and as colourless, dust welling higher and wider towards the sun and also to the ends of the earth, corroding the voices of men and battening their vision, ever present and ever raw; it gave a new flavour to breath; it sealed everything in a light film and made all surfaces alike to the touch. Riding the high crest of it from day to day, Vijay watched it engulf the landscape underneath; the blue and green strands of the coast disintegrated slowly and space became an imperfectly remembered dream. On the ground the dream hardened; dust was a hush that gave a new quality to the brilliance of May.

Even the trees felt it. Each day the gulmohars kindled their fieriest flame and each night the dust quenched them to stillness. Along the seashore of Bombay the contest spurred the forest to better and more dazzling efforts every day, but dust hovered above it and bided its time. All vegetation seemed to be in it. The hot sea breezes swishing inland in the early afternoons shook the scarlet rash of the asoks and revealed their fever, and the mimosa plumes swayed with a strong yellow glare. Obstinately they clung to the last remnant of spring, hidden in the black earth of the shade, but all the sky and certainly all dust proclaimed a summer drunk with itself, pressing hotly from above, spreading a little more each day and a little whiter each new morning.

The question why the month should have been picked for a mass political meeting addled many people. Leaders said that it had become inevitable. A deadlock was developing over the point whether Congress should put its electoral victory to some use in the reformed government, or whether the party should abstain from office altogether. Hotheads from the left wanted an open revolution; conservatives were all in favour of some real work at last and for paving the way to complete autonomy; middle-of-the-roaders urged for the best of both worlds: going into office, but only to wreck the new constitution. Decision was the greatest need of the moment and a conference was necessary. Meeting under the seething skies of May the leaders would also prove to the people that work was the same for all and that the sun beat down alike on the heads of politicians and peasants. And a great event it turned out to be for Bombay.

'We shall never get in,' Salim said, rounding the circle at Tardeo. 'Have you ever seen such a crowd? There must be half a million people on this road alone!' Saying this, he steered the car into Gowalia Tank Road and stepped on the brake immediately. Driving on became a thing of much restraint and patience.

Neither Salim nor Vijay nor Lakshman, all three of whom still hoped to reach the meeting tent at the Gowalia Tank Maidan, had ever seen anything quite like it.

Perhaps only the Magh Fair of Allahabad and Kumbh Fair of Hardwar surpassed it, and they had not seen either. Up the sloping road went this dense stream of men, women, children, young and old, Hindu and non-Hindu, and Vijay could feel them crushing the car and almost lifting it; he could hear them breathe the heavy air of the evening and smell the clouds of musk, tuberose and frangipani one after another. But for the fact that the sun had just slid beyond the jagged bastions of Cumballa Hill and nothing of it could be seen save the glare, they might have been marching straight at it, so staunch and indomitable they seemed. With their gleaming heads and white robes they made the road into a razed anthill, they even hummed like a marching army; the double rank of houses on both sides seemed to wedge apart to make room for them. A vast tide of heat rose up from them and it met the heat of the air, and the sultry result of the fusion sat on the town like an immense lid.

'Bas! Not an inch farther!' Salim said and pulled up at the left kerb. 'I am not going to have my car squeezed like a lemon!'

'Lakshman was right,' Vijay said. 'We should have stopped at Tardeo and walked from there.'

'We shall walk now, and Allah have mercy on us!' Salim said.

They got out with some difficulty and Vijay had to lean against the door to keep it open for Lakshman. Then, it was only a case of letting the flood carry them.

'Had I known it was like this, I would never have come.' Salim pushed out his elbows to secure a margin on both sides and the other two advanced in his ample wake. He had come with them from curiosity, not any patriotic urge, and had feared the heat, the smells and the pickpockets; now there was an abundance of the first two and imminent danger of the third. The upper part of his face pictured astonishment at the sight before him, the lower distaste at what he smelled. His huge head bobbed on the tide like a coconut shell of water, for he was almost a foot taller than the Gujaratis, Marathas and Marwaris who made up the mass. 'The question is,' he added over his shoulder at Vijay, 'what is a Muslim doing in an exclusively Hindu crowd?'

'It won't do you any harm,' Vijay told him. 'Have you forgotten that there are Muslims in the Congress? It is an all-India party.'

'Arre, bhai, don't give me that!' It was well known among the Muslims that this was another trick of the Hindu Congress to get their vote.

'It is a fact, Salim, whether you like it or not.'

'In that case, perhaps you will look around you and tell me how many fezes do you see?'

'Not many,' Vijay had to admit.

'That is what I mean,' Salim said. 'The only reason I do not go home is that I cannot. I am trapped in a sea of Hindus.'

He did not seem concerned with the curious scowls of some of the people around him. He wore no headgear himself, only a pair of white pyjamas and a tan silk shirt. But for that, and for his frequent use of the Urdu and English idiom, he might have passed for an Irani or Punjabi of mixed descent.

Near the tank the stream debouched into channels, each destined for a different gate of the meeting enclosure. Here the air was stiller, because the maidan lay in a hollow at the foot of the hill, and because the breeze, if there was any, blew over it at some height. However, the noise was greater. Loudspeakers had been installed in the trees and on lamp-posts, and they cracked in a fast grating Hindi; in the main tent one of the leaders was speaking to the assembly, but Vijay couldn't think who it was. The voice came over them like the first harbinger of a hurricane; it tried to say something about the suffering of the Indian peasant and his bottomless poverty, and it brought in religion and the staggering birth rate, which would have been good signs for the future save that they were defeated by general misery, and presently the faulty installations made it sound like the raving of an awakened Gargantua. Men and women at whom it stormed went on milling around the little square, their faces showing no anxiety; they laughed and felt reassured by the nearness of the leaders; after all, the voice was not addressing them, but only a small and chosen audience in the main tent. They listened to it with one ear, for they were still outside the conference grounds, and with the other they listened to one another and enjoyed themselves. It was fun to be in the street, pushing among so many laughing faces, and it was good to know that the fate of India was in such capable hands. They had cast their vote last winter; now it was up to the leaders to use it as they thought fit.

'What could he be saying?' Salim asked the other two. 'He sounds very angry.'

'It is Subhas Chandra Bose,' Lakshman said, reviving. 'He doesn't want the party to have any truck with government. I have heard him before.'

'How can he speak so fast?' Salim said.

'He is a Bengali, don't you know,' Vijay said. 'They all talk fast.'

The thought of the radical leader's harangue led Vijay to his own present problem: How to find father and Tara in that multitude? They had gone to the meeting earlier in the afternoon and he was to join them as soon as he got back from Juhu; they were to be in their reserved seats in the main tent and wait for him. But he was beginning to feel doubtful. It was hard to see how any organization, however thorough, could outlive so great a mass of people; he thought that anyone venturing into the spawn pool would be sucked up instantly and swallowed without trace. Anyhow, Salim seemed to have that opinion.

'Let me wait for you right here near the gate,' he said diffidently. 'What will happen if we should get in and find that we cannot move?'

'I must find them,' Vijay said. 'And without you we couldn't push through at all.'

'I would prefer a glass of water to any speeches.'

'I am thirsty, too,' Lakshman said. 'Let us have a drink.'

They pushed through to the southern side where vendors had set up stalls of refreshments. They found the sherbets too vividly coloured and the aerated waters too fizzy, but Lakshman nevertheless had an orangeade; Vijay and Salim preferred the crush of bamboo shoots made on the spot. The seller, a Surti with a grimy cap tilted over a cowlick of lustrous black hair, stuck the shoots into the press and worked the lever; the juice poured into the glasses full of air bubbles, tepid, but tasting good. While they were still guzzling, a bevy of snickering Hindu girls stopped by and ordered a round for themselves. They wore the plain white saris of students and their hair was oiled and beflowered, and their slender bare arms reminded Vijay of spring vegetables. They tossed their plaits and shook their wrists as they prattled, and their bangles tinkled like a troupe of dancers getting into step. Salim's dour frowns vanished like magic.

'Now that the sun is down, bhai,' he said to Vijay, 'I am beginning to feel much better. I am also thinking that any politics with pretty young girls in it cannot be so bad.'

Lakshman saw his ogling and it made him restless. He emptied his glass and gave it back to the Surti. Among the girls there was a fresh outburst of giggles.

'I told you there would be many things of interest,' Vijay said to Salim. He, too, inhaled the dry, flowery scent which now overpowered all other smells.

'One might think men ruled the world,' a girl said brazenly.

'One doesn't have to think,' he said. 'One knows for fact.'

'Well spoken, bhai,' Salim said. 'It is for men to do things and for women to put flowers in their hair. A due and proper ramification.'

'Are they not too swollen with pride!' the girl exclaimed, tacking the sari to her shoulder. The movement revealed a shiny yellow bodice and a full upturned breast.

Lakshman looked away, hot around the ears. The real thing was always so much more poignant than the bloodless similes which he laboured so hard to put in its place. 'Breasts like ripe mangoes' had seemed apt when he last thought of it for a poem of his, but now the quivering pullulation of the bodice outshone it so utterly that he vowed never again to use the expression. He had not the nerve of Salim or Vijay; they had had many women and when they looked at a girl they knew what to look for and how to value it. He was a virgin, racked, among other things, by too sharp an imagination; forms to him were chance embodiments of a set of words whirling inside his brain without respite, and sometimes they appeared so suddenly and vividly that the words refused to fit them. It was in those moments that being a poet struck him as a painfully vicarious existence. He edged away in a huff, tortured by the scents and the giggling.

'What a waste of time to listen now to a dull politician,' Salim said.

'I could almost agree,' Vijay said. 'What would you rather do?'

'Arre, bhai!' Salim gave him a sidelong glance. 'Is this a real question . . .?'

The girls paid and sauntered off, preening and glancing back. Vijay watched the arrogant sway of their hips and remembered Chanda; she, too, ambled along a little like that, with the soundless heave of a cheetah, and her hips rocked just as rhythmically. That seemed to be peculiar to Indian girls. It was an old Indian belief that the lifelong wearing of sandals made a woman's step fluid, her thighs round and desirable; they flowed onward sensuously, where the Western woman bounced and jerked. He felt that the difference had never been as apparent as at that moment.

Then loudspeakers poured out another voice—a persuasive, soft one that sounded as though it were weaned on profound philosophical texts and twilight. Where the previous one had crashed and whipped, this one fluttered over the square like a rare bird, so that scores of people stifled their laughter to listen to it.

'Maulana Kalam Azad,' Lakshman explained, moving along towards the gate. 'We must go in now or we shall miss the best speeches.'

'Do you hear, Salim?' Vijay said. 'Here is a Muslim who is not afraid of being an Indian first and Muslim only afterwards.'

'I hear, bhai. What of it?'

'I like his voice. He sounds trustworthy.'

'One Muslim on top doesn't make the Congress any less Hindu. What does one voice like that mean? Does it speak to this rabble . . .? No, my friend. It speaks merely to itself and from habit.'

Lakshman made a piqued grimace; he was finding Salim's disparagements a little tiresome. 'Can you once stop thinking of numbers?' he said wryly. 'It doesn't matter how many Muslims or Hindus are in the high command. This man would die for India any day. You may be a Muslim like him, but I don't think you would do the same.'

'He would die for less than that,' Vijay said. 'He sounds that kind of person.'

'I would not be too sure,' Salim said. 'Dying is a one-sided business.'

'Everything on this earth is one-sided,' Lakshman said, coughing and putting his hand to his mouth. 'You should not mind dying if you have left your mark behind you.' He went forward, waiting for Salim's reply, but none came. He tried to confine the itching to his chest, forcibly, by holding his breath as long as he could endure, and the odd sensation finally passed. 'Dying,' Tara had told him one afternoon as they walked out of college reading an afternoon newspaper, 'should not be hopeless when one has accomplished everything else.' They were talking about the death of a famous Sikh poet in the Punjab, and she thought that poets were particularly exempt from the usual sorrows of death.

'After all,' she said, placing him on the same plane with the dead laureate, 'you will only be going to where you came from. You came down here only to give us a little beauty and help us to understand ourselves!'

It was this simple faith in his future that made him first realize what a good friend she was. With her he was never shy or awkward. They talked freely about everything that interested him, and never quarrelled. When he coughed before her for the first time, she didn't stare at him as though it were an impolite thing to do; she heard his poems with closed eyes and could often repeat whole lines several days afterwards; he liked that about her and naturally wanted to meet her oftener. He was going to, now, though the meeting had not been planned. He did not know if he loved her, but it was certainly significant that he thought of her whenever a lyrical image rose up in his mind, or whenever he coughed.

Then the sun must have gone down finally because the flaming pinnacles of the street went out and the dusk set in incandescently. Contours softened, hues sobered down. All the heat of the sky seemed to sink into the earth's own and all the smells seemed to trickle into the bowl of the maidan and lie perfectly calm. Walking towards the gate of the enclosure Vijay stirred it like a liquid. He had known it as a boy and had thought it a part of himself, but had later become unused to it: this smell of his own people crowding together in common excitement, this fountain that sprang up so swiftly in a few hours, invigorating all who bathed in it. It was full of women's perfumes and men's sweat, and of their boisterous laughter and fraternization; politics simply gave it a devil-may-care quality. Breathing it again after so many years in all its teeming potency gave him a sense of anchor; he felt again that being Indian was synonymous with the beginning of the world; he felt older and safer.

Salim was taking it less well. Dark stains disfigured his silk shirt under the arms and on his chest, and he shoved more roughly and made fewer apologies. As they passed under the loudspeaker and neared the gate he stuck his fingers into his ears and made a wry face.

'We will not get out of it alive.'

The efforts of the uniformed volunteers to regulate the traffic at the entrance had long ceased to be effective, but they kept up a hoarse chant and waved their arms. Two lathi-armed policemen did their best to deepen the confusion; they said little but used their hands generously. Salim brushed past them and Vijay saw him sailing through a tight knot of angry young Muslims, one of whom raised an arm to hold him. He wore sunglasses and his face was pockmarked.

'If you want to push, we can push too,' he said in Urdu.

'Arre, brother, take your arm away,' Salim answered, pressing the fellow's hand downward.

Even as he did it, a little island formed in the stream and friends of the pockmarked boy swarmed around him.

'He is Salim Haq,' the first one said loudly. 'I know him.'

'What of it?' Salim said.

'Salim Haq, the renegade Muslim, that is who you are! A traitor to your own people.' He turned to his mates and added shrilly, 'Do you not see him standing here in all his shame . . .? He even admits it, he cares so little. This offender of Islam, this befouler of . . .'

Salim smacked him across the mouth with the back of his hand. 'Enough of the spluttering!' he said sharply. 'Get out of my way!'

The boy took off his glasses and threw himself on Salim. For a split second Vijay saw his eyes and thought that their look was familiar, then he was seized from behind and brushed aside without ceremony.

'Traitor of Islam! This time you are not dealing with a Parsi!' The boy slashed out at the tower of Salim rather ineffectually.

'Unnameable misfit of a she-camel!' Salim cried.

'Go away, leave us alone!' Vijay shouted from the fringe of the island.

But the others closed in uttering ugly words and invoking the Prophet, and Salim staggered under the onslaught. Although it was an unequal combat, he seemed to be strengthened by an accumulated rage that had been dormant up to that moment; he growled and reeled about first to dislodge a boy who had jumped on his back and then to grapple with the original offender. Each time he pushed one of them or dealt a blow he groaned a two-syllable obscenity. Some women nearby began to scream and their babies howled.

'Police! Police!'

Lakshman, too, screamed 'Police!' He could not move from astonishment. He clutched in vain at the shirt ends of the assailants, and they paid him little attention. 'Arre, bhai, this is an outrage . . . !' he shouted towards the volunteers caught in the swirling stream.

Vijay lunged into the cluster and fought through with all his force. He didn't know the reason for the attack, but he had got over his first shock and felt himself strangely roused over the unfair odds against his friend; a dozen men fighting one was not in the Rajput tradition. He called encouragement to Salim and disposed of the two nearest boys in short order.

'Stop, stop, or I shall arrest you!' a policeman said as he elbowed himself forward.

His wooden stick went into action and the turmoil boiled up briefly. A posse of volunteers appeared at the same time. The knot loosened, came undone, stopped fighting. The pockmarked boy jerked out of the policeman's grasp and slipped away and two of his comrades managed to follow him. When the order-makers began their inquiry, there were only Salim, Vijay and some unknown puffing youths to answer the questions.

'It is no place for rioting,' the senior volunteer said. 'Are you trying to discredit a Congress meeting before the authorities? What was it all about?'

'I don't know who they are. I have never seen them.' Salim brushed his hair back and pulled his shirt straight.

'He would not let us pass,' a boy said, with a bleeding scratch on the side of his chin.

'Liar, it was you who wouldn't let us pass,' Vijay told him.

'We cannot have rioting on these grounds,' the volunteer said pedantically. 'Now kindly get out and stay out.' He began to muster his men for an escort.

'In the first place, I had no wish to come,' Salim told him. 'In the second, now that I am inside, I shall remain inside.'

'Then you did cause the disturbance?'

'I did not, positively.'

'Breaking the peace of a public place,' the policeman said. 'I have a good mind to take you to the chowki.'

'Just you try.'

Vijay explained that they were peaceful visitors to the meeting and were looking for their family; they had no quarrel with anyone. The constable seemed relieved, but the volunteers glanced questioningly at their superior.

'If there is any more trouble,' this last said, 'you shall be taken off the precincts and handed over to the police.' When no one answered, he signed to his men and they fell back among the crowd. The boys who had been in the fray went after them sullenly.

The island dissolved as quickly as it had come into being and the stream surged up as before. Vijay and Salim moved along, while Lakshman, whom the upheaval had washed some distance away, called after them and joined them a little later. They walked in the direction of the speakers' tent, brushing their hair and straightening their clothes. Heat, noise and humidity reigned supreme.

'The hot-tempered little brats!' Salim said. 'I never saw them before in my life.' His anger was gone; he did not look at Vijay but stared ahead and sounded merely peevish. 'They have not yet come out of school and already they think they can judge all and sundry. If it were the first time, I wouldn't mind. But it has happened before. A fortnight ago someone left a blood-stained Koran at the door of my flat. There was a note in it. It seems my novel has upset some people who have not bothered to read it entire.'

'These boys were Muslims.'

'That is what makes it so unbelievable.' He attempted a grin of irony and almost succeeded, but his heart was not in it. 'You have heard them call me a despoiler of Islam. Brother, it would be hard to think of a more stupid accusation.'

Vijay recalled the fanatical fire in the eyes of the pockmarked fellow. It was unbelievable and yet apparently true. Men who had lived peaceably side by side all these years were beginning to forget that they were all Indians; if you were one of their kind and refused to feel as they did, they hated you just as much as an outsider. In public they were apt to put it down to a fault of the British—'Divide and rule, an old trick, don't you know?'—but in moments like these the glint of their hate betrayed them. He said nothing more to Salim as they neared the tent.

Soon the squat, canvas-shaded auditorium rose up before them and there was Tara waving a sheet of paper at them, trying to attract their attention. The sight of her lively face braced them up considerably.

'You were so late, father sent me to look for you. Vijay, did you see Rajuram? He is supposed to be looking out for you at the eastern gate. . . .'

'We came through the northern gate,' Vijay said.

'How are you, Tara? Have you been heckling Gandhiji?' Salim grinned at her.

Lakshman bowed over his joined palms and flushed. She returned his greeting and ignored Salim's question.

'You are here at long last, but you can't go in just now,' she said. 'Each and every seat is occupied, even the aisles are full of people sitting on the floor. Gandhiji has not spoken yet . . . he will probably speak to-morrow. We are all waiting to hear him. . . . Oh yes, Vijay, I nearly forgot. A letter for you, I think from Chanda.' She gave it to him with a significant look and a pout of the lips. 'It came this afternoon as I was leaving home.'

He stuffed it in his pocket.

'Bhai, what an inspiration for a great patriotic poem,' she said to Lakshman. 'I have been thinking about it all afternoon, but all I could think of was *Bande Mataram*. I hope you will do better than that.'

He nodded and looked into her bright and alert eyes.

227

3

THERE was a thunderous ovation and the enclosure shook like a ship on rough sea. On the speakers' pandal—rostrum—several heads came together and sheets of paper passed hands; they were too far away to be seen clearly and the garish light, beating down on them from bunches of bulbs on the ceiling, flashed on their spectacles as they moved, making them even less discernible; when Vijay screwed up one eye they began to look very much like a group of big woolly ewes prodding each other playfully. They were in white and either sat cross-legged or drooped backwards on their elbows, in clusters and irregular rows.

The pandal was large, draped also in white, with a huge Congress flag as backdrop and a microphone in the foreground; one flank of the rostrum was given to the press, the other to the party secretariat. The tent was an oblong of tightly packed chairs, strung together with bamboo poles, rope, canvas and sheets of jute sacking; even though its sides were open to the maidan, it reeked of perfume and heat. White was the dress of an overwhelming majority of men and women, but there were many fashionably dressed Hindu ladies and Europeans in silk suits. These were the paid seats. In the open field, a park common otherwise, was the humble mass who came not to be seen but to hear the message, and they squatted on their own mats and on the parched grass.

'That one with the elbow on the bolster is Gandhiji,' Tara pointed out. 'He looks so much younger than he ought to be. I wish we were closer so that you could see him better.'

'I can see him quite well. Where is father?' Vijay said.

'In the seventh row . . . on the left. Can you see him . . .?' He could, and she went on singling out the people worthy of note. 'By the side of Gandhiji is Jawaharlal . . . still very thin from the jail, poor man. . . .' She used the affectionate suffix 'ji' with the tenderness of one who not only knew these men but also loved them, and she could not help a flapper's note of awe. 'Look well, bhai,' she said. 'When Gandhiji goes, Jawaharlal will be the leader of India. He was speaking just before you came . . . what a pity you missed him. It was the finest speech of the day. And, you know, he has the most beautiful eyes I have ever seen . . . and such a soft, cultured voice. His hair is becoming grey, but I think it suits him very well.'

Now the applause died down and a tall, rugged-looking man stepped up to the edge of the pandal. He had the scraggy beard and hooked nose of a frontiersman, and he wore a voluminous white shawl loosely over his upper body.

228

'Abdul Ghafar Khan,' Lakshman whispered in the sudden silence, leaning towards Vijay.

'Seven feet at the very least,' Tara said impressed. 'How can a giant like that be non-violent, I ask you?'

'He is, all the same,' Lakshman said. 'No wonder they call him the Frontier Gandhi.'

The giant spoke up and his throaty bass came out of the nearest loudspeaker like a man-devised waterfall; there was power in it, but it was being used carefully and for a pre-ordained purpose. The meeker Hindus in the audience watched him with a mixture of fascination and disbelief, for, although a Muslim from the most intractable part of India, he was also one of them and an invaluable showpiece for the creed of One India.

'That one there, looking like a professor of archæology, is Maulana Kalam Azad,' Tara continued. 'Isn't he sweet, bhai? Black-rimmed glasses . . . a beard, moustache . . . just like an Iman. And never, never loses his temper, something wonderful. I do think he would make a very good president, don't you, Salim?'

Salim rolled his eyes, phewed comically, then slouched. 'I assure you, it would make no difference to me whatever,' he said. 'It would certainly not make me a Congressman. If Vijay here were a president . . . well, that would be something else.' He had recovered his good humour, but this atmosphere of resolution and efficiency was alien to his temperament.

A Marwari who looked like a cotton broker turned stiffly in his seat and glowered them to silence; the gold braiding of his turban glimmered briefly and richly. Salim stared back, then shrugged and said nothing more. Lakshman leaned on a bamboo pole, trying to listen to the speech and at the same time hear what Tara was saying. Every now and then his eyes would sidle to her neatly wound tresses and to the flowers in them, and he would think again what a pretty and stately girl she was.

'S. C. Bose, the stormy petrel of Bengal,' Tara was saying close to her brother's ear. 'The fattish, young one behind Jawaharlalji. You can see he is a Bengali, can't you? They are all round and plump . . . and so sleek, but their tempers are something awful. I heard him once before and he screamed just like an angry woman.'

'Isn't he supposed to be a radical?' Salim inquired.

'Radical . . .?' She gave him a long and indulgent look, which he brazened out with a grin, then added, 'He is a revolutionary, no less. All Bengalis are revolutionaries, don't you know? They are not fighters like the Rajputs, but they always know how to rebel.'

Observing her with guarded longing, Lakshman thought that a very acute remark. It accorded so well with his admiration of her and with all his sketchy knowledge of far Bengal, and it sent his mind ticking in a vague metrical rhythm. *Methinks what glorious deeds of yore, are thine, O voluble rebel of Barrackpore* . . . and then words brimmed up in his head in a mild whirl and a mist drew over his half-closed eyes. Leaning on the bamboo pole more comfortably, he straggled off in quest of rhymes and images.

'Where are Premchand and Rana Prashad?' Vijay said, wishing to wind up the catalogue of leaders. 'I thought they would be in the meeting this afternoon.'

Tara narrowed her eyes towards the rostrum. 'They are hard to make out,' she said after a pause. 'If you can see Sarojini Naidu . . . there on the right, yes the fat one . . . Rana Prashad ought to be right behind her. Anyhow, she was, before I came out. She spoke this morning, I was told . . . there were a few catcalls on the maidan.'

'I wish her daughters were here. Chanda says in her letter she's full of envy.'

'Uncle Premchand has a desk all to himself by the side of the pandal,' Tara said, missing the point altogether. 'He will not speak . . . he is making a record of the meeting. They are supposed to stop at seven, and then we will meet him . . . and her. By the way, what is the time now?' And when he showed her his watch: 'Goodness, six o'clock already! Then it is almost the end. It serves you right for coming so late!'

'If I knew what it was all about,' Salim said, shifting, 'it might not be so boring.'

Tara searched his face, but restrained herself. Ignoring the pointed stares of the Marwari gentleman and some other disturbed people besides, she summed up the day's speeches for Salim's benefit. 'You might as well think about it intelligently, if you think at all,' she told him by way of reproof. It was all so simple that a child would understand it, really. 'You do see, don't you,' she said, 'that a national ministry could never get going if it knew that a governor could veto their work at will . . .?' Well, all this talk was about that, and it was important that everyone had his say. They were all inclined to form national cabinets and go to work, but they wanted at the same time to guard themselves against any tricks or breach of promise. 'And let me tell you, Salim,' she wound up pertly, 'you ought to be ashamed to be so ignorant. Apart from the Marut's Hour, which, thank God, you don't write any more, haven't you ever read anything else . . .?'

'I read my novel, Tara. It is satisfying and I can understand it better.'

At this stage there was already much throat clearing and fidgeting in the audience, and the gaunt frontiersman on the pandal seemed to sense it, for he speeded up the rest of his delivery in a heightened voice. Vijay heard him out, wondering at the force of his logic and his smooth tone, so unusual in a Muslim from Peshawar. And behind him the sheep swayed this way and that, and glasses shone like sudden looks of recognition. Then he folded his notes and stepped back and another hurricane of clapping almost raised the roof of the tent. Tara, Vijay and Lakshman joined in, while Salim crossed his arms and looked more bored than ever.

Afterwards the party secretary came to the microphone and made a short announcement.

'Adjourned until to-morrow morning,' Tara echoed him. 'Oh, I wish I could come right at the start.'

'You can read about it in the papers and you won't be crushed to death,' Salim said.

'It is never the same as being here.' She said that with a real and sincere regret, causing Salim to gaze at her in wonder. But Vijay and Lakshman knew what she meant and Lakshman murmured a ready approval.

Then everyone lumbered to his feet and the man at the microphone began to sing into it. He was nervous and the first line of the song rang out falsely.

'Mother, I bow to thee . . .'

Skipping along at first, then gaining in confidence and enthusiasm, the slow graceless bars of *Bande Mataram* flowed out of the tent and over the maidan, and the night itself seemed to take it up and lift it higher and farther, enriching it with a music and power of quite another order. Vijay sang it too, and so did his sister and Lakshman. He knew only the first lines and only a portion of the repetitious melody, but that didn't seem to matter. The secretary gave the rest; his husky rendering withstood even the rasping importunities of the loudspeakers. Then all sang and hummed it, and a great number of people closed their eyes and relished each for himself the great welling of patriotic oneness.

'Rich with thy hurrying streams,
bright with thy orchard gleams,
cool with the winds of delight,
dark fields waving, Mother of might,
Mother free . . .'

Stumbling in the broad and plangent wake of the anthem, repeating the lyrics after the leader as though he were learning a vow, Vijay found himself tingling once more with the old sense of belonging. His thoughts fuzzed over and seemed to float on the bore, feathery, as if cut loose from all weed and undergrowth, and their airiness was as real as it was sudden. At his side Tara and Lakshman raced on ahead of the main wave, each warm and clear, as though pleading to be recognized. There was rapture of an unknown kind on Tara's face, and it was mirrored on all the faces around her. Salim sulked mutely, his hands folded on his chest in the polite posture of non-participation. From outside came a massive undulating echo of the song, and he heard it lag behind the loudspeakers, sometimes an entire bar;

231

the people outside sounded determined to take their own time and sing each word to the full. The white bundles now stood upright on the pandal and the large-eared old man stooped no longer but drawled lustily after the rest.

Yes, it was a great, hair-raising, goosefleshy moment, the like of which he could not remember. It was another way of saying what he had felt from time to time, but saying it in a melodious all-Indian language: that being Indian was being endless. He had no doubt that all of it was karma yoga in its stoutest and most uprooting essence and that men at all levels of life were groping for something common to all, and that this gesture was a proof of their prime unity. Not only that, but the song took that unity far into the night and raised it up towards the stars, so that it became a unity of cosmos at the same time, and Indians from all four corners of the land could see it plainly and write its absolute truth into their nobler souls.

He was startled by sudden silence, then by another gust of thunder. Heads rocked and bounced. Several white caps soared towards the ceiling, accompanied by shouts of 'Gandhiji-ki-jai!' 'Jawaharlal-ki-jai!' 'Congress-ki-jai!' A loud and fervent voice said, 'Inquilab Zindabad!' and others chorused it from all parts of the tent. Some thronged the rostrum, while chairs rattled and scraped wildly. Then all became blurred, like a street square behind a wet pane, and one part of it began to bulge and another melt away. The maidan trembled, the herding began; all faces seemed to beam. Presently the loudspeakers spoke up again advising moderation and a peaceful dispersal. When Vijay turned round to talk to Salim, he was not there.

'He left during the singing,' Lakshman said. 'Muslims do not like *Bande Mataram.*'

'I didn't think he was that kind of Muslim,' Tara said, surprised.

'I didn't, either.'

'He just got bored, I know him,' Vijay said in excuse of his friend.

Then he waited for Jagnath, in order to help him find Rajuram and the car, after which he thought he would look for Salim; the rush was too great for anything more methodical. At that moment it looked as though it would be hours before the stampede sorted itself out.

'Come with me,' Tara said and started to shove forward. 'I know father wanted to speak to Uncle Premchand before it was all over. He is bound to be near the stage somewhere. . . .'

They waded through a jungle of chairs and the skirt of her sari stuck frequently on the protruding leg of an overturned seat. They saw a couple of volunteers help Mr. Gandhi from the rostrum, while a great many more hovered about in attitudes of hawklike apprehension; the old man stopped at the canvas flap to join his palms and bow to his applauding admirers. Vijay saw him much better now. The toothless grin was not pretty, but it was charming in another way; it reminded him of a fairy story of Mr. Varma's, in which a stone Jain saint came down from the temple freize to mingle with men and beam pleasure at what he saw; only the gold-rimmed glasses gave the legend a modern touch. He bowed humbly a few times and his lips twitched nervously, then he waved his skinny arm and vanished, with the hustling escort at his heels.

'A great, great man . . . the father of Bharat Mata,' Tara said.

When they finally ran Jagnath to earth another excited upheaval took place outside. They could not see what was happening, they only heard the screams of women and the shouting of men, but the noise was mixed and too far away, a part of the larger lake of noise. There was whistling that sounded as though the police were on the scene, then more and louder screams and a new swirling of the hot and jam-packed mass. The edge of the maidan seemed to recede as the turmoil within it boiled up. Anxiously, Jagnath stood up on his toes and tried to look over the sea of heads.

'We shall never get home at this rate. I hope no one is behaving badly. I hope there is no trouble of any kind.'

'We must expect some,' Premchand said, gathering the papers on his official desk. 'There has been no trouble so far, thank goodness, but it would be unnatural if——' The loudspeaker drowned him out. He listened tensely, his eyes moving from Jagnath to Vijay, from Tara to his stepson, and the lenses over his eyes seemed to magnify his worry. He strummed the paper he was holding.

'This is the chairman of the reception committee speaking,' the voice boomed. 'In the name of peace and order I ask you to leave the maidan and go home. . . . Men and women of Hindustan, show that you are good citizens. . . . Remember that the authorities are waiting for something like this . . . so that they can stop the meeting and silence the voice of the people. Disperse in good order, I implore you . . .!'

A volunteer rushed past and Premchand made a swift jab at his sleeve and caught it.

'Hooligans making a row,' the man gasped. 'Muslims, I think . . . government agents very likely. Refused to sing Bande Mataram and the people got upset. . . .'

'What is being done about it?'

The harassed little fellow freed his arm and stood up on his toes. 'We are trying to stop it, but the police have started to meddle . . . what stupidity . . .! I must go. . . .' He went off, wiping his face with a tomato-red scarf.

'Wait here!' Premchand said to the family. 'We cannot afford to have this kind of trouble . . . it would be unforgivable.' He climbed the panald from which all leaders had gone by now, and spoke to the man at the microphone. They had a short argument which the loudspeakers rendered as a disjointed staccato dialogue in singsong English, and then Premchand clutched the stem of the apparatus and spoke into it with an altogether new voice.

'Fellow countrymen, calm down and go to the exits,' he said slowly. 'Remember the words of our great leader Gandhiji . . . love and non-violence conquer everything. This is a peaceful assembly of the people and we want to keep it peaceful . . . we must be strong and show discipline if we are to gain our goals. We must be the living examples of ahimsa to others. . . . Now hear this and do as you are told. . . .' He went on in a soothing low drone, without a single inflection, and the words poured out over the field from a dozen points at once and their combined mesmerism took on some of the languor of the hot summer evening; under its weight the screaming lost its terror and the upheaval began to falter. 'There are four gates in all . . . one at each side of the maidan . . . and many emergency gates,' the drone explained tirelessly. Yet the man who intoned so calmly was himself a picture of pent-up intensity and the hand that gripped the stem of the microphone was almost without colour. It seemed to Vijay that if this was non-violence in action, it was all a human being could stand at one time.

'How foolish, how foolish of them,' said Jagnath. 'What good is such scuffling to anybody! How can people get so excited over practically nothing. . . . Imagine what the outside world must think of us!'

He had sat in a hot, cramped position all afternoon and could not understand why anybody should not be glad of an opportunity to go home; behind his irritation, too, there lurked an official's instinctive aversion to disorder and commotion; though he would not admit it, rowdyism stood in his mind for childishness.

'How can you talk of nothing, pitaji?' Tara said reprovingly. 'If you were against something, would you not say so openly?'

'I would, Tara, most certainly . . . but without the police. Truth does not always have to mean a disturbance.'

'That is just it, pitaji. Our truth always brings out the police.'

'Well, it's getting quieter,' Vijay said. 'We might try to get out now.'

But Jagnath wanted to wait for Premchand and for Rana Prashad, if she was still around. They were to drive up to Premchand's home for a cup of tea before dispersing for the day. Transport had to be arranged and tickets secured for the following day. So they lingered on a little longer and wiped their faces and fanned themselves with anything they could find. At length the uncle wound up his appeal and stepped down to them; his forehead was wet, but the awful tension was gone from his face.

'I hope that you made them see sense,' Jagnath told him. 'Where is Rana?'

'Left with the others. I told her to meet us at home. . . .' He discovered Vijay and added: 'How are you, Vijay?'

'Very well, uncle. That was fine work you just did.'

'I only hope it helps, dear boy. A crowd of these proportions is like a dragon without a head. It is afraid, so it lashes about wildly and usually hurts the innocent. Well, let us leave then,' he added, shining his glasses on his white shirt. 'We have done all we could . . . now it is up to the people themselves.'

The crush was still on as they ventured into the open ground, only now the terror seemed to have gone from it for good. Humidity had increased; there was a slight breeze that ruffled but did not cool. Policemen and volunteers were in evidence. They also came across a few Eurasian sergeants, looking very harassed and very crimson. Vijay resented their pushing and their proprietary airs.

When he asked himself why he did, he found he could not answer. They were there on an ostensible mission of public peace, yet that was only a minute facet of their presence. It seemed to him that they had no right to be there and that their unsavoury grimaces were a crude and uncouth denial of all that had occurred during the last few hours; he believed that he resented them not only for himself but also on behalf of his family and Uncle Premchand, whose impressive performance on the pandal was still fresh in his memory.

4

SALIM sat smoking in his car when he found him. They were to join the others at Uncle Premchand's on Cumballa Hill, Vijay told him, and have refreshments before going home; but the Muslim declined politely. He would drop him there, however. He put the car in gear and began to crawl forward at a pace no greater than that of the milling crowd.

Night had already set in, but heat did not abate. There was dust again, too, kicked up by thousands of sandalled feet tapping slowly in one broad direction, towards Tardeo. Shop lights burned brightly on both sides and some merchants could be seen leaning precariously over the heads of their customers. Trams stood marooned in the middle of the road, packed to a hot and patient capacity, while the white-clad stream tore happily around their bows. Frail, unlovely Gujarati women shrieked to their husbands, who shrieked back; babies, riding pickaback above the current, shrieked for their supper and their tired little bodies sagged and shook like the dolls'.

At the circle, Salim forded over to the left and turned off. He blew a huge sigh of relief at the windscreen.

'Never again, brother! Never!'

The new street was darker and he put on the headlamps. The beam cut out a wide slice of pavement and trees on both sides.

'What became of you at the end of that speech?' Vijay asked him. 'Someone said the singing made you run.'

'Hundred per cent. correct, my friend. *Bande Mataram* is a foolish song, which ever way you look at it.'

Vijay let the rudeness pass. 'You missed a lot of excitement, you know. It seems there was a fight on the maidan. . . .'

'I am not surprised,' Salim said. 'I spoke to a man at the gate and he said some of your people beat up a couple of Muslims for refusing to sing. What else did you expect?'

'We didn't hear about the beating,' Vijay said and, wishing to be fair, added: 'If that is true, it is very bad of course.'

'It is more than that, my friend. It is very stupid. You cannot go round begging Muslims to join the Congress and then feel offended if they will have nothing to do with *Bande Mataram*. It has been happening too often lately. Listen to this'—and he paused a second to concentrate:

> '"Who said thou art weak in thy lands,
>   when the swords flash in seventy million hands
>   and seventy million voices roar
>   thy dreadful name from shore to shore . . .?"

'You think a Muslim likes to be compared to a mad highwayman in the national anthem? Do you expect him to sing such a stupid song?'

'But Salim, those words have been scratched long ago. What we sang was perfectly harmless!'

'That will not fool anyone. It remains the same song.'

'Well, I don't believe you. That's no excuse for leaving a meeting,' Vijay said.

They pulled up on a corner and Salim bought two betel-nut rolls from a biddi-wallah. They chewed silently and spat the juice out of the open doors and found the ritual refreshing. Vijay, who used pan seldom, found the flavour a pleasant antidote to dust in his mouth; it quenched his thirst somewhat. It also toned up Salim's spirits, so that when they continued the drive the air in the car sparkled noticeably less.

'I hope you understand me well,' Salim said, cruising along leisurely. 'I do not defend anyone at the expense of someone else. I do not care for politics . . . and especially I do not care how many Muslims or Hindus there are in the Congress. I am against hypocrisy in any shape or form. Logic is logic, after all.' And when his friend challenged this cryptic statement, he went on to elaborate. 'I do not like labels. I think that all this League talk of the Muslims being a different nation is the blackest reaction.

236

It is tactical eyewash. We were born here and of course we are Indians. And as for your Congress'—he spat out of the window and wiped himself with a silk handkerchief—'I like them even less. No matter how hard I try, I see no future in their tune of non-violence.'

'There is so much else they believe in, Salim.'

'No doubt, bhai . . . but they cannot hide their Hinduism . . . just as the Pathans, Momins, Sikhs and Parsis cannot help being what they are. Too many labels, too many parties, too many different costumes and kinds of worship . . . that is the undoing of India. Classification comes first, brains only afterwards. I should like to be an Indian without being classified. I do not force my songs on anyone, and I do not wish anyone to force his songs on me.'

'But that is India, Salim. We must give in and hope for the best. We can't have unity without some trouble to each of us. I once thought we could, but I have come to change my mind. You cannot remove our differences by sitting in a chair in Juhu. You must organize and fight them.'

'Sorry, bhai . . . no organization. I can also ignore them. Juhu is a good place for that.'

'A terrible picture, Salim. Really terrible.'

'On the contrary, my friend. A sober and sensible picture.' Sighing aloud, he bent forward over the wheel and peered into the darkness beyond the beam. 'But enough of it for now,' he said in a changed voice. 'I do not wish to think of politics until next month.'

He sheered off to the right and slowed down to enter a narrow byway, and Vijay saw him smirk indistinctly. The beam uncovered a winding ribbon of asphalt cleaner than that of the road and a line of gardens marked by tall walls of bougainvillæa. Behind the trees and their creepers were the pale residences of the neighbourhood.

'Where are you going?' Vijay said.

'Where there is music and people talk about simple and charming things my friend. Follow me and profit by it.'

They passed a ramshackle gate and pulled up under a banyan tree rising suddenly out of a cobblestone drive. Salim cleared his throat and spat for the last time.

'What about the Premchands?' Vijay asked.

'I shall take you there too, have no fear.'

They climbed out, and Vijay followed him along the dark and uneven drive in mounting wonder. He thought that one part of his friend, the irrational and easygoing one, was still the same as in the old days, but that the others were becoming hard to fathom. Certainly he had become more petulant and conflicting, and his moods changed more quickly, so that one seldom knew which was the real Salim and which his fitful shadow. School texts were wont to suggest that Islam finally went down in a blaze of glory in the Indian Mutiny of the 1850s and that the Indian Muslim had not salvaged his soul since, but Vijay was not quite so certain. Salim had had everything necessary for full success and he, too, had brought back from Europe a more acute view of his own potential. What went wrong, when and where?

'Follow me, bhai,' Salim said climbing a broad verandah where a naked bulb shed light on some wicker furniture and a striped durrie. Beetles buzzed around the light and a mouse scuttled across the entrance ahead of them.

'Salim, I mustn't be late, please remember.'

Indian music came from one of the back rooms. They stopped in an ornate salon, spread with disintegrating Bokharas, lighted by a pendant in the shape of a Mogul tower, and Salim gave his name to an old red-bearded servant. The music died away. They took off their slippers and trailed the old man to a large, hexagonal room in the rear of the building, where the floor was done up with clean white sheets and a kind of thick matting that sucked in the step in a softly opulent way. Several divans had golden-brown and crimson rugs thrown over them, and the lamps were again shaded by Mogul lattices and bakrum of a warm, honeylike hue which blurred every shadow and kindled every fold. Cushions had silk tassels and mounted warriors painted on them; an incongruous table fan purred quietly at them, as also at the young woman lounging picturesquely in one corner.

She flashed a hospitable white smile at Salim's introductions and seemed pleased to see him. She wore billowing salvar trousers of the Punjab, pleated together at the ankles, and a long kurta shirt of red satin, cut out dizzily at the breasts; her veil was all over the bolster, its tail trembling in the fan wind. She was surprisingly pretty.

'You are handsome too.' She returned Salim's preliminaries with languid grace. 'So is your friend here. I knew he was a Rajput when he stepped into the room.'

'A Rajput is a half-Muslim,' Salim said. 'Rajputs and Muslims are the cream of India, and you have them both.' He flourished his long arm in a gallant wave of surrender.

They prattled on and Salim told a story of the Rajput who died and was reborn Muslim only to find that the ladies liked his love-making better. They laughed over this and the girl playfully beat Salim with the end of her plait. They all had pan and simply smiled at each other until the first business of chewing was over; then Salim talked to her privately. Her trinkets jingled as she shook them in his face.

'Do you know Arabic?' she asked of Vijay and, when he denied it, added, 'you should, it is a lovely language.'

'I will translate for him,' Salim said. 'He must hear it as it was written.'

Then she recited in the throaty and clipped tones of that language, touching herself and her garments, cocking her head and rolling her eyes to score the meaning of each line and phrase; Salim listened rapturously, said 'Shabash!' a few times at the end and then kissed a fold of her salvar in a theatrical gesture of appreciation.

'On that particular evening,' he began, but she broke in laughingly.

'Not "particular," ' she said. 'It is not a business letter you are reading, it is a poem. Let me do it.' Then she began to translate slowly, shutting her eyes and frowning whenever the going became difficult.

> ' "She was lovely that evening and gay. . . .
> In little games my hands slipped her mantle,
> I am not sure about her skirts;
> but in the night's curtain of shadows, heavy and mute,
> I asked and she replied: Tomorrow.
> Next day I came saying: Remember!
> Words of a night, she said, to bring the day. . . ." '

She curled up on the bolster, permitting Salim to kiss her arm, while her silk rippled and glinted, and her smile seemed to take on the same shiny, teasing quality.

'Shabash,' Vijay said politely, admiring her. He was beginning to think that there was much truth in the saying that Mohammedan women redeemed sex by an instinctive artistry which was almost glamorous, and he wondered if that was because they were bolder than the Hindu women.

'She can do that for many hours,' Salim explained. 'In Pushto, Urdu, Persian, in short, all languages of fine culture. And she knows many Soufits too . . . don't you, my dark-eyed one?' he added, stroking her breast shamelessly.

She rapped his hand and pushed it away.

'It is a notion of hers,' he continued towards Vijay, though still smiling into her face. 'Ask her and she will tell you openly. They are the most perfect pair in all Bombay. Are they not, my dove?'

'They are, and you shall not rough them for nothing,' she said half-seriously. 'If you will stay, I shall let you play a short time.'

'How do we know they are the most beautiful? It is only you who says so.'

'You have said it, too, I remember.' She made a starlike breastplate of her hand and watched him in feigned defiance.

Warmly awkward at that stage, Vijay got up and gave an involved account of why he must go even though he would have liked to stay. Salim offered to take him to the nearest gharry stand if that were sufficient, and he winked broadly when Vijay said that it would be. The girl, whose name was Aisha, hoped that he would come again some evening and stay longer, much longer, she added with a sultry smile. Any friend of Salim's was welcome in this house, and especially a Rajput. Then, as Salim rose to accompany his friend out of the room, she said after him:

'The monsoon is very near and the roof of my parents' house must be thatched before it begins. It is good you came, Salim. Muslims are rare nowadays . . . it seems they are either happily married or too busy with politics.'

'I shall be back in no time,' he said, waving.

The same servant gave them their slippers and took them out, and Vijay pressed a ten-rupee note into his hand and asked him to take it back to his mistress.

'She went to the zenana high school at Lahore and might have been a teacher by now,' Salim explained as they walked through the garden. 'Altogether a clever and accomplished girl, believe me. I too was taken aback when she first gave me Omar Khayyam in Persian.'

At the car Vijay said he did not mind walking alone to the gharry stand and he advised Salim to go back and get politics out of his mind. The Muslim shook his head vigorously; he wanted a short walk himself and a promise was after all a promise.

'Her father is a zamindar's driver in the Punjab,' he continued on the street. 'One summer she came home on holiday and met the zamindar shooting partridge in the fields. She had a child by him, which she killed before it was born . . . and the father threw her out of the house and went to Mecca and became a hadji . . . to wipe out the dishonour. She has not seen them for five years, but she sends them money and presents whenever she saves up a little. . . .'

'That didn't seem to break your heart overmuch,' Vijay said.

'It did, bhai, certainly . . . in the beginning.' He sighed with feeling. 'It is a terrible thing, how true . . . but how was I to change it? I wrote a short story about it and gave her the money which they paid me. Thirty rupees it was, I remember. Not only that, but they said that it was sentimental and unrealistic.'

'Was it?'

'Was it, he says! Let us not talk of realism, my friend!' The growl seemed to rake up the ashes of an old impatience, so that his voice warmed up accordingly. 'Whenever I hear a reviewer say that a book is realistic I always think that it is full of smutty old monosyllables. It was a true story, certainly, but they said it could not happen in these enlightened times.'

'And now you're going to have the roof thatched?'

'Yes, if you like, I shall. It is better than having my blood sucked by a designing Parsi widow. She is a Muslim, after all, and a pretty one. Brother, if this was the age of Akbar, she would have a court of her own and her name would be known all over India. But Akbar is dead . . . a great misfortune. The British do not care for gazals, and your Congress will only be happy when all misery of this country is equally divided and every man spins his own idiotic charkha.'

'You know, Salim,' Vijay said laughing, 'they write of us that we are a race of sentimentalists. I think that we are, by and large. But there is surely no Indian more sentimental than a Muslim crying for his Moguls.'

In the glare of the lamp under which they presently passed, Salim's face softened perceptibly. He made a small clucking sound and shook his head.

'Bhai, I am not crying, though maybe I should,' he said. 'Let this be quite clear. There is no Muslim to-day who does not remember how great he used to be.'

Farther along the valley a match flickered close to the hedge and a male cough tore the silence. The asphalt vanished in a bay of darkness at the foot of towering trees on both sides and the sky became a mere strip of deep purple, and on it the stars choked in that diaphanous haze which a hot summer day hung between heaven and earth. The air sagged with the exhalation of flowers and moist lawns; rodents rustled in the thick undergrowth. Vijay pondered the remark of his friend and found it not without contradictions.

'At last we learn that you have an ideal,' he said. 'A Muslim raj backwards. To me especially this is very disappointing.'

'You are mistaken, Vijay. I have no ideals whatsoever.'

At that moment several shadows loomed out of the dark, faintly, like shapes thrown on to a screen from behind, and Vijay realized that they were men; they spread across the alley in a semicircle and barred the road. They were hatless, but wore trousers of a light colour which showed better than the rest of their dress.

'What is this?' Vijay said and stopped. There was no answer. The extreme ends of the barrier moved up silently and formed a dim ring.

'If this is a joke, we have not time for it,' Salim said.

Again silence. 'Come on, bhai,' Vijay said to his friend, stepping forward once or twice, hoping against hope that a gap would suddenly open and they would be able to pass through. But the barrier stood firm and he faltered, while Salim moved up behind him.

'Is it an ambush by any chance?' he asked sarcastically, yet all who heard it could feel the tenseness behind the sarcasm. 'If it is that, at least let us know by whom?'

This time the rejoinder was a snort, followed by a loud laboured breath; Vijay shifted on his feet and his heart began to throb very fast. From far off, beyond this tomb of foliage and shadows, the faint voice of the main road filtered through as if it, too, were diminishing before the unknown threat, and it struck him as mocking. Are we dreaming? he thought in a swift access of outrage. It was inconceivable that they could stand in the very middle of the town and yet be so utterly isolated.

'Very well then,' Salim said deliberately, anger giving his voice a sharp and jagged new edge. 'I don't know who you are, but I see that you must be cowards. No one but a weak-kneed jackal would do this in a place where he cannot be seen.'

'Son of an untouchable father and a she-hyena!'

The snarl sounded as though it were uttered by the nearest shadow; it was in a quaking Urdu. This almost certainly meant that the person was a Muslim, like Salim.

'You evil-smelling king of literary dunghills, you talk of cowardice! Who reeks of fear now?'

'You do, unless I am mistaken,' Salim said. 'And of other foul things too.'

'It is the one from the maidan,' Vijay said, recognizing the snarl. The sudden memory dilated his sense of outrage into another, more familiar feeling, and he licked his dry lips and swallowed hard; he was getting very impatient with fanaticism and with the Muslim brand of it in particular.

'So these sons of camels have taken the law in their own hands!'

Saying this, Salim swiped at the nearest shadow and caught him full on the ear; there was a loud thud and a gasp as the man landed on the asphalt. 'Come on, Vijay!' he shouted, swinging at the next man. 'We shall teach these jackals . . . they will not forget it so soon!' He felled the second one with a glancing blow and growled savagely.

'You cow-butchering bastards!' Vijay heard himself as he began to slash out at the circle. 'Offspring of darkness everlasting!' He smashed his fist in the face of one shadow—square on the mouth, he noted grimly— and followed it up with a much lower blow which came out more muffled than the first; his knuckles went dead and he rubbed them quickly and shouted another challenge. Then the ring tightened less comfortably and he could only half-swing to defend himself.

'Stay out of it, Hindu!' a voice said nearby.

'Try and make me!' he said, more furious than he had ever been.

'Fool, I am warning you . . .!'

'And this,' he spluttered, jerking his right arm and almost wrenching it from the shoulder, 'this is the answer!'

From the ground a hard blunt object flew up between his legs, grazed his knees with a sting and got deflected towards the top; its aim was unmistakable. He caught it level with his thigh and twisted it brutally, sandals, toes and all, and heard the scream of pain with satisfaction. The apparition toppled over and was immersed in the crush.

'Unspeakable mouth of a urine drinker!'

'Fanatical sons of funk!'

'You shall pay for this!'

'Get the Hindu first . . . this one here!'

More kicks, aimed at the high point between his legs, landed stingingly in his groins and on his thighs, but one was more accurate than the rest and it managed to bruise him painfully; this was too much. He careened round, kicking back fast and viciously, and his own rasping breath was soon drowned in the moans of the assailants. The cluster grew more entangled by the minute, the pace more relentless. Somewhere in the midst of it, Salim's low growl turned to a running commentary, spaced out with gasps and groans. 'Drivelling . . . infamous jackals . . . you think you can use police methods on me! I have had . . . enough, by Allah! You shall remember Salim Haq to your dying days! Here . . . you cannot threaten me . . .!' There followed an interval of strenuous moans and breath sucking, thickened by slaps, thuds and an occasional ripping of cloth.

As he wrestled and punched away it suddenly struck Vijay that they were outnumbered by far; this had a sinister significance of its own. He could still not see the faces of the attackers; they were mere blotches against a sheet of absolute blackness; they spoke little and then only brief insults so packed with hatred that they seemed to swat about in the shade like malignant bats. As far as he was concerned, they were all pockmarked and their lips were purple, and their unbridled murderous spleen was like a disease that called for instant and rough extermination. More and more he felt it as a decisive combat in a larger sense. Presently the two glowering youths from the bookshop came to hover before him and he thought he was fighting them as well; he was hot and they were hot; each thumping blow or clinch took place in a dark shroud of sweat and effluvia.

Then he tripped and attempted to save himself by clutching a body next to his own, but a hand propped against his Adam's apple forced him inexorably over and backwards. Falling, he kicked once more with all his strength; his foot tore into a bundle of softness at the level of his own thighs, and the subsequent shriek proved the success of it. All the same, he was now on the asphalt, too concerned with his own safety to savour the triumph. He was stepped upon, squeezed and gouged; he raised his elbow to his face and tried to crawl away through the shifting obsessed tangle, but another slippered foot met his temples with a wallop and he had no time even to gasp. He lay down flat on his face, out of it for the time being.

'From behind . . .!' panted the man who had grasped Salim around the waist and was now ramming his head into Salim's belly and jerking his knee up to his groin.

'Come on, brothers!'

'Unnameable scum!' Salim snarled, realizing the intention.

He smashed both his fists in the ears of the man and went on pounding them like a drum; he called 'Vijay!' twice and waited for the reply, but none came. There seemed to be more of them now and they clung to him

243

like a monstrous swarm of leeches burrowing for his blood. He knew he was alone then and decided to break away. Reeling around ferociously, invoking Allah and damnation, he dislodged himself and flailed his way out by strenuous inches, then ran back towards the alley shouting for police, holding his broken waistband to keep it from falling.

'Don't let him get away!'

'Arre, beating will never stop him!'

He was out of breath and his head pounded unbearably. One of his sleeves hung down from the shoulder and he tore it off completely with his free hand, lest it impede his speed. But they came after him and when he glanced back to see how many, they had already passed the nearest lamp and seemed to be quite a group; he swore obscenely and pressed on, disregarding the stitch in his side. He ran through yet another tunnel of blackness, catching his breath halfway up his throat every time his guts twisted and seemed to change position, and past many other street lights partly concealed in the trees, until he reached the gate of Aisha's house. Here the crowns grew apart and the light was fully exposed; this was bad, but he had no alternative. They saw him enter the gateway and vanish in the recesses of the garden.

At the car he leaned on the door and doubled up helplessly. 'Ai, Salim . . . Salim,' he rasped to himself, stretching his mouth for more air. 'They will . . . kill you, bhai . . . kill you, like a rat.' The notion of having to die, normally so terrifying, worried him less than the uprooting agony of having to choke for lack of air or from pain; he made a more systematic effort to breathe and the strain brought on a wave of coughing made up of tickling and smoker's hoarseness and lungs torn to shreds which seemed to erupt all the way from his toes and storm through his insides with the searing violence of a gale. He flung open the door and reached for the steering-wheel and held on to it for all he was worth; now his chest felt like bursting wide open at any moment and he began to beat it with his other hand. 'Ai, brother. . . . Ai, Salim . . .!' He shut his eyes, not feeling the tears in them; the ripping pressure kept up, his body felt like a bag full of explosive gases; they continued to tear at his lungs and escape through his throat, nose and ears with a grazing fiery pain. At length he managed to pull himself up and lean over the seat with one buttock, then laid his elbows on the wheel and dropped his head between them. His chin sent the horn blasting through the darkness, deafeningly but intermittently, for he could not yet restrain his convulsions.

'Merciful Allah . . . help Salim . . . Bismillah!'

When the knife gleamed above him, there was nothing to stop it; his shoulders even heaved up a little to receive it better. The sharp edge slid in between the shoulder blades and seemed to come right out in front. He gasped out loud and arched himself stiffly, and the little air which was still in him seemed suddenly to rush out and leave him absolutely dry and lost. This he remembered as happening three times in all.

When Vijay tottered to his feet the alley was empty. His head buzzed and one of his eyes was nearly closed, but there seemed to be no other damage immediately assessable. He called Salim's name softly, expecting no answer, and then, none too steady, made his way back to the broken gateposts. Above the lane the sky was a thicker opal hue and one side of it looked paler than the other. The car was still under the banyan, with the doors flung open and no one in it, and next to it was another empty one which he couldn't remember seeing before. The house struck him as much brighter; the hum coming from inside seemed to be made up of many voices. He wobbled in and called his friend's name in the corridor; an unknown menial rushed out, gaped at him for an astonished second, then vanished. He took off his shoes and went towards the voices.

'Who might you be?' asked an elderly Muslim in a fawn tunic, as he stepped into the room.

'Looking for Salim Haq, my friend,' he said, dropping into a chair. He gave his name and added that he had been here a little while ago.

'Then maybe you can explain . . .'

But the bearded servant interrupted with a rapid speech in Urdu, making the face of the questioner relax somewhat; he was joined by three others and by an old woman, all in various stages of undress, who tried to outshout the bearded one. Then came the tapping of other feet and shrill female voices, which Vijay ignored by asking if anything had happened.

'Oh yes, plenty. I am Dr. Nurredin Ali,' the man said. 'If you were with Mr. Haq to-night, perhaps you will tell us how such a terrible thing could have happened. . . .' He went on to say that the servants had found Mr. Haq in a pool of blood in his car, that he himself had come as soon as they telephoned him. 'A dastardly, heinous outrage, Mr. Ramsingh,' he said in a trembling and indignant voice.

'It can't be!' Vijay said, stupefied. 'We were attacked on the street. Salim would have fought two dozen men. . . .'

'All the same, he is now dying,' the doctor said.

Then the girl Aisha came in, wiping the hair from her eyes, tousled beyond recognition, and there were big wine-red flowers on her salvar. 'What a horrible thing!' she cried seeing him. 'We were laughing together only a half-hour ago, Allah have mercy on us . . .! What did you do, where did you go from here? I have known this to be an accursed house from the day I took it. . . .' She broke off, sobbing 'Oh mother' into her cupped hands.

'We heard the car horn and came out,' the bearded servant volunteered. 'He was lying on the seat . . . not speaking . . . we carried him in and called the doctor sahib.' He clapped his hands to his ears and swayed from side to side. 'Bismillah . . .! What have we done to suffer such a misfortune!'

Vijay staggered up and said he wanted to see his friend.

'Come with me,' Dr. Ali said. 'I need your blood for transfusion.'

Salim lay quietly in the room next to the girl's, amidst the same kind of low-slung divans and drooping rugs, and the glare of the ceiling lamp streamed over his bloodless face. They had undressed him and thrown a clean sheet over his lower body, but on his chest lay a pile of swathe and some of it had blossomed out in deep crimson. One of his arms dangled to the floor. Lying so simply in this ludicrously ornate museum he looked like a dead nawab brought into the tent from a battlefield. An ayah fanned him with her veil and she simpered when they approached the bed.

'Let me test you quickly,' Dr. Ali said. 'I have tried these others, but they are not of the same blood group. It is probably too late anyhow.'

Vijay sat down at the feet of his friend, while the doctor made a hurried test and examined it under the lamp. 'Praise Allah, it is all right!' he said, busying himself afresh. 'I had given up all hope when you came. Now there is no time at all. . . .' Ordering everyone save the two women out of the room, he took out his instruments and tied a chewed-up piece of rubber hose to Vijay's arm. 'It will not hurt you, do not be afraid,' he said. 'Tell us what happened after you left here,' he added pushing the needle into the vein with deft, sure fingers.

Vijay told them all he knew. While he talked the face of Salim seemed to grow more composed and serene. It was ages since he had seen it so mellow, and the change struck him as profound; it was smooth and free of all frowns, the mouth slightly agape and russet at the corners, where blood had been wiped by an awkward hand; the upper row of teeth glimmered faintly under a withdrawn mauve lip; the broad-ridged nose seemed to have caved in at the nostrils ever so little. In their shadowy sockets the eyelids resembled a pair of wax bulbs; his breath came slowly with a slight rattle. The hair on the pillow and over the ears seemed too long and artificial.

The girl stopped crying. A fateful hush settled on the room, defied only by the doctor's fussy hands and by a couple of purple moths chasing around the light. Aisha shuddered several times but grew rigid afterwards. Her scent, mingled with ether, rubber and the doctor's perspiration, heaved up in Vijay's head and stomach; he turned away to look at the swab on Salim's chest, where the bloodstains seemed to spread wider and become more sinister almost by the minute, and then he raised his eyes to look at the girl, only to find that there, too, red was the predominant colour, for the lamplight set her blouse aflame and one of her half-hidden breasts seemed to gather it all and throw it back at him. He belched helplessly. This was followed by an interval of utter peace, after which Dr. Ali's voice sounded as though it were battling a head wind.

'My dear sir, just what we needed . . . look at your face! Why did you not tell me you were not well?'

He drank from a glass held by Aisha and suffered himself to be helped up from the floor. A litter of gauze cast-offs now lay over the carpet. He stood up, still shaky on his pins, and saw gratefully that the operation was over.

'Concussion, if I am any judge of black eyes. . . . Sit down here!' Dr. Ali said. 'I shall look at you in a moment.'

'How is he?'

'How could he be with those terrible wounds in him, the poor fellow . . .!' He laid his stethoscope to Salim's chest and his finely arched eyebrows hunched together in acute distress. 'There should be some sign of life one would think, after two pints of nourishment. . . . Well, we must wait a little. Did you call the police?' he asked the girl suddenly.

'I have not. Should I?' She fidgeted with the glass in her hand, once more on the verge of tears. 'I am afraid of them. . . . I live here alone with the servants. My parents are in the Punjab.'

'That has nothing to do with it, my girl. Do you not realize a murder has been committed?'

'They will ask questions, doctor sahib. . . .'

'Naturally they will, it is their duty,' and he narrowed his eyes at her, for the words 'doctor sahib' had been a plea; then he seemed to grasp the meaning, and turned away shrugging resignedly. 'I am very, very sorry,' he continued with more sympathy, 'but if you do not call them, there will be trouble. He will assuredly die . . . I cannot do anything more for him. I dare not even move him to the hospital, he might die before we put him into the car. I shall have to state in the certificate that he died of knife wounds.'

'Better call them,' Vijay then said.

She nodded without a word and went out. They heard her ordering a servant to run out to the nearest phone.

'Ah yes, good God! that reminds me!' Dr. Ali said to Vijay. 'We found this in his pocket when we undressed him.' He took a crumpled piece of paper from his pocket and gave it over. 'What do you think of it, Mr. Ramsingh?'

Reading the note with his one good eye, Vijay experienced another wave of indignation: it was an anonymous typewritten sheet, addressed to Salim at his flat, and its single paragraph struck Vijay as characteristic of the writer:

*You have dishonered Islam and made leag with shaitan like a infidel.
Despite of each warning you do not moderate your anti Islamic action,
your attitude is offensive to each and every Muslim, it is a pity on the
good name of Haq. We have ofttimes asked to withdraw objectionable
matter from your book Unveiled City but you have not deemed one reply.
Our patience is exhausted. Islam is great and his victory is a crescent
moon over whole India. Allahu akbar. Inna sahn'akka huwal abtar.*

'The last line means "Your enemy is the one cut off from good," said
the doctor. 'It is a prayer . . . a common Muslim prayer. It seems Mr. Haq
had received many such letters and not paid them any attention . . . a plain
case of intimidation and murder.'

'Yes, doctor,' Vijay said, gulping his impotence. 'We are back in the
Middle Ages.'

'Unbelievable, absolutely unbelievable! It is just as well the police are
coming.'

Aisha re-entered and came towards the divan; she had changed her salvar
and thrown a pink veil over her head in preparation for the visitors; she
listened to Dr. Ali's promise to deal with the authorities, all the time standing humbly and watching Salim. Blood was again oozing from Salim's
mouth and his rattle was louder. The paleness had not gone, but his chest
rose and fell with greater regularity. Vijay touched his hand.

'Salim, wake up. It is I . . . your friend.'

All three bent over the bed as his eyelids trembled for the first time. It
was as though he resisted the awakening and tried to tell them so. Aisha
stroked his temples, tenderly, as she would those of a fevered child.
'Salim, dear friend, what have they done to you?' she said. 'Wake up and
tell us . . . you are safe now . . . you are in my house, Salim.'

'Coming round, I think. This is all we can expect, I am afraid.' Dr. Ali
mopped the blood, then the eyebrows.

Salim's first look was terrifyingly glassy, and it rested on Vijay for an
uncomfortably long minute; later a light of recognition seemed to widen it;
then he attempted a smile, but the result was merely an awry twitch of the
lips. Vijay squeezed his hand reassuringly.

'We'll find them, bhai, don't you worry,' he said. 'Even if we have to
turn this town upside down. No one can get away with such a thing.'

'No moving, Mr. Haq, please. Just lie still,' Dr. Ali said.

Vijay peered deep into his eyes for a proof that he was attending, but
came up against an opaque gloss; tiny reflections of the ceiling lamp
burned beside the pupils; it was like staring into the polished kernel of a
slab of malachite.

'One of them kicked me in the head. I must have lost consciousness,' he
went on, murmuring almost into his face. 'They found a letter in your

clothes . . . a threatening letter. . . . Salim, do you understand . . .? You have had it all the time and didn't tell me. Do you know these people? Who are they? Salim . . . if you know them, you must tell us. They are murderers. . . .'

The mouth moved weakly, but the sound it produced was grating and not like a voice at all. At the door the servants had come back and were huddling together in silence. They waited tensely.

'Tell us, tell us, please!' the girl echoed in panic, kneeling down and pressing his other hand to her forehead. 'The police are coming, Salim. They will send me away from Bombay. Think what my father will say . . . I shall disgrace him forever.'

'Hardly pertinent,' Dr. Ali said testily. 'If he knows and can speak, he will tell us.'

The watch of the doctor ticked away, but neither it nor the strong perfume of the girl, nor even Vijay's soreness, could intrude on the breathless pause. At last Salim shifted his gaze until it was level with Aisha's, then moved his head from side to side.

'Young . . . fanatics . . . hooligans,' he whispered. His hand slid along the edge of the bed, slowly, laboriously, as though a heavy chain held it back, then stroked her cheek and flumped into her own raised and expectant hands; the gory half of his mouth curved up tortuously. 'What . . . matter . . . anyway,' he added.

'Why, why, Salim. They were your own people,' Vijay said.

The look returned then, a trifle clearer this time, and the face seemed to relax in a hard-won quiet of its own. 'No place . . . any more . . . for Salim Haq,' he enounced with rattling but dogged effort. 'You said ideals were . . . you said. . . . You were right. . . .' He licked his lips with a red tongue and tried to swallow. 'No ideals . . . no place. Exit Salim Haq. . . .'

'Don't say that, please. Try to tell us slowly.'

'Yes, bhai. . . . Place for you . . . because ideals. . . . They will . . . you shall do well. . . . They must. . . . I told you . . . one good point. . . .' Then, shutting his eyes, he mumbled more feebly, like someone with a full mouth but too sleepy to chew: 'Indian first, Muslim . . . but Rajput . . . just the same.'

And finally, as they still clung to his lips, he rattled off in a sudden fit, slurring the rest, and only the name of Allah managed to make itself intelligible. A red trickle sprouted in the lower corner of his mouth and slithered down his chin; Aisha carefully lowered his hand on the sheet.

'That is all, I fear,' Dr. Ali said, pushing the stethoscope under the gauze. 'Now it is a question of minutes. Allah have mercy on his soul.'

'Bismillah!' Aisha cried and covered her face.

'Bismillah,' murmured the ayah and the servants at the door, and their voices had a ring of terror in them.

'Oh Allah! Whomsoever thou keepest alive amongst us,' the doctor said in Arabic, wiping the mouth slowly, 'keep him alive on Islam . . . and whomsoever thou giveth death amongst us, give him death on faith. Oh Allah, deprive us not of his reward and test not after him. Allahu akbar!'

'Allahu akbar!' The bearded one clapped his ears and began to pray.

Vijay stared at the pale face and at the shiny quivering strand on his jaw and couldn't think of anything to say. His head ached desultorily, still wrestling with Salim's last speech. He remembered Salim telling him once that a dying Muslim is turned towards the Kaaba and exhorted to pray Tashahhud, for which the Prophet granted an entry into paradise, and he was moved to tell the good doctor about it, but gave up the idea for lack of daring. But if the doctor had forgotten, the girl still remembered it.

'Ayah! Abdool Rehman!' she called between sobs.

They lifted him awkwardly and faced him the other way, and Vijay stood up to help them. There was no argument; they all knew where Mecca was. They laid him down again and drew the sheet up to his chin, while the doctor used his stethoscope for the last time. 'What he needs now is an iman,' he said tiredly, rubbing his hands on a towel; he pressed Salim's jaws together and tucked his arms under the sheet. 'Generous Allah . . . Receive him full of mercy!'

'He must be washed and prepared,' Aisha said. 'Abdool Rehman, the faithful ancient one, you and ayah shall wash him. Go and bring the clean sheets and send someone for the iman.' She dropped her forehead on the divan and began to pray, racked by her own sobbing.

Vijay crossed over to the chair and flopped down. He was no longer sick or indignant. The savage ferment in his head seemed to beat against his eardrums and throat, defeating all bids for coherent thinking, and the still head of his friend, now facing full into the light, had an eerie, compelling fascination. It was not the head he had known; death and Mecca seemed to give it a perspective all their own; the bundle of silk and girl near it, the vivid red flaming in patches on the whiteness, the stiff rustle and weird-sounding chant of words and sobs, these gave it a bizarre flavour. He shut his eyes wondering what it was that made it different from that previous watch at Villa Ram. As long as Salim had still breathed, there was a deep sorrow in the scene which held him spellbound in the familiar old way. The manœuvering of the body, the prayers, these had somehow broken it. He thought, Why is that? and groped earnestly amidst the buzzing and jangle of his mind. It was as though a couple of strangers had taken charge not only of the corpse but of friendship, too, and their proprietary actions had blotted out a long and valuable past. It was odd that the dead Salim should contradict the live one, yet it did; now he was merely a dead Muslim. It was a different end from that of Nand or Kandubai, whose trends of continuity would not be snapped either by certificates of death or by gathering years.

'I think the police are here!' Dr. Ali said at length. 'Let us have a look at your head now, Mr. Ramsingh.'

He rose unwillingly and let himself be propped under the lamp. He thought, These same fingers were on Salim just now, and hoped that the recollection would soften the aridness of his feeling; it did not. The fingers merely probed and hurt, and their grossness was of a piece with the rest of that improbable night; they even stopped him from remembering altogether. Salim was gone; this lumbering, quarrelsome, cynical, sentimental giant who had meant so much until this night was gone; that which the girl and the servants prayed for, which lay askew under the stained sheet, was the Prophet's ransom. They were separate entities, these two, divided not only by their natures but also by the inflammable tempers of India and by the forward fingers of the doctor and by a head so sore that it could only generate flashes of blinding but unworthy brilliance.

'The truth is,' Dr. Ali said finally, as if meeting him on the same cerebral beam, 'the truth is . . . your friend needed more than your blood.'

5

In the beginning of July the monsoon set in dramatically, first invoking the rain-god by a mass offering of singed fields and melting asphalt, then by raising its sluices. All the way up from Cape Comorin it lashed the west coast into spume and the surf into a frenzy of pounding, arriving in the stream of Bombay one evening when the air was stiller than usual. Men driving along the Ballard Estate saw it poised over Uran on the mainland, mustering its gaseous cohorts, but then it blew up into the sky and crossed the stream and stuck the city like a prelude to doomsday. Throughout that night and the following morning Rajuram, his son and helpers dashed about the house fastening windows and spreading rags in the spots where its soaking fury could not be withstood.

'The wrath of Lord Rudra and Lord Siva together,' Rajuram the Elder told his son. 'It is to let us know that we have sinned unforgivably.'

Torrents of rain ushered in another year for the peasant, but over Bombay the clouds continued to break like some mountainous eggs and the outpour hit the ground without bothering to refine itself to a sprinkle. It swamped the fallow areas of the town and made silted lakes of public gardens, then sprang leaks without number in the old flat roofs, oozing to the innermost chambers. On Malabar and Cumballa hills the last of the gulmohar lay rusting at the foot of the trees, and the poinsettias curled up sickly; branches dripped, flowers dripped, grass dripped; of a morning the air was dank with the wetness of peat and earth and a myriad beetles, small

251

and big, in all hues of the rainbow, came to haunt it without respite. Scent of cassia soared on unseen levels of a ranker, heavier breath; all that was frail and delicate lay drowned. It was the drenching, sopping intermission between two seasons, when the teeming lust of the soil could be read into every tremble of leaf or stem of grass, the end of a long abstinence, when the reckless guzzle went on until both the sky and the earth gasped Enough!

Above the town winds scraped at the dark ceiling and cloudy scars flowered forth hugely, while through them oyster-grey tufts drifted into the outer abyss of space like escaping Jinn. As every year, men gladly inhaled the wet earth; their spirits rose in the first fortnight of the break and then wilted in the harsh monotony of greyness; they glanced skyward hoping for a patch of blue and a gleam of the sun, but the hope was wistful, for the clouds writhed on, sending ever more rain earthward. They tucked in their dhoties and went on gadding under their black umbrellas resigned in the knowledge that their discomfort was hope for the peasant, that the hills would be green again and grass thick and lush, that there would be no more dust for a while, that the air would be magically clear and horizons more remote. A slaked and muddy soil was a bounty from which all other boons proceeded.

At first Vijay found himself with nothing to do.

The Delhi and Trivandrum services would be closed and would not reopen before September. He loitered around Juhu and took to visiting political meetings with Tara and Lakshman. In the third week the company gave him Salim's job, with a bonus and slightly improved pay, and with it went a year's contract with option of renewal. Jagnath recorded the event with a sober celebration, to which he invited the Premchands and Mr. Varma of the Congress headquarters. The uncle was moved to remark that India never forgot her young men, if they did not forget her; the statement was more wishful than logical, but Vijay took it to mean that he was willing to forget the past. Then Chanda wrote again and the sight of her scrawl warmed him very much; the letter contained a snapshot at which he looked closely: Chanda against the railing of the Mussoorie Mall, sharp and different, against a vast sunny bowl in which the green sediment was Dehra Dun. The camera saw her artlessly, it knew nothing of her wit or the Portuguese man-o'-war, it noticed only the most obvious, in obvious black and white. The pale sheer sari draped her flowingly, with scarcely a crease and its hood hid all but two locks of hair and framed her face so roundly that her loveliness seemed to be on exhibition; the face was more mature than he remembered it, for up to the time of their last meeting she had not covered her head, and her tresses, weighted down with flowers, had given her a girlish, collegiate air. The grown-up dress brought with it a sophistication which even the two-dimensional flatness of the print could not quell

Yet, after he had noted all the points of detail, the general impression persisted: that of a svelte and proud figure, virginal and disturbing at the same time, stilled in the accident of wind's modelling.

She wrote:

Your praise was too generous. What made me graduate was the simply awful amount of solid sitting I had put in during April and May. A well-trained myna would have done just as well.

You don't know how beautifully Ranjit's house here is placed and how good it is to rise early (once a week) and see the pink snows from the terrace. The garden is coming up fast since the first rain fell about a week ago and already the cosmos is up to my window and the snow range seems to grow out of it. There are clouds over Landour and long trails of mist along the hills, left by a train, I often think. There are hours of sunshine after each shower when we scale all the summits around us to look ever farther at the Himalayas. 'We' is Hira and a couple of friends. Mother and Ranjit lie in the terrace chairs or go riksha riding on more level ground. The crowd is something enormous, from all parts of India, and they never let up. I suppose this is the secret of life in a hill station, this light and dry air which makes us feel that we have left our consciences in the plains and are free to get as giddy as we wish.

We were having tea the other day and the talk turned to the Bombay meeting and your friend's death. All were deeply shocked, I more than anybody—it seemed I had talked to him only recently. What luck, wasn't it, that they knocked you down early in the fight? You say that it was a vendetta and that the police could not find the murderers, but from here it certainly looks as though it is all bound up with this poison of communalism. And it is sad, but how true, that there is an awful clannish stiffening among the Muslims, just as there was among us at the time of the Muslim invasions, only that the Muslims are less forgiving by nature. No, I have not read Salim's novel. You must be right to think that only an organized civic life can put a stop to such wasteful passions—I agree with all my heart. The man without a political programme is a man with too much leisure; mother says that it is often he who makes his own law and enforces it with the utmost fanaticism. It is too bad that you were made to see this through the death of an old friend, but you would have seen it sooner or later, anyhow. You do not agree with all the policies of the Congress—all right, Vijay, but their main ideals come nearest to your own convictions, don't they? So you will do very well to join them, although it will be hard for us to picture you as a party member.

Have you read of the riots in Aurangabad, near Gaya? We have always had clashes with the Muslims, but never with this kind of regularity and fire. Ranjit explains it logically: First India had a Muslim raj and the

Hindus resented it, then came the British raj which both resented, and now it is the start of the Hindu era and the Muslims are up in arms. How unlucky for India that our differences are still religious first and last!

If everything goes well, mother and I may be in Bombay next month. It is almost decided that I shall study law, but we don't know whether in Allahabad or Bombay. There is a daily discussion about that as we sit on the terrace and watch the sun go down beyond the Siwaliks. Ranjit is for Bombay; mother is afraid of the distance. I should simply love Bombay. When we have guests, they put in their own pennyworth and then I just sit quietly and wonder. We had such an argument the other night and it all started with poor Salim; everyone rushed right in and, really, Vijay, you should have heard us! We were a go-ahead and backward people. We knew life and knew nothing about it. We had a glorious history, but it was nothing compared to the future. We were wiser and more stupid than the rest of the world; India was fast asleep and very much alive. We thought progress was a stage, portraying other people. Mankind would not exist without our spiritual message, but we needed motor cars to present it more forcefully. The motto of Hinduism was live and let live, which meant that some of us live comfortably and the others are at the mercy of karma. We were here before the Muslims were born, and now we must teach them to live peacefully and obey the majority—they are fine people save for their beef-eating habits, which must be stopped at all costs. And so on and so forth—thunder, crushing logic, salvoes, heat, shouting and speechlessness —until Ranjit called for more tea and changed the subject. Believe me, it was unbelievable! What strange gymnastics we Indians sometimes perform! How easy it really is for the foreigner to conclude that our thousand voices will be our undoing. Well, let us face it: there is some truth in it. Salim was such a voice, and others drowned him out.

You ask what made me decide to study law. I have been thinking about it seriously for many months, but I made up my mind only lately. Here is one of the many reasons—and don't you dare to laugh! A couple of weeks back, one of our malis, who comes from Gulistan in Kashmir, beat his wife so mercilessly that they had to take her to the hospital. Poor, poor woman, I thought afterwards! I remembered all the trouble mother had in the beginning and all the things she had been telling me from time to time. I then saw clearly that our women will have to work hard for every privilege and that our men will try to hold them back at every turn. It is they who have invented the glorious Indian mother, the suttees, the purdah and the rest of the poetic flummery, which they pulled over the eyes of the women with such tender raptures. They have done that for so long that women have forgotten when and how it all started; now they are trying to live up to it because they don't know better and because they have been numbed by the habit of security. I always think of them as of people who

refuse to get up in the morning because it is warm and cosy in bed,
because outside the sunshine is too stark and the world too large and
dazzling for their comfort.

Of course they will have to get up sooner or later and face it, and it
might be necessary to wear dark glasses for a start. A day is twenty-four
hours long and there are many other good things besides lying in bed.
When they do that, they will read Manu with different eyes—and so will
the men. That beating certainly made me think. My husband will never
treat me like that! I shall explain the Laws of Manu to him as they
should be explained—and that is why I want to study law and become
very good at it. By the way, the ruffian mali was discharged forthwith and
the police took him in for 'assault with malice aforethought.'

And now I must stop or this will become a treatise. I wish you were
here to see these lovely views and breathe this good air. Until your last
letter I did hope that you might be put on the Delhi run and maybe come
up for a day, but that was simple ignorance, as I now see. I was thrilled
about Tara's matriculation and Munu's success at school—please give
them my love and good wishes. And do write again soon. All your news is
like a gust of salt air in the thin atmosphere of this unreal life up here. . . .

He had read the letter in a deserted corner of his father's club and
paused over some passages trying to imagine what she would have looked
like if she had been talking to him instead of writing. Now it was quite late
and Tara and Lakshman would walk in at any moment.

On the long verandah skirting the lounge, twilight sopped the sports
field a pellucid indigo. A squall was creeping up from the south, maybe
even a storm, and there were frequent flashes through the clouds that threw
a polarized image of the opposite street on the dark screen. House lights at
the other end had a watchful, odd clearness, as of a pack of jungle prowlers
in abeyance; they stared and didn't bat an eyelid. A string arpeggio at the
end of the verandah sent an unearthly trill into the field; the musicians had
arrived; soon there would be a lively awakening throughout the building
and green-braided servants would post themselves at all entrances. He was
not sure if his seclusion could withstand such an onslaught. He wanted a
little more time to think about the letter, and to look at the picture, so
different from the one he had carried in his head, before Tara and Lakshman found him.

Especially the picture. The past correspondence had given him a curious
sense of title to Chanda, now the snapshot gave her to him as another
person, a passer-by with familiar features, whom it was permissible to
observe without embarrassment. The gist of this observation could never
be mistaken for anything else; it was the thought that she was handsome
and desirable. Did she know that the picture would have that effect on

him? If so, she must plainly have wanted to please him—and this he would have liked to believe. He looked at it once more, noticing the sharply moulded breasts, the long and slim thighs, the impeccable little jewel of her face, and didn't know what to think.

She had peeled off the cocoon of the Juhu episode and emerged chrysalis-fashion with a set of new features and an attractive mature body. She existed separately for the first time. The newcomer was a provoking, inestimable quantity; it thought and it made him think; it wove in and out of his life, each time a little more suggestively. The knowledge that up to that point the whole sequence had been planned by his father and only imperfectly understood by himself seemed to become less important. He told himself that it was perhaps bound to happen, that at this moment he was actually watching it happen, and doing so with a clear new pleasure, and he thought: Not only that, but I am rolling it up and down my tongue like a piece of sweetmeat. I am just another sentimental Indian, he thought. Yet the picture of a tall, softly-curving Chanda survived even this pang of scepticism.

It loomed suddenly into a vivid memory of her. He thought how good it would be to talk to her again, on this greasy settee if need be, before the band struck up, to face a torrent of her questions and try to answer them and then fire his own, before all the lights came on in the lounge and abashed them both. What would they talk about . . .? Oh, but there was so much to say and admit, and he would probably start by suppressing the vision of that snapshot and taking her in afresh, without any overtones, so that all impressions would be brand-new and yet a complement to his present feelings, and all exchange chemically pure, as it were. And he would not make the last mistake and offer resistance, but go whichever way seemed the most promising.

The band did strike up, what a pity! A flippant little English ditty, in which the bass doled out all sentiment with stern precision—but it was a lesser intrusion than he had feared.

He smiled to himself in a warm resignation: He would not see her for some time, maybe months, for Mrs. Prashad might have decided to wind up their uncertain relationship. And while he thought that a pity, he dared not alter it wilfully at this stage. The pleasure of getting her letters, the sensual effect of her last picture, none of these entitled him to meddle in Rana Prashad's plans. He would have to meet Chanda once more to learn the whole truth.

It was more than a pity. The last four years had been an introduction to something he believed was there, yet when his fingers nearly closed over it, it was not there at all. It seemed to him he had been lonely one way or another for an awfully long time and that the blame for that was not altogether with other people and things. First loneliness of outlook had brought with it a narrower and more tactile personal distress, something he was wont to liken to life in a cave just below the earth's surface, with the sun and stars in full view, yet out of reach for all true purposes—a time he was now beginning to see in a sensible light. Mother's death had rent the hole wider open, and out of the crack had surged not a rescued spirit but a gush of flames and anguish laying waste everything around him for months. Then, Salim's death gave that waste an imprint of fate. The Muslim had not been all a friend should be, especially towards the end, but he had been a link with the bright space about the cave. Perhaps for that reason he missed him more than he had been prepared for, with a dull pang of regret and the familiar old emptiness. Salim's eyebrows bristled no more, his sentimental bluster no longer gave perspective to a picture already frankly one-sided. Now he would have to keep his head and fend for himself without help; there would be no companionship, no fun and zest that went with it, but another stretch of wasteland towards the open ground. Yes, he thought, glancing back at the letter on the table, it was more than a pity. It was phenomenal bad luck besides. It was more appalling than wearying. Here was Chanda, another half-realized moment, invitingly suspended between the past and the future, and she was to be given away. It was regrettable that Hinduism gave the heart so nominal a chance!

Tara thrust her head through the curtained entrance and seeing him made for his corner. Lakshman, in a khaddar jacket and cap, came shyly after her.

'We are very late. I wonder if Mr. Varma will wait so long,' Tara said swishing up in feminine haste. 'Vijay, you look an image of wretchedness!'

6

IN THE brightly lit office of the Bombay Congress groups of young people in homespun clothes loitered in the corridors; many had miniature flags pinned to their shirt collars. Mr. Chandrakant Varma sat in a room stacked high with newspapers and leaflets, and he was in telephone conversation when they entered.

He was a paunchy northern Brahman, rather dark under his tousled grey hair. Vijay, who had not seen him for several months, found him looking tired. He was scanning the typewritten sheet in front of him with long, tapering fingers. One-time government clerk, journalist, political pamphleteer, story and film scenario writer, Mr. Varma was now a man of general usefulness in the local organization, a rôle which spared him the limelight of platform politics and rewarded him with a lively sense of participation, even power. It was said that he sometimes polished and even drafted the more important announcements of the provincial leaders and that his honourable record of two jail sentences made him a figure of some standing. Vijay didn't know about that. Of a more intimate meaning was Mr. Varma's record as teacher of the Bhagavad-Gita and teller of the Ramayana and Mahabharata in the days when the Ramsinghs were newly arrived in Bombay and Vijay was still a small boy. It was somehow in the nature of things that Mr. Varma happened to be in every noteworthy event of the Ramsingh family life: he had witnessed Vijay's flight to England and Kandubai's death, and he was at hand now when the death of a close friend had pushed Vijay towards another considerable decision; outlooks changed and people died from time to time, but the old gentleman survived serenely, to an as yet unrevealed end.

'Welcome here, dear boy. I have been expecting you for some time!' he exclaimed, opening his arms patriarchally. 'Your papers are quite ready . . . all we need is your signature, or fingerprint, in the books.'

'You don't know how much it took to bring him here,' Tara said.

'You seemed sure that I would come. How did you know?' Vijay asked.

'How did I know . . . ?' He held up an open envelope and his beaming face broke out in mischievous wrinkles. 'Young men always think their lives are exceptional. They forget that we oldsters were also young once . . . that we might have had the same difficulties. In our youth we all go away, and each takes his own time to return. You came back sooner because you have not the talent to be complacent.'

'You must not flatter him, Mr. Varma,' Tara said.

'I flatter nobody, young woman. Not to be complacent is painful. So you have decided to follow the precept of action to the end, Vijay? Here is your passport for the next stage.'

Vijay took it, explaining that his decision rested on nothing so coherent or philosophical. He still didn't think that all the policies of the Congress were right or good for India, but they were better than no plan at all. He signed his name in the register and also on his new membership card and then stuffed the latter in his pocket. Discussing his aims before his sister and Lakshman was still like airing a love affair before the family.

'That is fine,' Mr. Varma said heartily. 'You are again one of us. The fee for the first year is payable in advance.'

He paid the regulation four annas and felt much better. He had thought that the moment would be melodramatic and had vaguely dreaded it, but the old gentleman was brisk and a genial soul, and the moment passed in joking and congratulations. On the other hand, there was much drama in the way a youth obeyed his greater destiny, a destiny laid down minutely in the old books, and in the manner in which he shaped it to overcome the obstacles of his day, and to this Mr. Varma now turned with a forgivable zeal.

'So the "wheels of this great world" are rolling again,' he said escorting them out of his office and through the building. 'The dharma of your great-great-grandfather was to fight Humayun and Akbar . . . yours is to become a Congressman. Not only that, but a very good Congressman. It is all in the karma yoga, if you look for it. Whether you fight with a sword or through an elected assembly, you are still fighting . . . you are still a true Rajput.'

'No one said that to me when I joined,' Tara said. 'I suppose women have no destinies to speak of. . . .' She tossed her head in a manner that could not escape Lakshman.

'Envy . . . don't pay her any attention, Mr. Varma,' Vijay said.

Mr. Varma would not have done it anyway. He took Vijay's arm and steered him down the passage, and when they came to the stairway he took out his box of pan and held it open for him. Vijay declined with all respect.

'Do you remember that talk on the night of your mother's death . . .? You thought that all India was against you, that we grudged you every new idea you had, that you were . . . I even remember the words . . . a tourist among your own people. It seems many years have gone by since then, does it not?'

'In one way it does,' Vijay said, remembering the strange softness of Salim's face on that divan of Aisha's. 'And not only years, Mr. Varma, but people too.'

'Yes, dear boy, only too true.' He put the box back in his pocket and moved aside to let Tara and Lakshman precede them downstairs; the jovial beam left his face, muffling his rich singsong in the process. 'You mean your Muslim friend among the others, do you not? And a terrible thing that was, no doubt. I could not believe my eyes when I read of it. Killed by his own people . . . to my mind the sorriest thing about it.' Holding the loose fold of his dhoti he began to climb down gingerly. 'But life goes on, dear boy. A friend dies nearly every day . . . someone's friend . . . but this is not to say that we must fret to the end of our own days.'

'I don't fret,' Vijay said, irked a little by the banality. 'A little while ago, in your office, I didn't tell you why I really joined. It was because of Salim . . . not because I like politics.'

'Motives matter only when they injure. When they are beneficial we don't talk about them.'

'Well, anyhow, Mr. Varma, save for that, nothing has really changed for me. I am still where I was. I am better used to it, that is all.'

At which the puzzled look of the old man cleared at once; that was all that concerned him for the time being.

'But not, no, dear boy, how can you deceive yourself!' he said, clucking impatiently. 'It is as plain as I am an old man that you are far from it. I told you then that you must first go back in order to go forward more easily later on. This you have done, I can see. And now you wear pyjamas and do not criticize our customs any more. It is where we start saying, That man has something, let us find out what it is.'

Downstairs, Lakshman went to find a gharry and the old gentleman glanced at the sky. A smell of rain wafted along the street on gusts of wind; the pavements still gleamed from the last shower.

'By the way, Vijay, what became of your marriage? Last time I saw your father, you were about to make a decision.'

'Not marrying. It's one of the customs I have not observed.'

'We all wish he would,' Tara said. 'Mr. Varma, doesn't the dharma of a stubborn Rajput include a wife?'

The old man permitted himself a broad and dignified grin. Vijay had to laugh too.

'It does, oh yes, it goes without saying'—patting Vijay's back. 'Marriage is one of the cornerstones of dharma, unless he wishes to be a celibate . . . a brahmachari . . . in which case he shall go straight to heaven without any trouble from Lord Yama. Chastity is a very commendable virtue.'

'He is just romantic, Mr. Varma,' Tara said. 'He broods too much and reads too many English books. We should never have let him go to Europe.'

'I have a gharry,' Lakshman said, stepping down from a hooded vehicle.

The driver, a Muslim, had a scarf tied around his fez to keep it out of rain; he eyed the little group curiously and blew his nose over the side.

'If the rain stops in time I shall try to join you at Baboo Premchand's later on,' Mr. Varma said, wiping the first drop from his face. 'And let us hope you will never regret coming here to-night.'

'Dear old Mr. Varma,' Tara said when the gharry moved on and the shower finally descended in full earnest dimming the lights and obliterating the streets. 'It must be fine to live so philosophically. To know that everything you do has already been done by someone else. He should have been a sadhu.'

'You are always trying to make people what they don't want to be,' Vijay said.

'Not always,' Lakshman said raising his shirt collar against the fine spray. 'Fair is fair, bhai.'

'I was thinking,' Tara mused. 'If we all lived our true dharmas, India would be the happiest country in the world. We would be half-gods.'

Vijay feigned a shudder. 'Don't say that even in a joke,' he told her.

They clattered through Kalbadevi and emerged on Sandhurst Bridge, where the rain lashed the pavements to a boil. Through long slanting sticks of water the horse plodded up Hughes Road and towards Cumballa Hill, and the carriage hood became one gigantic drum. They lowered the side flaps and huddled together, while the horse cantered in a vaporous shroud and its driver had to bundle up on his seat and hide his chin on his chest.

Scurrying shadows glinted here and there in the mist, their umbrellas tilted forward, heedless of one another. Trees swayed and creaked, cars hooted shrilly, water poured everywhere as though the town were submerging inch by inch. Then a flash would rip the low ceiling and a blinding paleness would lift the road out of the night and leave it in mid-air, so that men would find its jagged outline etched vividly in their minds for some minutes afterwards; then more wind, and other bucketfuls, and street lights melting down the sloping roads as though in a crucible—the monsoon was still young. It was the only kind of rain India knew, and it was indispensable at that; one had to be grateful that it fell at all.

On Cumballa Hill they dashed into the house and found it thoroughly alight; their dampened spirits rallied at once.

'We thought you might be caught in the downpour and never come,' Premchand said, receiving them.

He seemed to have lost some weight since Vijay last saw him, though none of his smooth self-possession, and he was also more leisurely and cordial. He was in a light shirt and dhoti and wore a pair of slippers, which gave him an aura of domesticity different from his usual preoccupied ways.

'Let me see, when were you last in this house?' he said, taking them aside.

'Last year, uncle.'

'Yes, yes . . . and it seems twice as long. So much has happened since.'

But Vijay remembered the house well—that sprawling slapdash labyrinth of rooms, floors and verandahs which so many builders had tried to stamp with their own ideas of comfort and luxury that in the end none succeeded. Now its lack of character gave it a huddled kind of personality, one third exposed to sun and outside influences, two thirds thriving on twilight, partaking of the character of the inmates.

It abutted on a large garden broken up by terraces of bush and flowers, for here the hill began to tumble more precipitously towards the rest of the shallow island, and on some rather gnarled and timeless banyans in which most of the birds of the neighbourhood seemed to nestle at one time or another. The only open view it could boast was directly to the sky. Its many wings clustered round an oblong cobblestoned courtyard within which, on sunny days, servants eternally ground out the spices, shifting from one sunny spot to another. The rambling medieval spaciousness impressed Vijay a little more each time he was faced with it.

This was how Indians built their houses in the days when every outsider was a potential prowler, when the family sometimes embraced three or four generations all at once and under one roof. Premchand had bought it from a Jain millowner about the time when Gandhi started the first Indian civil disobedience movement, and he had given it a water system and electricity. Deaths and births had qualified it in due course. He and his next of kin shared it with nearly two dozen near and far relatives without any noticeable overlapping or dissonance, and room still remained for an intimate meeting of associates or politicos called at short notice, or for a traditional religious celebration which required a pandal, sacred fires and priests. It was a family within families, a city within a city, a comfortable and admirable vehicle for the old Hindu instinct of family cohesion. Its lasting impression, however, derived not from its vast and haphazard bulk but from an obvious air of indifference to its own lack of graces.

'I cannot even begin to introduce you to everyone,' Premchand said upstairs. 'Some you already know, the others you need not know. The ladies are observing Nag Panchami, I think mainly for the purpose of a little gossip. So . . . whether I like it or not, I must observe it too.'

Vijay and Tara found their father talking to Radabai Premchand. Other unfamiliar men and women strolled in and out of rooms, snickering and conversing loudly; they all wore the customary spotless white; they smiled and joined their palms together during the introductions, but dispersed just as easily afterwards. Lakshman presented Tara to some of the ladies and they drifted away together.

'We were so taken aback about your luckless friend,' Radabai Premchand said to Vijay. 'Were you badly injured?'

'Only some bruises, Shreemati.'

'Poor Salim Haq . . . pity his family and friends. What a terrible blow it must have been to them.'

'To tell you honestly,' Premchand said, 'I do not remember such a black crime in all my years of journalism. Such an untimely end for the talented fellow. We have all liked him so much.'

He shook his head gravely and let the rest go unspoken. He had attended the coroner's court after Salim's death, amidst his other duties and party work at the time, and had been genuinely grieved. His *Morning Herald* had assigned the best reporter to cover the proceedings and cry for justice in article after article, causing the Criminal Investigation Department to go to great lengths with their inquiry, but all of it had yielded only the usual handful of vagrants and shady characters on whom, however, nothing could be pinned; half of them were illiterate, anyway, and could not be squared with the anonymous letter found on Salim. Of the real assailants there was no trace. Premchand deplored the crime in his two newspapers and his various writers dwelt on it so long and so skilfully that the authorities finally gave up all hope of blaming the tragedy on the excitement of the Congress meeting. Privately, Premchand was apt to resent the Muslims for resorting to ancient methods of intimidation.

'But let us not talk of sad things to-night,' he said presently. 'The thousand-hooded cobra has been propitiated, the ladies tell me . . . and we ought to be happy.'

He brought Vijay a glass of orangeade and some curry-kooftas, then left him to go and receive a telephone message, of which a servant had just informed him.

'That is how it goes from morning till night,' Radabai complained to Jagnath, nibbling dutifully at a sweet. 'It is a holiday for everyone, but not for the telephone.'

'Jee-huhn . . . yes, it is hard on a man,' Jagnath conceded.

'Once it is the office, then a friend, then someone from the party . . . we hardly see each other all day. I am proud to know that all this work is for the good of the country, but often I am not happy about it. A family man must have a little time to spare for the family.'

'Yes, yes . . .'

Yet another spotlessly dressed servant came up to say that supper was ready. Then Premchand came back in a jovial mood and took Vijay's hand in both his and patted it vigorously.

'What is this I hear from Mr. Varma, Vijay? You do not breathe a word of it . . . not to anyone . . .?'

He broke the news of Vijay's enrolment with great gusto and precision. 'It is a great day, Vijay, very great,' he said emphatically.

Jagnath embraced his son, moved to tears. 'I wish your mother were here to hear it,' he muttered. 'It would have made her very happy. Why did you not tell me . . .?'

'I have been meaning to, but it took some time to arrange it.'

He told him how Tara and he had discussed it and how she had spoken to Mr. Varma, who in turn had offered to arrange it. They had decided to keep it quiet until a suitable occasion arose. In telling it, he enjoyed their obvious pleasure and his own warm thrill.

'We have observed the day you took your job and it is proper that we mark this day too,' Jagnath then said, beginning to rub his hands. 'It is a proud day for all of us.'

'I think so too,' Premchand said. 'I shall announce it with a speech.'

'No, please, uncle! No speeches!'

'No speeches, then, if you wish. But I say this ought to be proclaimed from all the towers of Bombay . . . to all our young men. Come now . . . let us go and eat.'

During the meal the spotlight stayed pretty much on the uncle. The people sat in two parallel rows on the floor of the austere dining-hall, men separate from women, each on a plain wooden dais with a large brass tray in front of him, while the servants walked endlessly down the aisle dishing out hot *dalpurries*, refilling the emptied vegetable bowls. The meal was strictly vegetarian. Premchand gave out the news chattily, but it rippled at once to the ends of the rows. Before long Vijay became the focus of many eyes and much well-disposed comment. 'You see, dear boy,' the uncle stooped companionably, 'they all know of you and many have thought you more English than Indian. Now they are not afraid of you any more.' He went on to sketch for them his nephew's idea of flying pilgrims and leavened his story with examples of orthodox resistance; the rough impression was that he and Vijay had fought mountains of prejudice and that all their efforts had been in vain. In the meantime, he said, with the partial autonomy around the corner, things were bound to liven up somewhat and the day was not far off when Indians of all castes would fly to the remotest corners of their country and also learn to be modern without cramping their piety or their sense of decorum. Vijay caught his sister's eyes across the aisle and they exchanged a small smile full of meaning.

By the time they rose to wash their hands, most diners felt that Vijay's accomplishment of the afternoon was a personal triumph for the host. Jagnath was quietly contented; Tara bubbled soundlessly; he himself shared her fun and the feeling was a good one on the whole. He had to laugh, because they laughed. They were certainly the most emotional people under the sun, but how well they meant! It was this side of theirs, he mused, recalling his old talks in England, which made them such a puzzle to an outsider and occasionally such a burden to themselves.

Much later, Vijay sneaked out to the verandah and had a quiet cigarette. The rain had ceased, but the sky was still starless. In the dense crowns reaching right around the house like a roof of umbrellas, water continued to descend to earth in a softly busy cascade; a million leaves barred the way, so it had to tick and drip with a sound of crushed pieces of paper left near the fire; he thought he heard the leaves stretch and open, not to heat, but to a sea of waterdrops teetering above. In the bushes of tropical evergreens bandicoots hustled in fits and starts; the air reeked of wet flowers and drenched moss, and when he began to breathe it deeply it sat on his tongue like the aftertaste of a kiss on wet skin.

'Your hair is the longest I have seen,' Lakshman said in the darkness below, in a voice so deep that Vijay did not recognize it at once. 'It smells of double jasmine . . . but finer and softer.'

A bat flapped close to Vijay's face and he hit out and missed it; he could hear it beating its way out of the treetop frantically, until it gained the sky and flew off.

'First time I have played with a girl's hair . . . no, truly. I have never told anyone. When my father died and I was adopted, we were five boys . . . no sisters. I played with other small girls in our village, but I was very small then and didn't know it. This is the first time I remember. I like to touch it, Tara. It is softer than the down of a young chick.'

'Is it?'

'It is softer than anything I know. It is like breathing on your fingers.'

'It takes too long to comb and brush it every day,' Tara said, veering back to the main subject with a jingle of her bangles.

'Maybe the brushing makes it so beautiful.' When he spoke again his voice seemed to have been shaken in its depths. 'Oh Tara, Tara . . . my darling. I write poem after poem about you . . . nothing is enough. I wait to see you for hours, often whole days . . . then the time passes like a second.'

'I wait, too.' Unexpectedly, her voice quavered. 'Often I don't think I can wait any longer.'

'I never dared to think that you would. You never showed it.'

'One cannot show everything. No, don't . . . no, just my hair. Enough, Lakshman.'

'Tara, my love. . . .' His mumble flowed into the low-keyed undertone of the garden and became indistinct for a little while, then he started to cough and choke, and presently the grove echoed to his wheezing.

Vijay moved quietly along the verandah and turned the corner, then planted his elbows on the balustrade and stared into the sky. Like the strumming of a hidden instrument, laughter and voices buzzed out of the open windows and doors, to flounder in the greenery. A sudden longing for a companion rose up in his throat and made him clasp his hands together. Tara's murmured sound had been so virginal that it had spoken to him across the gulfs of night and walls of taboo; it was a tremble and a plea, both tender and inexplainably rousing. Only once before had he heard the same quailing whimper, on the Juhu sands, but then his own excitement had somehow diffused it and given it another tone. Now the vivid imminence of it was like a sudden blast of current and he grasped the stark meaning with every shred of his consciousness. Without wishing to, he remembered the evening when he had crept up behind Thelma, leaning out of the window of Salim's flat on Marine Drive, and pressed against her taut warm back. They had been making love all afternoon and when night came on from behind the house she went to the window and became pensive.

'Whenever you look at me afterwards,' she told him, 'I think that you regret I wasn't a virgin.'

'I regret nothing,' he said. 'You imagine things.'

'No, try to be frank for once, please, Vijay. . . . You Indians think so much of virginity, don't you . . . even if you don't admit it?'

'Ask me a simple question,' he said. Yet he was full of resentment and that was the most curious aspect of the query.

'Well, look what it means,' she said. 'Absolute possession from the beginning to the end. You are brought up on that, aren't you? Can you imagine not having to think of the men who were there before?'

He began to dig his fingers into her waist, but thought the better of it and returned to the bed; while he dressed, she watched him with a cool, speculative stare.

'There, I knew it. You can't even talk about it,' she said, as though establishing a racial trait. 'You do care very much and I knew you did. You can't help yourself, can you?' She joined him on the bed and lay flat on her back, apparently fascinated by the finding. 'The more you know about love, the more you come back to it. If I were virgin, you'd worship me . . . I don't think you'd ever want to go away. All you Indians want a complete course . . . from scratch to finish. It's in you, I think. You bring it into the world with you when you're born. And you know what, Vijay? I think you'll probably marry a nice little high-caste virgin and think yourself the cat's whiskers for the rest of your life.'

Then he had merely been irritated; now the words had all the trappings of a prophecy and their truth seemed to be an inescapable fate. Now the cloud of yearning was abroad and he felt himself swept away before it. He felt the garden arch with it and grow limp in slow waves. He imagined Chanda making such a sound, but the thought took his tension aloft; he thought of love so vestal and pristine that nothing could ever jar it to the end of time. He cracked his fingers, leaning over the damp void of the grove and later raised his face to the cool air, and little by little the loneliness thinned to a more tolerable haze in his head, enabling him to move on again and think of other things. He turned into the house by an unfamiliar door.

In one of the halls, Uncle Premchand was wiping his glasses on the hem of his dhoti when he came across him. He peered at him with friendly myopic eyes, hooked the spectacles back on his nose and put his arm on Vijay's shoulder.

'I did not wish to say this before the others,' he said ponderously, walking his nephew back to the main living-room. 'I cannot tell you how relieved I am that you have finally made your choice. Strictly between us, it was high time that you did.'

Vijay made an assenting sound; he was still unnerved by his eavesdropping.

'Do you remember your last visit at Juhu . . .?' The uncle faltered at the door; the bland eagerness of the host was gone from his face. 'It is odd how similar things come to pass at the same time, is it not? I told you then that no one can sit on the fence and remain convincing . . . that the people will ask for accounts sooner or later. I thought of it just now. Salim was an example of what I mean . . . a most unlucky one, to be sure. You and your father saw the light in good time and now you are both safe, thank God.'

'What do you mean, uncle?'

Premchand gave him a matey pat and push and, when they were inside, raised his arms imperiously.

266

'Quiet, please, everybody!' he exclaimed. 'Silence, please! I have to make an important announcement.'

At the far end of the room Jagnath and Radabai leaned back in their chairs. All doorways filled instantly and young mothers shook their babies to silence. When the noise was down to a few whispers, Premchand dropped his arms and cleared his throat. His eyes roved over the assembly with a fine sense of timing.

'I have just been called by the office,' he said slowly, enouncing each word with a speaker's care. 'They gave me certain long-awaited news which I know you will wish to hear at once. For over a month we have waited for an assurance from the British that the emergency powers of the governor would not be abused in the working of the new constitution. That assurance has now been given officially. Mr. Bhargava, my editor, has just informed me that the old cabinet of the Central Provinces has resigned this evening and that a Congress cabinet has been formed. Dearest friends . . . this is the end of the deadlock . . . the start of a new chapter in our political life . . . the last fight in our struggle for complete freedom.'

'Shabash!' Jagnath said, and rose.

'Shabash! Shabash!'

'Well done, Congress . . .!'

'Long live Bharat Mata!' Radabai said, and tears came to her eyes.

Exuberant cries broke out and some of the younger men clapped. A woman lifted her baby into the air and the child squealed happily. They all pressed around the host and began to ask questions, and he shook their hands and grinned at them.

'It is not all we fought for,' he said, 'but it is a big step forward. Now the people shall be the government. The British are not leaving India, but they have given it back to the people. If we work hard, they will give up the rest. Inquilab Zindabad! Long live free India . . .!'

'Vijay, my son, this is a great moment!' Jagnath said, and his eyes sparkled. 'I never dreamed I would live to see it happen!'

'You did, pitaji. You shall live to see much more.'

They embraced again, stroking each other's backs, and Vijay had a momentary but hopeful impression of his parent finally emerging from the long lacklustre daze which had veiled him since the death of his wife. His feelings were overwhelming; they seemed to spring from a vital eagre within him; and his joy was of the moment, not of a memory, and the moment itself seemed to command his full participation.

'Everything is working out well . . . better than we had dared to hope. Yes, let us sing by all means. How else can we show our happiness.'

They caught up with the chorus of *Bande Mataram* which the uncle had started in the middle of the crowded room, and Jagnath did not release his son's hand.

If there had been any restraint between the men and women relations before, this now vanished completely. Husbands held their wives, mothers rocked their babies, and they sang aloud, with gay and catchy exhilaration This time there was no loudspeaker to guide them and they either rushed their lines or lingered over them with too much emotion, and there were brief seconds in which Premchand's false lead was the only clear voice in the room, but that worried very few of them. After a while their faces fell into a uniform mould of rapture and they stared dreamy-eyed into space and began to look all alike.

Vijay saw his sister and Lakshman in one of the doorways, singing the last stanza with the rest. Tara's hair was in order. She met his eyes across the crowd and smiled proudly.

Eighth Chapter

❧❧❧❧❧❧❧❧❧❧❧❧❧❧❧❧❧❧❧❧❧❧❧❧❧

1

THE breaks in the monsoon had grown to long intermissions of sunshine and green lushness. Huge white clouds raced northward at all hours and the hills rose daily mistier against the blue dome of India. The heads of the Premchand and Ramsingh clans chose one such day to show the famous Brahmanic caves of Elephanta to the family of Rana Prashad.

The crowd on the steamer was a colourful mixture with a strong sprinkling of local fisherfolk. The women were particularly fascinating. They wore maroon saris tucked between their legs Maratha-wise, which allowed them to squat beside their menfolk in identical postures, their legs wide apart, their clasped hands between their knees. The loinpieces of the men girt them tightly and their purple-moist skins shone in the slanted sunshine of the early morning. Their shrill voices reduced the ship's engine to a dull subterranean grumble; they seemed blithely indifferent to the upper deck and the curious stares of the Europeans. Some women bared their breasts and fed their babies with a functional kind of oblivion which in turn amused and repelled Vijay.

'The poor creatures have never learned otherwise,' Chanda said in their defence.

Upstairs some tommies played cards near the railing, sunburnt and serene, as only the men of an idle garrison can look. The other passengers were the usual Sunday assortment: picnickers, both Indian and European, with their wicker baskets of food and boxes of sodas on ice, their cameras and sunglasses. They surveyed the landscape with a possessive gaze and discussed the brightly-hued ships anchored at random in the stream.

Vijay's own people made a lively circle on the forward deck, with Jagnath its centre of quiet dignity and repose, in a white shirt and trousers which took years off him and made him almost of this generation; his daughters Tara and Munu in light blue saris, flushed with the thrill of the excursion. Then Premchand and his wife Radabai, the hosts for the day, and Lakshman, their foster-son, skinnier than ever but responding to all

269

that girlish flurry with a shy smile and an occasional quotation. How well did their hilarity compare with the stolid huddle of the Europeans! Lastly, Rana Prashad and her two younger similes Chanda and Hira—but here, for some reason, he desisted from further comparing. They were the sheen of the party; they made it so decorative that one of the European tourists aimed his camera at them on the pretext of recording the upper deck. Mrs. Prashad, Premchand and Jagnath had started talking on the ferry pier and they were still at it with undiminished interest. If some of the foreigners did indeed wonder what made the talk so absorbing, Vijay might have told them that it was politics, that conversational evergreen of the Indian middle class, that yeast which fluffed and held together a long bun of gossip, patter, memories and opinionated enthusiasm. They made it into a fine art!

'I said to him, Bapuji, how can the people expect . . .'

Inflated by a sudden gust of breeze, the engine throb drowned her voice. He saw his father lean towards her with a cupped hand behind his ear.

'You promised to show me the view,' Chanda said just then.

'All right. Come along.'

On the port side the wind met them with more force. Without looking at her, he knew that it was implacably draping the silk around her tall body and that the sari was not thick enough to veil her from inquisitive stares. He went half a pace ahead, screening her and hoping that this hint of urbanity would induce the tommies to look the other way. It did not, unfortunately; a sergeant glanced up and his mouth pursed up in eloquent appreciation. A moment later they were aft, out of his view, leaning over the railing and facing the glimmering see-saw of Bombay on the horizon.

'So this is the Gateway of India,' she said, looking at the bright and impressive arch at the far end of the shining surface. 'Is it true that a new viceroy must pass under it when he arrives?'

'Yes, it is a custom. Also when he leaves. It is meant to impress the poor Indians who are supposed to love pomp and pageantry.'

The arch seemed to grow out of the sea, flanked on the left by the enormous turreted cube of Taj Mahal Hotel and on the right by the red tiles of the Yacht Club and its bedizened flagpole, against a line of those architectural crocuses for which Bombay was justly notorious, the Raja-bhai Clocktower, the museum, the municipality, the high court and others, all in the advanced stages of germination.

This was Bombay, he told her, the second city of India, the melting-pot of the future and yet less Indian outwardly than any other city, which he knew better than all the rest put together. He had not been born in it, but had breathed its humid air ever since he could remember, and whenever he now came back to it after a long absence he did so with a pleasurable twinge of homecoming. He didn't love it as he might have loved his father's house in Indore had he remained there, or the weird home of Ranjit in

Dehra Dun or even a township in the Western Ghats had he lived there as long. 'I can never think of the reason for that,' he said truthfully. Was it the sea, whose impartial magnitude thwarted all provincial feelings, or simply the many-facedness of Bombay? He didn't know, and this was not a moment for inquiry. But he was proud of it and this was another odd power of this vigorous and sprawling town; he could show it to a stranger or friend and share a little of its pulse and fascination, for Bombay had not one soul, but several and all Indian roads led to it sooner or later.

'I wonder what living and studying here will be like,' she said.

'One thing is certain,' he answered. 'You will not love it. Life here is like sitting on a high wall between two fields. You won't be of the sea . . . and not of India either. But then, if you said that to some of them'—tossing a thumb over his · shoulder—'they would probably think you terribly ungrateful.'

Swirling about them the wind filtered her scent and brought it to his face as a tickling sweet-moist whiff, which he inhaled with relish and gratitude. A mind at rest—what a rare holiday that was! How exhilarating sudden gifts could be! This journey to Elephanta was something he had not expected so soon, if at all; this morning, so clean-washed and blue after the downpour of the past week, was a gift too; most surprising of all was Chanda herself, resurrected from the pages of recent letters, a gift which, but for the merest accident, might have been deferred for several weeks. After seven days, his mind still dwelt on it pleasurably. He thought yet again about the uncertain quantity which men called the psychological moment, that whimsically exact stage at which the loose emotional strands were spliced with such a persuasive show of finality, and came to the conclusion that he would never fully understand it.

'You know, Vijay,' she said, 'we have been here only a few days and already it seems so much longer. Is that good or bad?'

'Good, I am sure,' he said.

This time her eyes seemed very near and bright.

Cleft at the bows the muddy stream lapped the hull like a long greedy tongue, then it fell off and frothed petulantly on and on. They were now three-quarters across; the green cone of Elephanta Island swelled out of the sea more sheerly every minute.

He thought, Talk of gifts! and wondered how much of life was shame-lessly casual when the illusion was that of careful willing. He was almost convinced now that chance was badly neglected by philosophers.

Somewhere between will and cosmic lassitude a crotchety old spook clapped hands at odd intervals and all the sleeping protagonists and hidden stage props came flying to their appointment; chance became coincidence wishes became fact, even though a little unsettling at first. The spook thought it would be a good idea to send Mr. Unwalla to bed with a mild case of 'flu; Mr. Unwalla was Vijay's pilot on the Delhi route. When this young man submitted a medical certificate and told Vijay he could not resume duty for ten days, there happened to be no reserve pilot on the roster; the flight manager ordered Vijay to leave his desk and deputise until suitable provision could be made. That was chance at its most teasing. He was on his way to Delhi within three days of Mr. Unwalla's becoming bedfast, and the sorting was afoot. On the day of his arrival at the Willingdon field he came out of the staff mess hall and was handed the list of passengers. There were three—Rana Prashad, Chanda and Hira. Half an hour before departure they were talking excitedly outside the plane. Who would have thought they were going to meet in that precise spot! It was surprising and delightful! 'And I thought you were still in Mussoorie!' he gasped. 'I thought you were no longer a pilot!' Mrs. Prashad cried, holding on to her sari in the rising wind. 'Well, I'm not, exactly. For a couple of days only, that is,' he told her. 'Imagine, my first long flight,' Chanda said with obvious joy, so that his heart leaped inadvertently. 'Mine too!' piped Hira.

Rana Prashad was flying to Bombay to attend a meeting of education ministers and also to settle the problem of Chanda's further study and Hira's departure for America. Chanda was to be enrolled at the Bombay University after all, for all kinds of reasons, and Hira's wardrobe had to be secured well in advance. They had wired Jagnath of their imminent arrival then packed in a few hours, driven down to Dehra Dun and Delhi, failed to secure sleeping berths on the two mail trains and found that the Bombay plane was leaving early the following morning. Delhi was like the rim of a volcano and Rana Prashad could not stomach a whole day's delay in that heat, especially not after the cool winds of the mountains. 'Let us try one of Vijay's airplanes and go completely modern,' she told Chanda, and Chanda pounced on the idea. So here they were, and this was the story of their escapade. As he taxied to the bottom of the field for a take-off, both she and Chanda screamed the more amusing details into his ear. The spook should have been gratified: the reunion was a great event for all four. They scribbled notes to one another during the first part of the trip and later Rana Prashad began to feel groggy and dozed off in her seat. Vijay found that he had seldom looked into the future with more thrilling anticipation.

With the glittering water before them and with Chanda's presence more real than at any time since he had known her, that thrill was a light, seeping kind of sensation through which his other feelings seemed to bubble up richer and more vivid. It was a week old and still magically sustaining.

'Tell me about Elephanta,' she then said, breaking a pause. 'Is it less than they say . . . or more?'

'I don't know,' he told her. 'The caves were forgotten for many hundreds

272

of years. Afterwards the British came and brushed them up and told us all about them. It is one of the few good things they have ever done.'

'Arre, Vijay, is that you talking! Could this be an anti-British remark?'

'Anti-British . . .?' He realized that this was just how it must have sounded, but the point wasn't interesting enough at that moment; he dismissed it with: 'I have been to so many meetings lately and heard so much anti-British talk that it has become second nature. Of course, a lot of it is quite true,' he corrected himself. 'But let us think of other things now, shall we? I'll show you the caves on one condition . . . that you come for a swim afterwards. I know a cove on the other side of the island where the sea is shallow and clear as a brook.'

'In my sari?'

'No, in Tara's swimming suit. I asked her to take it, when you forgot.'

'I have never done it before, Vijay,' she said lamely. 'If you promise not to look at me, I will try.'

'I promise,' he said.

They went aft, with the breeze behind them this time, and found the elders still immersed in each other.

Now the breakwater pier of the island floated on to the bright surface in the shape of square buoys. On the beach beyond it the upturned and tarred country craft gleamed brightly; the stone stairway that led to the caves below the summit cut the cone like a wide heat crack, but the slopes on either side were bedded with that plush verdure which two months of rain can impart to all foliage; in the north the revived turf was beginning to heal the few remaining glades. Vijay pointed to the old tower on the western promontory; it alone stood naked and white against the swarming jungle; every few years a mysterious agency gave it a coat of whitewash and thereafter it could be glimpsed all the way from Bombay on a clear morning.

'Chanda has promised to swim,' he told his sister. 'Tell her, Tara, that we all wear European swimming suits at Juhu and think nothing of it. Anyhow,' he added, 'we do it when we're alone. She doesn't believe me.'

'I do believe you, Vijay. I just don't know if mother will let me.'

'We'll just go away in the afternoon and have a quiet swim, not telling anybody.'

'What if the costume does not fit me?'

'It will, don't worry,' Tara said quickly. 'We are the same size. Besides,' she added with a gurgle, 'how would you look swimming in a sari? Here in Bombay only the low-caste women do it.'

'That ought to convince you,' Vijay said and looked at her. 'Let's see how modern you really are.'

'Oh, you two . . . it is not that.' Flushing, she reached for the border of her garment.

273

The old picture of her at Juhu rose up in his mind, a visage of abandon and laughter which he now failed to reconcile with the present person, and he was amazed again at the change in her; yet he liked what he saw. She had become statelier and more demure and—this he found entirely gratifying—she seemed to trail around her a new delicate shroud of coyness, which was more provocatively feminine than even her scent. Did that mean that his instincts were every bit as selfish as those of the average Hindu? Shyness in a woman was a sign of purity, and what Hindu male did not experience a pang at the thought, especially if he believed that that purity was his own rightful preserve? If that was an explanation—and it was perfectly plausible, since he no longer thought of himself as a spearhead of all progress—it was also well tainted with the comfortable feeling that even in Europe, where sex was very much a thing of chance, men never tired of longing for complete innocence.

But now the boat was swinging to in a wide rippling arch and its engine had fagged to a slow, faint throb. In the small bay the sea was smoother than outside and seagulls dipped over it and streaked up into the brilliant canopy. On the mole, a breakwater of cement blocks placed at intervals of a few feet, chair coolies waved and shouted frantically. Naked boys stood in the dugouts tied to the head block, their brown bodies and smooth-shaven skulls glinting like polished metal. At the beach village women came out of their huts, shielding their eyes from the strong sun. Then Uncle Premchand strolled over to the railing and slapped Vijay's back playfully.

'You and I shall arrange transport . . . a chair for each of us. You had better hop ashore first, before these European ladies corner all the coolies.

'The girls want to walk, uncle. I will keep them company.'

'Well, if you like. A little exercise is all to the good.' He turned to his foster-son, a shadow of concern creeping over his smile. 'Anyhow, Lakshman, you should not walk. The climb might be too tiring for you.'

'I would like to. I can go slowly,' Lakshman said.

Then they moored and Vijay walked down the gangplank ahead of his people and engaged the requisite number of chairs, and some of the coolies made a dash for the shore to make the chairs ready; the ladies stood by and held hands in the tumult. The shrieking continued throughout the stormy transaction. Little by little they went ashore, hopping from block to block, trailed by a chattering legion of mixed humanity. Chanda and Hira caught their saris at the knees and permitted Vijay to assist them in hopping; Lakshman took charge of the Ramsingh sisters.

'Watch me!' Chanda said.

'No, wait! You better be careful!' Vijay gripped her arm more securely. 'We must do it all together or we'll end up in the water.'

They leaped on; she moved lithely and her weight was no more than a twitch under the fingers of his hand. He saw the unhampered bounce of her breasts under the slipping sari and thought briefly of the swim ahead. They reached the land panting, in fits of laughter

'Now for those wretched chairs,' Rana Prashad said, arriving after them.

The pier vanished at the foot of the massive stairway, where the chair-wallahs awaited them one above the other. A lengthy palaver ensued about the wages and duration of engagement, during which the women sat themselves in the chairs and spread their parasols. Finally Uncle Premchand spoke up with iron authority and the coolies sighed loudly and went to work; they lifted the chairs to their shoulders, four to each chair, and began the long ascent. The youngsters brought up the rear at their own leisure.

In the shade of the hill the greenery was more prolific and more heavily scented. They climbed along a tall avenue of neems, simuls and dangling woodbine that looked as if they had been there a thousand years, while yellow and white butterflies flitted overhead.

2

The large quadrangle of the central courtyard was still in the shade and its stone floor sent up a delicious chill in which all fatigue dissolved as in a bath. At the lower end the sun was flooding a pool of bright green and yellow, and above it the rock appeared even more forbidding. Towering over the steps and the colonnaded entrance to the main hall, the granite boulder rose abruptly to a height of one hundred feet; trickles of moisture had wrought its face into a maze of scallops, which the afternoon sun would touch up into a fable of decorative pattern; at present it was still grey and merely turgid. Beyond its tortured front, in its deep and cold belly, were the caves which the Brahman monks had carved out to form one of the masterpieces of the ancient Indian rock sculpture; there were several caves, and one housed the famous bas-relief of the Trimurti.

'Let's see the best first, shall we?' Vijay said to Chanda, slowing down to allow the family to gain on them.

'All right. You are the guide.'

He took her hand and led her into one of the reredos of which the cave was full. Somewhere in the dark nooks Radabai's voice piped like a small flute out of tune and Jagnath's baritone echoed in and out of niches with a strangely plangent bounce; their steps sounded fainter and fainter; were they going away . . .? He hoped they were. Although his father had been to Elephanta several times, he still didn't know the order of chambers and corridors, and in any case his favourite sculpture had always been that of Goddess Durga afloat in a universe of pious intoxication, to which he would no doubt lead his guests first of all.

'How cool it is in here!' Chanda said presently. 'The monks truly knew how to be comfortable.'

'They were the fathers of modern air conditioning. This is what I wanted to show you,' he said, swinging her into the crypt. 'What do you think of it?'

'Goodness me! You didn't tell me it was so big!'

The granite Trimurti seemed to thrive on the faint half-light that somehow outlasted the sieve of successive aisles and chambers. At that moment it was more impressive than either Chanda or even he was prepared for.

'When we were new to Bombay, we came here more often than nowadays,' he said. 'It is a great image, isn't it?'

'Great, Vijay? It takes my breath away! I have never seen anything like it.'

'This panel on the left is Vishnu and Lakshmi . . . the preserver and the grace of the universe. On the right, Shiva and Parvati riding the bull. Two ways in which the first Indians pictured the universe. This is all I know about the caves. I think just looking at them is quite enough, don't you?'

She nodded and walked to the base of the colossus, to read the wooden plate with the legend. 'Brahma, Siva and Vishnu,' she said, and her voice had a haunted hollow quality. 'The Vaishnavite conception of the universe. . . .'

Carved faithfully and lavishly out of solid rock, the dome of the statue's triple head touched the ceiling of the cave and faded into the shadows; the lips of the foremost face pursed in blissful disdain at the world at large. Why should stone, he thought fleetingly, lend an image more imponderable serenity than any other medium of the artist? The soft shimmer of its surface seemed to be a mere gossamer over a dream more peaceful than coma; the monolithic stillness spoke of a strength held in check at the instance of a bland idea. The very crannies of it seemed to echo a whisper as primeval as the rock itself. Many years ago, as a small boy he had believed he knew its secret; he could still see himself walking into the crypt with a piece of chalk in his hand, faltering in terror and fearing that if he wrote his name on the statue, as he had been dared to do, it would most certainly crash down on him with unmentionable wrath.

To-day the three countenances were distinctly friendlier, and he responded to them with understanding and dignity. They seemed to say, You have grown up remembering us and we like you better. The accident of being closeted with them gave him only a lightness of mind and feeling, rather than awe. And Chanda, swishing silkily between the two moods, as live as the giant faces were stony, seemed suddenly to span them with the easy and graceful flair of an elf.

'There is a story about this island,' he said, watching the crypt pile the dusk on her. 'There was once a king called Banasur, who had a daughter by

276

the name of Usha . . . Dawn. She was very beautiful and he wanted to marry her off, but couldn't give her a wedding fit for a princess. You see, the island was as poor then as it is now. To spare him the worry, Usha vowed to remain a virgin all her life. This pleased the gods and they rained gold on the island and Banasur became rich and powerful.'

'What became of Usha?'

'She kept her vow and became holy. Afterwards the people named the island the Golden City.'

'Very pretty, Vijay, but I am sure a man invented the story. A sacrificing woman is always a noble sight.'

He laughed, but she only glanced at him quizzically. Her features seemed somehow reversed. Highlighted by sun and youth in broad daylight, they had always tended upwards, so that their whole effect was a lovely pointedness, but here in the cave the twilight cast them in a low key, carving the mouth sharply, hiding all but a minute and uncertain light of her eyes, under the brightly ridged but otherwise dim forehead. Here, even though she might laugh, she was more vividly a woman than a friend.

'And talking of gold,' he went on, 'I have never properly thanked you for your amulet. Am I to wear it as a charm against evil or according to the old Rajput custom? Do you want me as a brother all your life?'

'Maybe you think it is too much worry?'

'No, I don't, Chanda. I like the idea.'

'Suppose I fell off the ferry on the way back, would you jump in to save me?'

'Without question.'

'Expecting absolutely nothing in return?' She sat down on the base and, folding the sari over her knees, raised her eyes to him.

'Absolutely nothing,' he said.

'Then you are a new man, Vijay. No more an Anglo-Rajput, but a real Rajput. I am very happy about it.'

In his pocket, his fingers caressed the silken bundle and he wondered again whether or not to give it to her; he had intended to give it as soon as he bought it, which was yesterday, but she and her mother had been out until late in the night.

'All right,' he said. 'The custom requires the brother to give a return gift . . . usually a kachli. . . .' He pulled the bodice out of his pocket, shook it out and gave it to her. 'Here it is, Chanda. You must take it and wear it.'

She took it and held it to the light. 'Oh Vijay, how pretty! A real kachli. Am I to wear it to-day?'

'That's up to you. I have never bought these things before, but you made such a point of custom. Listen, I'll turn my back and you can put it on here.'

277

'No, not here,' she said, folding it hurriedly. 'What would mother think!'

He sat next to her, tapping his sandals on the floor, listening to the echo. Her scent was again all around them; he thought that it came mainly from her hair, now gleaming moistly below the border of the sari; he thought how six months ago he would have put his hand out and stroked it, and how this time he held himself back with a clear and yet confused anticipation. The gap between the two emotions was an oblique measure of the new Chanda. He saw again how their correspondence had turned his big-brother indulgence into something like respect and a feeling of parity, and how, finally, the flesh and blood counterpart was beginning to live up to the fancies of his mind. They were now less free with each other than in the past, but that was because they knew one another better, and each perhaps sensed that any deliberate advance ventured at this stage would be equal to a formidable commitment. It was pleasant for him to cavort on the fringe of the fire, look into it without singeing himself and yet find the flames endlessly rewarding.

'Do you remember the last time at Juhu?' he said, trying to sound light. 'You mentioned how everything can be found in a thing smaller than itself . . . I think it was a verse. I didn't know what you meant, but now I do. You see, Chanda, I feel now that I have been dashing about in small circles for a long time. I expect I must have looked silly to a lot of people. But no more. . . . I wanted to tell you that, because you were the cause of it all.'

'And now you are over-simplifying?'

'I don't think I am. I am just taking it easier. I don't blame people any more, and they have stopped blaming me. There is a kind of unspoken truce between us.'

Drunkenly a moth flew into the cave and its wings threw little slivers of light into the dusk; they both watched it with studious concentration; then she got up, strolled over to the opposite wall and leaned on it. 'I think I liked you better when you were angry,' she said.

He could just about see the blurred greyish pillar of her sari, though not her face any more. Then, from the right a pair of tapping feet approached with a hollow echo that flew into the crypt and batted around with a cadence of fainter echoes; they ceased abruptly. Whoever the intruder was he must have stopped before one of the reliefs in the reredos, and Vijay wished he would change his mind and turn back the way he had come.

'Listen, Chanda,' he said, coming towards her and taking her hand. 'You really must make up your mind about me. An angry man is not happy. You'll never know what it means to be a stranger in your own family . . . and I don't wish it on you. I was a stranger for a long time, but now I am no more. Do you know why?'

'I think I do.'

'There you go . . . you only think you do . . . you can't really know. Because I gave in to them, that is why. Because of the things that happened. You see, Chanda, when I started to give in, they did too . . . and that made us square. I still have my ambitions, and some day I hope to make them work, but I hope I'll never again be angry as long as I live. Tell me you see that.'

'There is someone coming.'

'I don't care. Tell me I am right.'

'You are right, Vijay. Let us go now.'

He raised her hand to his chest and then, not realizing it, put it behind her waist and pressed it; the unintentional force made her get up on her toes and lean on him fully. There was a long and rushing second—then the steps started again and a dark shadow filled the oblong of the entrance. He wheeled her round so that she stood by his side, and tried to sound calm.

'Let's go and look for the others. They must be wondering.'

They passed the mute stranger and came into the corridor where the carved majesty of old kings and their courtiers protruded from the walls, then turned into the central hall and walked from there to the outer cave where a bright shaft of sunlight made them both frown. But the family had not yet returned.

'We'll wait for them, and if they don't come we'll go for a swim,' he said.

'Vijay, I should have told you this before,' she said evenly. 'Please don't be angry now. I am half-engaged to a man in Delhi. Mother wanted to keep it secret until it was final. No, no, please don't say anything just now'— and when he didn't, she pulled the sari over her forehead and added almost defiantly: 'Now you know. You can be angry, if you like. I was too, but it didn't help me.'

In the blinding glare of daylight her cheeks flushed deeply.

3

'WHEN I say one, two, three . . . push hard!'

Floating on his back, he paddled himself between the girls and lifted his feet to theirs. Tara laughed all the time and swallowed water, but thought nothing of it. When the tendrils of the star were more or less in position, he began to count. 'One, two . . . three!'

As Tara pushed off with all her ineffectual strength, she also bent her knees and upset the heave. Vijay went down and overhead first, and when he came up again and tossed his hair back, the girls were already wide apart.

Tara was on her feet, the sea up to her shoulder strap; she coughed and wiped the water from her eyes. Chanda was still struggling to float, though not very successfully, and the top of her wet head glinted in the harsh sun.

'You spoiled it,' he said to his sister. 'It is a very simple trick, if you'll only wait until I say "three," and then push. Look, let me show you once more.'

'Nothing doing, bhai! I have already half the bay in my stomach.'

'Sea is good for your inside.'

'No, thank you very much.'

She stopped choking, but her eyes streamed with more than mere sea. He waded over, slapped her back lightly and had to laugh; the hair had stuck to her cheeks and made her look like a whiskered lady from a circus. Then he swam back to Chanda and lay back again on the water. The surface was warm in the afternoon sun, and if one swam horizontally one avoided the cooler layers near the bottom. The little cove was embayed in a crescent of coconut palms and forgotten by the larger sea outside, and its waters were clear, its sands bright and pure. Looking straight up he saw an army of hurrying white clouds and a seagull performing on a current of hot air; a couple of kites soared watchfully in the heights, a ballet chorus awaiting their cue. But for the splash of the bathers and this other world of the sky the drowsy peace might have had no beginning or end.

'Where did you learn to swim?' he asked Chanda. 'You're much better than I thought.'

'At school in Bareilly. We never learned floating.'

'Oh, that's very easy. Let me show you.'

He planted his feet in the bottom and took her waist from both sides, and she leaned backwards until her body was almost level. He dropped one of his hands and held her up with the other. 'Now put your arms behind your head,' he told her. 'Don't be afraid.' She obeyed and shut her eyes at the same time, so that he laughed again. 'You must trust me. I am not going to duck you. Lie still and breathe slowly . . . through your nose.'

Her hair came awash, dissolving like a cluster of black anemone, and she gradually limbered up and breathed more easily; the water rippled around the atolls of her chin and breasts; the costume clung very neatly, outlining even the nipples with a sharp realism. 'That's all there is to it,' he said, forcing himself not to look. 'Just go on breathing and resting and you'll never sink. Once you are used to it, you can do it for hours.'

'I think I have learned now.' She folded up quickly, stood up and threw her head back to let the hair fall down in one solid wet braid. 'We have been in the water for an hour at least. I must be blue in the face.'

'You are. Like a wet dove.'

'Psh-h-h . . . you are not much prettier yourself!' She hit the surface with a rounded palm and sent a squirt into his face, but when he sprayed back quickly, she covered her eyes and reeled away. 'Stop, Vijay, stop! I can't drink any more!'

'Enough? This is what I get for teaching you to be a good swimmer.'

'Please, I won't do it again.'

They all waddled out to the surf, where Lakshman and the two smaller girls had smacked together a sand fortress, and then higher up to the pile of their clothes. Tara took her wrap and returned to the group on the surf. Chanda threw a vast towel over herself. Vijay flumped on the sand and lifted his face to the sun, still high up in the dome and burning. He thought how beautiful the heat could be when one used it sparingly. Soon only the cries of Munu and Hira and the sound of Chanda's rubbing were full perceptions; all the rest mellowed to a lazy stream of thoughts and a fine peace endlessly prolonged. When he opened his eyes again, she was at his side, drawing the comb through her hair with a rhythmical sway of her upper body; her plain maroon suit was still remorselessly revealing, as though she had chosen a pose that would temper its great daring. Wrung and tamed now, the plaits were slithering sticks of ebony.

'You know, Chanda,' he said, staring at her, 'in Europe a man sees his girl in a swimming suit and he knows what he is getting. We Indians still take some awful chances. Any cripple can look good in a sari.'

'Again . . .?' she said. 'You promised not to stare, and you are doing it all the time.'

'You look at me, don't you?'

'That is different. You are used to it. I am not.'

'Oh God,' he said, 'where is the difference? Are you ashamed?'

She kept quiet, and he turned away and remembered her confession back in the cave. He had forgotten it in the sea, and now the heat and her vivid presence had somehow blunted and stowed it away at a painless distance; now it was only a half-baked discomfort nibbling away at the outer glow of his physical exhilaration, and he could ward it off if he wished, or face it as one faces a dutiful encounter which can still be dodged. Of course she was going to marry one day—didn't he know it and expect it? All Hindus married as surely as they went to temples and discussed politics; what was wrong with that? But something was, in the case of Chanda, only that he could not yet admit it to himself clearly and without sentiment.

'Who is this man you're going to marry?' he said. 'Do you know him at all?'

'I have met him. His family are Merwar Rajputs.'

'Does he love you? Is he happy to see you?'

'He wants to marry me.'

'You said you wanted to study law and go into politics. Will he like that?'

'He won't have any choice.' She started to twine the combed tresses into a pair of sleek braids. 'I will consult him, naturally, but he will have to agree.'

'Oh!' he said. 'You wouldn't boss me like that, I can tell you.'

'Why should I? I am not marrying you.'

Now his lukewarm acceptance of the fact faded into the heat and he scrubbed the loose sand off his chest and began to imagine himself in the rôle of the other fellow. The notion was exciting, bodily at any rate, for as he squinted at her quietly out of the corner of his eyes the bountiful profile of her breasts seemed very near and desirable; but it was not uprooting, as he still hoped it would be. Wading through the surf with her, teasing her and arguing with her, even this feeling of tolerant superiority about her toilet—these were wholly good. Moreover, the thought that another fellow should share them as intimately, perhaps even more intimately—wholly inconceivable and bad! He remembered the Vedic phrase about the perfect couple: where each is both—and it seemed to him that his jealousy was a much stronger emotion than his urge to marry her, it must have amused the Vedic versifier to fling that catchy line at the host of intending brides and bridegrooms down the centuries, but how much could Vijay be Chanda, and vice versa? and for how long? That was the acid test, he thought. Unity there ought to be, one that sprang from an unquenchable need of each other every hour, every day, in bad times as well as good, but how was one to find it? And now that the question had crept up on him again, he thought it better to have it out once and for all.

'We Hindus,' he said, 'are supposed to be level-headed about our marriages. I thought that you were not, but what you said just now shook me.'

'Never mind about me. Let us hear what you think.'

He stretched himself stiffly, digging his toes into the torrid sand.

'We have talked about it before, do you remember?' he said, opening his eyes on the sky; the dome was unbearably bright, it seared his pupils, so he shut them again. He thought of the old and new epigrams that would sum up the lazy chaos in his head, but nothing quite seemed to fit. Marriage, wedding of two souls . . . why was it that only the dramatists and poets had anything permanent to say on the subject? Why not a soap manufacturer or airline pilot, whose wisdom would be so much closer to his own?

'We know all about the lips like cherries,' he ventured, wondering where he was going, 'and about the dovelike shyness . . . and the grace of a lotus at dawn . . . and kisses like scented unctions. These things sound very pretty in a Sanskrit drama, but you don't find them in our marriages.'

'Go on, sage.'

'All that happens is a lot of children . . . and that's what frightens me.

282

I could never think of my marriage in the shape of little Vijays . . . or little Chandas, if you like. I still say it must be more than that.'

'For instance?'

His toes began to burn and he raked the sand briefly and reached a cooler layer. 'Marriage and procreation . . .' the old injunction ambled through the attics of his head, then evaporated. 'Well,' he pushed off again vaguely, 'I don't want to think of the preservation of the community when I take a woman. We can leave that to the people who don't fly. . . .'

Bogged again, he yet realized that that was plainly the trouble with poets, swamis and lawgivers; they never flew. And now what were his other views on the formidable topic? What did Manu write, the first lawgiver? That woman was one half of universe? No, he got that garbled; that was because the sun was still rather withering and her rocking body so unbelievably alive in its aura of scent and moisture.

'What else do you ask of the little wretch?' she said. She placed the comb on the towel, then lay down alongside.

But nothing terribly new or pithy occurred to him for some time. He smiled towards the sun. What else . . .? Complete possession of her for one thing, that went without saying; anything less would not do at all. And if he thought of her as Chanda and wanted to be honest with himself he, had to confess that that alone would be well worth looking forward to. As for the rest, he wanted actually very little more than was already his, and that was it; he raked the ground as if burying that conviction safely. His mind was at last set on that one point, and the point itself was like a legible passage in an old manuscript, revealing and suspended at the same time. If all this buoyancy, this ragging, floating, confessing and tingling, would still be there after years of 'household' life, he probably wouldn't ask for more; if ten years from now Chanda could lie like this in the same sun and on the same hot sand, and disturb him and please him just the same, why, no man could feel cheated. However, none of it could be stated in these same crude terms, unless he wanted to trespass the ground already ceded to another man, and this he wouldn't do from conventional decency.

'Let me sleep a little and I'll tell you later,' he said.

'You had better.'

He stirred with a groan of pleasure and his hand touched hers, limp at her side, and the touch produced a warmth far removed from that of the sun, at which he presently scowled with one eye. He wondered how relaxing sheer twaddle could be. This was the sensual beauty of words, like those early readings of the Gita, only more rousing in another sense, all sounds, twitchings and prickings, tantalizing and yet somehow truthful. He thought, How hot her hand is! and squeezed it lightly and then checked himself, because Beauty began to quicken into an altogether more throbbing sensation, the one he had been baulking ever since they undressed for the swim; he wasn't going to be ruled completely by incalculable moments. Then, forgetting his earlier promise, he rose on his elbows and bent over her. The sun now gilded her from a more depressed angle and the shimmer of moisture and perspiration frosted the peaks of her body like a change of seasons.

'And if I don't tell you,' he said, 'what will you do to me, you underfed little hillwoman?'

Sensing his stare, her lids trembled. 'You will see, don't you worry. We hillmen have more wars to our credit than you people of Rajputana.'

'You have, have you? Look how you cringe instead of answering my question. Is that the character of a hill Rajput?'

She pulled the towel from under her, covered herself up to the chin and laughed. 'Anyhow, we at least keep our promises. You keep them only as long as they suit you. . . .'

'Why shouldn't I look at you? For a mountaineer, you have a beautiful body.' He was on the point of adding, Too beautiful for that Delhi yokel! but he restrained himself; he wound a wisp of her hair round the small pearl ear-ring and then blew at it. 'You know, Chanda,' he said, 'there is one good point about your swimming suit. I can see your legs are not crooked . . . they are very shapely. I was afraid they wouldn't be. Did you know that very few of our girls come up to the European women in that respect?'

'What silliness is that!'

'I am telling you. I know.'

Beyond the wavy horizon of her body, Tara and Lakshman waded at the bottom of the beach; they trailed a greenish-white wake which seethed for a while behind them and then settled by rippling degrees. In the far corners of the cove, where the palms kept the jungle from spilling over the sands, several fisherwomen filed out of the grove and began to toddle down to the surf. He peered back into her smiling face and sank down on his elbows.

'That's why I can't help looking at you,' he said. 'You should never be ashamed of a swimming suit . . . and I don't care what tradition has to say about that.' All of a sudden the thought of the other man loomed huge and incongruous, and he made a violent snatch at the towel and tore it off. 'Here . . . ! You don't have to hide yourself from me,' he said thickly, watching the frantic attempt of her hands to replace the cloth. 'I know how you are. I know you from here to there . . . every little part of you. . . .'

The vein on her smooth neck pulsed faintly, and he wondered for an inane second whether there was a way of stopping it; then, like Beauty some time ago, Jealousy began to swell into another distinct feeling, up and up, so that he soon heard it in his head, and he bent closer and strained to keep his voice free from undertones.

'You may be married a hundred times,' he said, 'but no vegetable-eating banya from Delhi could break this ripe body of yours as I could. Just you remember that when he puts his arms around you!'

Before he could finish, the fisherwomen toddled nearer, wedging their shrill cackle into his emotion and splitting it; the pitch itself came pecking closer and louder, overpowering his bluster, and from the far ring of his vision the latent detail came pressing forward with an equally unconquerable zest—Lakshman and Tara crossing the frothy surf, waving towards him; the two smaller girls dusting their saris; the angle of the sun and the first bluish shadows at the bottom of the cove; the memory of his father, uncle and Chanda's mother on that blanket in the quadrangle of the cave, still talking for all he knew. He sat up unwillingly.

Chanda did, too, reaching for the towel in the same movement.

The burning split second was gone. If he had been less startled he might have recorded its passing with more than just an idle, passive stare. The women chattered past, and he recorded instead, quite separately, the absurd heave of their buttocks and the crimson chafe of the saris in the hollows; up and down they moved, one up, the other down, dropsically, like the stuffed limbs of cotton dolls; high up on the heads of the women, against the very sun it seemed, were stacked the empty baskets, and way down below them they seemed to walk only with their lower bodies, so rigid were their backs and shoulders; then, off they went, never once swerving out of the perfect file, and off went their wriggling, tightly draped bottoms, which the sun presently painted a shinier red as though in soundless laughter. Then Tara and Lakshman stood above him in a cloud of watery coolness, the sand browning under their dripping feet.

4

TRYING to recapture it afterwards was like an attempt to remember the riot of a flower bed by invoking botanical names.

While all the colours and smells were still there, each as redolent as the next and a triumph in itself, from a distance all was simply a blaze of effulgence and a cloud of attar which he would inhale deeply with a familiar tickle in his chest, but before which he would at other times shut his eyes like a man whose finest fire burned in the draughtless space of his mind and for him alone. He told himself that he had foreseen it, as one tinkering with the gates of a dam might foresee a flood, and yet this could not explain his unpreparedness when the flood did finally break through. Would he ever remember it whole? He did not know yet. For the present he could say to himself, A little of this and a little of that, and hope that this would not only sum it up but also remain a cabalistic password in times to come, allowing him to re-create and relive any part of it at will; by then, too, he learned that the way the poets have been saying it all along was after all the best anyone could do, and that nothing in life possessed the clear-cut elegance of an algebraic equation, most of it being truly a little of this and a little of that, and that all personal symbolism endured only as long, and not a moment longer, than the 'littles' on which it rested. These truths now struck him as eternal, but his intimate avowal of them was a fresh revelation. For days afterwards such a 'little' had only to straggle through his memory and all at once the other 'littles' would glow up one after another, like the June oranges after a low-drifting cloud; but where by themselves they only gleamed against the green canopy, together they seemed to kindle the earth and the sky in one blaze.

He didn't doubt that old India would have scoffed at such a profusion of feeling, for the ancients had a sensible way with life and earmarked all great emotions for the minstrels; always, they insisted, the main duty of a man was to speed along the march of the clan with due regard for God and forbears—not to wallow in exaltation. So he would be generous and admit that the present was an extraordinary time in many ways, and he would even go farther and place one small concession on the altar of proportion: He would own that such a luxury of feeling might not be good for all people at all times—for it was truly staggering. He would do that because generosity was a mere crumb from his overladen table and because in all great adventures of the senses there always lurks the smug wraith of exhibitionism. But to himself and for himself he would not deny it. Denial would have been sham. Moreover, the great adventure was something he had set himself as a goal many years ago, and in this sense it was his birthright. So it came about that he presently abandoned the ancients and gave up all comparisons, and in that intimate vacuum his memory shone with a lustre that had all the promise of permanence.

Reaching the top of the hill after a rambling climb under the fronded heads of the jungle, they had flopped on the new turf at the foot of the old tower and waited for the return of their breath. That was one of the colourful family of 'littles' whose happy fitness was borne out by later events. They were hot and wet from the walk, and she turned her glistening cheeks to the cool breeze veering in from the sea. It was mid-afternoon, when the world lay prostrate and crushed in the sun, when even the kites and vultures could not bear to look at it.

The stream and the open sea shimmered like a wash of watercolour which had not been allowed to dry, and they had to screw their eyes up to peer at it for a few seconds at a time. The strain of looking was great, but he remembered thinking even then that more imminent than the view was his own lively sense of expectancy. The skyline of Bombay was a puckered fringe of a mirage, with a moonstone set here and there as by an immense necklace stringer; he felt that if he lowered his gaze the work of those million hours would vanish without trace. On the water the currents were then beginning to bristle and lose their sense of orientation, reminding him of the wheel tracks on a windy desert plain of Rajputana. Then a cloud would screen the sun and the water would mirror it as a lake of bottle-green within the sea, and whole stretches of the bay would seem to sense the restlessness of the open ocean outside. This went on for hours through the afternoon, only they could not watch it all. And once he saw it as a vast plate of pea soup and the shirring of its surface as a giant simultaneous breath from all sides; there in the west the plate curved away into the Indian Ocean, but here it meandered among a dozen light blue creeks off the main-land and drifted into the craggy presence of the Ghats.

He showed her the way they had come—'There by that gully, do you see, in front of our little cove?'—by now entirely in the shade, beyond which was another pear-like little hill tumbling into the sea rashly, in a spate of greenery, and beyond all that the pier at which they had landed that morning. 'The one you called funny,' he reminded her—a long line of low-slung cement blocks now invisible and merely imagined. In the valleys of the island the shadows were deep green, next to sloping patches of an unbelievable lushness; from their present height both seemed to be the exultant work of a child and his paintbox.

He told her of the year he had come up here as a boy in another squally monsoon, and he and the other boys had sheltered in the tower until the storm abated. 'Funny how I remember these things,' he said to her, no longer concerned with her betrothal or anything connected with it. 'I wonder why that is'—and he told her the rest of the story, as indeed many other stories from that time of his boyhood. She listened, mostly with her eyes shut, munching a stem of grass, and although she was sympathetic she couldn't help laughing now and then. Later he asked her what made her smell the way she did, and she told him: 'It's a secret, but I shall tell you since you know me so well already.' It was an old family formula brewed of plant and flower extracts, which her mother had received from her grandmother and she herself was hoping to pass on to her daughter one day. Then he asked her why she didn't smoke. 'Well, I just don't,' she said; there was no special reason, and definitely not because of public opinion; she put some emphasis on the point. They forgot all their quarrels and he let himself be influenced and often dominated by each following moment; his sense of well-being returned and he let it enclose him in a hermetic void of care-free isolation, while one other 'little,' a striped yellow-brown bumble bee, buzzed a while overhead and drew many ecstatic but faulty figure-eights against the eternally brimming clouds. 'I wish we had a pillow,' she said, moving the handkerchief which he had spread for her head.

'Try this. Anyhow, it will be a little higher,' and he put his arm under her head.

They lolled in the humid fragrance of the grass, happy to be alive, and he began to twist the escaping end of her plait. The hair was duller and brittler after the sea bath. He recalled another time long since forgotten when he had lain abed with a peculiar kind of slow fever that somehow pared a big event to absolute triteness whilst inflating a perfectly petty one, like the wisp of her hair, for instance, with a tremendous new importance. He thought that all talk of the sense of proportions was made by men who had not lain close to a lovely sweet-smelling virgin. The finding impressed him as another indefeasible truth. He remembered, too, parts of their talk that morning and the story Uncle Premchand told of the jail experience of a leader friend of his; and this led him to a lazy rumination on politics and jail in general. He had to smile again. If one happened to be an Indian A.D. 1937, love and politics were likely to agitate neighbouring cells in one's brain. He asked her if she thought it likely that her mother would be imprisoned as a 'political' in the future.

'Goodness me, I hope not,' she told him. 'Mother is not a real politician . . . as some of the others are. She was drawn into it quite by chance.'

'What if they jail you sometime?' he asked chortling

She straightened herself delicately, still with shut eyes. 'I don't think there is a chance, Vijay. If they should, someone said prison was very good for meditation.'

'Oh no, not that,' he said. 'No more meditation. One Uday in the family is quite enough. Did you notice how a man who meditates always thinks he is above all others?'

'I have not. How?' She moved her head away from him and sighed contentedly; her breath began to warm his bare wrist. He tried to think of how meditation played that trick on a man and how to put it in words, but he no longer had the requisite mental discipline.

'I'll tell you another day,' he said. 'Look straight up and tell me what you see.'

'Nothing. What do you see?' She had to shade her eyes at once, so brilliant was the glare.

'Nothing, absolutely nothing. That's what I like about the sky. There is no trouble in it.' He followed his raised arm and thought it over, and the glare scorched all his attempts at coherence; a flashing processional passed through his head, each picture overlapping another as if set not to stop at all.

Then she yawned and remembered her younger sister, who was about to leave India and go to an American college. 'Poor darling Hira,' she sighed, and the sigh had a ring of sleep, 'how unhappy she will be. I wish mother wouldn't send her away so far.'

'One or two years isn't such a long time. It will be good for her.'

'She is too young, Vijay. She will grow up away from us and won't know us when she comes back. You were much older when you went and look how you changed.'

'All boys and girls must change'—but instead of continuing, he yawned too.

Change, change, change, he said to himself and the word grew into a tall column that rose higher and more pointed until it faded among the mists of the firmament. He decided that it was impossible to think when one's look went so far and there was nothing to stop it. He closed his eyes and came down shakily, and the descent became a streaked rainbow of shimmer and stillborn ideas. The ground coalesced; her neck grew again firm, her skin turned warm and moist. Change . . . now the banner fluttered closer and he could read it more clearly. All was change, and without it there would be no seagulls, no grass, no tower, no Chanda or Vijay . . . and then he knew and was happy about it. That was how in the steady flame of that old fever he used to say, I know, in the dark and then he knew. He shut his eyes to draw a magic sheet between the ground under his back and the sky, so that certain things were again simple without mental effort; they seemed to be winnowed and strewn all over his mind by a compassionate spirit. Should I be grateful? he thought vaguely, finding that gratitude would be in bad taste. Nothing that helped one most was ever completely conclusive.

In the same way, and without having to open his eyes, he realized that she had fallen asleep. 'Good for you,' he muttered under his breath, with a tender brotherly concern.

He listened to her breathing and to his own, comparing the sounds like some minute but vital items of property, and this led him astray once more on a musing about children, whose sleep was just as easy and quiet. He spun a coil of her hair around his finger and then put the end of the plait under his chin; he was glad that she slept, for it was the first really fatuous thing he had done for months. Now that it was so close, the hair exuded a sweet cloud which did away with the last need to think. Then, like a mysterious tug at the sleeve in a dark passage, the smell took him on another unplanned trip and then the feeling of motion changed to an airy surge that was like the slow rise of spume; that was already much farther than he had reckoned on going; nor could he stop himself short of a stupendous effort of mind and body. There was a fine sense of freedom at the moment when he regained light and could once more hear and see distinctly.

They were clambering up a new wooded slope, like the others they had climbed and in some ways curiously unlike them, and she walked in front parting the bush and bending the branches for him, being especially careful of the karle creeper which was said to bring bad luck to anyone who passed underneath, while sunlight fell through the dense green roof and set a bright mango-orange fire to the nape of her neck, where the tresses were divided. He wondered whether it was her scent that gave the trees their rousing bouquet or whether it was they that mulled her own fragrance. She wore a thin batik sari as though it were a shawl, and the veil filtered the light mildly but did not arrest it altogether; behind that pellucid greyness her figure was a buff ghost, now sharp, now blurred. An immeasurable time went by and he remembered that she paused on a sudden and cried aloud; the next clear image showed a squirming brown coil topped by a darting forked tongue that gave an outraged hiss. Cobra! he said soundlessly, grabbing the first handy stone under his foot; but she caught his hand in the middle of the swing. Don't, please don't, let him go! she implored in a voice full of fear. As he boggled and scrupled the snake slid off under a fern, and a brief swish was followed by silence. What came over you? he said afterwards, too bewildered to notice the fallen sari and the breasts aglow in the sunlight. I don't know, she said sheepishly, it didn't seem right. He might have been the Shesha, and killing a Shesha is a terrible sin for anyone. He then picked up the fallen garment and spread it around her saying, Are you the kind who still believes in legends?

I do, on one particular day in the year, she said.

Which day?

To-day, she said, nodding wisely. It is Nag Panchami, the day of the snake worship, don't you remember?

He didn't, he said, and anyway what did it matter. They went up the rude trail as before and she told him the story of Shesha, the king of snakes, the thousand-hooded one, whose coils made an eternal couch for Lord Vishnu, the preserver of the universe. It seemed that a peasant once ploughed his field and killed a whole brood of young cobras when the share cut a new furrow. And seeing blood on the plough the mother snake went and bit every member of his family save a young daughter engaged in snake devotion at the time, for those praying were immune to venom; she coiled up to wait until the puja was over; while she waited she lapped up the milk and ate the offering of parched pulse which the girl had placed on the floor; she cooled off by and by and owned the killing of the girl's relations. The pious one begged that they be restored to life, and Shesha gave her a divine potion, and this the girl put on the lips of the family, reviving them completely. Since then it had been ruled that no one should plough his field on the fifth day of Shrawan or cut vegetables in the garden or cook any kind of food, and that rule was still observed.

He had to laugh over that, saying. You're a funny girl, Chanda, so young and yet so old. They climbed a little and he presently heard her say that she had a theory of her own, that snakes were really lovers from another incarnation, repenting the sins against their loves, and that she did not want to make their punishment any harder than it already was.

What rubbish! he then exclaimed. But what nice rubbish! You don't expect me to believe it, do you?

I don't, she said, but why mar this day with an act against life, which would be an act against love?

Why indeed! he said, quite willing by then to forgive her. He also remembered thinking: Love is another kind of knowledge, something the sages had in mind when they talked of man's realization in this hothouse of the great Maya . . . but the rest of the conjecture faded into a fresh whiff of her scent. Then the jungle brightened up inexplicably, like a stage of great depth in which the lights hung concealed behind the drooping foliage, and the sinuous rocking of her hips kindled him anew, and then he discovered himself wishing in some mysterious way to be a part of that movement and inside it. Very soon that urge stretched from one end of him to the other and he saw himself soaring onward arrowlike, just above the ground, and a keen warmth filled him all the way up like the pouring of tea over a dry throat.

When he again glanced straight up, the two worlds were equally real for a time, except that the first was now visible while the other flashed only in his head. The minute act of seeing with his eyes was the only separation of the two. If he shut them for a moment, both became enduringly fused and the pulsing of either streamed in both directions smoothly and vividly; in the first all was hotly imminent, but in the other he was carefully freeing his arm from the weight of her head, for it had gone dead on him while he slept, and leaning down over her face, wondering whether the noise of his heart was loud enough to wake her. A spindly, ginger-hued ant stumbled over the twined hurdles of her hair. He took it between his fingertips, saw the frantic waving of its legs, threw it off into the breeze.

She slept on peacefully, with a mouth so much like a cowrie shell, glossy and notched on top, softly outcurving at the bottom. He propped himself on his elbows and kissed her. He meant it to be a light and tender epilogue to his dream, he didn't mean to wake her. But when her pouting lip slipped between his, tasting surprisingly full and velveteen, he forgot his intention and remained quite still. Now there was a greater rush of heat through that mouth and he gave himself up to it completely. Presently she was awake. He raised his head and looked deep into her eyes and they were at once mirrors and skylights towards a greater brilliance; he had never looked deeper into anyone. Then she shut them and he imitated her instinctively, sinking lower once more. Her lips came together and lost their pout; he pursed his own and strained to pry them apart, but they resisted; he lessened the pressure a little, and the lips became again pliable; the tip of his tongue brushed the warm corners of her mouth and the tiny caress touched off a fresh gust of heat. She clasped his neck fitfully, as though unsure of the limit of her participation, and later a little more resolutely, until the weight of her embrace grew more explicit than her faltering kiss. That was when the last hedge between his two worlds wilted away lamely.

In the days that followed he would not be able to shake himself completely free of the impression that the most uprooting moments of that time were the most esoteric chapters of the memory as a whole; he would suspect that memory of a callous hoard of things electrifying and unimaginable. He would only remember scattered fragments, jumping to attention in a helter-skelter fashion, in which his acute perception gave him no clue for what was to come. In many ways this was the most unexpected thing about it, for if one knew a game thoroughly one could anticipate retaining a certain coolness of mind even at the height of passion; he retained none. It was this that afterwards weighed with him and made him believe that it was unlike any previous experience.

Parts of it were clear and indelible pictures, the others swamped each other too swiftly to be remembered; he talked to her in brusque stifled sentences and she answered him tersely, whilst the overall import of the sound hovered in mid-air like a fateful decision. She lay back, out of her sari at last, a live gift out of a billowing silken wrap, and her blouse, open save for the lowest button, over which he had fumbled violently but in vain, shone with the stark tilted light of the afternoon; he even noticed the blade-like creases radiating left and right from that button. Swelling gently to a pair of hard barbs her breasts would sag in a gilded gourdlike fullness when she rolled on one side to escape his caresses; he stared at them and fondled them in hurried turns, as if to make up for all the time he had not dreamt of their faultless shape. His blood pumped away toilsomely. He wanted to go on cupping and caressing them, but his possessed hands chose to be on their own; they shifted from spot to spot, from the breasts to the face, from there to the small taut belly and farther down over the black bun of hair, and then all the way up once more as if worried she might not be there if he gave up for an instant. He kept saying 'Chanda, Chanda . . .' and she gasped back wildly, striving to stop him. He bruised his lips harshly against all protuberances, soft and hard, and once his teeth jagged a nipple and nearly closed over it. With every limb of his body about to snap, he presently raised himself and waited for the moment when he could tear himself away.

'Don't look . . . please, Vijay . . .!' she said, clenching the shirt on his shoulder. He glowered at her, so near and flushed, and at her arms joined like a shield over her nakedness, and could not bear to remain still.

'We can't . . .' he said thinly, in sudden agitation; he could not bring himself to utter the words as they alighted on his tongue. 'Chanda darling . . . you've never, have you . . .? You're . . .'

'No,' she breathed, 'but now, yes.'

'You don't know what you're saying. We mustn't . . . we've gone mad, both of us.'

Don't look, please. Just come to me!'

Pulling at his neck her other arm dispelled the brief moment of indecision; his trembling elbows gave way and he collapsed, burying his face in her sprawling hair. He muzzled her neck and bore himself to be kissed in turn, impulsively but erratically.

He shut his eyes and opened them, and each time the tang of moist skin went more to his head; by then his breath was running away with him and inside his temples several questions flitted feebly and failed to materialize. This was another quaking 'little' he would always remember: No girl had ever done so much to him with so little conscious effort; he realized this with the rest of his witless mind and with all his fingertips and bursting body. And one more image singed his brain so very close that he bated his breath: Her glowing face uplifted at the peak of strain, her eyes shut, her bared upper teeth viciously blanching the lower lip.

'I love you, Chanda. Look at me!'

'I too. . . .' The urgent command made her open her eyes, though only a narrow, dazed slit.

Her head slipped farther back and she gave up talking. Through the seemingly unstoppable heat of his impatience an inexorable new feeling dived uppermost and it was that of a burning solicitude. The wrenching chaos in him fell apart once more and some of it forged ahead with a troughing momentum, while the other took hold of itself. She stroked his face and dug into his hair in fitful succession, gasping, 'Don't hurt me, please.'

Halfway through his mouth the words slurred their own likeness and he shivered. He felt himself frittered, then ground away in huge pieces and the potent core of the moment fused with a chafing sensation that brought new power to the outermost parts of him. He only remembered that one half of him was being driven before it, while with the other he caught breathtaking glimpses of her and they aroused his pity and spurred him on at the same time. She writhed, tossing her head from side to side, swallowed and caught her breath. Other glimpses were even more poignant, though also more fleeting—her twitching eyelids, that other hand first crushing a fistful of sari then tearing at the grass, those white clenched knuckles from which not only all blood but also all veins seemed to have gone. Her mumble became a thing of pain and endearment and she swept her forehead of hair, as though it were in the way of her breath. All this he saw and it shook him more than anything ever had, but the reckless part of him would have nothing to do with it. From then on and all the way to the end his love remained dual; out in front a rough wanton race, behind it a pang of compassion so clear that the consummation found him muttering into the hair of her neck.

They lay side by side, divided by heat and their own distances. The sky descended in a rainbow of pastels, full of splintered sounds—yet another 'little.' He abandoned the far land and took it all in on the way, cloud by cloud, colour by colour, form by form, and later the stillness ebbed away gradually and he made a fresh discovery of his limbs and felt the evening breeze frizzle the hair on them. No longer ringed with heat, he could again raise himself up without any great effort, even crane over and push his nose into her inert face; he kissed her eyes, cheeks and chin, then her neck and breasts, now heaving slower once more; the taste was pleasantly brackish but the scent was that of dry figs. At length she took his head in both her hands and forced it back towards her own face, not daring to look at him.

'Shut your eyes, Vijay.'

'Why . . .?' He blew gently at the soft black down on her neck. 'You married me after all, Chanda.'

He ran his fingers through her hair and tucked it behind her ears, in sleek curving ringlets, and the hardest thing seemed to be the awful gap between what he felt like saying and the way he knew it would sound when he said it; all kinds of conventional and intimate words rushed through his mind, and he shrank before them. Then gratitude overwhelmed his reticence and he began to think of it as a burn in his chest.

'Once you will know it just as I did, I promise,' he said.

'Oh, don't say it. Don't talk about it.' She groped for the sari underneath, but he caught her hand and held it.

'Not yet, Chanda. Don't be shy now.' A wave of protest rose up in him; he drew her to him, all the while racking his brain for the right sentence.

Again she hid herself and turned away. 'I thought I would spoil it. . . . I didn't . . . did I?'

'You could never spoil anything.'

'Yes, the beginning . . . I could have spoiled that. At first I thought of you . . . I said, Vijay, Vijay, Vijay, and thought the name would choke me. I thought too much . . . and I thought you would know it and would not like me. My heart nearly burst . . . I thought you were flying away and would never come back. I thought you had forgotten me for good.'

'Forgotten you? How could I?'

'It seemed like that. That is all I remember. Now I am glad.'

'Glad, Chanda?'

'Yes, I am. I thought of it in the morning and wondered if it would happen. I wanted it . . . then I got scared, I don't know why. I thought that when I told you of . . . that thing'—and she tried to invest the jarring communication with an impersonal ring—'I thought that you would not want me any more. It was awful even to think of it.'

Speaking, she had lain back and now her moving lips stirred him again strongly; he reached for the end of her garment and spread it quickly over her, looking only at the cloth; but the sheer fabric moulded her crossed legs faithfully, leaving a lotus-shaped cut-out of buff uncovered.

'Wouldn't want you . . .?' he said. 'My darling, I've wanted you from the day you came, what are you saying? I must have wanted you before I even knew.'

'But now?' she said. 'Will you want me again?'

'Listen.' He cupped her cheek in the hollow of his hand. 'From now on I will want you more and more, don't you know? Now I have seen you like this, I won't sleep at all. I'll see you day and night, every part of you . . . and I'll want you every time I see you like that.' Bending so near that her face was a mere blur, he said: 'I love you, Chanda, don't you feel that?'

'Oh yes, yes.'

'It happens only once, you should know. Now I can't let you go, I want you for always. . . . I don't even have to think about it. I know it through and through.'

'That is how it ought to be,' she said, closing her eyes. 'We should never have to think about it. We should have each other every time we are together like this.'

'Like this, or any other way.'

'Any other way . . .'

He ruffled her hair to recall her, and now the words which had rung so fatefully in his head during the last few minutes came out perfectly easily, stripped of all pomp and self-consciousness.

'Listen, my beautiful darling . . . there is only one way out of it. Do you want me as I want you? Do you want us to be together again and again?'

'I do, Vijay, I said it just now.'

'Then we must marry at once,' he said, looking at her intently. 'Next week, if possible. Do you hear, Chanda? It is not only love, or that I hate to lose you to another . . . now you have become my wife. More than my wife. We must marry at once.'

She said nothing, but pressed him to her. They lay like that for a long time, the vein of her neck throbbing softly against his lips; he returned the pressure several times and later made a move to kiss her, but she held him possessively. Finally she spoke up in a whisper.

'Darling Vijay, I have waited to hear you say that. You will never know how long I have waited. . . .'

The sound filled his ear as a warm moist puff.

Then, from the depths of the little harbour, a whistle spiralled upward and around the hillsides, a sudden reminder of a world still uninitiated. The ferry—there is that, too, he thought unwillingly. He listened to the thick forest absorbing the last baleful shriek, then raised himself and kissed her on the lips.

'We must not be late. They are waiting for us.'

'I should best like to go to sleep again.'

But they sat up back to back, a trifle self-consciously, and began to dress.

He felt her warm shoulders wriggle against his as she shook the sand out of her sandals and struggled with the bodice and petticoat, and he mused about the last sailing of the boat and about the trail back to the caves, but most of it was burbled and serenely inconsequential. The sun had fallen behind the tower; in the shade the air had become more fragrant and humid. This then is love, he thought, recoiling before the shoddiness of the word; he didn't want it; he wanted this afternoon to endure for ever and to think of it in a simple way of his own, for he knew by then that simple memories had a better chance of lasting. He decided that he would think of it as Chanda Hill, Grass, the Old Tower and First Time. And of the future, too, he would think as She and something else and something else again, and then nothing that the future might have in store could ever bedraggle it. He thought that 'love' was as drab as the rest of the community's sophisms, and as for the poets—well, that was on a different plane, they worked with such primitive tools indeed!

'And so an end comes to our short brotherhood,' he said, noticing his rakhi amulet for the first time. 'You won't have to give me one at the next Rakhi-Purnima.'

'This holds good for a whole year, Vijay.' She rose, paying out a length of the sari, then twined it around her hips and pleated it in front; her tone became more confident. 'Besides, I like to think of us as brother and sister,' she said. 'Yama and Yamuna were real twins and they started the human race.'

'You don't believe that too, do you?'

'I don't. Only it is moving to think of it . . . to me, anyhow. Do you remember the story in the Rig-Veda? Yamuna loves her brother and wants a child by him. She says, "Like chariot wheels let us spread to meet each other." '

'What does he say?'

'He saps;

> "Embrace another, Yami; let another enfold thee,
> Win thou his heart and let him win thy fancy
> and he shall form with thee a blest alliance." '

'You see!' he said with a laugh. 'Unlike you girls, men always remember the law.'

'Still, I like it. It is a beautiful idea . . . it has nothing to do with law. Yama and Yamuna were half-gods, law was nothing to them.'

'It is very much to us, unfortunately.' He got up and stepped into his white pyjamas.

The grass lay flattened all round, some of it gleaming a dull russet. For some seconds he could not take his eyes off it, and he swayed a little to keep his balance. Then he straightened himself and finished dressing and presently another old legend came to his mind; in that one the tear from the pain cry of a god fell to the ground and burgeoned into a splendid tree, destined never to grow old. He wondered what Chanda's tree would have looked like if this had been a century of fables. Would it have been a tall one, with a sparse crown and an exquisitely slender and glossy trunk, or a lush, dense kind, weighted down by an opulence of blossoms and leaves? Then she finished combing her hair and they stood holding each other by the waist, looking across the pea-green stream.

'I never thought it would be a hilltop,' she said, a little sadly.

'Nor did I. We never know anything much, do we, darling? I would like to put a stone here and engrave on it: Chanda and Vijay, on the fourteenth day of September, in broad daylight . . . something that happens only to shepherds . . . both for the first time.'

'Only one for the first time. . . .' She shut her eyes.

'No, both. Vijay too.'

'How I wish that were true,' she said, moving away suddenly.

'It is, my love, believe me,' he said earnestly, stopping her and fondling her hand in both his. 'I tell that to myself all the time. It *is* the first time, truly. It is like going down the same street every day, then seeing it again on a beautiful holiday morning. That is when you really see it for the first time.'

'Please, Vijay . . . let us not say anything.'

They embraced fiercely once more, though he couldn't again bring himself to muss her hair. Also, although he tried to put it off loyally, the thought of the ferry and their families back in the cave loomed rather formidable. He squeezed her firmly, evoking a loud gasp, and said:

'All right, my darling. We will not. But now we must run!' As they started down the hill, still close together, he added, 'Think of something we can tell them.'

'You think,' she said. 'I can barely walk.'

The woods were cooler and more heavily exuding. He went into the lead with his hands outstretched to ward off the thorny bush; she gasped every now and then over loose stones. Near the bottom of the slope the trail opened into a coarse path and they resumed walking abreast and holding hands. He thought again more or less collectedly, and as the theme in his head hardened well enough he put it in words.

'You must let me talk to father, first. Yes, darling Chanda, you must. As soon as we get home, I will take him into his daftar and talk to him. I'll tell him we are engaged and want to get married as soon as possible. As soon as we can arrange it. I can just see his face when I tell him!'

1

AND that seemed to be the end of the road—one road, at one time, anyway.

Compared to the accounts of most people it was not an elaborate one, nor could he truthfully say that the overhead exceeded the returns; there were some long and rather forlorn columns on each side of the line, yet the grand totals managed to tally roughly; in them was the best and worst of both worlds. Gazing into the mauve bay of the evening he could now often see a greatly magnified map of his life, still somewhat chequered and also much more readable, and take comfort from it where once he would have fretted. Was there a dot in that kaleidoscope which he would care to relive . . .? He thought there probably was, but he was not certain of the practical ends of such wizardry. Some deep thinker had written that life and soul had one thing in common: they never duplicated themselves; while men often fooled themselves that they could re-create a moment of past enchantment if they set a suitable stage in the present, they were in reality infatuated with a mere crude likeness. Man is a wheel forever treading on fresh ground'—and indeed it was hard for him to see how one revolution could approximate another with so much fresh ground between them. To try and go back with the equipment of the present was an example of the snaring Maya.

A conventional retrospect, a wise and tolerant attempt to focus its hard core, was an altogether different sort of pastime, legitimate and profitable; that he could always do without believing himself a fool. And it was rather revealing how a few years unfailingly boiled down to a couple of super-charged hours, the last two weeks for example, and how the towering mansion of time waned away to disclose the slender piles that had bound it together so impressively. He had to ask himself whether nature, spirit, Brahman, or whatever tag the Thing bore on itself, chose to waste all that alarming effort and time for the simple purpose of making those few minutes, the costly ferment of the good, bad and indifferent, blaze all the more gaily, and whether that waste was intelligent and not simply a proof that Design was a Simple Simon whose goals were barely more creditable than his fumbling techniques. But as often as he pondered it, the answer was lost in pictures whose power was more immediate and definitely more attractive.

'It is what I had hoped and prayed for,' were Jagnath's first words on the night of their return from Elephanta. 'Oh Vijay, Vijay, what happy news! If a king himself tried, he could not have chosen better than you have.'

I didn't choose, pitaji. It chose itself.

I love her, pitaji. I didn't think that I would, but I do . . . more than I can ever tell you. . . .

Yet he didn't say that, or anything else in that vein, for he was still too dazed for a rough and ready confidence, and words still made him fidget.

He thought about it on another plane. Chanda was only a few weeks out of several years, yet she seemed to have become their synthesis just as his first solo flight, after a roundabout of training, had become flying for him. She had arrived slowly and after a prodigal misuse of effort, but once there she affirmed its truth in a moving voice and the truth at once forged ahead of all the previous ones. His life in England, the months with Constance, his hopes, mishaps and rallies, were so much hesitant spring cleaning for her ultimate arrival, seen in retrospect. How could he now help dwelling on her to the exclusion of all else? Was this emotional induction a virtue or an error? He thought that an old Hindu would probably see it as an error, but, fortunately, there was also the Hindu man of the world. 'All bliss is of two kinds, the joys received through the body, and those imparted by the peace of the spirit.' Some would have it that the latter was above the former, like the pipal tree which overshadows its own naked roots, yet no Hindu in his right mind would dream of belittling either in its proper sphere. And that, he realized with a new and warming insight, was the most comforting thing about Hinduism; it sheltered all manner of people and all sizes of stature and encouraged all notions of happiness. And if the ranking of your personal 'bliss' on the roster of merit caused you no headache, you could lead a very full life and justify it before yourself. Until you came to the next stage on the road of spirit, for which, anyhow, a greater than average curiosity was the first need.

He felt no such curiosity yet. It seemed to him that the stagnation of months and years was at an end, and that all now flowed in one broad direction and carried him with it. Action now showed itself as basically uniform and monopolistic; he thought that it and peace crossed each other out. He felt—as he always had, now with more, now less conviction— that he preferred to move forward and that such motion was in his temperament, that it made him most happy and that it was his dharma, as the sages would dryly remark. In surging on and letting himself be shoved by forces greater than himself he also had the sensation that nothing else existed, and that feeling also was a part of his gratified pride. He relished every moment of it. More than anything he relished the evening when the news swooped on the family like a falling star and burst into fireworks. What a splurge that was!

'So you have changed your mind at last!' Jagnath said after the first silent minute in which his bewilderment ranged freely over his countenance. 'I am so happy for you . . . for myself . . . for Chanda and everyone. It is what your mother had so dearly wanted to see. If only she were here now. . . .'

'She is, father. I know she is happy, too.'

They embraced joyously and Jagnath cried a little, holding his son's hands, and the event somehow took on an importance beyond its simple sights and sounds. His ageing face mellowed as he dabbed his eyes with a crooked forefinger; but he took hold of himself soon afterwards and then all his pent-up frustration poured out in a stream, now happily lightened to effervescence.

'When did you decide? What made you? And all of a sudden like this? Have you talked to Chanda . . . did she agree . . .?'

'We talked it over fully and she agreed.'

'But when, when . . .? They have been here ten days and you never even gave a sign that you were going to. Does anyone else know? Did you tell Rana Prashad?'

'You are the first one, pitaji.'

'Then we must tell her right away. My goodness, how surprised she will be! She gave up this marriage some time ago. We dropped the matter and didn't discuss it this time . . . and now here it is again. . . .' Then he tapped his temples suddenly. 'My God, Vijay! You don't think she has gone and accepted another proposal for Chanda?'

'She did, but not finally.'

'How do you know? How is it you are better informed than I?'

'Chanda told me.'

He paced up and down the daftar, gathering speed and wrestling with the hurdle, emerging triumphant at last. 'Yes, of course, yes,' he said and stopped before his son, peering at him craftily. 'It shall be cancelled, naturally . . . what other way is there? Yours is a prior claim in the eyes of everyone. But we must tell her at once, this very moment!' He strode to the door and beckoned to Vijay with more resolution than he had shown for months. 'That is what we shall do. Talk to her right away!'

No one in Villa Ram could remember another such uproarious night, nor could anyone stand on his dignity in the face of those tidings. They barged into the guest-room just as Rana Prashad was starting her pedicure and broke the news from the door, while she ran for cover and re-emerged respectably attired. Most inmates heard Jagnath's bellowing baritone and in fact—although he did that on the sly—Rajuram the Elder tiptoed from the pantry to the staircase to hear it more clearly.

'Men, men, one at a time, I beg of you!' Rana Prashad cried. 'Who is marrying whom, and for what reason? Why was I not told?'

Patiently but tersely Jagnath explained, stopping only for breath or a turn of phrase, while Vijay stood by and occasionally smiled sheepishly. Then they embraced, emitting delighted grunts. 'I hope you will approve, Shreemati,' Vijay said to her.

'Nothing will make me happier, dear boy. It is really up to the girl herself. If she wants to have you, I shall bless you both. But why did she not tell me?'

'We agreed that I should mention it first.'

'Let me call her,' Jagnath offered, shuffling off at once.

When Chanda came, already combed and dressed for the night, she passed Vijay with dropped eyes and threw her arms about her mother. They rocked together in tearful understanding and their loose tresses commingled, as if resisting separation, and neither could bear to look at the men at whose hands their bond was destined to come undone. Vijay tugged his father's arm and they quietly went downstairs where, in no time at all, the whole family was gathered in the living-room.

'Oh Vijay, I am so happy, congratulations, you lucky man!' Tara said, bravely staving off a breakdown. 'You will never know how lucky you are. Men can be such fools . . . why did you go and make her miserable all these months?'

'Miserable . . . Arre, I never dreamt . . .'

'We are all exceptionally happy,' Jagnath intervened, at the same time ordering Rajuram to make tea and bring all the sweets hoarded up for the Divali holidays.

Vijay accepted the stammered wishes of his little sister and of Chanda's sister Hira and afterwards, though more formally, of the two Rajurams and other servants; these last had expected it all along, for to them birth, marriage and death were simple and inevitable phenomena.

Then there was hot tea on the carved teapoys and a whetting feast of silver-foiled sweetmeats, and then Chanda and her mother came down and the jollification started in real fast earnest. How they sat up into the small hours of the morning chewing betel nut, shrieking their views on marriage, wedding arrangements, guests, quarters for the couple-to-be and a hundred pertinent and impertinent details! How this eruption impinged, as always, on every conceivable subject under the sun, including politics, Hindu sociology and the inevitable issue of supremacy between the hill and plains Rajputs, until they laughed and ragged themselves into a happy stupor, which finally sent them to their beds in warm anticipation of the new day, Divali, as it happened, when another celebration would be added to all that was in the air already! And when the pale dyes of dawn filled the window of his room, Vijay thought how rewarding the grooved life of the Hindus could be at times. They undoubtedly tried to boss one, but how lavish they were with their love when one did the right thing, and how readily they assumed the best and responded with the best in them.

'I have written to Mr. Kurla to-day,' Mrs. Prashad announced in the morning, in a temple of all places; Mr. Kurla was the father of the Delhi boy to whom her daughter had become almost betrothed. 'All negotiations will be broken off forthwith,' she said emphatically. 'What is more, we must proclaim this new engagement without delay. We ought finally to agree on the wedding itself. I think that we can dispense with the customary period and fix it for next month.'

'Next month, Rana . . .?' Jagnath said. 'It is not the proper marriage season! We must see an astrologer and make sure of the date. After all, he is my only son. I should like the wedding to be remembered by all Rajputs of this town.'

'Bother the Rajputs. We must be sensible about it.'

'When I married Kandubai at Indore we had over two hundred guests. We had even a state military band playing outside the pandal. I remember when . . .' and on he went, like a man who turned up a crust of earth to prove that the soil was fertile.

They were coming out of a temple in a very crowded section, having coupled the Divali thanksgiving with a few words of their private gratitude. It was Kartik—October-November—in which, farther back than anyone could remember, King Bali was forced to abdicate the universe to Lord Vishnu, and lotus-skinned Rama climbed the throne of another kingdom on earth, and Vikramaditya, the last of the imperial Guptas, was crowned in yet another part of India, thus setting the ball rolling for the famed era of Vikram. Earlier that day Jagnath had phoned Uncle Premchand to give him the joyous news and Rana Prashad had made up her mind to return alone to Bareilly, to prepare Chanda's dowry and Hira's departure for America.

'It should be a sample of the new Indian trends,' she therefore pressed Jagnath. 'The wasteful old weddings, those hundreds of food-consuming guests, that awful hullabaloo . . . all that is out . . . old-fashioned! I know how dear they are to the hearts of Rajputs, but look where they have got them! As a caste we are bankrupt . . . and may I tell you why?'

'Why?' Jagnath was labouring over the steps of the temple passage.

'We have always fought on the wrong side and cut each other's throats for all sorts of silly reasons . . . and thrown huge parties at the slightest provocation . . . that is why. In this new India we are mindful of the poverty of our peoples. And Vijay does not care for a large wedding . . . neither does my girl. They only want it as soon as possible.'

302

Jagnath shook his head. 'Dear Shreemati, I have duties for a first wedding in the family.'

'Besides, I cannot go on record for giving an expensive party on my pitiful government salary. Some people might think I have embezzled public funds.'

The quip went half home, because that was a line of persuasion the official in him was most sensitive to. 'Time is so terribly important,' he said, floundering but stubborn. 'The cards must be printed and sent out, relatives must be informed. And what of the right day?' he added, thinking that his pundit would have to be consulted about two horoscopes, instead of the usual one; these matters required much time and forethought. 'The part of the father is only just beginning,' he wound up, giving a nervous wide berth to a bunch of boys huddling over their Divali crackers. 'Who knows when it shall end?'

Rana's answer went up in smoke and explosion, for just then the street urchins began to fire and whoop hugely; Vijay piloted his parent past the din and on to the waiting car on the street proper. 'All the same, it is not right, son,' Jagnath summed it up in the car. 'What would your mother have said?'

He went right on resisting, with that mixture of nostalgia and decorousness which had lately emerged as his final frame of mind, and in the meantime Rana Prashad left for Bareilly, taking Hira with her after all but entrusting Chanda to the care of the Premchands until she returned. Wholeheartedly, Jagnath plunged into the preparations. Closeting himself in the daftar one whole evening, he composed the text of the announcement and wrote three dozen letters to the relatives, real and supposed. He went to see the astrologer and the solicitor, and then engaged three priests to conduct the nuptials; he even called an architect to study the proposed extension of Villa Ram and was restrained only at the last moment, by Vijay, from incurring an unforgivable expense. He could not sit still for any length of time, but rubbed his hands and scowled incessantly.

'Is it not appalling,' Rana Prashad wrote him from Bareilly, 'that I must be mother and cabinet member at the same time? For years we have blamed the British way of doing things, and now that we have taken over, how do we behave? Go and cheat the wretched taxpayer right away! I have to leave the office for a couple of hours every day lest Chanda's things become neglected. Is that not awful, I ask you . . .? No wonder foreigners say that we are only too willing to sell out to the family. Yet what choice have I, what *can* I do?'

Jagnath showed the letter to Vijay. 'She is busy, a good sign. The Prashads are not wealthy, they spend too much on themselves,' he said with tentative malice, 'but Chanda will not come to you a poor bride.'

'I don't care what she brings with her, pitaji. I have a job. We can both live on that.'

'That is all very well, son, but what if there is a fire, or flood, or famine? A reserve is a welcome thing. But do not worry about it . . . Rajputs always know what is expected of them.'

'Maybe even a small ceremony will be too much for them.'

'That is not an affair of yours. We are all of us trying to do our best. Even your uncle has offered his help.'

'Has the date been fixed?'

'We shall know it to-morrow, the pundit promised. Son, marriage is not one of your airplanes . . . one cannot rush it, it is not proper.'

Next day they were again able to inch forward. The horoscopes had proved that the week of the full moon in December was singularly free from malignant influences and that marriage could be consummated with the best hope for the future; they scheduled the event for the three days beginning December twenty-sixth and wrote to Rana Prashad; Uncle Prem-chand offered his town house in token of the bride's paternal home, where in accordance with custom a good part of the ceremony would be enacted. Meanwhile November crept up on them with a dry nip, and the jacarandas and balsams on Cumballa Hill burst out in a heady new rash; the last autumn winds decamped over the Indian Ocean, abandoning the coast to its own gentle breezes, while up in the North the Hindus beat up the Muslims in a few places and vice versa, and the country had a foretaste of a Hindu raj.

'You know, darling,' Chanda said one evening as they walked home from an open-air performance of *Ramleela*, that fine melodrama of the demi-god Ram's deeds, 'sometimes I cannot imagine that we are really getting married. I read Manu the other day and it seems we do not fit into any of his chapters.'

'Yes, we do,' he said and took her arm. 'You gave yourself of your own free will, with a single robe . . . to a man of learning. That makes it a Brahma marriage.'

'We are not Brahmans, so that is out. On the other hand'—and she lowered her voice to escape being overheard by a passer-by—'you took . . . no, I mean we had our real wedding before the formal one. So our marriage is Ghandarva . . . Manu calls it the reciprocal connection of a youth and a maiden with mutual desire. It sounds terrible, but in our case it is quite true.'

'Are you sorry, Chanda?'

'Oh no, no! Please, can we not just think about it?'

'Sure, darling. Only it is too late for names.'

They climbed the hill leisurely and loitered in the Premchand garden before turning in. The rustle and stirring, as of a legion of ants marching through fallen leaves, was finally gone and the neems held their cool breath to themselves and eavesdropped in dank silence. Unseen carpets of camphor scent received them at all levels of the night, inviting and softly caressing. They tore them slowly and their heads seemed to float as they went. Remembering how he had longed for her a few weeks ago in this same garden, he kissed her eyes and hair impulsively.

'Never mind what anyone calls our marriage,' he said with a beating heart. 'I love you and that's all I know. If anyone took you away to-morrow, I would go after him and break down his house.'

'And kill the guards and elope with me?'

'As surely as I hold you now.'

'My lord, my love, how wonderful,' she said, sliding her nose along his open shirt neck; but when he tried to slip a hand under the sari she foiled him with a demure, 'No, not now,' and moved nimbly away. 'It also seems you are not pleased with one kind of marriage alone,' she said. 'Are you now trying the rakshasa kind . . . ?'

'Which is that?'

'Marriage by force. And let me tell you, darling, Manu speaks of it very slightingly.'

'He wasn't a Rajput. If we Rajputs want anything, we go out and capture it.'

'How true. Must you remind me of it?'

He joined her by a bed of begonias and took her to the house. There was bright light in all the windows and the verandah railing on the first floor went like a pale sash around the broad waist of the building; again he saw himself crouching over it late one night, listening to the soft cries of Tara somewhere in the darkness of the garden, aching for the warm untouched firm-smooth virginity of this girl walking now beside him, and he felt tolerant towards himself and thankful that the soothing of the ache had not fallen short of his expectations.

2

'I CALLED you here, dear boy, about an important matter,' Uncle Prem-chand said. 'Important for you, to be exact. Sit down while I finish this.'

His private sanctuary in the humming newspaper office was a plain, sparsely furnished wing of a verandah, shut off from the editorial rooms by a swing door and from the street by a curtain of bamboo shutters that hung there throughout the day creating an illusion of privacy, where in reality the whole verandah was a cratelike outgrowth of the building directly above the street pavement. It was plainly an afterthought, typical of the days when newspaper owning was an insecure and unrewarding way of life. But although not imposing, the cubicle was at least cool and restful, in spite of its hideous brown walls. There were Indian, British and American periodicals on one side of the desk and a signed silver-framed photograph of Mr. Gandhi on the other. The rear wall showed a large map of India, with a tinted shadow of Europe superimposed, which the uncle occasionally showed to foreign visitors and journalists to impress on them the size of the Indian problem in relation to the local European squabbles; it was a telling visual argument and effective against the critics of Indian disunity. From the ground floor and right through the guts of the building throbbed the ancient rotary of the *Morning Herald*, now coughing up its sister evening sheet.

The uncle flourished his pen for a decorative signature, then screwed on the cap.

'Knowing how busy a bridegroom must be, I shall not waste your time,' he began amiably. 'I have been asked by a friend of mine, a well-to-do Parsi gentleman . . . to whom I happened to mention your improbable plan of flying pilgrims . . . to find out whether it was practical. Perhaps you will remember our difference of opinion some time ago,' he smiled artfully, looking down on his fingertips. 'Well, this time I said I would find out from you and let him know.'

'Most kind of you, uncle,' Vijay said. 'I will tell you all I know.'

'Very well, then. How much money do you really need?'

'Fifty thousand for one machine and the work of two flying strips. A few more thousands later on, to get it in good running order.'

'When do you hope to earn it back?'

'Four years . . . maybe five. You see, uncle, it is a seasonal service, from May to October, when the pilgrims . . .'

'I know that, dear boy. Who would fly and who would manage?'

'I myself, in the beginning, anyway.'

Premchand took off his glasses and glanced through them against the light. 'You seem to become more modest with time,' he said pleasantly 'That is how it should be. I too started in a very small way. This person would like to study your papers for a day or two. Could you let me have them?'

'Yes, of course. This evening?'

'To-morrow will do.' He got up and made his next point walking towards his nephew: 'I hope he will find it interesting. What will you do if he really does agree?'

'What will I do, uncle! How can you ask?'

Just then the uncle's editor, a Mr. Bhargava, a gaunt man in glasses and hand-woven dress, leaned over the swing door and interrupted them. 'I have a Rajkot organizer in my office, will you come?' he said in a gently gelded voice. Premchand shepherded his nephew into the next large room. 'We can finish talking in the hall,' he said. 'Come along.'

Walking after the two men, who presently indulged in a brief and confidential shoptalk, Vijay tried in vain to appear casual. Calm and his uncle's news seemed to be in opposite camps for the moment; he had not been prepared for the interview, had in fact thought that the summons would be in some regard or other to the wedding. But now his uncle appeared to him in an altogether new light.

Then Mr. Bhargava shrugged his tall frame and, with a breezy wave at him, strode back to his editorial lair.

'Used to be a revolutionary,' Premchand said on the way out. 'Even a terrorist, for all I know. And look at him now! Such are the blessings of patriotic work . . . let that be an example to you, my boy. As we get to grips with our trouble, we grow humbler too. That is why an ex-rebel makes a most suitable practical politician.'

'You were never a rebel, uncle.'

'No, not that kind.' He took Vijay's arm, crowding most of the room and boxed-up desks into a single lingering look of pride, and his tone gained in dignity and self-esteem. 'We are like the wheel of life at Sanchi, turning round full every thousand years,' he said. 'Each spoke touches another part of us. This is the part in which we work hard and do useful things . . . instead of rebelling. For that reason Bhargava is not a dynamiter . . . and you are helping a rich Parsi company to become even richer . . . and I, a Jain by conviction, choose a public life which is bound to land me in jail one of these days. It is very good while it lasts. It makes everyone happy. It makes the British wish they had never allowed Mr. Hume into this country.'

Amused but respectful, Vijay smiled. Allan O. Hume was the Bengal civil servant at whose nudging in 1885 the Indian National Congress had been formed; it was a standing joke in nationalist circles.

'I used to think it would be a good idea, when I am sixty or seventy, like our Gandhiji, to dress in a saffron cloak and read the Gita of Dhanmaharaj. Now I am not so sure. Once you mould the public opinion, you always wish to do so. And my son Lakshman will marry one of these days and have children. There will be no place for an old man to read holy books.'

'And India will be free by then.'

'I hope so sincerely.' He scribbled his name in a book held up by an office peon, then swerved into the boarded passage and towards the lift door; deprived of the sight of his achievements and of the scribing sweat-labour on which they had been built, his swagger waned somewhat; he became his old jovial self.

'By the by, you never answered my question,' he said. 'What if this friend of mine agrees to your plans?'

'Oh uncle, I couldn't wish for a better wedding present.'

Premchand laid his hands on Vijay's shoulders and grinned almost coyly. 'Then you shall have it, dear boy. Are you surprised?'

'What do you mean . . .?'

Comprehension flooded back into Vijay's mind, like the glow of a flashlight after the first blinding stab; he stared at his uncle, beaming interest and a delighted benevolence behind a thick-lensed myopic gaze, and found himself at a loss for words. The lift made a clinking sound as it passed the floor above, its canvas-sewn cable dropping stiffly beyond the grille of the door. A sepoy bell rang out sharply in one of the offices.

'Uncle, you are not joking . . .?'

'Why should I not joke? Have I not led a good and proper life? But it is true all the same.'

The pan-chewing boy who ran the lift flung the door to one side and turned his face to the switch; he remained in that humble posture to the end of their talk.

Vijay gripped his uncle's hand and shook it vehemently. 'If it is true, uncle, then I . . . then it is wonderful. I wouldn't know how to thank you. I never dreamt when you called me. . . .'

'I know you didn't. In a sense, neither did I. It is one of my principles never to conduct business with a member of the family. But we shall be a new kind of firm. I shall be a silent partner and you will only take your own orders. We must prove it to the British that we can modernize even a pilgrim, must we not? They shall not say that we Indians are not enterprizing. But you had better go and give it some more thought,' he added as Mr. Bhargava's voice piped up in an adjoining room. 'We will have another chat after your wedding.'

Vijay stepped into the lift, uncertain even of its floor; the grille closed.

'Uncle, I don't know what to say,' he said. 'I know Chanda and her mother will be terribly pleased to hear it.'

'My dear Vijay, I should say so, of course! These two females have been after me like a pair of tigresses.'

The lift started and they shouted good-bye to each other, and then the bulky figure of the uncle shot skyward and vanished from view.

Outside, the sun clung to the buildings in dazzling vertical sheets and to the street in a row of greyly luminous shingles, and the air had the dry and thirsting tang of November. A line of chokras had already formed at the gate of the machine room, waiting for the first batch of the evening paper. Pigeons again rutted and crows dickered in the treetops of Elphinstone Circle, whither now, light in the head and none too certain of his immediate intentions, he turned his groggy steps.

IN THE middle of December, Rana Prashad and Hira returned, bringing along a somewhat sheepish Ranjit: he had been entrusted with the safe delivery of Uday at Bombay and had gone and lost him in Central India, probably to Ujjain, one of the seven holiest cities in the land. He assured the family that it was all Uday's fault, that his weakness for holy places would surely become his final undoing, but he felt pretty certain that the sadhu would show up sooner or later—he always did, anyhow—and be there for the wedding. They echoed that hope with mixed feelings. So great a red-letter event was simply unimaginable without the family sadhu.

They were put up in the house at Cumballa Hill, formidably enlivening the existing life there, and Rana Prashad set about applying her native talents of persuading everyone to share her problems and haste. Ranjit was not forgotten; after his last remissness he was quite willing to renew her faith in his worthiness. 'Isn't it true that when it rains in my life it always pours,' she was wont to exclaim on more than one occasion, drawing freely from alien idiom. 'Who will remember all the things I am supposed to do! What have you done with that Benares sari I gave you yesterday'? Ranjit had driven all the way to a silk mercer in Phydonie and had it exchanged for a paler colour; it now lay among the heap of Chanda's dowry. 'You never told me!' she said, and he wondered yet again if all this high fever could ever be resolved into the calm dignity befitting so final a ceremony.

In between such flimsy assignments, the catering provision, too, had fallen to his lot. One would think that one joint reception would redound to the good name of both the marrying families, but no: Jagnath had at last won a major point in the nuptial etiquette, as though in compensation for his other denied ambitions, and the bride would now be collected by the bridegroom at her symbolical home—Premchand's house—which meant an extra feast on behalf of the male who gave the bride away—himself, awkwardly enough. Thus he had to spend long hours with Radabai Premchand and other eager females of the household, and waste his time on an oily Indo-Christian caterer discussing the faloodas, curd sweets, rasgoolas, dyed gram balls, curried dainties, pappads, English-style cakes, biscuits, muffins, tea, ice-cream, sherbets, beer, whisky, gin and sodas— because a few Europeans had also been invited—when he should have thought of his own gifts to the couple, or gone to a painting exhibition or two, or spent more time with Sarojini, the exquisite Kathakali dancer whom it had been his good fortune to come across quite recently. But duty was duty, especially to a Rajput in whom the notion of smooth family feasts was a second instinct, and he went about his errands with commendable grace and even allowed himself to become engrossed in some of them. So it happened that his own present for Vijay remained unbought until quite late and he had finally to consult him, lest a duplication be made somewhere along the line.

'I should never give it away like this, but I know you are a modern young man,' he adorned his procrastination one morning, after dragging Vijay halfway across the town. 'How would you like a statue of Nataraja from my collection ... or maybe an old Jain prayer book, beautifully painted, eh, Vijay?'

'Very much indeed, Ranjit. But why should you go without it?' Vijay was duly enthusiastic, though the real munificence of the offer escaped him completely.

'A sixteenth-century work of art, bound in gold brocade, set with six rubies ... and Apsaras, heavenly dancers, such as you never saw, drawn all over the thing?'

'I can see that you love it very dearly. I shouldn't want to ...'

'Well, perhaps not,' he said with a cluck of the tongue. 'Nowadays all gifts must be practical. They must be wearable and gapeable-at ... or they must run, so they tell me. Yes, I think I know of a present after all, a very modern one ... and you shall come along and pick it out for yourself.'

And he took him to a motor-car showroom on Sandhurst Bridge and stood him in front of a small British family four-seater, still smelling of the factory and bearing the customs tags, and demanded slyly to know if such an object were more to the point in these days of locomotive societies.

'Ranjit, I know you're the most generous of men, but I really can't allow you to ruin yourself,' Vijay said.

'You cannot, it is quite true. I am already ruined. A decent last gesture will not do me any harm. But do you like it?'

'Do I like it? Are you out of your mind?'

'Do you propose to have a large number of children?'

'——?'

'Because if you do, this may be too small in a few years. However, that is your problem, not mine. Your present shall run ... just as Chanda's will be gaped at, it is hoped.'

Vijay mopped his forehead wildly. 'Chanda's ...? Ranjit, dear fellow, you have not gone and ...?'

'I have, I have, though it is nothing on wheels, thank God! You must know that I am very fond of Chanda. Rana Prashad is one of the dearest friends I have.'

And back in the car he thrust a small plush box in Vijay's hand and directed its unwrapping with a livelier, almost brotherly concern. From the mass of tissue emerged a pair of ear-rings of an old Oudh design, done in crescents of small emeralds on hand-wrought Indian gold, the copying of which, he owned with a collector's true glee, he had personally superintended in Old Delhi. 'Here at least,' he said largely, 'they shall have something to gape at. I am told that Nassiruddin Haydar of Oudh . . . a famous debauchee, you will remember . . . gave such a pair to those wives of his who bore him sons. The pattern is a rarity. Practically nobody remembers it to-day.'

Vijay tried to protest, only to be hushed up as soon as he began. Overwhelmed, he thanked him in simple, totally inadequate words, wondering whether after all the reckless soul of their common great ancestor had not been distilled in Ranjit to an extent which no one yet realized. They drove home by a big detour of the Parel film district and after a while Ranjit clucked again gently—something he rarely permitted himself, for the sound had a low-caste connotation.

'It is good to welcome you on this side of sleep,' he said.

'Sleep . . .?'

'Have you forgotten? Once . . . I think on a train . . . I told you that blood counts for more than brains. I said that we prefer sleep to being awake. You are becoming a good Hindu at last. Welcome to our dormitory.'

'Uncle Premchand thinks the contrary. So do I.'

'Your privilege, to be sure. I see you lying down in a corner together with Uday, your father, myself and others. Do not be shocked. It is a pleasant life and you will live longer.'

'And you?'

'I . . .?' He waved airily, both acknowledging and dismissing the topic. 'They say that not one of Nassiruddin's bastards were his own . . . that his eunuchs were unreliable . . . and I feel like saying, What matter! Giving those ear-rings away gave him great pleasure and he died a happy man.'

They drove into a quaint-looking enclosure, parked the car and went into a long shed of corrugated iron sheets. 'But for the unfortunate patties of Rana's, I should have been here yesterday,' Ranjit said, forgetting about the presents. 'I hope it is not too late now.' The dwelling was one of a random number in a well-known film colony, and he found his way without any apparent trouble. He knocked on a door from behind which issued nothing more make-believe than the angry sobs of a woman. The crier turned out to be a frail and dishevelled young lady who answered to the name of Sarojini.

'Oh Ranjit, I shall poison him, I shall, you will see!' she exclaimed, sitting forlorn on a pile of flamboyant costumes, ornaments and open containers. 'He is doing everything wrong . . . forcing me to do it too. It cannot be borne, I tell you! I will not be ruined on his account! I do not want his contract, I am going away never to see him or speak to him again. . . .'

'Calm yourself, Saroj,' Ranjit said. He sank beside her and patted her hand compassionately. 'I take it you mean that stalwart of well-intentioned ignorance, Mr. Kooka? Tell me everything.'

Mr. Kooka, it transpired, was the director of the all-vernacular production called *Apsara* (English title, 'Heavenly Dancer') in which a court dancer achieves her recognition in the face of much intrigue and slander. Mr. Kooka worked with an eye to effect, an ear to the tinkle of silver rupees, neither of which left room for the subtleties of pure Kathakali—a dance form native to South India, at which Sarojini excelled. Since the film was her first and so much depended on her performance, a clash of ideas was inevitable, had in fact taken place that morning, so that at this moment all was actually over and she was merely trying to pack her trunks. Did he not think it was the only course left to her?

He did, and said so mellifluously, drying her swollen eyes in the meantime, stroking her pretty head until the sobbing ceased. 'I shall speak to Mr. Kooka forthwith,' he declared firmly, for he knew him well and had some influence with the fiend, 'but you are not to move or do anything until I return, promise me now . . . and especially you are not to think of poison.' Great artists, he added, must bear with exploitation and the ignorance of the exploiters, since the greater number of mankind was, anyhow, made up of grocers and clerks. And he would find out if Mr. Kooka meant what he said.

'Take my car and go home, Vijay,' he said as they came out of the shed. 'I will follow you in a gharry later on. For all I know of our friend, you may have quite a long wait.'

'No, let me. I'll sit here and have a cigarette.'

So Ranjit vanished in the two-storied brick and stucco building which housed the company's offices. Afterwards a group of medieval rajas and veiled princesses strolled about the courtyard smoking and munching betel nut, and teams of coolies carted entire palaces from one shed to another, and mango trees, complete to the fruit, sprouted from the cement pavement. As worlds go, this one seemed to fit Ranjit every bit as faithfully as his own homestead in Dehra Dun; he was of it as much as Vijay believed himself to be of that larger one without. And still later a brass-buckled watchman brought a cup of turmeric-tainted tea with the salaams of Mr. Kooka and then a frantic gong sent the whole plumed fauna of the colony flapping into the hazy glare of noon. Then Ranjit came back and they drove out of the premises.

'Mr. Kooka was happy to see me,' he said in high humour. '*Apsara* has been saved for the future generations of Kathakali lovers. Let us hope there will be no more talk of poison.' The old glint played over his handsome pale brown features, irradiated no doubt by the same whimsical flicker of his forbear which kindled his general inexplainable glow.

But as they neared Worli, Vijay could not resist asking a question which had climbed foremost in the course of his musing. 'Are you in love with her?' he asked gently.

312

'Arre, my goodness, certainly not! She is a very fine dancer and that is all.'

'Are you never going to marry again? Is there no woman beautiful and accomplished enough for you to want to marry?'

'Maybe, Vijay. If I can find her, I shall most certainly not speak to her of matrimony.' He smiled and sighed one after the other, as if the subject were an ancient one, exhausted long since. 'Anything so perfect would be like the work of an artist. It would make me jealous . . . it would snub and make me small. Wait, I know what you are going to say . . . why not marry the opposite, am I right? Unfortunately, the opposite does not attract. As for a happy medium, I married one when I was very young and it was not a success. Does that satisfy you?'

'No,' Vijay said. 'I often think you are laughing at the whole world.'

'Dear Vijay, do not speak to me of anything so exhausting,' he said, and laughed.

And as the red-purple cliff rose from the unlovely horizon of Worli and the glimmering river of asphalt wound away northward, palmward, Juhuward, and Villa Ram, that steady bulwark of everyday sanity, craned her dappled and bright cheek to them, he sighed like the man whose secret joke was too revealing to be shared, who yet neared the bursting point several times a day and overcame it only in the nick of time.

'Do you remember the "rolling wheels of this great world"?' he said. 'I was going to say that they now seem to be rolling for you at full speed. I am delighted to think that my wedding present shall multiply their number . . . by four all at once.'

4

THEN Hira sailed and the cream of three families saw her off in the Alexandra Dock. It was the week before the wedding, a couple of days before Christmas—there were advance signs of it all over the steamer, tuning the farewell in a sadly lustrous key which would have dismayed even an adult steeled to such pathetic moments.

'You are not just a student going to America to learn all you can,' Ranjit told her by way of encouragement. 'You are an ambassador of goodwill, the youngest ever to leave these shores. My onyx-eyed one, do not forget that ever.'

Tearful, frightened, lost, Hira betrayed the ambassadorial vision by burying her face in Chanda's sari. How could he know the agony of loneliness to which this ship would resign her before long, despite the fact that a good friend of mother's was to be her companion and protector?

'They will ask you where India is, and when you tell them, they will probably mix us up with the Central Mongolian camel thieves. Those

Americans know more about their screen actresses than an old culture like ours. But you will tell them . . . you will tell them all you know.'

'She will, don't worry,' Chanda said, barely holding her own tears.

'They are a lively people, Hira . . . talkative like ourselves. They build tall houses and fast trains and splendid roads, not only to live in them and move on them . . . but to talk about them too. They can do that because they are free, not like us. Because no one tells them, This is too much, or, What do you know about this or that? And they understand our struggle for freedom so well.'

'It is a pity they admire the British so much,' Premchand said. 'That is because they don't know them as well as we do.'

'Vijay, is all the luggage in the cabin?' Rana Prashad asked, shielding her younger daughter from excessive limelight.

'All of it, Shreemati.'

'Then let us come off politics and cheer up a little.'

They commented on the gaily bespangled decks and the funny drawl of the American steward and the possible gales in the Atlantic, while Vijay settled with the coolies and Premchand devoted some time to the Brahman gentleman in whose meek charge Hira had been placed. The last passengers came aboard, weighted down with the customary garlands, and the tugs came on, hissing and wallowing a little way off the starboard. Hira snuggled closer to her sister—someone had mentioned the wedding, a particularly painful subject just at the time.

'Never you mind, darling,' Chanda said with a choking catch. 'A wedding is like any other holiday. I will write and tell you every little thing, I promise.'

'That promise came first,' Hira said.

They had been thinking of it all the week, Hira with a sharp and rebellious twinge that outlived all appeasement, her sister with a pang of pain and love, now more, now less mingled. While still at school together they had made a pact to attend each other's weddings and name their first daughters after each other. Now one half of the promise would never be kept; together with their general feeling of loss, this broken pledge rose like a grievous solitary cloud over Chanda's other happiness and she found it hard to keep it to herself.

'At least I will be at yours. I swear nothing in the whole world shall keep me away.'

'Ah Chanda . . . Chanda . . . !'

They cried into each other's saris and promised to write regularly, while the others looked away. Then a loudspeaker admonished all persons without tickets to go ashore; they embraced frantically and Hira threw her last bravery to the winds.

'Don't, my precious,' Rana Prashad said, herself on the verge of a breakdown. 'I shall see you next summer, if everything goes well. Only a few months from to-day.'

'Ama, don't let me go . . .'

'It is the best for you, my darling, believe me.' She pressed her into her lap and stroked her hair, crying openly now. 'Good-bye, my precious! Remember all that we talked.'

'Good-bye, darling Hira,' Chanda said.

They all took their leave and each managed to say something heartening over a strangling lump in his throat, for they all loved her and shared her sorrow as only Indians can; milling around her, pinching her cheeks, pressing small go-away packages into her arms, flurried, swishing, apprehensive, they made a sanguine and unforgettable group. 'Remember the women of old,' Ranjit said valiantly, as though dispatching his own sister or even his own child. 'Do not be afraid. They never were.'

Then the siren went off and the hawsers flipped into the water; the dock lascars picked them up and rowed them to the tugs. They scrambled down the gangway and on to the pier, leaving Rana and Chanda to say the last farewells. While they huddled there, looking up at the towering upper decks, the siren shrieked twice more and the sound careened inside the oblong dock and broke out towards the city. Presently the two women came down too and the ship cast off, and the tugs nosed at the dock gates; steam blew out of the bulk in half a dozen places at once; signals strained to windward. A small wisp of white, itself a-flutter and waving, leaned over the railing in an attempt to stave off the inevitable, and to it the group on the mole directed its last shouted communication.

'Good-bye . . . God be with you, my darling!'

'Farewell and Godspeed!'

'Don't forget to write . . .!'

'Send a telegram when you get there!'

'Bye-bye, Hira . . . take care of yourself!'

'Look at her . . . she will fall into the harbour!' Rana Prashad said, motioning wildly at the ship.

'No, she won't. Mr. Raman is holding her.'

The pretty voyager, however, had drifted out of earshot. The white and black palace floated majestically on the mirror of the dock, her human cargo reduced to speckled strings along its white balconies. Then through the gates she inched, coughed and hissed, pecked at by the tugs, and later into the open stream, while they jumped into their cars and raced out of the dock and around to Ballard Pier to behold her for the last time—a shining, preening sea bird on the waves.

'A beautiful child . . . in body and mind,' Rana said afterwards. 'I wouldn't live a day if something should happen to her.'

'Arre, dear Rana,' Ranjit said. 'Why should anything happen to her?

She is not going to the aborigines. We shall all miss her, but we shall see her again.'

'Hira is gone. This one is getting married. I shall be all alone in that house in Bareilly.'

She trembled, suddenly visited by a loneliness which she had not felt since the death of Professor Prashad, her husband. Fear twittered in the part of her heart which had once been in the exclusive ransom of her elder daughter, a fear the more poignant because she realized that she may have lavished too much on Chanda and too little on Hira. She wondered why motherhood was so full of contradictions, why a big loyalty sometimes displaced a smaller one, and why, when the big one was fulfilled as God and men ordained it—as now with Chanda's marriage—the small one knocked on the heart like a waif and filled the vacancy again completely.

'Hira is going to have everything Chanda missed,' she said in defiance of the ghost, now close at hand. 'It is good for her to see another country and hear of other things besides caste and religion. She will be modern and without prejudice.'

'She could have learned that right here, like Chanda.'

'It is never the same thing, Ranjit. Education of the girls is a big worry. Even if I told you, you wouldn't understand.'

'How do you know I would not?'

'You would not, really. I know,' she said. It was one of the few things she had never discussed with anyone and least of all with a friend so near that he automatically barred certain intimacies. 'Please, let us leave it alone,' she said in a shaken voice, glancing away.

She had been determined to do well by her daughters ever since Professor Prashad passed away, and she had led many an uphill battle against his clannish relations, who had wanted the girls to be brought up under their wing; they could not forgive her forcing the professor to give up his own friends and family and devote himself to hers to the exclusion of all else. The memory of a whole family was more implacable than an individual's, and more specific; being old-fashioned, they subscribed to just retribution; they dangled disinheritance over her head, for most of the professor's estate had legally passed over to his male descendant, as yet unborn—an appalling medieval law, that. She had fought them tooth and nail and also vowed to have the girls out of their grasp as soon as humanly possible, and all kinds of things, bright and otherwise, had come in the wake of that decision: She had turned feminist, then politician, wanted to send the girls to England, then become queasy and chosen neutral America instead. Later, as Chanda was about to sail, she had run a-foul of New Delhi and Chanda's student permit was cancelled. The next few years went into making Chanda the most accomplished young girl in Northern India, so that the Prashad clan would think twice before claiming her as their own.

She finally succeeded, but the tussle had been a long and wearying one, and her maternal emotions had been severely tapped; all that could be given to a child had been given to Chanda; little was left over for Hira. Public life and fame had also taken up a lot of space in the interim. Now Hira was on her way to the States because that seemed to be the best all-round solution and because there she would receive a good liberal education and imbibe the spirit of independence and maybe even follow in her mother's rigorous trail.

'It is an old promise, and I must see that it is kept,' she summed it up for Ranjit when they reached Cumballa Hill.

But her heart was no longer in it. Going first to her room and then into the garden she thought: Has the rush of the last four weeks been too much for me? Am I simply exhausted? The shadow of her love for Hira crossed her path mournfully, as if blaming her, and Hira herself seemed to say: Ama, why did you let me go? Politics and the feeling of confidence begotten by fame receded all of a sudden; her eyes filled with tears.

She paced the path between the bushes and used her handkerchief freely and the thorns jabbing at her skirt gave her an abstract but sweeping sense of injustice. By degrees, the scent of sultana-champa cleansed her grief to a more purposeful emotion; she thought again that it was not the men but the women who invariably found themselves at the receiving end of all pummelling; she had resisted that infamy ever since she knew how, only to find another indelible confirmation of it in her own flesh and blood. After five thousand years, Hira's future was in reality just as cramped as that of the legendary goddesses had been; for a woman it had always been one vicious circle after another, save that each century made it a little wider. Then it occurred to her that the male was almost wholly to blame and because this thought was a familiar standby, it brought her some comfort. She broke a flower branch and carried it back to the house, feeling emptier and also mysteriously stronger.

She kicked the splinters of a broken bottle from the stairs, thinking: Look, even the ordinary safety of a strange house devolved on the woman! She went to her room, opened her bower and found her various presents for Chanda. One was a fine, intricately embroidered sari, which she fingered vacantly, held up to the lamp, then replaced in the almirah. The sight of her own wardrobe touched off the thought of to-morrow's tea meeting with her ladies; she had been inveigled against her better judgment into addressing the Bombay Beggars' Rehabilitation Centre. Well, now she would cancel it and hang the consequences! They might try to talk to one another for a change! She would stay home and give the little time that was left to her daughter Chanda and, incidentally, corroborate the wise old man who said that enlightenment began right in the middle of one's own parlour.

317

❀❀❀❀❀❀❀❀❀❀❀❀❀❀❀❀❀❀❀❀❀❀❀❀❀❀❀

1

VIJAY slept very little that night and was up long before the dawn, waiting for Rajuram and the tea. Over the chair near the window lay his new ceremonial tunic, a gaudy affair of gold brocade and gold buttons, which Jagnath himself had chosen and committed to the family tailor and which, he later said regretfully, was nowhere near as sumptuous as his own wedding garment had been in the good old days. On a chest were the turban, as yet only a length of sheer pink cloth, and his new churi-dar-pyjamas the narrow white trousers named after the bangle effect which they formed over the ankles; his silver embroidered slippers, jutis, with curved-up tops; and the piece of muslin which would be tied to the sword scabbard to mark its peaceful mission. The diamond ring and the gold bracelet, both bearing the family insignia, and the ceremonial sword were still with Jagnath. Looking at this finery in the first pale flush of dawn and seeing himself fully caparisoned before the guests, he had to smile. So ended the subtle tug o' war between tradition and reform! What set out to be an example to the young marrying Indians wound up as an emulation of the past vainglory! With a quietly patient disregard of his original promise, Jagnath had achieved what indeed should have seemed inevitable to all who knew him.

'A great day, baba . . . a day of joy for all!' proclaimed Rajuram the Elder as he brought the breakfast. He too wore a clean shirt and a fresh pair of pyjamas, and moved with a deliberate new dignity. 'It is already six o'clock. You must rise and hurry. Lalaji has ordered me to help you with the dressing.'

He had his tea and then his bath. From the first diffusion of orange and primrose the morning fled into a colourless haze warmed by the sun and mirrored by the sea, and when he returned from the bathroom the day seemed to be several hours older. Rajuram was dusting the slippers and shining them with the end of his shirt.

'No need for that now,' Vijay told him. 'It seems to me enough time has been spent on it already.'

'Jee-huhn . . . so it has.' This he murmured into his chest, as was his habit when something challenged his sense of fitness. 'By the sword and the way you carry it, they shall know that you are a Rajput. Shoes are also of prime importance. When lalaji married I cleaned his shoes for many days . . . also the saddle and silver-plated harness.' He clucked softly and shook his head. 'For truth, baba, when a Rajput rode to his wedding in those times the whole village turned out to see him.'

'Nowadays riding is old-fashioned, Rajuram. Anyhow, the police wouldn't allow it.'

'Jee-huhn!' with gruff emphasis. 'Nowadays they have cars and carry their swords as though they were ashamed of them. A great change has come over us, baba.'

'A good thing, too. We do our fighting with pens and speeches.'

'Jee-huhn . . . for shame! Now you must start dressing.' He held up the white trousers as if they were treasure.

'If I dress now and sit around for an hour or two, they will be crushed, Rajuram.'

'That is so, baba. All the same you must dress.' Rajuram's reasoning was often remarkable for its two parallel streams of logic; he now exemplified it further by not relinquishing the garment. 'If you dress and get ready,' he said cajolingly, 'I can return to my work. Otherwise not.'

So Vijay began to dress, allowing himself to become infected with another kind of nervousness, the one he had hoped to spare himself by being superior about it: Would he appear ridiculous in these satiny furbelows? Would Chanda laugh when she saw him? He began to wish again that his father had been less zealous. He stood up, refusing to put on more than the undergarments. 'All right, Rajuram,' he said. 'Go now and do your other work.'

The old one left after a protest. Vijay spent another half-hour paring his nails and grooming his hair in a concentrated effort to calm himself. The outcome was only a mild drugging; when the job was over the palpitation came back at precisely the same pitch. He walked over to his father's quarters and knocked on the door, but Jagnath was still bathing. He went down to the ground floor and found that only Tara and Munu were around, the former in workaday clothes and driven to virtual distraction by the tasks at hand.

'We should never have taken on so many extra servants,' she complained 'They only moon about or fall over each other And where is that impure caterer? . . he was supposed to have been here at seven o'clock. . . .' She looked out of the window towards the road, but the man was not to be seen.

'Where are the aunties?'

'Asleep . . . where would they be? They were in the kitchen until midnight last night.'

She rustled off into the garden where the workmen were putting the finishing touches to the wedding tent and pandal, and he followed her slowly, feeling unwanted and rather abashed. One might have had the impression that a ruling sovereign was marrying off his heir, so harassed were the servants hustling past him, balancing tray after tray of food, so little attention any of them could spare for the half-dressed figure of the bridegroom. The hurly-burly was a fitting climax to the nightmare of the past few days.

Three uncles and their wives had come down for the wedding, two Ajit Singhs from Indore, Vijay's maternal uncles, and one Ramsingh from Central India, Jagnath's only surviving brother; they had been crammed into the vacant rooms and their wives had been recruited to the kitchen. The dozen-odd hands hired as help to the Rajurams had to be broken in, trained and watched over. The construction of the pandal had been given to an outside firm, yet even so Tara and Kunti Ajit had to superintend it from hour to hour. 'Just you try and leave them alone,' Tara said to her father when the work had been in progress for a day, 'and the tent is bound to crash down in the middle of the ceremony.' Tara was respectful to her little-known aunts, but she knew the peculiar conditions of Bombay and could therefore impose her will and tastes on them without once appearing haughty; their enthusiasm may have been boundless, but were they not after all too provincially simple for so exacting a task? She swayed between a master-of-ceremony zeal and the dumps during her waking hours, and had terrifying nightmares during the rest of the time, yet somehow the fever increased her womanly stature in a way that could not be gainsaid; she seemed to regard this busy eruption as a dress rehearsal to some greater and final event. Her prodigious fuss seemed to lend colour, at any rate in Vijay's eyes, to the adage that no woman is whole until she has buried and married someone.

Other ladies fluttered to and fro with scarcely a smile of recognition. On the rear porch Rajuram the Younger bent his mechanical talents to the polishing of brass bowls and platters, to be used in the fire sacrifice. In the pantry, Manu helped an aunt with the selection of leaves and flowers for the ritual: a basket of balsam for an offering to Goddess Gauri, kusha grass for a mat in the worship of the Ramsingh manes, betel-nut leaves for the gods generally, tuberose and jasmine for Lord Krishna, the very special family deity of the Ramsinghs, and bel leaves for a homage to Siva, the Rajput god extraordinary. Dressed only in a shirt and pyjamas, Jagnath stalked about munching a cereal sweet snatched from the brimming shelves.

'Not ready, Vijay?' he said astonished. 'I sent Rajuram to help you an hour ago. Has everyone lost his mind this morning . . .?'

A short while ago he had peeped into the pantry to see if everyone was at his post and Tara had dispatched him summarily; now he vented his accumulated concern on his son. Was everything by way of dress prepared? Did he still remember the priestly directions for the kanyadan and satpheri, those vital parts of the ritual? How would he hold his sword when he took the bride's hand to lead her around the fire? 'Never you forget,' he said in answer to his son's nod, 'that it is by these small but all-important points that a Rajput's breed can be recognized.

'And talking of swords,' he continued, signalling Vijay to follow him, 'yours is ready to be fastened on. Let me give it to you,'

In the daftar he took the gleaming weapon out of a teak chest and drew the blade out of the sheath; passing his finger over it, he brandished it once or twice absentmindedly. Vijay had to grin, however deferentially; from Jagnath the official to Jagnath the warrior was a far cry.

'Of course, it was a long time ago . . . I have never had it in my hand since,' his father harrumphed, plunging it back into the scabbard. 'But your great forefather Jaswant knew how to use it, and did use it quite often. It is written in the annals of Indore that his father got it from the Rana of Jaipur, for his fighting against Aurangzeb. That is something, my son. Let no one tell you that we have not earned the title of Rajput.' He wiped the finger stains off carefully, then added: 'Here you are, Vijay. Go now and finish your dressing.'

Vijay took it, but stopped at the door. 'This luncheon at Uncle Premchand's . . . will there be any guests?'

'Only the family and relations. We are going there to bring our presents for Chanda. It is a custom. Then we shall return here for the pucka ceremony.'

'Father, are we getting into debt?'

Jagnath flipped him into the hall with a blustery pretence of firmness. 'Arre, what shall you ask next? These things are a father's province. To-day you are a bridegroom, you should think only of that. The family izzat is my worry.'

Then Tara crashed the conversation and dragged her father into the garden, where one of the attendant priests desired to inspect the pandal preparations.

'What might be passing through the head of the bridegroom?' coyly inquired Kunti Ajit as she crossed the hall at that moment; she gave him a wicked look and vanished out of doors, not waiting for an answer.

'What indeed! Who would not like to know that!' said her moustachioed husband, toddling down the stairs just then. 'Is the girl beautiful enough for you? Has she hair on her back and warts on her body? All this will be learned soon enough.'

He did what was expected of him: grinned modestly. This banter was one of the smaller discordances which tradition decreed a bridegroom should bear with good grace. In the backwoods of Indore State where the

Ajits lived at a still leisurely medieval pace, such bucolic touches were another way of wishing well to someone. He drifted away self-effacingly and the uncle's laughter died down gradually.

Then the phone rang and he heard his father answer it. He went up to his quarters and resumed dressing, and presently a hot and breathless Tara came up.

'They are beginning to ask about you,' she said, blinking at the swanky form that confronted her. 'My God, Vijay, you look like a raja! I would never have known you in this puggree and achkan!'

'How do I look?'

'I am telling you, like a prince! All you need is an elephant and a howdah. The sight of you is enough to blind any poor girl.' She ruffled up the loose end of the turban and pulled the back of the tunic straight, also bending to touch up the wrinkles of his pyjamas; the harassed edge of her manner first blunted, then softened. 'You look fine, bhai,' she said. 'Chanda's heart would have burst with pride even if she didn't love you so. I hope you both live to be a hundred and never stop loving each other.'

'Thank you, Tara. I wish the same for you and Lakshman. When are you going to marry him?'

She fingered the silk bow on the sword and brushed the hair from her forehead as though suddenly very conscious of her appearance. 'He has asked me and I have told him yes,' she said quietly. 'Had he wanted it, I would have married him long ago. But he does not want it because he is not well.' She waved at a fly circling her face and her look filmed over. 'If he goes to the mountains, I shall go too,' she said. 'He cannot be left alone. He needs someone to look after him.'

'Would you like me to speak to father about it?'

'No, no, that would not do! It is not so easy . . . and our pitaji has too much to think about just now. When we are ready, we will let you know, bhai.'

'All right. Only remember, Tara, if you need help . . .'

'I will, bhai, thank you very much. My goodness, look at me standing here and keeping you from your wedding! I will tell them you are coming down immediately.'

He stroked her cheeks affectionately. 'If you love each other, Tara,' he said, 'you must marry him and leave Bombay together. It is time you think of yourself, too.'

'Yes, bhai. Hurry up now.'

Watching her go down swiftly, her shapely bangled hand on the banister, her head high and resolute, he wondered yet again if the diehards weren't right when they said that home life gave a girl full scope to realize herself completely.

On Cumballa Hill the traditional meal was in full swing when Chanda came out of her bath and started the bridal toilette. Alone in the room, she stood before the looking-glass in a moment of indecision, her freshly oiled hair about her neck and shoulders, her skin aglow with the scrubbing. She shed the bath towel with a quick and daring flourish; the result was like peeping in on a stranger whose eyes she dare not meet for fear of being spotted.

The mirror recorded a tall sinuous body of an eggshell hue, a pair of calves so well shaped as to seem almost un-Indian, round column-like thighs and lofty hips and a partly shaded ripple of curves welling from the pit of the groin and ending in a round double bulge which she could not resist cupping and pressing apart to achieve a semblance of bigness, even though Kanji, her ayah, or her mother might open the door at any moment and surprise her. She remembered a remark of Vijay's at Elephanta and wished that he had never made it. 'Don't you know that we Indians exaggerate all we like?' he had said before a buxom stone carving of Parvati, Lord Siva's wife. The statue did indeed prove him right. Not only that, but most Indian visual art seemed to bulge enormously behind that explanation: Fertility was huge breasts and bridgelike hips in a woman, vigour, broad shoulders and a massive frame in a man, while power and knowledge were extra arms, eyes and heads. She had thought about it every day since, and now this was the only critical comment which the mirror seemed to volunteer. But the whole image was pleasingly sensuous, even with one's eyes half shut, and she hoped fervently that it would remain so for a long time to come. The words of Sita—of the Ramayana epic—came to her suddenly and seemed to make up for the improbable idealism of Indian art:

My hair is fine and smooth, and black; my brows do not run together; my legs are rounded and not hairy; my teeth are close-set; my temples, eyes, hands, feet, ankles and thighs are well proportioned and have a fitting fullness. My fingers have rounded nails, they are well shaped and glossy. My breasts show no gap between them, they swell up plumply and have the nipples well centered; my navel is well sunk and raised up at the edges; my flesh is hard, my skin taut. My colour is like the precious stone and the hairs on my body are soft. I stand erect on my ten toes. So I am called a woman with blest bodily forms. . . .

But now there was a tapping of sandals in the next room and she drew the towel around her and sank on the dressing stool. In came Kanji with a heap of silk over one arm and a silver casket under the other. This was panch-pala, the five-partite box of traditional bridal toiletries, which the Premchand womenfolk had prepared on their own initiative.

'Arre, dear child, the lunch is almost over and you are not even covered!' Kanji dumped her load on the bed and stripped her arms and head for action.

'Where is mother?'

'Now she asks . . .! Where would she be? With the guests, naturally!'

She began to braid Chanda's hair with hard deft fingers which forty years of incessant fussing had gnarled into something like ginger roots. When the plaits begun to take shape she wove into them white flowers of jasmine and pink petals of rose with the same touch of the master craftsman, so that Chanda, regarding her in the looking-glass, had to admire her despite her own excitement. Then she stripped her of the towel and busied herself with the henna dye; this had to be painted on the soles and palms so lightly that it adorned the skin rather than covered it.

'Three kinds of people are well received everywhere,' she said grudgingly. 'A gallant warrior, a learned man and a pretty woman. I am to see that you are not only pretty, but also clean and sweet-smelling. And if you are not thankful, your husband will surely be.'

'He loves me as I am. I don't need a perfume to charm him.'

'Never be too sure, child . . . until he either goes blind or dies. And stop fidgeting, baba!'

The painting over, she ordered her to stand up and submit to a detailed scrutiny of her complexion, for she had known both the Prashad girls from babyhood and would not be put off by any squeamishness. 'You are clean, anyhow,' she muttered with a tentative nod, 'but no bride should smell only of soap.' She substantiated that statement by rubbing her down first with one scent and then with another, wheezing asthmatically in the act, until not only the girl's skin but all the air of the room tingled sharply. 'Do this every night and take care not to grow fat,' she summed up, 'and you will not have to worry about his mistresses.'

'He has had them before I knew him,' Chanda said. 'Now I am the only woman in his life.'

'May the gods grant it, child. It is easier to find flowers on a banyan or footprints of fishes or white crows than to know about the love of man.' She reached for the new petticoat and kachli on the bed, puckering her nose wryly. 'Enough of this prattle, child. Put on your clothes and become a lady.'

The bodice was of a heavy yellow satin, embroidered around the neckline and armlets. The ayah buttoned it tight at the back; the tailor had obviously known his craft, for now the breasts filled out in a mould of frank provocation. Pleased by the result, Chanda stepped into the first petticoat skirt and pulled three others over her head, and Kanji frilled up the copious folds so that the outer skirt—a stiff gold-woven ghagra which Rana Prashad had saved from her own wedding—might fall in an eye-catching flare and show to the best advantage. They were still tacking the fabric and squinting at the successive effects in the mirror when Mrs. Prashad burst into the room with a fresh armful of boxes.

'Oh, Chanda my precious, let me look at you . . .! I would have come ten minutes ago if only some people were less talkative. But now they are leaving, thank goodness! Turn around . . . darling, you look sweet. Is this my little Chanda who left school only yesterday?'

'The same stubborn one,' Kanji said, tying the last knot at the waist.

Chanda swished around and the mirror captured it all as a streak of flash and billowing loveliness. Rana Prashad dropped her stack on a chair and threw her arms around her.

'You are a beauty,' she said, her eyes filling up without warning. 'No Padmini of old could have been as beautiful.'

'No, truly, ama . . .?'

'Truly, my darling. Would I say so if it were not? And this is only the dress . . . wait till I show you what is coming on top of it!'

She opened some of the boxes and spread them on the bed. Rings, bracelets, necklaces, pendants and brooches spilled over the silk, jingling richly, and each new piece drew a more amazed gasp from Chanda and Kanji. 'Your heirlooms, my precious,' she said. 'Five generations of our women have worn them at their weddings, and you are going to be the sixth. If you will only stand still, I will put them on at once,' she added, clasping a necklace on her. 'And this . . . this . . . and this . . . all to make my darling the most ravishing bride of all time!' She fixed a pearl string on her head, hanging the studded pendant full over the middle of the forehead like a glistening third eye of Siva, then loaded her wrists with bracelets of gold and uncut gems, and put two rings on her fingers, one with a big hexagonal ruby and the other with a Ceylon sapphire. 'And this is not all, imagine!' she said. 'Close your eyes and don't open them until I tell you.' With the ayah's help, she inserted Ranjit's ear-rings in the lobes of her ears, then smacked her bottom lovingly. 'Look what Ranjit thought would be a fi.ting gift for you!'

Chanda peered into the looking-glass and caught her breath. 'Oh mother, are you sure? You mean a gift for to-day only, or a gift for good?'

'What do you mean a gift for to-day only . . .! A loan would not be a gift, would it? Of course I am sure. What is more, he never breathed a word until this moment . . . he is absolutely mad, the dear fellow. It is supposed to be after an old Oudh pattern . . . I have forgotten which . . . I was too thrilled to remember. Look closely, darling! There is more money on you right now than any honest minister could hope to make in a lifetime!'

'As if such a man could be found,' Kanji said.

'Oh, ama, you are wonderful! Ranjit too . . . I shall never forget this day.'

'Now let us get on,' Kanji said more softly. 'You heard, the guests are leaving.'

'She is right, my precious. We shall all be leaving in half an hour. Where is your dopatta . . . your sandals, your handkerchief . . .? Kanji, you had better go and tell Radabai to expect us downstairs in a little while.'

Through the crack of the door, which the ayah failed to close, came a high-spirited hustle and the unmistakable sound of guests on the move. The house began to sound as though it were populated exclusively by hysterical women, rattled dishwashers and roaring men, and the noise brought home to Rana Prashad the sharp imminence of their separation. They embraced again in silence. Chanda strained hard not to weep; Kanji would raise a hue and cry if the kohl around her eyes were to require any more retouching. Then a new stage fright came to haunt her other worries, big and small.

' 'Ma, you saw him downstairs. How did he look?'

'Like a prince. Even Europe could not spoil the Rajput in him.'

'What did he say?'

'Nothing. A bridegroom is supposed to sit quietly and mind his own business.'

'Will he like me, ama . . .?'

'Should he not, child, I shall be very cross indeed. You are more lovely than any man deserves.'

'And his relations? Those Ajits from Indore . . .?'

'They had better, that is all I can say.' She dug into the rustling heap on the bed for a matching veil and her voice curdled quite against her will. 'Your family is every bit as good as theirs . . . and I do not care what they are saying privately. If they should tell you that a hill Rajput is not as good as a Rajput from the plains, it will be your duty to laugh in their faces. Caste would be a very good thing for this country if people were only less snobbish.'

Later Radabai Premchand came in, trailed by some wide-eyed women relations, and Chanda had again to twirl in front of the mirror and accept their good wishes and advice.

'You are fit to turn the head of a saint,' was Radabai's goggled verdict. Forthwith she began to mop her eyes, for nothing in this life refreshed a woman's memory of her own mysteriously lost wonder like the sight of another would-be victim.

'If Tara and Lakshman do marry,' Rana Prashad said with sympathy, 'this home will see another fine wedding. Tara will make a lovely daughter-in-law.'

'May the Lord grant it,' Radabai said, drying up. 'I love Tara as my own daughter.'

Pinched, stroked, stared at and overpowered, Chanda was finally rescued by her mother. 'Now get along, ladies . . . you shall see her again this evening,' she said with chairwomanly firmness. 'We must get ready soon, or we shall never be in time for the ceremony.'

'Her sons will be real handsome Rajputs,' one young woman said.

'Arre, they might all be girls, who knows!'

'Not if she walks around the asok tree at full moon.'

'Is it true that he has never kissed you?'

'He looks strong . . . did you see his legs?'

'Arre, would you not like to be the bride for one night!'

'I did not say . . .'

'There . . . it is most kind of you . . . thank you very much. . . .' Rana Prashad piloted them into the hall and shut the door on them. Together with Radabai, she set about repairing the damage on Chanda, then veered her round to face the mirror and gazed at the image appraisingly. In the courtyard a car hooted three times.

'You are pale, darling, but you are dazzling.'

Chanda's temples began to throb all of a sudden, her limbs loosened and a dry heat pressed down on her palate. She clenched her hands. The notion that it was still not too late to call off the whole thing, that Vijay would surely understand if she explained it to him, that no one seeing the face of her mother at this instant would have the heart to proceed with it, for this was the end of their companionship, their unquestioning confidence and love, their identity of hope and feeling, behind which it had been possible to taunt the harsh winds of orthodox disapproval, the notion that this exposure to priestly interference, critical stares and whispered remarks was too high a price for the exchange of one love for another, blazed through her mind with the suddenness of a crushing light and made her quail. She took a step towards her mother and shook her head dazedly.

'Take hold of yourself, daughter,' Rana Prashad said. 'There is nothing to cry for.'

'I feel ill. . . .'

'So you should, like a good bride,' Radabai said and opened the door. 'Fresh air will cure that.'

'It is time, child,' Rana said. 'They are waiting for us. . . .'

With an oddly rigid bow of the body, she kissed her on both cheeks and pressed her hand. 'Show them how a Prashad carries herself,' she said 'You are more beautiful than you have ever been'—and she gathered the veil in a full and showy fold on her shoulders. 'When you walk into that pandal, they must all know their good fortune. They must cringe from envy . . . all India must hear of this wedding. And they will sit up and take notice, never you doubt, precious. They will not only say, There goes Chanda, They will think, Look, it is the proud daughter of the widow whom we all but shaved and cast off! They will wish that they could have had you for their own weak-minded boors of sons. . . .'

She led her to the steps, where Radabai looked up at them in round-eyed wonder.

2

How remote everything seemed to be even though they squatted in the midst of it . . .! Vijay passed his scarf along his face and took a sidelong peek at her, but she refused to acknowledge it.

The senior priest read from the book of mantras and stirred the sacrificial fire, homa. He was a barrel-chested, smooth-looking Brahman of about Jagnath's age, the serenity of his profession written into his leisurely deportment and the pudgy curve of his belly. Little slivers of fire wagged on his eyeglasses and, when he bent to feed more rice and ghee to the flames, on his clean-shaven pate. His chanting seemed to be confined to labials only . . . mummmm . . . vummmlummm, but he managed to make the most even of this limitation; after a time his lips fleshed up somehow into a thrumming instrument which Vijay found hard to watch without falling under its spell. At either side an assistant sat in charge of the homa paraphernalia, but they had the peaked countenance of young priests as yet susceptible to great and flashy gatherings. Topping the edifice of banana and fig branches directly above them hung a toran, the mystical triangle emblem of the Rajputs, tied with sacred silken cords.

'. . . Mumjmmm . . . vallaballa . . . vumummmm . . .'

It was the pitri-puja—worship of the ancestors—without which no ritual of this magnitude could begin. Now the Brahman motioned to Jagnath, who passed him a dish of coloured rice and coconut; Ranjit did the same on behalf of the bride. The priest tossed the pile into the cauldron and intoned afresh.

'Oh ye dwellers of ancestral paradise, deign, one and all, to come to this pandal, be ye present at this marriage feast and grant it a happy ending.'

More rice, more rolls of betel nut, a fresh crop of tongues along the walls of the grimy vessel. Then, a throaty echo from both sides of Vijay, and also behind him, in which separate strands belonged to his father, uncle, Ranjit and Rana Prashad.

He didn't see any of them. He gazed either at the Brahman or at the fire or, unseeingly, straight ahead over the dense rows of the guests' heads stretching all the way to the entrance at the far end. The small group of family and relations behind him he sensed only by their fidgeting and coughs and a sweet-smelling rustle; he shut his eyes for a moment and moved his inner knee closer to Chanda's—for they squatted side by side—and although the touch was the merest kiss of two kinds of fabric it sent an intimate signal to the ends of his body. Was she awe-smitten like himself? What did she think, sitting so still in that warp of gauze and sheen?

328

This is it, my love . . . just as you imagined.

If the touch spoke to her at all, she was careful not to show it. Her bejewelled hands lay clasped in the labyrinth of her skirt pleats, the long half-moons of her nails white and shining. The sight of them loosened his own tension. His insides came slowly out of a long cramp, his chest lightened, his stomach steadied. Now that the first hair-raising exposure had been weathered, the rest might be almost bearable.

With the mysterious ease which a Brahman casts over any rite, the worship of the ancestors flowed into the next worship, to the gods and family protectors generally. No time at all elapsed between the two; there were no awkward lacunæ in the chant; round and round spun the ladle under a shower of bel leaves and rice, thawing yet another clump of butter in the hallowed gruel.

'O God of gods! with our wives and kinsmen, our hearts overflowing with the nectar of your dance, may we live and rejoice a hundred autumns.

'. . . redotums . . .'

'. . . dotums . . .'

Ranjit chose the moment to clear his throat; he had been smoking like a chimney all morning.

Then came the Krishna devotional and every member of the family passed a token flower to the priest, who in turn heaped them on a dish of curds—this to the smiling god of the milkmaids and to the lover of Radha in the fond memory of his sylvan dalliances. Presently a quiver of expectancy shook the assembly and Vijay's stomach twisted again nervously; gods and spirits had been honoured, the path lay clear for Kanyadan, the wedding proper. Now the Indo-Christian orchestra which Jagnath had engaged over the heads of Rana Prashad and Ranjit, who would have preferred an Indian company, glided into a waltz of unmistakable alien flavour, and Vijay saw the bald domes of the European guests come together discreetly; many of them were officials from his father's office, but a few ladies were Rana Prashad's feminist friends. The comment, he knew, would be on whether such music was suitable or not. But music there had to be at a wedding and a Western band was better than none at all.

'Son, pay attention,' his father admonished gently.

The brocaded apparition of Chanda stirred at last and he caught a glimpse of her pallid face and her look which, even behind the flimsy ripple, seemed reluctant to linger. Warmth returned to his head and the gnawing in his gizzard became more distinct.

'Who giveth the virgin?' said the Brahman.

'I do, in the place of the father,' Ranjit answered.

'What is her name?'

'Chandraleika Prashad Singh.'

'Throw in the rice,' the priest ordered.

They did, scooping it from a bowl.

The assistants began to arrange other trays and containers. Vullumm . . . mullum . . . pullum . . . but now the prayer was a lengthy one, in Sanskrit, which no one understood, but whose meaning set everyone on edge all the same. Vijay's own heat seemed to spread towards the ceiling, his eyes filmed over from the sheer strain of holding still, and all the time the Brahman's look rested on him mildly, as though wondering about the wisdom of all this fuss.

At the fore end of the pandal the band leader watched him closely and next to him, filling the broad entrance entirely, stood both the Rajurams and all the other servants.

'The gift of the virgin,' Mr. Varma explained to his European neighbour in the first row. 'The bride's father—in this case a friend—gives away. The boy's father accepts.'

'And the boy?'

'He considers himself greatly favoured by the arrangement.'

The guest nodded. 'I thought they were to walk round the fire?'

'They will, presently. That is another part of the ceremony. Formerly the bride's father used to wash the feet of his future son-in-law, but this custom is now observed only by the lower castes.'

'Interesting, very interesting,' the guest murmured.

Out in front Rana Prashad bit her lips, whispered, 'Good luck, my darling,' and sighed deeply. She moved as if to assist in the rite of uniting the couple's garments, which Vijay was completing at that moment with a haste typical of agonized bridegrooms, but recalled herself in time. Hindu mothers were supposed to behave heroically; well might she rail against the unfair traditions in her spare time, but it was a fact, at this time only too painfully plain, that all the highlights of a Hindu life were the exclusive preserve of the male, be he aborigine or ascetic.

'Now the hands,' the Brahman motioned to Ranjit. The music swelled suddenly and a gust of wind stormed the tent from outside and some of the loose sheets of canvas flapped violently.

'Hath-leva . . . the joining of hands,' Mr. Varma explained to his neighbour. 'The same as your ring giving, only our brides get their rings afterwards.'

'And now they will walk around the fire three times?'

'Seven times. It used to be three in the old days, but we . . . like every-body else . . . have become more complicated since then.' He gave him a swift look, to see if his humour was appreciated, but the guest still nodded as though witnessing a natural history revelation.

Ranjit wound a gold and silk cord around the couple's clasp, to a loud chant of the priest—the highspot of the Kanyadan—and the band underscored it with a gay flight of its string section, which drove it home even to the most ignorant of the guests; it was the moment for which Ranjit had patiently coached the musicians for many hours. The knot made, he bobbed the flower attached to it on a last-minute artistic impulse, then, still bowed from the waist, retreated and sat down on his cushioned dais. Then, as the strings soared lower and Jagnath flashed a comforting smile to Rana Prashad, who was beginning to jab her eyes once more, as Lakshman turned a mute but tender visage upon Tara, squatting at the other end of the pandal, the priest took over again in a voice first helpless against the music but later more ringing and authoritative. He also poured holy water over the couple's hands.

'Let this union flower forth, made this day in the presence of gods and ancestors, in full accord with the sacred texts and with the consent of those here assembled. . . .'

One after another, they all sprinkled saffron and flowers over the couple's hands, mumbling after the Brahman.

'Be ye not parted . . . dwell ye here and reach the full time of human life. . . . With sons and grandsons sport ye and play, rejoicing in your abode.

'Signs of good fortune mark the bride. Come all of you, look at her and wish her prosperity. . . .' He looked at Vijay and added in a whisper: 'Repeat after me, please.'

'I take thy hand in mine for happy fortune,' Vijay said after him shakily, 'that thou mayest reach old age with me, thy husband. Gods have given thee to be the mistress of my household. Thou wilt share of my pleasure and twine thine loving arms about me, and welcome all my love and mine embraces.'

He went on saying this sort of thing after the Brahman, less shaky after each new line but aware of the huge stares across the gulf, and his hand tightened unbearably around the small and hot one to which he was tied. How false he sounded, what would she think of him! Did she, too, squirm at these appalling declarations? Where were Juhu and Elephanta now, those high marks of reckless spontaneity which had been laws unto themselves? One thing was quite clear to him even though his head spun like a prayer wheel: The breathlike touch in the hollow of his palm was worth a carload of prayers. It was a relief to hear the priest say, 'Get up and walk around seven times!' and he obeyed him hastily, maybe even a little too hastily, for he was still tied to her and she, in her voluminous robes, had not as great a freedom of movement as he.

'Ah, here we go!' said Mr. Varma's neighbour.

'Yes, indeed. Sat-pheri . . . seven circumambulations.'

'What a lovely match,' Ranjit said to Chanda's mother.

'Aren't they!'

Once, twice, three times, Vijay led her around the priestly group, around the toran and the fire, looking neither up nor down but straight ahead, and the stares became a whorl of shiny blades converging on them from all parts of the tent and all his efforts to count were absorbed in the all-important endeavour to moderate his pace and hold himself with dignity. The looks of his family said different things at each new turn. The music mounted once more—when did it start? Ranjit was leaning towards his father and saying something; Premchand and Radabai bent to Mrs. Prashad, while the Ajit ladies snuggled together; Tara whispered to Munu, the young priests clinked among the bowls. It should have been a great moment. It probably was. In years to come he would never quite recapture it, because it would flutter inside a whirligig of flash and glitter; of his own feeling he would only remember the awful tension and the parched throat.

'Enough!' said the Brahman, ever so gently. 'Put the tali around her neck and the sendur on her hair.'

When they were reseated, Ranjit loosened the cord on their hands and Jagnath proffered the necklace called tali, an affair of gold thread, semi-precious stones and flowers; Vijay eased it over her head until it sat securely on her shoulders, then took the tray of red oxide of lead and, with everyone looking on raptly, lifted Chanda's veil and rubbed a fingertipful into the parting of her hair. This was Sendurdan, the formal taking possession of the bride. With it the rite of wedding was completed, though not before the priestly adjurations had been listened to in complete silence.

'Win thou his heart and let him win they fancy, and he shall form with thee a blest alliance.

'Over they husband's father and his kin bear full sway; over the sisters of thy lord and over his sons and daughters rule supreme.'

This to Chanda—as full and vigorous authority in her future home.

'Speak as lady to thy gathered people. Happy be thou and prosper with the children in your lord's house. Closely unite thy body with this man thy husband. So shall ye both, full of years, address your company.'

And, together with Vijay:

'Come now, thou from the gods obtained, thou beautiful one with tender heart, thou of the charming look, thou good to your husband, kind towards other men and animals, thou destined to bring forth brave sons come!

'Be ye not parted, dwell ye here for a hundred autumns . . .!'

Then Chanda drew the dopatta back over her face and the ordeal was over.

Nodding humanly for the first time, the Brahman flipped a fistful of saffron rice at the couple. The orchestra resumed in a livelier tempo; the parents and relations added their own showers of rice, crowding around them, congratulating, laughing and murmuring. Rana Prashad patted her daughter's cheeks, Jagnath the back of his son. A buzz filled the tent and chairs began to squeak.

'Blessings on you, son and daughter,' Jagnath said shakily. 'Be happy with each other.'

'Vijay, Chanda . . . let me wish you from the depth of my heart . . . After this, Rana Prashad could only squeeze their hands and try vainly to smile.

'Oh, bhai, you are such a lovely pair,' Tara said.

After them Premchand, his wife, stepson and all the others.

'May you have all you desire. . . .'

'Accept our best wishes. . . .'

'Blessings . . . to the end of your days . . . sons and daughters. . . .'

'Stand up, son . . . Chanda . . . and receive your other guests,' Jagnath said after a while. 'They are all coming.'

They were indeed—and the lesser kin stepped back self-effacingly to make room for them. Rana Prashad uncovered her daughter's face and padded the veil into a silky plinth around her neck, so that Vijay broke off his reception and stared at her in astonishment. Was this shining vision the person he had coached to swim and made love to under the old tower?

'Let them go home and talk about you for the rest of their natural lives,' Rana Prashad said.

Presently the swarm boiled up to a pitch. Brahmans, Rajputs, Jains, Parsis, Europeans, all passed by muttering variations of the same formula Throwing off the last restraint, the orchestra bounced off into a merry march. Servants began to disperse to their points of duty under the eagle eye of Rajuram the Elder and lights came on to brighten the opalescent twilight of the pandal, to cast a tinselly glare over the decorations and the tumult. The houseladies withdrew to the kitchen. The young priests began to muster their equipment, prior to receiving the customary gifts of cloth and money. The untapped pockets of perfume broke up, wafting hither and thither, making the heat more noticeable and also more intimate.

'Come, children!' Jagnath said at last, leading them to a trapdoor in the side of the tent. 'You shall now refresh yourselves and then come back.'

In the house, Vijay put away his sword and Chanda her tali.

'We had better remove some of this heavy jewellery, too,' Rana Prashad said, divesting her of the headgear and the more cumbersome necklaces.

Then the servants filed in to pay their homage and Rajuram the Elder touched their feet in token avowal, followed by his son and all the others; the Brahman's instructions to Chanda thus became an established fact and one to be reckoned with. Afterwards they were led to the new quarters upstairs and there Jagnath bade his son break the silk knot on the door. This accomplished, the parents withdrew and they were alone on the floor.

'Until I build a home of my own, this is where we are going to live,' he said awkwardly, taking her hand. 'Before we go in, I want to tell you I couldn't look at you down there . . . you were so beautiful.'

'And you so strange. . . .'

'All those people. . . .'

'Yes, I know.'

He took the doorknob and twirled it uncertainly. 'They have had it locked for ten days,' he said. 'I don't know what is on the other side. Shall we go in?'

'Let us.'

'Look,' he said, and pushed the door open, 'you are so beautiful I have forgotten how to talk to you.'

But now she said, 'O—oh—oh!' and stepped into the room behind him, and all their embarrassment seemed at an end.

It was a bedroom, newly and lavishly furnished. Rich new curtains screened the windows, a crimson-bordered rug lay on the floor. All free space was taken up with flowers and presents—silver fruit bowls, gold-capped flagons of toilet water and scent, jars of unguents, rolls of Amritsar carpets, painted Kashmiri lampshades and, piled in separate heaps on the beds, fold upon fold of silk and brocade. They waded into it and read the inscriptions half in awe, half in delight. The tissue-paper exhibits on the dresser yielded two sets of gold and ivory bangles and one engraved gold cigarette case. They touched every package and bundle, but couldn't open them all; this would need more method and leisure. They sat on a bed and held hands, gloating and snickering rather foolishly. It seemed to them, dizzily enough, that all this magnificence was a just reward for the hours of tension downstairs.

'Go on, take your pick,' he said. 'I don't mind what you take.'

'Vijay, I feel suddenly faint.'

'Oh no, my darling, not now, please,' he said. 'You are supposed to enjoy this.'

'I mean really faint, Vijay. I have felt like this every day for a fortnight. I worried about it during the ceremony, but it didn't come, thank God.'

'Look at me, Chanda!'

He raised her chin and peered into her face. The pallor seemed to make her eyes grow larger and blacker even as he looked at them; her neck, stemming from the sheath of veil like a sleek flower unfurled for the first time, was colourless, too, and unsteady. Then she shut her eyes and pressed her face into his achkan, muffling a little groan.

'Darling, listen to me . . . could it be . . .?'

'Maybe. . . . It has happened every day . . . sometimes twice a day.'

'Oh Chanda, darling, why didn't you tell me . . .?' He stroked her head and went on muttering endearments, as if that were all he could think of. 'My beautiful darling Chanda. . . .'

334

Now a fresh strain of music poured in through the window, bringing laughter and voices, and he remembered the pandal in the garden and the guests in it, but none of it could make him move and get up. Inside his head all was a fuzzy whirl, as of a hidden source of emotion suddenly uncovered and sent radiating. So this was it—the old pious orders fulfilled on the very day they were uttered! He wanted to think and ponder and grasp the whole lofty meaning of it, but he caressed her instead and held her desperately and his nostrils seemed to widen in the sweet unforgettable tide of her fragrance. My sweet, my own beautiful Chanda! My one and only, how can I even begin to tell you! He kissed her eyes, forehead and the red stain in the parting of her hair, and then both her cheeks and mouth, not daring to break his hold.

Hear ye, Kishore-, Ram-, Ranjit-, Ajit-, and Pratap-Singhs, whose sraddha we have remembered in all these years! Hear the good news!

Whether they did or not made finally little difference. His embrace seemed so complete that it left no room for ghosts, however well disposed. He was to be a father, that massive being of unrivalled excellence on whose broad shoulders the kingdom and salvation of Hinduism rested for now and for ever after. It was a new feeling, inseparably bound up with power and a sense of endless potential, one that blotted out his old sophistication without trace; it gave no warning as it rose and swept him, save that all hardship seemed to fly before it like so much dust. When it finally lapped to the crest of him, he could no longer recognize himself. He was all things at once, and none in particular. High, high above it he was immensely tender and experienced, and also inaccessible. Darling, darling . . . wait till we can tell the others! At length he got up and saw that her paleness was redeemed by a shy happy smile.

'Darling, shouldn't you lie down and rest?'

'No. Open the fan and let me cool a little. I will be all right then.'

He did. They stopped in the middle of the glittering room, heads thrown back in happy self-sufficiency, and let the wind bathe their faces with a steady swish.

'Ah, the proud bridegroom . . .!'

'Where is the ravishing bride?'

'With the ladies,' he said, laughing graciously at the badinage; then he drifted over to Ranjit and Mr. Varma, where the merriment was quieter and less exacting.

'Your father is not to be recognized,' Ranjit said. 'One would think it was he who got married.'

'A royal reception,' Mr. Varma added, sipping a purple beverage through a straw. 'I hope that our English guests are duly impressed.'

Vijay sat down to rest his feet for the next round.

No one had noticed the sun going down or the evening thawing away into the ocean beyond the garden's hedges. Now the meticulous labours of the pandal builders began to reward in fanciful strings of bulbs, so that the jolly blaze could be watched from such distant vantage points as Malabar Hill and Bandra, several miles to the north and south. Handsomely rewarded, the priests had departed long ago, delivering the company to a more reckless spirit. Pictures had been taken, toasts given and received, and the guests had broken up into groups, some feasting in the tent, others inspecting the presents in the house. As was proper, to them Vijay and Chanda had given much formal attention, he confining himself to the men, she as much as possible to the ladies. Now the strain was beginning to tell on both.

'To-day the Ramsingh izzat stands very high indeed,' Ranjit said. 'A Rajput has done his duty in fine style. . . .'

They laughed continently. Izzat meant the prestige of the family, a notion which the Rajputs prized as highly as personal honour and fighting prowess; it was even said that the less a Rajput possessed the more avidly he looked to his izzat. Certainly his father was ruining himself to uphold it in due style, and it was not improbable that he himself would be heir to some of the debts incurred on this day. Such was the power of tradition; no one could alter it in one night. He knew that even a tactful question about it would have discomfited his father no end, and he had no intention of asking it just yet.

'But is it not true,' Ranjit said, reading his mind shrewdly, 'that our birth, marriage and death are the only proofs that we have lived? All right then . . . let us don our silks and do well by our guests. To-morrow they will be gone . . . the flowers will fade, the music will stop . . . only the izzat will remain.'

'And the future . . .?' Mr. Varma inquired half-mockingly. 'Are we not to think of our poor and starving?'

'My dear friend, but naturally. Only it would be well to remember that the greatness of India does not come from the starving.'

'From the izzat, maybe?'

'Well, let me tell you . . .'

And as the fray was joined, Vijay got up feeling refreshed and made for the next cluster of guests.

Beneath the toran his father and Rana Prashad paused likewise to exchange notes and get a breather. Jagnath still wore the ceremonial tunic but she had changed into a light sari of shimmering leaf-green.

'I have been wondering what came of all our good resolutions,' she said. 'How can our youngsters grow up sensible on such gaudy examples?'

'They are all friends, yours and mine,' Jagnath said. 'Is Chanda not your first daughter . . . is Vijay not my first son?'

'And Uday has forgotten us after all. What could have befallen the boy, I wonder?'

'Arre, dear Rana, you must not worry. You know how Udayji is.'

Ranjit's last search for him by letter, wire and telephone has been in vain; all they knew was that Uday had got stuck at Ujjain and that there his tracks vanished into the thin air. 'Probably lost in some new penance,' Jagnath had thought peevishly, then promptly dismissed him from his mind. 'Sadhus are that kind of people,' he said to Rana, partly in defence of his own happy callousness. True, he would have liked Uday to be present, if for no other reason than that a family ascetic was always an asset at a family occasion, but otherwise he nurtured no lasting regret. Men turning their backs on life made unreliable counsellors, even, he was apt to confess to himself, in things that had nothing to do with life. 'Miserable abortion,' a cynic once cried, 'dost thou believe thou canst taste death thou who hast never known life?' That was how he felt, too, especially on this day when one of the goals of his parenthood had been reached in safety.

The rest of the mild sting was soon lost in his deep-felt concern for the guests.

'And how are the ladies getting on, Rana?'

'As well as always. You should have seen their eyes popping at the presents.'

'And our dear Chanda?'

'Tired, I think . . . and very pale. She must have a long rest after this.'

'A beautiful bride, we are all so proud of her. Excuse me . .'

And off he went again, mopping his brow, towards the nearest table, where someone had waved at him—a genial figure of a tireless host, upon whose forehead the years no longer hunched but seemed to slide as though losing their foothold.

In the garage at the end of the garden Tara was showing Lakshman the new car gift of Ranjit's. She had at last escaped the kitchen, the servants and all the gossip and racket which the senior family ladies in the throes of a marriage feast were prey to, in order to be alone with him even if for a moment only. Night, descending with the surprise of a curtain, and leave-takings of the English official guests had made it easier than she had dared to hope.

'Is not Ranjit the most generous of men?' she asked him.

'He is, but your brother is the most fortunate.'

They touched the cold steel of the car, tested the door handles and put on some of the switches on the instrument panel. Lakshman was in a silver-grey tunic padded at the shoulders and cut in tight at the waist, which made him seem even more slender; his abundant mane for once neatly brushed, his neck encased in a high collar lined with white silk, he looked older to her and somehow more masterly—both pleasing observations. She had compared him with her brother during the ceremony. While not possessing Vijay's good looks and assertive manliness, he was yet attractively lithe and could actually turn his shyness of strangers to good account, almost to dignity. Taking this appraisal to a logical feminine conclusion, she had thought that she had made a good choice on the whole. He was going to be a poet of renown, perhaps even national fame; the reviewers of his recent collection of Gujarati poems had prophesied that much with a rare singleness of judgment. And he had big plans for the future.

Now he was going to get well, going away to Panchgani, where the pure mountain air was said to cure even the most obstinate 'chests.' If only his notions of propriety and filial duties were a little more sensible . . .! If only he would let her come along!

'My darling, I have worried over it so much I don't care any more what anyone says,' she began. 'Let us get married quickly, without fuss . . . then go away together.'

'No, Tara,' he said dreamily. 'At our wedding, too, there shall be guests and music . . . and gifts. We shall not sneak away like thieves in the night.'

'But if we are together?'

'No, no, no!' He braced himself with a deep, slow breath. 'They shall not say of you, Look, she has gone and got herself a coughing husband.'

'Oh, dear Lakshman, don't!'

'It is the truth, is it not?'

'No, not like that . . . why do you say it? Why do you break yourself all the time? It is not your fault . . .' Realizing that this would get her nowhere, for every tiny aspect of this obsession had already been thrashed out a thousand times, she snuggled up to him and went on more fervently. 'Think of us in a little house, all by ourselves . . . you writing, I cooking. How lovely that would be, darling! All alone for a whole year. . . .'

'No, Tara, enough of that!' He disengaged himself brusquely and switched off the headlamps, plunging the garage in blackness. 'Come, let us get out.'

She should have been angry, at least hurt, over the snub; but a great wave of pity swept over her, clouding all her sensible intentions. What bundles of unreason and false pride men really were! Here she was quite set on flouting every shred of family orthodoxy with the simple aim of serving only him, and he insisted on being her conscience! Yet he was also high-minded in all his idiotic misery, and realizing that she said, 'All right,' and groped for him in the dark. That was the worst of pity—one gave in so easily, so without a murmur, often to the most outrageous unreason, because one loved and could not harp on a wound. Blind or not, he was hers after all.

'Let us not be cross,' she said at the door. 'What is a year of waiting, if it is what you wish.'

'It is not what I wish. There is no other way,' he said.

'Then I shall wait, darling . . . one, two, three years, what does it matter how long . . . if you love me and want me to wait.'

'Will you?'

'Oh yes, yes. I promise.'

The words seemed to dye his tension a more lurid hue and he stopped, hesitant, mutely unhappy with the unfair burden he had placed upon her, then succumbed to self-pity and recoiled before the apparition sprouting in its wake. She heard him fidget and sensed another quiver of torture—what was it now? But when he put his arm around her waist and wrenched her over backwards, she was not ready for what came.

'When I go away, some other will kiss you,' he said through his teeth. 'You will let him stroke your hair and caress you, as I did.'

'No, no, my darling!'

'And he will be strong . . . he will not cough. He will tell you how lovely you are, and put his arms around you!'

'There will be no other! What are you saying!'

'How can you know there will not be? Can you divine the future . . .?'

Of course he had lost his mind, but now it was too late to tell him. Besides, his passion was contagious—it strummed all the way down her spine in an altogether gusty and surprising fashion.

'Light of my eyes, my love, my darling,' she said with a moan. 'There will never be anyone else. I am yours, if you want me.'

'You said that before. Will you swear?'

'Yes, yes. I swear a thousand times!'

'By what . . .?'

'Everything, my love, everything. . . .'

He began to kiss her, with a crushing roughness she had never expected of him. My mad darling, light of my eyes! she thought, slumping weakly, wishing that he would never stop; never before, O wonder of wonders! had her knees responded with such utter wobbliness. 'I will keep myself . . . you shall be the only one!' she said over and over again. She would have let him do as he wished then and there, had servants not approached along the drive laughing noisily.

The younger Rajuram found them sitting behind the steering-wheel of the car, absorbed in the instruments. He took the hand pump off the wall, said something about a puncture, salaamed and vanished. They waited until his footsteps died out, then left the car and came out of the garage.

'I shall be going next week,' he said, still in a stupor. 'We have ten days to think about it.'

'My mind is made up, Lakshman. I shall wait for you.'

'I have no right to . . .'

'Oh, don't!' she said. 'All the rights I have, you have too.'

They walked down the drive, then back through the main entrance and into the blazing garden. He let go of her hand and hurried away without once looking at her. She watched him pass the gate of the tent, sidling hurriedly to accommodate some passing guests, the old haunted look back on his face, and her heart gave a quick leap. How much wilder and more aggressive he seemed!

Later that evening the chattering Ajit aunties made remarks about her vacant air, but she made no attempt to deal with them as they deserved. Let them grouch! she thought. What do they know! They had never been smitten over the head, and indeed how could they have been! What did a couple of practical peasants from Indore—with all respect to her father—know about passion and wretchedness, about love and self-denial, all whipped tempestuously into a few brief seconds? Had they ever walked the rim of a precipice in the belief that they had the upper hand, then found themselves hurtling down headlong . . .? She was sure they could not have. That kind of uprooting accident came only to those willing to pay for it with all they possessed and pay for it long in advance.

By ten o'clock the band was gone. In the house, the ladies were resting and comparing notes; a gramophone let out a tuneful but elegiac ballad which set everyone relaxing in a thoroughly Indian manner. On the roof, Ranjit, Mr. Varma, Vijay and Chanda cooled themselves under a round December moon.

'He said he was new to India and would like to know us better,' Mr. Varma reminisced, telling them of his European neighbour during the wedding. 'I told him to read the Mahabharata. There is not one of us, I said to him, who would not find his spit and image in that glorious epic. Everything we do has already happened to the people of the Mahabharata.'

'Thank you, I prefer the hookah,' Ranjit said, declining the betel nut which the old man was pushing towards him.

Mr. Varma, the chubby home philosopher, yawned with that deliberate luxury which marks a happily concluded rumination. 'The English have an adage,' he went on. 'Everything comes to him who waits. I think the Mahabharata puts it even better . . . to him who lives fully.'

Ranjit stirred up a long bubble in his water pipe. 'Are you not forgetting something, Mr. Varma? Most of the epic's heroes died a violent death.'

'I was just thinking the same thing,' Chanda said.

Vijay crushed her hand playfully, but she only turned more fully towards the other two.

She was happy that she no longer felt faint, that she could lean on him and not have to hide it; from now on these possessive familiarities would not invite scandalized or dubious scowls, even though the more old-fashioned among the relatives still frowned on them as unseemly. Not for her the scraping and bowing and blind obedience of the old Hindu wife the modest, self-effacing vegetation in the shadows—she loved him too much for that. Nor, she was certain, would he want such a wife after all he had seen in Europe. Theirs was to be a new and better Indian marriage and they were not to bury it under a heap of medieval prejudices. And if men paid her the compliment of engaging in thoughtful talk in her presence, she would acknowledge it by talking right back, even though at this very moment she would rather listen to Vijay and tell him how handsome he looked in his brocade achkan. But Mr. Varma was addressing her again.

'My dear child, all of you make the same mistake,' he said, not talking down to her, but up, as to an equal. 'The carnage of the Mahabharata is a hopeful thing . . . not a hopeless one. When our heroes die, they do not vanish. They become godly and live forever . . . and that is what they strive for on this earth. There is far more happiness than blood in the story of the five Pandu brothers. As a Rajput, you should know that better than I, a Brahman. As a matter of fact,' he added, crackling his toe knuckles, 'any of those women could be you, just as any of the Pandus could be Vijay. They fought, made their mistakes and finally won, just as you have, Vijay. Change the chariot for the airplane, the Kurus for flying pilgrims, Draupadi for Chanda . . . and it is the same story.'

'Save in one thing. Draupadi had five husbands,' Ranjit said.

'A simple embellishment,' Mr. Varma said placidly.

The moon soared higher each minute; now it revealed Ranjit curled up in his chair beside his snaky hookah, Mr. Varma leaning back in another, his arms behind his head, the newly painted water tank in the background, and beyond it the parapet of the terrace and some other houses on the ridge of Worli.

'Recently,' the old gentleman went on, 'I came across the Iliad and read it once more. I was struck by the terrible difference between the old people of the West and East. In this book, dear boy, the people are far from happy. Their suffering and despair does not let up for one moment. The flower of manhood in both the camps is dragged away from the battlefield one after another . . . women weep and pray for them in deepest sorrow. Slaughter is practically non-stop . . . so that finally the besiegers forget what they have come for and dream only of the destruction of Troy. Of course, they succeed . . . but it solves nothing. I thought they were like the men who spend a lifetime breaking down a door only to find, when it topples, that it separated them from an abyss without bottom.'

'Have we not done the same things?' Ranjit asked. 'Was not woman the cause of the Mahabharata war too?'

341

'A mere accident, dear Ranjit. Poets need a scapegoat . . . woman is a popular device.'

Chanda clapped delightedly. 'Shabash, Mr. Varma! It is time someone spoke the truth.'

'However, my child, the violence of the Mahabharata helps man to find his place in the scheme of things, and here we Indians are different. Like children, we fall and bruise ourselves and get up again remembering what our parents have said. Do you remember Arjuna doubting if he should fight his kinsmen in the other camp? And Krishna's reply to him? He must fight, he was told, because a soldier must fight, because battle is the dharma of a Kshatriya . . . or Rajput, if you prefer. Because, naturally, if a Brahman stopped being religious or learned, or a Kshatriya refused to fight, be he a simple levy or a king, if a Vaisya left his business to look after itself and a Sudra struck work in the fields and cities . . . India would not be here to-day and the last of us would only be a wild forest tribe.'

'And we might have been better off,' Ranjit sighed languidly.

Mr. Varma ignored him. He picked himself a pan.

'And this dharma is what our heroes battled for, and it gave them hope. Men must do well by their God, king, nation, clan, family and themselves, not expecting any rewards, for these duties are automatic. They must go on functioning without covetousness of any kind. This is Krishna's answer to Arjuna, the part of the epic we call Bhagavad-Gita. According to that blessed song, he who follows his dharma lives a full life indeed. And how could it be otherwise. . . .'

'Otherwise?' Vijay echoed.

'That is what I said.' He rolled the selected nuts and condiments into a leaf, but did not put it in his mouth, as chewing would have silenced him. 'What do you see behind all that unbelievable strife and warring, behind those fears and confusion? I shall tell you,' he added at once, the question being purely rhetorical. 'You see the pinnacles of the Upanishads, those bright beacons that light up every part of our lives from birth to death, our sloth as well as our promise, trifles as well as goodness. They point the way not only for Arjuna and his charioteer Krishna, but for every last man on the field no matter how lost he may feel when the battle is joined, to-day just as much as then, for you and your young wife just as much as for me and our dear Ranjit here.'

'With all respect, I point my own way,' Ranjit said.

Mr. Varma ignored him again.

'So the Mahabharata finds duty fully discharged on all sides. Common sense, propriety and devotion prevail; man learns the art of living together with others despite all differences of opinion. We do not destroy senselessly. We do not mature either, it is true, in the sense that our veins do not harden as they did with the old Greeks and Romans. We are the children of this world, and like children we are happy most of the time. We give in to superior force knowing that it is a mode of survival . . . knowing, too, that force must spend itself. In this way we have become indestructible. We rise and fall like a wave, not the one that dashes itself to foam on a rock, but one that is thrown up by the solid depth beneath it, one that blossoms forth in the winds blowing from distant shores.'

He stuffed the roll in his mouth and dusted his hands with a gesture of finality.

'Very, very interesting,' Ranjit said softly. 'I wish we could persuade our Muslims, Parsis, Buddhists and Jains to see it like that.'

Now the servants took charge of the pandal downstairs. Their tidying up, their carting of crockery, glassware and banquet left-overs rose up to the roof together with the music, now even more wistful, as if recalling the golden era of Vikramaditya. Ranjit coiled the pipe round the water bowl and stretched himself stiffly. Chanda hopped down from the wall, then thrust an arm through Vijay's; moonlight painted a fragile, far-away tenderness into her face.

'All is well but one thing,' she informed him in a whisper. 'No woman in the epic could have been as happy as I am.'

'Truly, Chanda?'

'Truly, my love. All is a dream, I think. They can have their heroes and dharmas. I have all I will ever need.'

'You are my dharma, and I am yours. Now you have learned. I once tried to tell you about it, but you didn't believe me.'

'I know now,' she said. 'From the bottom of my heart I know.'

She gazed at the smudgy line dividing the sea from the sky and thought that love did indeed make a world of difference. She now knew the passion and marriage of the Mahabharata, and also the love of her own time—which made it a trifle difficult to breathe at times, but was incomparably wonderful.

Now the ceremony came back to her in all its disjointed trepidation—the Brahman's plea for harmony couched in those awful phrases, her own flickering doubt whether to love a man as much as she did was treachery to all she had maintained so staunchly. And what if it was? The thought was no longer distracting; elation had adorned it so richly that it was of one piece with the rest of her mood. In these four last weeks, men had ceased to be the blanket sort of menace she had been brought up to believe. Above all, Vijay was not one of them. He was a hand in hers, a breath in her ear that sent her all logical principles scattering pell-mell; he was lips on her lips, a warm weight crushing her own tremble—who could possibly remember all that and not live it again at the same instant? She raised his hand to her cheek and leaned on it lightly. The live throb rushing to the innermost part of her *was* Vijay, was love, was oneness, was all she ever wanted.

Ranjit rose. Mr. Varma spat into the cuspidor.

In the house a vessel dropped with a whopping crash, but a quick chatter drowned it. Music faded out likewise, resurrecting a host of smaller noises Down the sea wall cars glided to and fro, rapiers of light clashing fluidly, exploding with a flash, then leaping on in contrary directions, unscathed, bright as ever. Temple bells from Mahim and Maha Lakshmi rolled up for their daily tryst above the cliff, delayed somewhat by yowling curs in the vicinity. The face of the moon wrinkled up into a semblance of a smile. Gazing at it dreamily she thought it much like the lofty mien of the Brahman in the contemplation of heavenly joys.

3

ALL by themselves, they drove up to Khandala in the new car just as the first cool weather arrived from Central India and the Deccan. It was a clear sunny day and a mild breeze blew the dust off the road and over the still green fields and jungle. They laughed and sang the whole way, even when the ground humped after the village of Copolli and splayed itself sharply on the eminence of the Western Ghats. No two people, it seemed to them, could have crossed from the past to the future in one such giddy leap.

To Khandala, the small hill station in the Ghats, the rich Parsis of Bombay were much addicted, but the vogue had spread also to other communities, who came in ever mounting droves and built their bungalows on the hill slopes. Such a house was Uncle Premchand's. It perched on a boulder above the river canyon, almost teetering, and looked to the conical hills of Poona and the cathedral-like peaks in the north. Ancient trees grew through the roofs of the outhouses and a cistern in the garden furnished its only water supply; it rambled along the precipice, sometimes thrusting a glassed verandah right over it, then falling back again and snuggling in the cliff fissures, full of oddly placed rooms and stepdowns, in which any kind of orderly progress was out of the question. They found it strung with jasmine garlands—the uncle was a good organizer, if he was anything. Inside, there were bowls of flowers, a pile of new books, a radio and a food supply fit for the marooned. That same night the fuses blew and they dined under hurricane lanterns and then built a fire in the living-room.

'Vijay, we are dreaming!' she said in the morning, flinging open the verandah windows. 'It is like living with the clouds and birds.'

'Like flying, too,' he said.

From the level of the plateau at the head of the gorge the river swashed downward in a steaming jet over which a rainbow played throughout the day; in the abyss there was froth on the sap-green rocks, and its noise came

344

up to them like the compelling voice of a mass human assembly; spurs and ledges pouted over it as though in petrified assent, and above them, at an impossible angle, woodbine knotted the jungle into vivid patches. A couple of clouds grazed the ridges of the plain in the distance.

'Do you realize that one of these fine nights we might wake up at the bottom of the river?'

'I have taught you how to float, haven't I?'

'It is enchanted . . . like a dream.'

That day, after a confusing instruction by the servants, they drove five miles to Tiger's Leap and picnicked on the edge of another thousand-foot drop, over which they threw stones and listened for the echo. As far as they could see, quaint volcanic slabs of the Ghats tortured one another for effect —towers, pagodas, stupas, pyramids and steeples, all with ribs exposed, their summits wearing little caps of greenery, often a single tree. They watched the slow grind of kites in the sky and afterwards made love to the whistle of a white-bellied drongo in a bush nearby, and then night fell suddenly as usual.

They returned to Khandala and decided to await the New Year awake, for this was one of the few Anglo-Indian customs almost akin to Divali and Hindu merrymaking. They telephoned their parents in the afternoon dined and dressed warmly.

A halo of hyacinth marked the spot where the sun had gone down and towards it the hills now reached ruggedly like the waves of a dead sea; when dusk poured into the valley a faint glow became visible over the hump just beyond the waterfall—the lights of the railway colony in Lonavla, two miles to the south.

'Which is the star Arundhati?' she asked him when the sky darkened completely. 'We should bow to it three times to-night and vow eternal faithfulness. Arundhati was the chaste wife of the saint Vasishta.'

He tucked the coat around her gently. 'I don't need a star to do that,' he said.

They put on the radio, while the servant built a log fire with a good deal of smoke.

The Congress party was at last knuckling down to its promise of reforms —was the grudging admission of the official broadcaster, for he was in the pay of the British. A large-scale educational plan, called Vidya Mandir, was being rushed through at the suggestion of Mr. Gandhi who, by the way, still refused to be drawn into government proper and preferred to guide his ministers from a straw hut in the country. The old system of land tenancy was being changed; experimental prohibition in Bombay and a few other places was working fine, save that it cost a lot of money; Indianization of the Army and Navy was proceeding apace; the shrill railing of the Congress left wing had been echoed sombrely by Jawaharlal Nehru, who warned the wire pullers in the City of London that their 'realism' towards the Nazis was a fool's game; there were Hindu-Muslim clashes in the United Provinces over the militant Hindu programme of the new cabinets; in Central India the monsoon had failed and famine was to be expected; one of the Rajputana highnesses had had a harrowing midnight encounter with a wounded panther; another had flown his sports machine into a couple of vultures while taking off and crashed with about twenty-five fractures.

'Serves him right,' Vijay said. 'He was most offensive about my lecture tour.'

'How the time flies,' she said.

There were also a few reports of looting in the outlying districts, one unsavoury complaint of rape and abduction, one birth to a woman of a baby with two heads. The rest of the country was barren of news; one had to assume that it was in passable shape. New Year's Eve illuminations were doing well in the bigger towns. . . .

'That baby, how too horrible,' she said shuddering.

'Everything happens here, darling, good and bad,' he said. 'We are the world in miniature.'

'Just a moment!' said the announcer. 'Here is a last report, just received. The child died in hospital after a few hours. This is All India Radio . . . good night.'

'There,' he said. 'No need to think about it any more.'

But she was crying; she buried her face on his chest and shook silently.

'Chanda, light of my eyes, what now . . .?'

'It is a bad sign.'

'Bad for what?'

'Oh Vijay, I told you!'

He shut off the radio and took her in his arms, his whole being going out to her. 'You're just wrought up, my darling, that's the only sign,' he said.

They lay cuddled and the fire burned down and his tenderness mellowed the more he thought of her tears; Chanda in a love shiver was moving, but Chanda weeping was more than he could stand. Then she fell asleep and woke up feeling much better. They went out on the glazed verandah and he opened the windows. 'Look, they're firing the first rockets!' he said.

'How pretty they are!'

A weak gauze of moonlight lay on the valley, veiling and soothing, drugging the stony agony of the peaks in the distance; into it seared rocket after rocket, to burst into brilliant sprays of blazing constellations and later to scatter earthward in showers of flashing filaments, and then gutter without trace. Each new burst burned out the stars and nearly the moon itself, but afterwards the peaks would loom again beyond the gauze and the waterfall would dive out of the crannies and murmur more suggestively. He looked at his watch.

'One minute to midnight, Chanda . . . then nineteen hundred and thirty-eight. From this minute onwards everything is brand-new. Are you not a little nervous?'

'There is time for that.'

'Well, I am,' he said, for her little outburst had turned his mind to the future and given his happiness a sharp edge of adventure. 'I get excited every time I think about it.'

'Tell me. . . .'

'About Hardwar, for instance, and the pilgrims. About all the work I must do before even the first one can take off.'

'You shall take your wife before any pilgrim. I have always wanted to see the real Himalayas.'

'I will, I promise. Then . . . about this new government of ours. Can you imagine, we might be a free people in five years from now.'

'Would that not be heaven on earth!'

At that moment the southern sky flared up magnificently and the valley seemed to leap into the air and each tree, furrow and bungalow became transfixed as in a lovely heliotrope dream. A few seconds later, a bore of sirens, whistles and car horns splashed over the gorge, then rushed on into the night. They kissed slowly and words proved bloodless as always.

For to-morrow, to-day, next week . . . for this peace and hope, and for airborne pilgrims and a new India . . . for everything and anything.

He smiled. Some of man's most ardent visioning was also the shyest. How good if one were a really great poet whenever this irrepressible tingle spread out of bounds!

'He will not fly two- and four-seaters, like his father,' he said, 'but great big transports with half a dozen engines.'

'Who, darling?'

'My son.'

'Do girls make good fliers.'

'I don't know. Very few have tried.'

'Oh, this one will; she will be bold, I am sure.'

'Is she named already?'

'Yes, Usha . . . "the Dawn." '

'Why not Chanda, Chandraleika . . . "like the Moon." '

'No, Usha. . . . All our women will know why.'

'It's getting chilly, come inside,' he said. 'I knew we would have propaganda even on our honeymoon.'

They opened the bedroom windows and undressed. From their large bed, smothered in unfamiliar eiderdowns, they saw a few faint stars in the cut-out of the sky.

'I believe that one there is Arundhati,' he said.

Gazing at it in silence did one more thing for him: Unlike the year before, he no longer saw himself as an outlandish meteor shooting this way and that, a slave to the pull of bodies bigger than himself, but as a lusty and considerable planet soaring under its own power and in its own orbit, obeying its own laws with a sense of dignity and pride.

'You know, Chanda,' he said after a while, 'if the first one is not a daughter but a son, I would like to call him Vijay, like myself.'

'Have you forgotten? It is supposed to be bad luck to name your child after anyone living.'

'I don't care. You and I are not superstitious, are we?'

'No, of course not. . .'

'And you know what else, Chanda? It is a good name . . . Vijay . . . "Victorious." It has come true for me, and it shall be true for my son too.'

She let out a long and deep breath and her voice softened.

'It is true for you, darling, is it not? In spite of everything?'

'Yes, it is. Varma was right when he said that I must go back a little so that the others can go forward and meet me. It all fits in now. If I had run too far, I would have lost them, or they would have lost me. That wouldn't have been good for anybody.'

'No, it would not. Mother said the same thing once, only differently. She said the first thing to remember about India is that it is made up of Indians. Anyone who forgets that can only blame himself.'

'I very nearly did,' he said, unable to take his eyes off the window. 'You came along and stopped me in time.'

She said nothing, but pulled the cover up to her chin. For a moment all scuttling and rustle ceased in the outer night and the rumble of the waterfall came into the room faintly but persuasively, like the stream of India herself—plodding, ageless and reborn with every new drop. He thought then he had never really stopped hearing her.

To him she was now not one thing, but things without number. She was vaster than Europe, she was four hundred million people; she was disease, famine, strife of all sorts; she was the small flying strip he would eventually carve out at the Ganges near Hardwar, and also the first man to fly to his God. That was one way of feeling her. She was the manner and scope in which one partook of her. In that personal light, she was one's life and duty—one's dharma—one's fate and its pursuit. Whether one loved or feared her, exulted in her or cried over her, prodded her on or held her back, she was finally inseparable from one. One did these things either weakly or forcibly, with the thought of oneself or without it, but one always did them and in doing them came to count for something. Surely this narrow and winding ribbon of ground which one chose on a broad highway was fulfilment, Indian version?

Let us think only of that, he said to himself, groping for her hand under the blanket.

GLOSSARY

achkan, three-quarter-length tunic.

ahimsa, non-killing; hence, non-violence.

Allahu Akbar, Allah is great.

almirah, clothes chest, wardrobe.

ama ('ma), mother.

Apsara, heavenly nymph.

arre, exclamation, rough equivalent of 'well then,' 'but.'

asok, one of the five holiest trees in Hinduism (*Jonesia Asoca*).

Atman, universal Self, whence all individual selves arise.

ayah, nursemaid, female servant.

baba, child.

bandicoot, large rat, pig rat.

banya, loosely: Hindu trader.

banyan, large tree of fig family.

Bapuji, little father (used of Gandhi).

bas, enough.

bhai, brother.

Bharat Mata, Mother India.

biddi, country cigarette.

biddi-wallah, vendor of cigarettes.

Bismillah, in the name of Allah

brahmachari, a celibate.

Brahman, first or sacerdotal caste of Vedic division; also, individual divine self.

bulbul, nightingale.

chameli, variety of jasmine.

champa, evergreen of the magnolia family.

charkha, spinning wheel.

chatai, matting.

chati, earthen waterpot.

chikoo, a fruit, potatoish in appearance.

chokra, youngster.

choli, bodice.

chowki, police station.

churi-dar-pajamas, a kind of narrow white trousers.

daftar, office.

dak, mail.

dak bungalow, resthouse.

dalpuri, fried unleavened bread-cake, made of pulse.

darbha, a grass.

dharma, religious and ethical laws binding an individual; hence, loosely, duties of an individual.

dharmsala, charitable resthouse for pilgrims and travellers.

dhoti, long loincloth.

dhow, an Arab sailing vessel.

dipam, oil lamp.

dol, a swing.

dopatta, a large veil worn by ladies as top vestment.

durrie, cotton carpet.

falooda, a kind of curried pastry.

gazal, a form of Persian verse.

ghagra, skirt worn by Rajput ladies.

Ghandarva, form of marriage.

gharry, one-horse hooded carriage.

ghat, steps leading to a bathing place; also, mountain range.

ghee, clarified butter.

Gita, Bhagavad, ethical and religious discourse occurring in the Mahabharata, the great warring epic; also called the Song Celestial.

gulmohar, the peacock flower; an ornamental tree with scarlet blossom.

guru, spiritual teacher.

hadji, a Muslim who has done his pilgrimage to Mecca.

Hara, a name of Siva.

Hari, a name of Vishnu (used sometimes of other gods).

Hari-bol, invocation of Lord Krishna.

hath-leva, wedding rite of joining hands.

homa, fire offering in worship.

howdah, a seat fixed on an elephant's back.

iman, a Muslim priest.

Inquilab Zindabad, Long live independence!

izzat, honour, prestige.

jai! long live! hail!

jee-huhn, respectful sound of assent (pronounced gutturally: jee hung).

349

jheel, swamp, lake.

-ji, respectful suffix, appearing after proper names, and also by itself.

kachli, kanchuli, kind of bodice; blouse.

kaman, well done!

Kanyadan, part of wedding ceremony in which bride is given away.

Karma-Yoga, action-concept of life and duties; eclectic philosophy-of-action outlined in the book of Bhagavad Gita.

Kathak, a dance form of Northern India.

Kathakali, a dance form of South India.

kevab, a kind of spiced hamburger.

khaddar, homespun cloth.

kohl, black make-up for eyes.

koofta, curried meatball.

Krishna, eighth avatar or incarnation of Vishnu, favourite deity of the Rajputs.

Kshatriya, second or warrior and ruling caste.

kurta, kind of blouse-shirt worn by Punjabi ladies over their trousers (salvar).

kusha, a grass with fragrant roots.

kutcha, raw, rough, crude (as opposed to pucka).

lac, one hundred thousand.

lalaji, respectful title.

lascar, native seaman.

lathi, wooden or bamboo stick (used by police in keeping order).

linga, phallic symbol of Siva.

Mahayuga, great era (age).

Mahabharata, ancient Sanskrit epic of the Great Indian War.

Mahar, a low caste.

maidan, open public ground, used for public gatherings, games, etc.

mali, gardener.

mandir, house of learning, contemplation.

mantra, prayer from the Vedas.

Marwari, a community of merchants.

Maya, illusion, deception, personified in a celestial female form.

meherbani, thank you.

mudra, hand poses in dance.

munuji, dear one.

Nai, barber caste.

nai (col. of nahin), no.

Narayen, another name of Vishnu.

Nataraja, Siva as cosmic dancer, symbolizing the cycle of birth and death.

nawab, Muslim ruler of a native state.

neem, the margosa tree (*Melia Azadirachta*).

pameloo, shaddock; a pear-shaped citrus fruit resembling grapefruit, but coarser.

pan (supari), betel (nut).

pancha-gavia, five products of a cow.

panchayat, old Indian 'court of five,' usually religious or judiciary.

pandal, pavilion erected from bamboos, banana leaves and jute sacking.

pappad, wafers with caraway seed.

pavitram, ring of plaited stalks of dharba grass, worn to scare away evil spirits.

peon, office attendant, messenger.

pipal, one of five holiest Indian trees (*Ficus religiosa*).

pita(-ji), father.

Pitri, soul of an ancestor.

prayashitta, rite of expiation.

priyaji, loved one.

pucka, firm, good, genuine, proper.

puja, worship, prayer, rite.

puratta, unleavened fried bread-cake.

purdah, screen, veil; hence, seclusion of women.

purohit, priest.

puggree, turban.

Put, hell.

putra, a deified ancestor who met violent death.

Radha, Krishna's favourite milkmaid and consort.

rajkumar, son and heir of a raja.

Rajput, medieval and modern equivalent of the Vedic Kshatriya; descendant of the Sun and Moon; native of Rajputana.

rakhi, charmed amulet.

rakshasa, marriage by force; kind of marriage.

Ramayana, ancient Sanskrit epic, celebrating the deeds of the hero Rama and his wife Sita.

rasa, Esthetic sentiments expressed facially in dance.

rasgoola, a sweetmeat.

rishi, a divinely inspired poet or sage.

sab-chiz, literally, all things; everything.

sadhu, ascetic.

salvar, loose trousers, gathered at the ankles, worn by Punjabi ladies (under the kurta).

samadhi, loosely, religious trance.

sannyasi, ascetic.

sanskara, domestic rite.

sari, one-piece garment of Indian women.

sat-pheri, seven walks around the wedding fire.

satyagraha(i), civil disobedience, one of Mr. Gandhi's political doctrines; (follower of—).

sendur, red oxide of lead; powder.

Sendurdan, portion of wedding ceremony in which bridegroom takes possession of bride.

serangi, a kind of North Indian string instrument, similar to fiddle.

shabash! well done!

shami, a revered tree (*Prosopis spicigera*).

shikar, hunt.

Shreemati, literally, Holy Mother; in daily conversation, respectful address of a lady.

shri, holy, revered.

simul, the silk-cotton tree (*Bombax Malabricum*).

sitar, oriental form of guitar.

sraddha, ancestor worship.

Sudra, the fourth Vedic caste of menials and agriculturists.

sultana-champa, the Alexandrian laurel.

suttee, widow who burns herself after the death of her husband.

swa-dharma, dharma of an individual.

swami, a learned ascetic, tutor.

tali, necklace.

tamarind, a tropical tree.

toran, mystical triangle emblem of the Rajputs.

Upanishads, collection of speculative treatises on nature of man and universe, forming a late part of the Vedic literature.

Vaisya, third or merchant caste of the Vedas.

vasant, spring.

Vasudeva, a name of Krishna.

Vedas, sacred books of ancient India.

vina, old Indian string instrument.

vir, Rajput hero fallen in battle.

zamindar, landowner, managing land and tax collection on behalf of government.

zenana, of, or concerning, the ladies; ladies' apartment.

351